The
Rocky Mountain
Company

Cheyenne Winter

*Also by Richard S. Wheeler
in Large Print:*

The Buffalo Commons
Deuces and Ladies Wild
Dodging Red Cloud
Downriver
Drum's Ring
The Final Tally
Flint's Gift
Flint's Honor
Flint's Truth
Fool's Coach
Incident at Fort Keogh
Montana Hitch
Rendezvous
Restitution

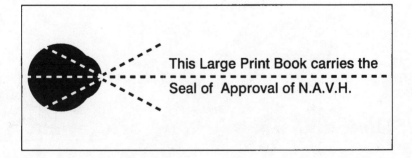

This Large Print Book carries the
Seal of Approval of N.A.V.H.

The
Rocky Mountain
Company

Cheyenne Winter

Richard S. Wheeler

Thorndike Press • Waterville, Maine

Copyright © 1992 by Richard S. Wheeler

The Rocky Mountain Company Book 3

All rights reserved.

Published in 2003 by arrangement with Kensington Books,
an imprint of Kensington Publishing Corp.

Thorndike Press® Large Print Western Series.

The tree indicium is a trademark of Thorndike Press.

The text of this Large Print edition is unabridged.
Other aspects of the book may vary from the original edition.

Set in 16 pt. Plantin by Al Chase.

Printed in the United States on permanent paper.

Library of Congress Cataloging-in-Publication Data

Wheeler, Richard S.
    Cheyenne winter / Richard S. Wheeler.
        p. cm. — (The Rocky Mountain Company ; bk. 3)
    ISBN 0-7862-4656-1 (lg. print : hc : alk. paper)
    1. Trading posts — Fiction.   2. Fathers and sons —
Fiction.   3. Yellowstone River Valley — Fiction.   4. Large
type books.   I. Title.
PS3573.H4345 C48 2003
                                                                2002073232

For Terry C. Johnston

One

There was still another matter to put before the partners. Guy Straus knew what their response would be, and he could override it if he chose. He owned two-thirds of the Rocky Mountain Company while Brokenleg Fitzhugh and Jamie Dance each owned a sixth.

This first annual meeting of the buffalo company, as they commonly called it, had yielded no surprises. Up on the Yellowstone, Brokenleg had weathered fierce competition from the American Fur Company and had broken even. Out on the Arkansas, Jamie Dance had managed a lively trade with the Comanches for robes, assuring an overall profit for the 1841–42 robe season.

Guy peered around the beeswaxed table in the salon of Straus et Fils, still astonished at the changes in his sons who'd been out at the posts; and in the rock-hard strength of his weathered partners, a pair of mountain men who'd turned themselves into buffalo-robe traders.

Sitting decorously along the walls were their wives, Teresa Maria Dance, looking lush and vibrant; and Little Whirlwind, as angular and haughty and unapproachable as ever. Guy felt a vast affection for them both, though only a year ago he'd wondered whether they might be serious liabilities. In a way they still were. Little Whirlwind of the Cheyennes — Fitzhugh called her Dust Devil — breathed fire against other tribes. And Teresa Maria had already shown Guy she could scold with the worst of them.

"Oh, your reports hearten me. Brokenleg, when all that bad news filtered down the Missouri I thought the company was finished before it had traded a robe up there. I don't know how, but you held off the Chouteau interests . . . And Jamie, your courage at Fort Dance — yours and that of my son David" — Guy saw his son stare at the burnished table — "fought off the Bents, the Comancheros, and the Mexican government, and won us a solid profit."

The thing that struck Guy was that they were all strangers. He'd sent two soft, inexperienced sons out upon the wilderness, and now, a year later, they were tanned veterans at ages seventeen and nineteen. They'd become strangers — as if they'd seen sights that Guy had only experienced through the whiskey gossip of fur and robe men at the Planters House. Not even his partners seemed the same: they'd come to him as beaver men, free trappers out of luck in the Rockies. Now, the passage of a year had turned them into hard, discerning managers of themselves and others.

"I should tell you that we have old Pierre *le cadet* worried down there in his lair on the levee. American Fur eats competitors. So do the Bents, I might add. You've both told me of buy-out offers. They must have been a temptation to you both — when things ran against you. Well . . . Brokenleg, you've got Pierre in a lather."

Guy unfolded the letter that lay before him, written in Pierre Chouteau's own crabbed hand, in French — a not subtle appeal to Guy, over the heads of Guy's English-speaking partners. It was dated just the day before, June 1, 1842, St. Louis. Timed perfectly, Guy thought.

"I will translate this as I go along," Guy said, donning his gold-rimmed spectacles. Brokenleg could read and write but Jamie couldn't, and Guy made a point of reading everything aloud at the annual meetings.

"My dear Guy. Chouteau and Company, along with Bent, St. Vrain and Company, propose to buy your interests in the Rocky

Mountain Company, along with those of your partners. We propose to pay a fair mountain price for existing inventory at the posts, as well as livestock, wagons, and furnishings. In addition we propose to pay two thousand for each post, and an additional thousand dollars, guaranteeing you and your partners a profit, to be divided as you choose."

Guy interrupted the reading. "That's an offer of fourteen or fifteen thousand by my calculations. I imagine after deducting what's owed Straus et Fils, we three partners would share four or five thousand — on top of the profits we've made this year."

"I ain't buyable," muttered Brokenleg. He glared at Guy.

Jamie said nothing but listened closely. That was the difference between them, Guy thought.

"We are also willing to buy your interests alone, Guy, and assume a majority partnership in the company. We assume your colleagues would be delighted to have a new senior partner if you should decide to protect your investment."

"Haw!" exclaimed Brokenleg.

Guy smiled. "There's more detail — time limitations and so on. But I would like your opinions about this much of it. I'll ask you

10

first, Brokenleg."

The mountaineer adjusted his bad leg and glared. As always when he was trapped in St. Louis he looked like a keg of powder ready to explode. "Old Cadet, he's fixin' to drive a wedge betwixt you and us. I mean, ah, there's you, friends of him and all — and there's Jamie and me."

Guy nodded.

"He say anything about what he's gonna do if he buys two-thirds of the Rocky Mountain Company? Him and the Bents, are they fixin' to boot us out?" asked Jamie.

A good question, thought Guy. "No, he says nothing of his intentions. That's for you two to infer."

"You'd git out clean. I mean, Straus et Fils. He's fixin' to give you a get-out profit."

Guy nodded again. "A rather good one."

"It ain't us that needs askin' then; it's you," muttered Brokenleg. "You gonna sell out from under us?"

"Would you like me to?"

Brokenleg Fitzhugh scrambled to his feet, a clumsy act because of his locked knee. "I reckon this is standing-up talk so I'll deal on my feet. I didn't go clear to the Yellowstone and work myself to the bone and git myself almost kilt half a dozen times to quit. And neither did your Max here. We got

11

buy-out offers all along — and damn, we fought instead, and we got us robes in aplenty and built a whole post — just a handful of us. I don't want to hear quit-talk. Not one more word."

That was vintage Brokenleg, Guy thought. He had picked his men well. He turned to Jamie.

Dance didn't rise; in fact, talking was his excuse to slouch deeper in the gilded conference chair until he was nearly horizontal, his legs poking out from across the table. Instead, Dance grinned. "We shore must be raisin' hell — pardon, ma'am — raisin' grief with their plans. I got us a mess o' prime robes, David hyar and me, and I plan to get a mess more right out from under the noses of them Bents and half the officials of Mexico."

Guy knew his sons would enthusiastically back the partners. A year ago they wouldn't have. But maybe they'd waver, even as Guy himself wavered, if they knew the rest. Guy found the buy-out a great temptation, a chance to clear a profit on this shaky adventure and return to the conservative financial practices that had been the hallmark of Straus et Fils for decades.

"There's more," Guy said blandly, adjusting his spectacles. "You filled us with admiration — this is Chouteau again — with admiration for your diligent efforts in the field. It took great skill and planning and courage on the part of your young men. But will it happen again? Who knows what the robe trade will bring? This year's profit could become next year's disaster. For our part we will compete by whatever means. You must let us know of your decision before your resupply goes out to the posts."

Guy waited for that to sink in. He wasn't even sure if his partners understood Pierre Chouteau's Aesopian language. Both Brokenleg and Jamie stared at him, not seeing much gravity in it. But David spoke up. How that young man, so lean and adult, startled Guy.

"It's a threat, isn't it, papa? He's saying more than is on paper."

"That's correct, David."

"He's saying that we've got to sell out or face — bad things. That's been the rule in the fur trade — erase the opposition."

David had a keen analytical mind, Guy thought.

"You gonna let threats whip us?" muttered Brokenleg, who was still standing.

"Threats become reality when the Chouteaus want them to be, Brokenleg," said Guy gently. "You know them all. I don't need to list the way property and lives can be destroyed in the wilderness."

"They sure fought back in the beaver days, but Bridger and Fitzpatrick and the Sublettes — they fought back and won."

"For a while. In the end they lost, Brokenleg. American Fur — Pratte and Chouteau — absorbed them all. Every one, except the Bents in the south. You might ask yourselves how that happened."

"We expected the old divil to try," persisted Brokenleg. "He tried last year and got whupped."

"Pierre Chouteau is a man who profits from his mistakes," Guy said. "Especially the mistake of underestimating the competition."

They argued it back and forth, with his sons hesitant to take sides. And the more they talked the more Brokenleg hardened in his belief that the company should reject the offer. Guy wasn't so sure. Jamie slowly sided with Brokenleg. He wanted another crack at the Comanche trade and a crack at the tribes the Bents thought were in their pocket.

In the end, Guy conceded. Actually he felt trapped. He couldn't quite bring himself to oppose two fierce mountain men who wanted to lick the two most powerful fur companies in North America.

"Well then, we'll try for another profit," he said wearily, filled with foreboding.

The Trapper, captained by Joseph Sire and piloted by Black Dave Desiree, whaled up the Missouri for the second time that year. The first voyage had departed from St. Louis March 27, carrying the resupply of the American Fur Company, destined for Forts Pierre and Union. It had sailed downriver a few weeks later bearing the returns — baled buffalo robes and pelts — of both Chouteau's American Fur and the new Rocky Mountain Company as well. And on board were Brokenleg, Little Whirlwind, and Maxim Straus.

Now it was flailing the Missouri again, this time on the second (or June) rise, and carrying the resupply for the Rocky Mountain Company, which it would deposit at the foot of Wolf Rapids on the Yellowstone, the practical end of navigation unless the river ran very high — which it didn't. From there, Fitzhugh's engages would wagon and keelboat the resupply to the company's little post at the Big Horn.

Brokenleg chafed at the delay. His giant rival would have its goods shelved and be trading weeks ahead of the buffalo company, but there was no help for it. Their annual meeting was delicately positioned to allow Jamie Dance to get in from New Mexico, which he could do only when the grass was up. It hurt the northern trade and endangered the resupply because the treacherous river dropped rapidly after the mountain melt-off and its upper reaches would no longer be navigable by mid-July.

Today, Sires told him, they'd reach Bellevue, and that was good news. Around Bellevue something began to change not only in the river but in himself. Below Bellevue the riverbanks were lined solidly with hardwoods, and the trees suffocated him until he could barely breathe. Down in steamy St. Louis he had to hold himself in like a caged creature, his mountain spirit wrestling with people, buildings, dampness, traffic, manners — not to mention coping with people like Guy and his family, Jamie and his, and that raft of slaves. It always made him crazy, like being assaulted by a whole hive of wasps at once. That was true of Dust Devil, too. She stood beside him on the hurricane deck high above the water, looking glad.

Near Bellevue the trees thinned and the air dried and became more transparent. The steam of the southern river gave way to dry

16

heat. The banks no longer crowded the river. The Missouri flowed through long stretches of prairie, open country where a man could see to tomorrow, and the grass pinned the trees to dense copses in low flats or cedar-choked islands. For Fitzhugh it was like freedom; jail bars falling. Soon they'd see buffalo. They'd long since seen the last vestige of civilization, the last farm, the last shack, so that the land seemed clean and pure, and as joyous as a rendezvous wedding. In St. Louis he'd survived on spirits, numbing his senses each day just to endure. He didn't need spirits so much here; only now and then when his bum leg tortured him, or he got the itch.

At Bellevue, too, they'd face their last hurdle. The Indian Agent there performed the final U.S. Government inspection of the packet, looking in particular for contraband spirits. At Fort Leavenworth the army inspected each packet, but leniently, with a knowing appreciation of the way the fur trade worked. Alcohol lubricated the business and no acts of Congress could prevent the passage of spirits up the river. There was rarely trouble at Leavenworth. In the days when General William Clark was Indian commissioner he gave the fur companies generous permits for the legal boatmen's ration. And the lieutenants at Leavenworth who poked and probed the mountain of cargo in the shallow holds never bothered to look closely at the compact rundlets marked turpentine or vinegar or lamp oil.

Still, they'd been careful. Not until well above Bellevue, at a certain wooding lot, would the Rocky Mountain Company's annual supply of two-hundred proof ardent spirits be boarded, along with several cords of dried cottonwood to fire the boiler. No company could afford to lose its license. Even Chouteau's giant company had once come close when a rival had tattled, and only the intervention of that friend of western men, Senator Thomas Hart Benton, had allayed disaster. Fitzhugh had six thirty-gallon casks awaiting upriver, carried there by mulepack at considerable cost to the company. The very thought of it built a joyous dry in his throat.

"Grass," he said to Little Whirlwind.

"Home," she replied. "The land of the buffalo."

She'd been as miserable in St. Louis as he, pulling into herself and glaring at the white men's world with ill-concealed scorn. She'd refused to don the clothing of white women, no matter that St. Louis summer was steamy and leather was clammy to the touch there. Instead, as an act of tribal pride, she'd adorned herself in the most elaborate ceremonial dress of her Cheyenne people, wearing velvety bleached-white doeskin fringed at the hem and sleeves; calf-high moccasins, elaborately beaded; and a heavy bone necklace. She'd worn her sleek jet hair in braids and wrapped each braid in white rabbit fur and garlanded it with a bow of red ribbon. And then, just to defy the customs of the whites, she'd streaked her forehead with vermilion, as if to announce that she was Cheyenne, and the Cheyenne were a finer people than any she set eyes upon in that filthy city.

Now she stood beside him feeling the throb of the twin steam pistons and hearing the thrash and rumble of the side-wheels of *The Trapper* as it fought the relentless river. But her face had softened, he thought. He knew why: the grass. The prairie, with its promise of liberty, running unfenced to distant horizons where her Cheyenne people lived and hunted and worshipped their everywhere-god, Maheo. And soon, the sacred buffalo, the commissary of her people. Her face would soften again some time soon when they spotted their first buffalo.

They passed the confluence of the Platte,

that shallow flow out of the Rockies far west, and Fitzhugh's mind leapt up that river to the beaver camps and rendezvous he'd known at the end of that highway. Then he heard the clang of bells and the muffled sound of voices erupting from the speaking tube that connected the pilothouse atop the texas to the engine room. The packet slowed and began slewing in the current. Ahead, around a bight, would be Bellevue and after that — freedom.

Even as the duckbilled prow of the packet slid toward the levee a small crowd of Otos and Omahas collected there, running down the steep paths to the water's edge. For years Bellevue had been run as a trading post for American Fur by Peter Sarpy. The comfortable post was still a trading center, but it had a new resident as well, the U.S. Indian Agent for the Omahas and other local tribes — the Reverend Mr. Foster Gillian, a portly divine of the Congregational Church. It had become Indian Bureau policy to appoint ministers as Indian Agents, supposing civilizing good would come of it. Brokenleg hawked up some spit and spat. He had his notions about all that.

From up on the hurricane deck Brokenleg eyed the fat cleric in his black clawhammer frock coat and silk top hat. The man was teetotal. And worse, he'd been imposing his morals on tribesmen until they brimmed with resentments, turning a happy, fruitful trading post into a seething mass of hatreds. Still, this would take all of twenty minutes and they'd be on their way upriver. Below, on the main deck, a motley mob of deck passengers, ruffians and mountain men mostly, swarmed to the rail. Brokenleg hardly knew any of them — the old beaver men, his rendezvous pals, had mostly vanished into some void. Oh, where had all them coons gone? Men he drank with, trapped icy streams with, told tall tales with through a wintry night? The Stony Mountains had become as silent as a trapped-out creek.

Deck hands lowered the stage and a welter of men boiled off the packet to stretch their legs and explore the loveliest of all the Missouri River fur posts. After that exodus the reverend proceeded forth, as stately as a whale, accompanied by a horde of factotums, mostly breeds. Brokenleg decided he'd better head down to the main deck even though descending the companionways was torture for a man with a leg welded straight at the knee by an old injury.

But Captain Sire was down there to greet

the agent, and young Maxim as well; the boat and the company were represented, so he didn't hurry. At length, after some babble, the deckhands opened the hatch and the Reverend Foster Gillian lowered his portly self down the ladder, a glassed candle-lantern in hand. Maxim accompanied him; no one else bothered. By the time Brokenleg limped up, the hold had swallowed the reverend.

Down there, Brokenleg knew, Maxim would steer the man along the two aisles through inky blackness, warning him not to bring the lantern close to casks of gunpowder, occasionally shifting crates and bales of trade goods to let the inspector examine what lay beneath. That had been young Maxim's duty from the start; he kept the books, did the clerking, checked the cargo against theft each day.

Nearby, Mrs. Gillian awaited under a white parasol, respectably isolated on the deck by cowed passengers. Brokenleg did not introduce himself. Something about Mrs. Gillian's manner forbade it. He wondered how she treated the red men in her husband's charge. He heard the scuff and scrape of shifting cargo below and knew Maxim was being put through a workout. And then he detected rising voices.

22

Maxim's head bobbed up at the hatch, looking worried. "We need two deckhands," he said, shooting an unhappy look at Brokenleg.

The mate sent down two deckhands, and in short order three rundlets were hoisted to the main deck looking like fat felons, followed by the lumbering bulk of the minister, who was helped out upon the planking, and stood puffing after his exertion up the ladder.

He had a bung starter in hand and proceeded to twist it into wood until he was able to extract the plug, which taxed his muscles to their limit. Then he bent his portly frame until his nose probed the hole, and sniffed.

"Vinegar indeed," he wheezed. "I smell foul spirits."

Two

Brokenleg was amazed. The company had no spirits aboard. He limped forward, plunged a finger into the bung, and sniffed. It wasn't vinegar.

"And who are you?" asked Foster Gillian, drawing himself up to peer down his aquiline nose.

"Fitzhugh. Partner in the company."

"Your full name?"

"Brokenleg Fitzhugh."

"Brokenleg? Have you no other?"

"Not as I remember."

"I must have a name."

"Robert, it was."

"You've violated the laws of the Republic."

"I don't reckon so. This ain't our spirits."

"Oh, fidd ededee!" The Reverend Mister Gillian wheezed out his scorn. "I suppose you'll tell me it was not on your cargo manifests." He waved the papers as if they were holy scripture. "Here! Three thirty-gallon casks of vinegar. A little legerdemain. A little chicane."

"What's that?"

"Fraud. Foul fraud. A base effort to debauch and demoralize the savages in our charge."

"I know nothing about it," said Brokenleg. He wheeled toward Maxim. "You know anything about this?"

The youth looked frightened. "Yes. I — the barrels weren't on the manifests," he stammered. "I thought a mistake had been made so I added them to it."

"Ah!" cried Foster Gillian. "A mere youth corrupting the savages! And toying with the law of the United States. What sort of company is this?"

Maxim reddened. "My task is to look for theft. Each day I check the hold for theft. There's often miscounts — differences between what's on the manifests and what's in the hold. I— it's nothing unusual."

"Stammering! A sure sign of a guilty conscience. Truth will out!"

"That isn't it — that isn't it. Someone put them there!"

The reverend wheezed, setting his whole torso to rocking. "I may be a minister, young man, but I'm not naive. I know that your foul trade is fueled by spirits. You fur and robe men think nothing of debasing

25

whole tribes — corrupting helpless inno-
cents, mere children, with your vile poisons."

Maxim stiffened and pressed his lips shut.
He was plainly through talking.

Fitzhugh felt like hollering but didn't. No
matter what he said he'd only dig their grave
deeper. As far as he was concerned
tribesmen were adults. They could choose
to trade a robe for some firewater or not,
same as any white man.

"I've caught you red-handed! That's
plain. Enough spirits to send whole villages
into the pits of hell!"

"Maxim, come hyar — I want to talk."
Fitzhugh dragged Maxim out of earshot.

"Stop!"

"We're havin' us a company meeting."

"Fiddlededee! Fiddlededee!" The reverend scowled but there was nothing he
could do. Fitzhugh halted at the roaring
firebox. "Maxim — what do you know
about this hyar?"

"Nothing! Nothing! Nothing!" he
screamed. "They've been on board for a
long time, Brokenleg," he mumbled. "I noticed them the first day. There's two manifests — one for the captain and my own.
The vinegar was listed on the ship manifests
but not on mine. I just thought —"

Fitzhugh growled. "You jist thought! You jist thought!"

Maxim looked so miserable that Fitzhugh wanted to calm down, but couldn't. "Maybe you cost us the license! Maybe you busted your pa and the rest!"

That was too much for Maxim. He wept.

"You coulda told me!" Fitzhugh roared. "You coulda said we got three casks of vinegar. Vinegar! Who the hell uses three casks a vinegar? I shoulda done it myself."

He knew he was cutting the boy to ribbons and he didn't care. Out in the wild lands anyone that made mistakes — them coons went under. The wilds, the Injuns, didn't give a second chance. This robe trade, with all its cutthroats, didn't give a second chance! He left the boy weeping spastically while firemen pretended not to stare, and stomped back to the Indian agent.

"I'm sayin' it and you can believe it or not. Suit yerself. I'm sayin' it for the record. We didn't put them casks in thar and we didn't know what they had in 'em. Someone else done it."

The Reverend Mister Foster Gillian looked amused. "I'll make note of your fiddle-faddle in my report to the Indian Bureau."

"Make plumb sure you do!"

"Oh, this heinous traffic in spirits will cost you your license. Don't you doubt it." He turned to Captain Sire. "I am confiscating this contraband. Have your blackamoors pour it into the river, sir. But leave a little for evidence."

Sire said nothing. At his nod two deckhands lifted the first cask and mournfully poured the pure grain spirits overboard. They gurgled out while men stared as if watching a fatal wound bleed their life away. And then the next. And the next. Indians, breeds, ruffians, mountaineers, boatmen, watched in agony. Mrs. Gillian, a tent under a parasol, pursed her lips. All three new engages who'd signed on with the Rocky Mountain Company studied the spirits as they departed the living.

That done, the reverend turned to Brokenleg. "I ought to seize your entire cargo and this ship as well. Believe me, this vessel's navigation license is in jeopardy. Oh, I'll put a stop to this traffic one way or another. Not a drop, not a drop of these poisons will touch the lips of these savage children of the West. One way or another I'll halt this nefarious traffic."

Bluster. Brokenleg stopped listening and turned to the business ahead: informing

28

Guy; defending the trading license; trying to prove somehow that things were less damning than they seemed. That was a task made all the more difficult because all fur companies winked at the law and circumvented the inspections. Everyone knew it, from David Mitchell, in charge of the Indian Bureau back in St. Louis, on down — and up.

"You're not even paying attention! I'll report your insolence as well."

Brokenleg focused on the man and listened to the rest of his sermon, or appeared to. The man irked him. Preachers had wrecked everything in Indian Country. The Indian Bureau's noble experiment had been worse for red men than the corrupt agents the preachers had replaced. The preachers, including this bubbling tub, had withheld food and treaty annuities from any Indians who failed to abandon their old ways and become Christians. The result had been seething hatred on the reserves.

After some interminable time, after Sire's impatient coughing, after deckhands had wandered off and spectators had wilted, the Reverend Mister Gillian concluded, swept the mountainous Mrs. Gillian down the stage, and marched funereally up the slope.

Brokenleg turned to Captain Sire. "I

reckon we've got to git word down to Guy Straus. Next time we pass a mackinaw or a keelboat give me a holler."

Sire nodded. "Monsieur, truly, those weren't your spirits, were they?"

"Nope. Some skunk put 'er there. This hyar was old Chouteau cadet's doin', sure as I'm standin' hyar."

"It is a different handwriting, *oui?*"

Sire handed him the ship's copies of the cargo manifest. The three casks of vinegar had been entered in a cruder hand than the rest.

"We must delay no more," Sire said. He waved to Black Dave Desiree high above in the pilothouse. Deckmen hauled in the hawsers. The twin chimneys belched black smoke that lowered down upon them all. The escapement pipe shrilled off steam. The packet drifted backward a moment. Then the eighteen-foot side-wheels bit water and the riverboat wrestled the violent current of the river.

He found Maxim still standing near the firebox at the boiler and hauled him out into the sunlight; to the duckbilled prow. On either side the river swirled by, a murky green color this far upstream.

"Now Maxim. You write your pa about this and we'll hail the next keelboat and send the letter down. He's got to know right fast. It's that or send an express. You write him good. You can say 'er a lot better than I can. Give him all the facts. Give him every-thing — every little thing. He's got to deal with Mitchell, keep the IB from pullin' our license. You up to it or do I haveta do it?"

"Oh I'll do it. It's all my fault anyway."

"I reckon it's not your fault that them spirits got put in there. That was old Chouteau Cadet."

"It's all over. The company's over."

"Naw. Maybe not. We're standin' in this hyar prow, cuttin' water. We're goin' up to trade robes. We're goin' to make us a profit. American Fur, they weasled out of it more'n once. Cost a fine or two but they kept on. We'll keep on. And we both learnt a piece."

"The fine could sink us."

"It'll hurt. Maybe we can lasso Senator Benton, like Chouteau did that time when ol' Wyeth visited Kenneth McKenzie at Fort Union in the beaver days, and peached on him — told the Indian Bureau they had a corn whiskey still runnin' juice up thar. They got out of it. We'll git out of it."

But he wasn't very sure of that. The next afternoon they closed on a mackinaw car-rying five men and sent Maxim's letter downriver in the hands of a buffalo-tongue

31

outfit. It'd get to Guy ahead of the reverend's report to Davy Mitchell. But what might happen after that was anyone's guess. Meanwhile, he reckoned he'd have a little palaver with the company's three new engages.

At each wooding stop along the river Captain Sire put every man on board to work, deckhands and passengers alike, and urged them to be quick about it. Woodyards were famous for sudden death. At this yard, a little above Sergeant Bluff, something unusual would happen. Maxim Straus stood at the duckbilled prow as the packet slid toward the riverbank. He felt moody and rebellious. He would not answer the clanging of the ship's bell summoning able-bodied men to work. Especially here.

Farther downstream woodcutters operated the woodyards, piling up cordwood along the riverbanks. At those stops the crew and passengers trotted the three- or four-foot lengths aboard while the mate or the captain settled with the wood hawks. But not here. Not out in Indian country where no wood hawk would survive long. Here and the rest of the way up the Missouri, the crews were on their own. They had to girdle living trees for future use and hack them down and into pieces as swiftly as possible. Some captains had a small sawmill aboard and cut the logs while they traveled. Captain Sire had no such equipment. An upriver wooding stop meant that the bankside cottonwoods and willows had to be felled and cut to length several times a day.

Occasionally Indians themselves prepared a load of wood and charged for it, often with a great deal of haggling because they were never in a hurry. Their presence in a wooding yard slowed things down so much that some captains preferred to avoid them if they had alternative sites — which enraged the tribesmen. As a result, a captain never knew when a volley from bankside rifles would rip into his boat, killing passengers and crew.

But Maxim wasn't looking for Indians here. He was looking for something else — three men and a string of mules bearing thirty-gallon wooden casks. He half-hoped he wouldn't see them. He'd come to hate the whole business of smuggling spirits past the federal inspectors. But there they were, waiting quietly in the shade of the dense cottonwood forest that spread east from the bank. The company's whiskey-runners. Delivering one hundred eighty gallons of two-hundred proof ardent spirits. Enough pure grain alcohol to make nine hundred gallons of firewater after it had been diluted. Nine hundred gallons of trade whiskey, consisting of spirits, river water, tea for color, pepper or ginger for taste, a few plugs of tobacco for bite, and anything else a trader felt like dumping into the pot to make the beverage entertaining. Enough to demoralize whole tribes. Enough to bring in thousands of robes, untold wealth.

Maxim hated it.

The ship's bell clanged and everywhere deckmen and mountaineers crowded to the stage, grabbing axes and saws from a box there. Even while the crew made fast the packet, wrapping hawsers around stumps on shore, the mob trotted toward the trees and began butchering them. High up on the texas, ship's officers watched for Indians, glassing the surrounding bluffs diligently.

Maxim didn't budge. He glared sourly as the whiskey-runners led their mules up the stage onto the main deck and began unloading the casks. Brokenleg was there to meet them and examine the bung of each cask, looking for signs of tampering, watering down, light weight, and joking with them all the while. In short order the six casks had vanished into the shallow hold, the whiskey men had been paid off and had vanished into the timber with their mules. An illegal transaction.

No one cared. No one among the mountaineers or deckmen even stared. Nothing was hidden. Any observer might have reported it to the Indian Bureau but no one ever would. No engage of the rival American Fur Company would peach because spirits were essential to the trade, not only to bring in robes and pelts, but to provide an occasional drunk, a Christmas or New Year's bacchanal for bored and hard-bitten men.

But Maxim seethed. He'd been wounded at Bellevue not only by the minister but by Fitzhugh. He dreaded the future; dreaded that his name would be entered in federal records. Dreaded that he might be arrested upon his return to St. Louis; tried, imprisoned, shamed. That was his handwriting adding those vinegar casks to the company's manifests. It'd been a terrible mistake. He felt he was always making mistakes and Brokenleg was always rebuking him in his savage way. He could never go home. He knew he'd get a letter eventually from papa, telling him to stay away, live in the wild lands for a few years. It broke his heart even to think about it.

But that wasn't what had turned him sullen as he leaned over the rail at the prow and stared moodily at the eddying water. The whole thing offended his sense of decency. His family was engaged in a corrupt enterprise. His own father! His brother, too. And himself. There was no subterfuge in banking and finance, and Straus et Fils had borne no shame. But this! Pouring out watered spirits to Indians, getting them drunk, enticing them to trade anything, anything, all the robes in their lodges for just one more cup of diluted firewater. Whole villages impoverished themselves in one big drunk, peddling every last robe and pelt to greedy traders for another drink. And the traders made each batch progressively weaker; the drunker the Indians, the more they were cheated, until at the last the firewater had scarcely any spirits at all in it.

Fitzhugh didn't seem to mind. Neither did Jamie Dance. And not even his father minded! It filled Maxim with disgust that the people he was with would not see what they were doing, ruining villages, turning proud, strong native people into sots. He'd done it himself last year through the whole trading season. He'd seen it with his own eyes, dipped the cups into the pot and poured out a robe's measure. A rogue's measure, he corrected himself. He'd seen them outside the post, staggering, bellowing, brawling like animals, the last restraint loosed in them all. And other things. The squaws drank, too. And when they did — he blushed to think about it. He'd seen it all and it had sickened him. And he had done it. He himself.

Fitzhugh limped toward him, fire in his eye. "You sick or somethin'?"

"No." Maxim turned his back on Brokenleg and stared into the murky water.

"Somethin' in yer craw?"

"No."

"Then git yer little butt out there and help. These hyar yards are dangerous. The faster we wood, the better."

Maxim ignored him.

Fitzhugh spat, snarled, and turned to perform his usual task. His limp kept him on board but he helped stack the wood into neat cords close to the firebox where firemen could lift each heavy piece and shove it into the blistering firebox. But he stopped.

"You upset about them spirits? After gittin' burned back in Bellevue?"

Maxim refused to turn and face his tormentor.

"I guess that's it," Brokenleg said. "I

figure if the government was serious about it they'd shut us all down. Chouteau, small traders, us. They ain't serious. They want us hyar. Helps claim the territory. Keeps the British out. Wasn't for us, the fur men, we'd have no claim to Oregon country. That whiskey law — that's just a little sop for the people back East. Don't you worry it none. And don't you worry about Bellevue, neither. Your pa, he'll pull a few strings. Him and Davey Mitchell. And it'll all pass."

"No it won't!" Maxim cried. "It'll never pass. We're ruining the tribes! We're stealing."

Brokenleg was startled, and sputtered something.

"It's not a sop. It's what decent people insist on. It's what I would want. We're so greedy we don't care! Don't care if some poor Indian trades everything — everything — for another cup of . . . of water with a dash of spirits in it!"

Much to Maxim's surprise Brokenleg didn't get angry, didn't bark harshly at him, as he usually did. Instead, he limped forward and leaned over the rail, peering down into the water beside Maxim.

"Them Injuns, they're adults," he said. "Nothin' compellin' them to trade a robe for a cup of spirits. A lot don't. The Crows don't hardly at all. They make their own choices. I reckon we're just providin' a product like anything else."

"It's not the same!" Maxim shouted at him. "They're not used to it. It's new. It's not in their — their ways. They're — savages."

"Oh, you got a point there, boy. Savages. Get an Injun drunk and he's likely to go mean, go crazy, start butcherin' and carryin' on like no white man I ever seen. Well, ah, I take that back. I seen a bunch o' white men turn savage, too, some spirits in 'em. Real savage. Like at the rendezvous."

"We shouldn't be doing it. It's against the law. It's against — decency!"

"I don't suppose it'd convince ye to say we'd go outer business fast; that we got to, or Chouteau's men'll take away our trade."

"No it doesn't," Maxim said. "Just because they're doing it — that doesn't make it right!"

Fitzhugh studied the water. Behind them the ship's bell clanged, summoning all on shore aboard. "There's two things, boy. There's what is, and there's what should be. The robe trade is. It just is, and no one knows how to change it. The Indian Bureau, it made Indian agents of a passel of ministers and it didn't do nothing except rile up the Injuns. They don't like having some white man hold back food and government annuities unless they start goin' to church, give up their ways, quit having two, three wives, quit huntin' buffler, start plowing the ground and sweatin' like no Injun never sweat before — naw. It ain't workin'. Nothing works good. I understand how you feel, boy. I feel real bad myself some times. But it don't do no good to feel bad. The world is. That's all there is to it. It just is."

Maxim turned to Brokenleg. "No," he said softly. "I won't do it anymore. I'm going back down the river with *The Trapper*, Brokenleg. I'm going home if they'll let me in the house."

Three

Little Whirlwind stood on the hurricane deck and thought about slaves. She had always wanted them. From the time she was a girl she knew she'd marry a powerful warrior who would capture enemies of the Tsistsista and give them to her. As a child she'd practiced being mean. She'd found a stick and beat ponies with it, pretending they were old Absaroka squaws she could bully. Or young Assiniboin girls. Or some stupid Gros Ventre boy she could whip. She'd always known exactly how to deal with slaves and she supposed it was part of her heritage as a Suhtai, a daughter of a medicine man.

She would make her slaves scrape hides and gather firewood, and if they weren't quick about it she would hit them with a stick and tell them they were dogs. Sometimes the warriors of her village made wives of the slaves, which was good. Then the oldest wife had lots of help. When her father had given her to the rich white man who laid blankets and a rifle and an axe before her lodge, she thought she'd have more slaves than any girl in the village!

But she hadn't known he hated slaves and wouldn't give her any. How strange he was. Didn't he know that the more slaves he had, the happier he made his wife? No, he didn't. She supposed it was because he had a bad leg and couldn't capture slaves in war. She scorned him for not making war. All he wanted to do was make love. Often, in the night, she'd scolded him: "Make war, nor love!" But he'd just laughed.

He didn't know how much he had hurt her. He was rich now, a trader, and he still didn't give her captives and swore he never would. Didn't he know that other peoples were just like dogs? What else was there to do with a Piegan woman? Or a Shoshone? Inferior people, fit for nothing!

She desperately wanted slaves now. She was the only woman in Fitzhugh's Post and she needed help. The white men expected her to do everything — cook, clean up, build fires, make them moccasins, tan hides, heat water, mend their clothing. But that was only part of it: she'd grown lonely without any female company. Slaves were always good for that. In her village the rich wives chattered through the days with their slaves, enjoying the gossip. But her man wouldn't give her any. It was like a slap in the face; like telling her she wasn't worth anything and didn't deserve help, not even one slave.

But Fitzhugh wouldn't yield. She had to reconcile herself to that. He might be rich but he'd kept her poor. She'd badgered him about it, and it got to be a sore point between them. He didn't understand her — and she certainly didn't understand his strange aversion to slaves. Other white men had slaves. Guy Straus and his wife had five or six.

Still, if she couldn't have slaves . . . he might accept wives. She'd tried that idea on him, too, but he'd scoffed and joked and asked her what he'd do with another wife. So she didn't tell him she and her family had some ideas about that, and that she wanted him to marry not just one other wife but three more.

The empty prairies released something in Little Whirlwind. The emptiness itself did it. The farther upriver *The Trapper* toiled, the less there was to see, and that is what appealed to her most. Except for occasional timbered flats, they traveled through a land of silence and grass with only the wind and clouds giving life to the universe. Not far west, beyond the distant green bluffs of the river, was the country of her people; a broken grassland that was still her spiritual home. Just now the fireboat traversed the land of the Lakotah, her people's ancient allies. But the fireboat would crawl up the river, taking her to the lands of her people's enemies, the Crow, the Blackfeet, the Assiniboin and Cree. She did not like living on the Yellowstone surrounded by her enemies the Crow. She had begged Fitzhugh to build his trading post farther south near her own people, but he'd said the new post needed a water route so the fireboat could bring the trade goods and take the robes down the river. That had ended the discussion in his mind, but not in hers. Each day a bitterness had grown in her.

She lived on the hurricane deck because she could see the wide world from there. When it was chilly she drew about her a Witney trade blanket, blue stripes on a cream ground. But mostly the days were hot and sun glinted off the water like knife-stabs, making her squint. From her high vantage she could lord over all the white men on the main deck. She could see Maxim at the prow, staring into the water, moody and unhappy. She could see deck passengers, smelly mountaineers mostly, who had bought only the passage and not a cabin. They argued and spat over the side, and waved their rifles or shot at deer on the banks.

How strange white men were: they toiled at women's work. No Cheyenne man would stoop to gathering wood or throwing logs into the fire of the fireboat. Women made fires and gathered wood and kept the fires burning. Women put up lodges and gathered food. No Cheyenne boy would think of bringing tea to her the way the cabin boy did. No proper Cheyenne man would dream of wrestling cargo or cooking or dragging up the anchor. That was women's work. Cheyenne men hunted and made war and gambled and gossiped, and that was how Maheo made them and how Sweet Medicine wished them to behave: with utmost virtue. She detested all white men.

Which reminded her of something that had been building up inside of her for many moons. She would not live this way anymore. And now was the time to talk about it, now while Brokenleg didn't have much to do except watch the banks for buffalo. She would not put it off or let Fitzhugh put it off.

She trotted down the companionways, feeling the fringes of her doeskin skirt dance over her calves. She found him aft, in shade, watching the prairie parade by. He

45

knew what was coming; she could tell that from the look in his eye when he saw her.

"Now see hyar —" he began.

"We talk about it," she said.

He started to limp forward but she kept up. "I going to leave you," she said. "I going to my people. You treat me bad."

That stopped him. He whirled, his blue eyes afire. "You what?"

"You heard me. And you know why."

He hawked and spat overboard. The green river whirled it away. "I don't treat you bad, Dust Devil."

"I'm Little Whirlwind."

"Yer my wife."

"You're rich! You can have anything you want. You can buy lots of slaves."

"I'm agin slaving. You know that."

She couldn't understand him. Rich white men like the Strauses had lots of slaves. She wanted some. "Then I go away. I have no one to help me. A strong Tsistsista warrior would have lots of them. And wives, too. You no good. No good white man."

"Dust Devil — I want you."

"I all alone. I have no one to talk to. No sisters. All winter I do not see another Tsistsista woman to talk to. Only white men, speaking French or English. I hate French and English is worse. I ask you many times, twenty times, a hundred times, for slaves and you just say later, not now. Well now is later."

"Well, you hang on. We'll git the trade goods shelved and git the season started and maybe I'll hire a Crow girl or two."

"Hire! Ha! I won't talk to any Absaroka woman. Unless she's a slave. I talk to a slave. No good, Fitzhugh. I leaving."

"But Dust Devil — maybe you'd like some red cloth for a new dress."

She glared at him. "That isn't what I want. I want slaves. I like to have slaves. It makes me feel good. Slaves or wives. You won't take either so I'm leaving you."

"But you can't! I paid your pap the bride price —"

"I going back to him. He'll have me. I tell him everything, how you treat me bad. I got three sisters, three Suhtai women. I stay with you if you marry them."

Fitzhugh stared. "Whoa up. Marry your sisters?"

"Yes. All. My father, he's waiting for you to bring him the gifts. He says no to all the Tsistsista boys that play the flute outside the lodge because I tell him you're coming for them."

"You told him that?"

"Yes. And they are waiting!"

"But one ain't ready yet. I mean, Sweet Smoke."

"It makes no difference. She marry you now."

"But Hide Skinning Woman, she don't think much o' me."

"It is for my father to decide."

"And — Elk Tail, she has eyes for a young feller — He's playin' the love flute for her last I heard."

"My father says you are for her."

"How'm I supposed to keep four wives happy?"

She giggled. "We take turns. We decide. You make one happy each night. We have a hundred children. Three sisters wear the rope, and all of them want to untie the rope for you. Are you a Blanket Chief or not?"

"I'm a fur man."

"I be happy again, Fitzhugh. With my sisters. We help you. Help the post. You need the help. We get wood and cook and tan hides and make moccasins and weave reeds and dig roots and plant corn and cut greens. I can't ever get enough greens and roots for so many men."

"I didn't say I'd git married —"

"Yes you will. Or I go away. I'll not even stay on this fireboat. I'll leave you at Fort Pierre and walk to my people." She glared at him, daring him to make a prisoner of her.

"You soundin' serious."

"After we get off the fireboat we take the trade goods and put them on the shelf. Then we take a wagon, you and me, and go south to my people with lots of trading things — and gifts for my father. We trade everything for robes. And you will give the bride-gifts to my father, and he is pleased and have a smoke with you. And we bring my sisters back. And you enjoy them."

"Sweet Smoke, she's too young," he muttered. "She's younger than Maxim even."

"That Maxim! He's unhappy. Maybe he needs Sweet Smoke. Maybe Sweet Smoke needs Maxim. We'll bring Sweet Smoke. If he don't want her, you marry her."

"How'd I git into this, dammit?"

"Because I tell you I leave you, you treat me bad, I'm lonely. Wives or slaves. You get one or the other and I stay. Maybe both. I want some slaves."

He grinned. "We'll git on up there and you'll be too busy to think on it."

"Wait and see!"

"How about I send for your sisters and we marry 'em to the engages? Then you can talk Cheyenne all you want with them."

"No. You're a big chief, a headman of the whites, and rich. My father waits for you to marry them. He wants rifles and powder and balls and blankets and hatchets and knives for them. My brother, maybe he come kill you if you don't, because he don't want his sisters to be never-married ones."

"I ain't makin' no promises, Dust Devil."

"Then I leave you now. At the next wood stop." She turned angrily toward the companionway and their cabin to gather up her things.

"Whoa up! I'll do it — soon as I can." He looked sulky.

She was exultant. "I have your word, Fitzhugh. You better not lie to me."

The June rise was ebbing and Captain Sire drove *The Trapper* relentlessly, beginning before dawn each day and not stopping until the last of the midsummer light vanished and Black Dave Desiree could see no more. They reached Fort Pierre at dusk, tarried only a few minutes to discharge several Chouteau engages and a few kegs. They pushed on for another two hours in the last light while Desiree piloted more by instinct than by vision.

Little Whirlwind did not get off, much to Brokenleg's relief. If she intended to walk to her people, Fort Pierre was the most likely starting point. She loved him in her own way — he knew that. And even though they'd had rough scrapes, Injun and white not knitting together very well, he loved her, too. And apparently was about to love her sisters. The thought started him squirming. He'd find a way out. He'd bring 'em to the post if he had to — an asset, really, free labor, companionship for Dust Devil. Bring 'em but not in unholy wedlock.

Sire drove the packet north again between arid bluffs with browning grass, past small herds of buffalo, some of them sun-bleached to chestnut and umber. Sire no longer stopped to pick up the buffalo the ship's hunters and passengers shot as they passed, except when the meat supply ran low. In spite of Desiree's gifted piloting they ran aground a bar that hadn't been there only a month before, a bar that had grown when the treacherous Missouri cut through an oxbow and rechanneled itself.

They lost a whole day grasshoppering over the bar, in trouble because of a sharp flow that quartered in from starboard and threw the vessel off its spars. Up above, on the texas or in the pilothouse, Sire paced, and Black Dave stood, waiting for the crew to free the vessel again. A harsh thunder-shower caught them just when the crew was lowering the spars into the sandbar for the third time. Lightning crackled and spat over the ship, an angry augury. On the fourth try Sire reversed the paddle wheels, pushing water forward and lifting the hull two or three inches. As any old riverman knew, the reversed force of the paddle wheels was no match for the forward motion of the packet as crewmen winched the boat upward and ahead. That time *The Trapper* slid off the spars planted into the sandbar, teetered on the bar, and then slowly eased forward and floated free, as emancipated as Black Dave himself. Men cheered. Within seconds the packet was churning its way ever north and west again.

They unloaded more American Fur engages, a few free trappers and some mountaineers, at Fort Clark along with five tons of Chouteau freight and then pushed on past the pox-killed Mandan villages. The lightened boat lost two precious inches of draft, which helped the pilot a bit. Each day the July sun blistered in, drying up the river, making Black Dave's work harder and more perilous by the hour as channels shrank and underwater obstacles, sunken root-systems called sawyers, rippled the glinting surfaces. Game disappeared by day, hiding from the brutal sun, grazing and watering only when dusk settled along the riverbanks deep into the night.

The land had changed. Trees and timbered wooding lots grew scarce. Bluffs showed their rocky bones. Prickly pear covered whole slopes. Nature's luxury had been scraped away leaving a spare landscape. Fitzhugh loved the change — loved anything that swept him away from the crowds of men thriving on fertile, watered soils. Here life was hard; the Indians who populated this country were mean, and it appealed to something at his center.

They steamed past the mouth of the Yellowstone in the morning of July sixteenth, surrounded by reddish and yellow bluffs almost naked of grass. An hour later, steaming up the greatly diminished Missouri, they raised Fort Union, the palatial Chouteau and Company seat of empire. It stood on the north bank at about forty-eight degrees north latitude, close to the British possessions. From behind its sixteen-foot stockades Major Alexander Culbertson ran Pierre Chouteau's Upper Missouri Outfit, a string of subsidiary posts that drew in the trade of Blackfeet, Crows, Assiniboin, Cree, some northern Sioux, Sarsi, an occasional Bannock and Flathead party, Hidatsa, Arikara, and Gros Ventres.

The post's six-pounder boomed its welcome and Sire shrilled the boat whistle. Surrounding the post was a sea of tawny cowhide lodges, evidence that the trading season was at its peak. Crowds of Indians swept to the levee, urchins and women arriving ahead of the men to gape at this intruder from the magical world of whitemen. And along with them a swarm of Fort Union's engages, ready to haul cargo into the post and baled robes into the hold.

It was the end of the line for Missouri River travelers and as swiftly as deckmen lowered the stage, thirty-seven mountaineers and a dozen of their Indian wives, most of them deck passengers, debarked for the hinterlands. At Sire's shouted orders sweating deckmen began hoisting cargo up and swinging it out to the levee while Maxim watched hawkishly to prevent errors and protect Rocky Mountain Company cargo. Brokenleg, standing on the hurricane deck, spotted Major Culbertson and waved at his rival, but didn't descend. Sire intended to pull out, not waste a minute, and there'd be no time for palaver.

An hour and a half later *The Trapper*, ten tons lighter and riding three inches higher, pulled free of the levee, wheeled around, descended the Missouri to the Yellowstone, and swung into the smaller river. Sire had contracted to deposit the Rocky Mountain cargo just below Wolf Rapids if the river was navigable — as far as Joe LaBarge had gone the year before. There, if things went right, Brokenleg would rendezvous with half a dozen engages from the post along with their big Pittsburgh wagons, and he, Dust Devil, Maxim, and the three new engages, Paul Lebrun, Pierre Grevy, and Jean Poinsett, would travel upriver to the Bighorn — and Fitzhugh's Post.

They passed a vast herd of buffalo lazing in the cool of cottonwoods. The cumbersome beasts clambered to their feet and fled as the riverboat closed on them, vanishing into timber and then trickling up a coulee in the far bluff. Fitzhugh thought it was a good omen, a sure sign of a good trading year, and rejoiced. They steamed past a small village of Hidatsa, cousins of the Crows, exciting them to frenzy. The villagers raced along the banks screaming insults. Sire didn't trust them and pushed into a moonlit night that taxed Black Dave Desiree's skills to their utmost as he fathomed and fought the narrow channel.

They reached Wolf Rapids the next day while Sire muttered that there wasn't even enough flow to turn the packet around. As they approached Maxim appeared to be more and more agitated and sullen, until Brokenleg finally made his way to the bow and collared the young man.

"You got some kind of itch?" he asked roughly.

Maxim wouldn't look at him.

"You got somethin' in your craw, boy. You git it out right now."

Maxim peered into the swirling green water looking miserable. When at last he forced himself to meet Brokenleg's gaze his eyes seemed haunted.

"I'm not going," he mumbled.

"You ain't going? What do you mean, boy?"

"I'm going back with the boat."

"Back with the boat! I need you! You signed on — you can't jist ditch the company. Your pa, he'd kill you."

"I'm going back."

The boy swung his gaze back to the water, and he peered into it so studiously that Fitzhugh sensed he was hiding tears. Tears or not he'd pull that smart aleck plumb off the packet if he had to.

"Lissen here, boy. You're comin' even if I got to hog-tie you and carry you off. You hear? You ain't a quitter. I ain't a quitter. Last year we didn't quit and we come out of it in one piece. Now you git to your bunk and put your kit together."

"You'll have to make me," Maxim muttered, gripping the rail with white knuckles. "Make me your slave."

Brokenleg's temper flared but he held himself in check. This was Guy Straus's little boy he was barking at. "We'll be hyar half a day unloadin'. You better damn well change your mind before we pull out!"

But Maxim huddled over the rail as if expecting Fitzhugh to smack him.

Brokenleg didn't have time for one spoiled brat's rebellion. As *The Trapper* slid close to the rendezvous island, a cotton-wooded acre connected to the bank by gravelly shallows, he discovered only silence. He saw none of his engages, not even Samson Trudeau who was as reliable as a good Hawken rifle. And no wagons, either. They hadn't met him. And that meant trouble.

Four

No one. Brokenleg studied the timbered island, hunting for the Pittsburgh wagons, for his engages. No one. They'd missed the rendezvous. He realized suddenly he was in a bad fix. Around him deckmen gathered at the rail, ready to lower a long stage and tie the packet fast as soon as the drifting boat, its giant wheels stilled, slid toward shore.

This was near where they'd unloaded the year before; a secret place well screened by timber from the river trace; a place well known to all his engages except Abner Spoon and Zach Constable, who'd joined him later. He reviewed what he'd told Trudeau: have wagons and men there by mid-July and wait.

The packet skidded into mud and lurched to a halt a dozen feet from the bank. Deckmen lowered the stage. It didn't reach the bank; it splashed into water two or three feet out but it didn't matter. Captain Sire barked an order from above and the crew sprang to work, hoisting cargo from the hold and swinging it on a spar over land and reeling it to earth.

Brokenleg hastened up the companionways, ignoring the vicious pain in his bad leg, until he reached the texas. "Cap'n," he muttered, out of breath. "Can you hold her a while? We got nobody hyar. Jist hold her up a day or two."

Sire shook his head. "Alas, Monsieur Fitzhugh. The river, she drops by the hour. We can't wait. Even now the risk is impossible — impossible. We may be forced to abandon her as it is. No — we'll unload and start back the instant — the very second we have fulfilled our contract."

"That's what I was afraid you'd say. I got me three men and a boy to defend fifteen thousand dollars of trade goods. And that village o' Hidatsa only a dozen miles away. And that isn't all, neither. I haven't got a bit o' sheeting to protect it. We were gonna put 'er into the wagons — under the wagon sheets. Keep rain off them blankets and cloth and all."

"Monsieur Fitzhugh, I wish I could help you."

"Maybe you can. You got any sheeting in ship's stores to spare?"

Sire didn't respond. Instead he bellowed something in French to the mate, who trotted off toward the storage bins aft of the boiler. Meanwhile, on the grassy bank the cargo grew into a small mountain. The crew worked feverishly, not wasting a second.

Then the mate appeared below and yelled up to the captain.

"We've none to spare, Monsieur. And the whole of it wouldn't begin to cover your cargo."

The news couldn't have been worse. Fitzhugh sighed and plunged down the companionways, leapfrogging steps to spare his tortured leg. The morning sky looked blue enough but it meant nothing. Thousands of dollars worth of cargo would be in peril, exposed to the elements there on the island.

He found his three new engages, Lebrun, Grevy, and Poinsett, on the deck, pulling their kits together. "Look hyar," he said. "We got us a pile o' trouble. No one hyar from the post. We got to protect them things. You git on down to the bank fast, and git busy. We've got to dig us a dray cache somewhere, which ain't gonna be easy hyar. Maybe back in them bluffs. We got to make her big and dry and then haul every blanket and bolt of cloth and what else gets hurt by rain into it, and do her before it rains."

They nodded. Caching was something every man of the mountains knew about. It was the time-honored way of storing beaver plews, weapons, and even food, safe from weather and Injun eyes. It was an art in its own right. A poorly built or misplaced cache would leak water and ruin whatever lay within. A poorly concealed cache would swiftly be discovered and robbed by any passing tribesmen — or wolf or bear.

Lebrun understood English best and spoke it. "We'll dig like badgers and haul like mules," he said.

They hauled their kits down the gangway, splashing the last few feet to land. Each carried a heavy pack of personal things and a good mountain rifle. On the bank they stood helplessly, waiting for spades and axes to show up from the hold.

Fitzhugh plunged into the hold, dodging swinging nets of cargo, and hunted down the spades, a dozen of them simply corded together. He grabbed the whole lot, struggled up the ladder to the main deck, and hauled them ashore, sweating fiercely. The engages swiftly grabbed them and headed toward the southern bluffs half a mile off. It'd be a staggering business to build a cache and carry the most vulnerable things on their backs to it, but Fitzhugh didn't let himself think about it. He'd been in tighter corners.

No matter how fast the crew worked, it wasn't fast enough for Sire, who paced the hurricane deck and scowled. Hours passed, and the lightened vessel pulled free of the mud and rocked at the end of its mooring hawsers. And on shore the heap of Rocky Mountain Company trade goods and post furnishings grew haphazardly. Sire put every man to work except the pilot. Black Dave was exempt. Sire collected the last scourings off his ship, the cook and cook's helper, the cabin boy, five firemen, the first and second engineers, the steersmen, and the sleeping second mate, and started them on firewood detail.

Brokenleg watched irritably, trying to keep the frenzied crewmen from smashing his crates and kegs. He couldn't help much — not with a leg that barely functioned. He glared at the crewmen lowering the six casks of illegal spirits to earth, daring them to swipe a drop, hoping they hadn't. Dust Devil appeared on the boiler deck, carrying her own things in a parfleche. He had to get his — and he had to deal with that brat Maxim. The very thought of the youth sulking in his cabin infuriated Brokenleg. He should be here checking off items against his cargo manifest as they were lowered to the grass. But Brokenleg couldn't be everywhere. He couldn't be watching the trade goods, couldn't be helping Little Whirlwind, couldn't be deciding on a place to dig a cache, couldn't be collaring Maxim, couldn't be down in the hold making sure every last item was being shoved over to the cargo hatch and dumped into the cargo nets. He couldn't be guarding the casks from pilferage by the boatmen.

Nonetheless he could deal with Maxim. He shoved his way up the stage like a salmon climbing a rapids, fighting past crewmen hauling firewood aboard or returning to the timber for more. He clambered up the companionways, ignoring the lancing pain he felt, and thundered to the boy's room. He jammed the door hard and found it locked.

"Maxim, you open up now!" he roared.

That produced only silence.

"I'll bust it down," he warned.

"You would," Maxim replied. "That's how you think. Just force."

"You're coming off this boat. Now git packed and git out."

"You can't order me around."

Brokenleg had had enough. He was running on a short fuse anyway with so much going wrong. He reared back and slammed into the door. The flimsy lock gave easily, tearing loose from wood, and Brokenleg staggered in.

Maxim careened backward into his bunk, wild fright in his face. Brokenleg pounced, grabbed him by the scruff of the neck and yanked him up.

"I knew you would. I'm not your slave," the boy said.

"You ain't of age yet," Brokenleg roared. "And you're in my charge."

Maxim sighed, his face twisted into contempt. "If you think you can keep me imprisoned at the post you're wrong. I'll slip away the first time I'm not guarded night and day."

"Git your kit packed."

Maxim did nothing. "I'm not going to participate in my own abduction," he said.

"Then do without," Brokenleg roared, collaring the youth again and marching him into the darkened salon.

"I'll — get my things."

"Be quick about it. And don't forget the cargo manifest. You can git busy checking off the lists."

"I won't. I won't."

"I haven't time to listen to yer reasons. You git, git it done, and then tell me."

"You wouldn't understand anyway. You know nothing about right and wrong."

Brokenleg felt like boxing the boy but instead helped him stuff his duds and books into a valise. That done, he marched the youth through the salon, down the steps to the main deck, and down the stage to land, Maxim sulky and slow before him.

"Now — check cargo!"

Instead, Maxim sat down on a keg and did nothing. Brokenleg had no time to argue. He grabbed the manifest and began checking off whatever he could find in the chaos on the bank, a task he knew was hopeless. But he did it anyway.

The spar swung the final load to shore and the sweat-blacked crew dumped it unceremoniously.

"Monsieur, that is the last, *n'est-ce pas?*"

Brokenleg didn't know. He scrambled back aboard and lowered himself into the low hold, his every step echoing hollowly in the dank dark. He lacked a lantern but with the light from the hatch as a guide he felt his way aft and then forward, seeing nothing but emptiness, hearing the slap of water on the hull.

He emerged into blinding light, waved at the captain, and debarked. Above him, steam shrilled from the escapement signaling the crew to free the hawsers and board. The vessel floated free, swung around, and thundered downriver with indecent haste, riding on a flow that shrank by the hour.

Brokenleg peered about him in the silence. The new engages were off somewhere. Maxim sat sullenly. Dust Devil smirked. And there on the bank sat a fortune unguarded.

On the first day of July, Samson Trudeau set out for the rendezvous site, about a hundred ninety miles downriver as close as anyone could reckon. He and his five engages would meet *The Trapper* near the place where *The Platte* had discharged its cargo the year before. He was due in mid-July and reckoned he'd have three or four days to spare even if the going was hard. In any case *The Trapper* was not likely to be early; not on a second trip up the Missouri scraping its keel most of the way.

He left Fitzhugh's Post in the competent hands of Abner Spoon and Zach Constable and a few others. He took with him the rough, hard Creoles who'd been with the company from the beginning: Larue, Bercier, Brasseau, Courvet, and Dauphin. He enjoyed them all, these seasoned mountaineers who knew the wilds better than they knew the alleys of St. Louis. They were all two-legged oxen, hardened to brutal labor and cheerful in nature, needing nothing but a pipe of *tabac* at the end of a rough day. The going would be good; the empty wagons easy on the oxen and mules.

That morning, none too early because nothing ever happened very early at a fur post, they yoked twelve oxen and hitched three yokes to a wagon. And they harnessed three span of mules and hitched them to the remaining wagon. These were Pittsburghs, designed for heavy freight, with a watertight box and well-oiled sheeting over the bows to keep the contents dry. An hour or so later they passed Fort Cass, the American Fur Company post just eat of the confluence of the Bighorn, and discovered a large collection of Crow lodges there and a lively robe trade in progress. The opposing company had already been resupplied with trade goods brought from Fort Union by a Chouteau keelboat poled and cordelled upriver by a dozen rivermen. In fact the keelboat was still there, anchored close to the fort. Soon it would float the summer's returns, a few hundred bales of buffalo robes, back to the sprawling warehouse at Fort Union.

Someone up in the wooden bastion at Cass shot a salute and Trudeau's men fired a piece or two in response. Scores of Crows paused, watching the wagons wend their way east. Samson wished the Rocky Mountain Company had a keelboat. It would be far easier to haul the trade goods from Wolf Rapids in one than it was to freight it with these cumbersome wagons over a nonexistent road with poor fords. He himself had come upriver as a boatman like most of the other French here. That was in the days before the steamboats; the days when sweating Creoles, rippling with muscle, poled the sixty-foot boats against the current; and when they couldn't pole they tied the thousand-foot cordelle to the mast and dragged the boat forward, stumbling along muddy banks, fighting mosquitos, scaring up bear, ending each day soaked and exhausted — and proud. Only the French could drag a heavy keelboat laden with tons of trade goods over two thousand miles up the Missouri. On rare occasions when the wind was right they could hoist a sail and push up the river on the breath of God, but that rarely happened. The pole and cordelle were things he and his colleagues knew; they didn't know the oxen and wagons as well.

They progressed peacefully down the Yellowstone, never far from its cold waters even though the bluffs were often a mile away. They scared up mule deer that lurked by day in the cottonwood and willow thickets along the river, dodging the fierce sun. Trudeau halted his party midday, let them sleep through the worst of the heat while the oxen and mules grazed and rested. They made good time, conquering fifteen or eighteen miles a day without gaunting the livestock.

Still, the peace was deceptive and did not fool Samson Trudeau a bit.

"Hobble the oxen, picket the mules," he told his men each dusk. "Who knows when the trouble, she comes in the night?" And the men did. They didn't need to be told; he said it because words were pleasant on the French tongue.

"Soon we will have a gill of spirits, *oui?*" he added. Men laughed. The trip had been fueled by their long dry run, and the promise of a rousing good time soon.

No moon illuminated the fourth night but it didn't matter. He'd found a good campsite well off the trace and close to the river, a few grassy bankside hectares screened from the world by a thick growth of willow and hackberry. They arrived at dusk, dusty from the long trek. The spring monsoons had vanished and now the country sweltered under a ruthless sun with only a rare thundershower to mitigate the heat.

His men patiently hobbled half the oxen and picketed the mules on long lines, and settled down to roast the antelope that Brasseau had shot earlier. They had enormous appetites, and the pronghorn would scarcely fill their bellies. But it was enough, and they settled swiftly into sleep under scattered stars dimmed by heat haze.

That's when trouble came; when the bawling of oxen and bleating of mules brought them up from the earth clutching their percussion pieces. The supper fire had long since died, the night offered no light, and they could scarcely tell what was happening. But their ears told them something, anyway: the livestock was being driven off. The braying and bleating of the mules diminished into the void. Oxen bawled in pain, and the sound of splashing reached the Creoles. There was nothing to shot at. Not a single one of the raiders had been visible to them although they knew it was a horse-mounted party. The whicker and snort of horses had accompanied the whole uproar, occasioning a few helpless shots from some of the men.

They had no lantern but spread out upon the meadows where the stock had been left to graze, knowing they'd find nothing. But they did stumble upon a few things — carcasses of oxen sprawled like black mounds, radiating heat. And poking from them, several arrows. Bercier tugged two arrows loose, losing their points in the carcasses of the oxen, and wearily the engages returned to their campsite and built a fire so that they might examine the shafts. Trudeau himself could often tell the arrow of one tribe from another. They all used different ways to fletch the arrows and dye them. Different materials, too. Feathers from different birds. Silently, when at last the fire careened high enough into the blackness to give them vision, they studied the arrows. He examined these, noting the long gray feathers, and decided he didn't know.

"Pieds Noirs," muttered LaRue.

"How is it that you know, Gaspard?"

"I know."

"*Sacrebleu!*" It was more than Trudeau knew, or the rest for that matter, but they accepted it.

"*Mais, pourquoi?*"

They couldn't answer that. These raiders had stolen the mules, which plains Indians coveted, and had shot arrows into at least some of the oxen — which they didn't really care about. They all despised the soft meat of white men's buffalo. Why, indeed? And one more thing chafed at Trudeau. Horse stealing parties traveled on foot, intending to ride off with their booty. But this party had been mounted. What did it signify?

They extinguished the fire, not wishing to make targets of themselves, and sat up, their backs to the wagon wheels or the heavy wooden yokes for the oxen. They smoked the *tabac* and waited for dawn, which would shed light on their dilemma. There was nothing to say; not among these old friends who knew each other's innermost thoughts without a word being uttered.

When at last dawn grayed the northeastern firmament and they could distinguish earth from sky, tree from prairie, they spread out silently, seeing the carnage that had been curtained from their eyes in the night. Of the twelve oxen, seven lay dead or wounded, pierced by arrows. The others had vanished. Of the six mules not a one remained. And back at the campsite sat three giant freight wagons, as useless as a canoe without paddles.

"This was the work of Pierre le Cadet, *oui?*" said Bercier.

No one replied. Trudeau thought they

probably all agreed. It had been an odd raid, well timed, four days from Fort Cass and Fitzhugh's Post, and six or seven from the Wolf Rapids rendezvous. Well planned by observers who had seen the wagons turn off the trace to this hidden bankside meadow. Pierre Chouteau's work indeed, or that of one of his underlings at Cass or Fort Union. And right in the tradition of American Fur, the ruthless monopoly begun by John Jacob Astor and later sold in pieces to the Chouteaus and others. Trade war, with Indians doing the dirty work.

"We will walk, *alors*," he said.

They loosened the sheeting from the three wagons and cached it nearby in the woods. The wagon sheets would be a prize for any tribesman. The wagons were a prize, too. Their wheels could be burnt to get at the iron tires, which could be fashioned into lance points and arrowheads. He would hide them if he could. Sweating and cursing, three men on the tongue and three behind, pulled and pushed each wagon off the meadow and into the timber. There in the shadowy forest floor they heaped brush against the Pittsburghs. It would not fool anyone for long but it might conceal them from the casual observer.

Silently they started walking, each man

carrying a heavy pack over his back laden with the food and robes and camp supplies from the wagons. No man complained. No Creole engage ever complained; it was not in the gallic blood to do such a thing. Trudeau was grateful for that. The walking slowed them down at once. They needed to rest their aching shoulders every little while. They had to send a hunter ahead and stop to butcher and eat whenever he shot game because there was no way to carry meat. They were used to walking; indeed, they had walked beside the oxen, driving them along with curses and whips. But this was different, now that each man was a beast of burden carrying his necessaries on his back.

Fur wars. Trudeau thought that this was just another small episode in the brutal battles of the trading companies. Still . . . an idea blossomed in his mind. If this was war, he thought he knew a way to fight back.

"We will stay close to the river," he announced the second day. The five engages eyed him curiously. It would make their work even harder and the trip longer but Samson Trudeau had his reasons. He laughed malevolently, enjoying his thoughts.

Five

Guy Straus read and reread Maxim's letter, absorbing the bad news. The master of *The Trapper* had hand-delivered it, and sat across from Guy.

"Captain Sire, this is about an inspection at Bellevue. Were you present?"

"*Oui*. I saw it all. Maxim took the Indian Agent, a Reverend Foster Gillian, into the hold. A bit later the agent demanded — in a most strident tone, I must say — that some deckmen lift three casks to the main deck — casks labeled vinegar. The reverend pulled the bungs, sniffed, poked his finger in and licked it, and proclaimed them contraband spirits. He was most indignant, *mon ami*. A volcano of righteous wrath."

Guy nodded, his heart sinking. The news was cramping his belly and he felt the dull pain of the ulcer jab at him again. "What did he say, Captain?"

"Why, that your company'd lose its license, of course. That he'd move heaven and earth to make sure of it."

That's what Guy feared most. Tens of thousands of dollars hung in the balance. "What did he do with the spirits?"

"Why, he instructed the deckmen to pour them overboard — a most mournful occasion, I might add."

"He destroyed the evidence?"

"Oh, not entirely. He saved back a little. He has all he needs for evidence. And of course he had his indictment penned and ready for me to deliver on the return run. Which I did. To the superintendent at the Indian Bureau."

"Do you know how those casks got there? Maxim says he had no idea."

"Not the foggiest idea. The casks are on the ship's manifest but in a different hand."

"Let me see, if you please."

Sire handed him the shipping lists. There indeed were the inscriptions, on page three — and not in Maxim's awkward hand. "My son says the company, ah, cargo, was loaded as planned some miles upstream from Bellevue at the wooding lot near Sergeant Bluff. Is it so?"

"Indeed. Your gentlemen were waiting there with six casks — which were swiftly loaded." Sire looked as if he was keeping himself solemn with some effort.

"My son says here that he spotted the

casks almost immediately upon leaving Westport. He noted they weren't on his own copy of the manifest. He thought it was simply a shipping discrepancy — poor bookkeeping. A fatal supposition it seems. Have you any thoughts about it?"

"None, Monsieur Straus."

"Could one of your crew have been paid to smuggle the casks aboard — and doctor your own cargo list?"

Sire laughed shortly. "Who of them can write? Only the mate, Bazile Bissonet. He reads and writes. But that is not his hand. I know his hand. He often keeps the log."

"Have you a passenger list — especially from here to Westport?"

Sire shrugged. "*Non.* The cabin passengers, *oui.* The deck passengers — none."

"With your permission, Captain, I'd like to have my clerks copy the cabin passenger list while we talk."

"Of course."

Guy rang a small silver bell and a clerk materialized instantly, heard his instructions, accepted the passenger list, and vanished. "They are very fast," Guy muttered. "Tell me the rest. You delivered our cargo?"

"*Oui.* Here is a release signed by Monsieur Fitzhugh. We discharged the cargo on the bank below Wolf Rapids as he required and made haste back. Even riding light we fought sandbars all the way to the Platte. An ordeal. One shouldn't ascend the Missouri in a low-water year. *Mon Dieu!*"

"The cargo was not damaged?"

"Ah, not by my company. We unloaded everything intact. But it was vulnerable there. The engages from your post hadn't arrived and everything was exposed to the elements. I wish we could have stayed . . ." He shrugged.

Another worry. A fortune on a streambank, poorly guarded and vulnerable to weather and any passing village. Guy knew he'd have to endure that clawing worry for months. It'd be a long time before news filtered down two thousand miles of rivers. It was as bad as owning a clipper ship out upon the terrible seas. "Is there anything else I should know?" he asked dryly.

Sire looked apologetic. "There is a small matter. A cabin door was damaged. The lock broken, wood splintered. I have a small claim here —"

"One of our men? But only Maxim and Fitzhugh had cabins —"

"Maxim's, monsieur. It was his cabin door."

"Ridiculous! He's a gentle boy — I won't pay this!"

"I was afraid of that. Monsieur Straus, a cabin boy saw Monsieur Fitzhugh smash it open and drag your son — drag him out. At Wolf Rapids."

Fitzhugh! A vicious anger stabbed through Guy, setting off his ulcer again. "I'll delve into this. And after I have answers, you may be paid or not . . . Did the cabin boy say what this was about?"

Sire shrugged. "Nothing. He merely saw it. Now as for the claim, it's not a lot. But my word is my bond —"

"I'll pay," Guy growled. He stabbed the quill into the ink pot and scratched his initials. "They'll honor it. I'll deduct it from Fitzhugh's share — if there is any share."

The clerk returned with the passenger list, and Sire made a hasty exit. Guy rubbed his eyes, scarcely believing the bad news, knowing that the company hung by a thread — and much of his investment as well. Sabotage. He'd march over to that grubby office of Pierre le Cadet and wring his slippery neck. Chouteau'd hired some thug to slip those incriminating kegs on board and doctor the cargo manifest. Chouteau or one of his suave, bland relatives, which he had by the score.

And Maxim. Witless child. For a moment the full force of his fury landed on his seventeen-year-old son, but Guy curbed it. He'd yank the boy down the river and put him to work here. Too young. Much too young. Not an ounce of judgment . . .

He swept out of his offices, grabbed his gold-headed walking stick, and pierced into the steaming heat outside. He marched straight down Chestnut Street, bringing up a sweat under his arms with every step. It didn't matter. He found the ornate federal building near the riverfront, the place where the fate of the Rocky Mountain Company would be decided. He pushed through the chipped brown double doors and turned right, steering toward the Indian Bureau — once the lair of General William Clark, who'd governed the Indian territories ever since he'd returned from his great expedition to the Pacific with Merriwether Lewis, except for a few years as governor of Missouri Territory. But the present superintendent, David Mitchell, was another type altogether.

Guy pushed in, swept past a clerk in shirtsleeves, and waited at the open door. Mitchell was reading something — and Guy knew exactly what. The man looked as weathered as any mountaineer — which Mitchell was. He'd tromped the whole west, befriended the bribes, worked for

Chouteau for years — and knew the fur trade. There'd be no pretending here.

"Expecting you," Mitchell said, waving Guy to a straight-backed wooden chair. "The Reverend Mister Gillian writes a remarkable report. Ninety-nine percent fulmination, one percent fact. But the one percent is bad news for you."

"May I see it?"

"It's your privilege. It don't say nothing you don't already know."

"I don't know anything for sure."

Mitchell grinned skeptically. "I can't stop this, you know. If it happened, you lose your trading license."

"We know nothing about those casks."

Mitchell scratched his brow with a pencil. "You're in an odd position, Guy."

"We didn't buy or load those casks. You might ask le Cadet who put them there."

Mitchell laughed. "I appreciate your indignation," he said slowly. "But you know how it'll go."

Guy knew. The evasions of all the fur companies were common knowledge. Everyone knew the companies shipped spirits upriver, contrary to several laws of Congress. William Clark had winked at it if it wasn't too blatant. Chouteau's American Fur had been caught at it more than once

81

and the great man had bought and politicked his way out, with the powerful Senator Benton bullying the administration and the Senate as well. If Pierre Chouteau had barely escaped, then Guy had no chance at all.

Guy sighed. "The reformers will love the whole spectacle," he muttered. "And I'll be ruined. And Pierre will go on, just as he has."

Mitchell shrugged. "You're in an odd bind. You can't claim innocence. Whether or not those casks are yours, I'm sure you'd made arrangements of some sort."

Mitchell stared directly at Guy. Guy refused to respond.

"Sergeant Bluff, I'd wager, old coon."

David Mitchell knew the robe trade, Guy thought. "What do I do to escape the licensing hearings?"

Mitchell shrugged. "You can't escape them. At least not unless someone confesses to the crime. It is a crime, you know. A serious one in the eyes of some."

"I have to find who did it and wring a confession?"

Mitchell scowled. "A *believable* confession, Guy. Not one that can be bought on the levee. And that might not get you off either. When the hounds start baying after witnesses, they'll find witnesses."

"You were Chouteau's man for years, David."

The superintendent stared back. "I can't say as I appreciate your implication."

Guy sighed. "I'm sorry. You're a man I trust totally. It's that — everything I possess is at stake."

"For the record, Guy — I play no favorites. I'm charged with governing a vast territory . . . and every enterprise in it. I do it as fairly as I know how. I worked for Pratte, Chouteau and Company for years, yes. I poured many a cup of diluted spirits upriver for my employers, yes. If that's what you want me to say, I'll say it."

"I misspoke, David. All right. I ask one thing. Could you delay this a while? I'm going upriver."

"You? What'll that do?"

"Maybe nothing. But I'm going to try." Guy astonished even himself because he hadn't intended to go upriver at all.

"Oh, I can sit on it a few weeks, Guy. Good luck."

Three days Samson Trudeau and his men trudged down the Yellowstone staying close to the river. And then luck floated by. Just as Trudeau had hoped, the keelboat wending its way from Fort Cass to Fort Union drifted around a bend. One man operated the tiller; six others lounged amiably on the deck fore and aft of the low cabin, watching the banks roll by.

Trudeau hailed the low vessel and it veered toward shore. Within moments, the engages had tied it and were pouring the *tabac* into their pipes and gossiping about their respective employers, Chouteau and Company, and Rocky Mountain. It was the amiable way of engages everywhere in that unhurried world. Trudeau hated what he and his men had to do but the fur wars were rough. He hated it also because he knew most of the other side's engages: he'd spent many a trapping day with Duchouquette, Labone, Dorion, Barada, Croteau, and Dubruille. The other two, Fecteau and Labusier, he hadn't met.

"Ah, messieurs, we have had misfortune indeed," he said, a signal to his own men, who drifted amiably toward their packs. "The Indians — Pieds Noirs, we think — stole our oxen and mules. A fortune lost! A thousand dollars lost!"

"Oxen? What Indian ever wanted oxen?" asked Duchouquette, who was the man in charge.

"Ah, Emile, it was a sad thing. They put

arrows into them. The mules they drove off in the night but our oxen they slaughtered. It is not the way of horse-stealers."

Duchouquette smoked silently in the late afternoon quiet. Trudeau knew exactly what all the American Fur engages were thinking, and they were right to think it.

"At any rate, *mes amis,* we wish to be transported down the river to Wolf Rapids. It would save us many a blister and spare our boots."

Emile Duchouquette considered that, puffing fragrant *tabac* as if decisions depended on smoke.

"We will have a party," Trudeau said. "At Wolf Rapids are several casks of spirits."

Barada and Croteau laughed happily, and knocked the dottle from their pipes.

"Maybe for a small consideration," said Duchouquette. "The Company would disapprove but there are ways, *oui?*"

Ways indeed. Samson sighed and rose casually. His men stood near their packs. He wandered towards his. When he lifted his rifle, his men would too.

"Oh, we'll make a little offering," Samson said. He lifted his piece swiftly, and his men did, too. They didn't like it much, and neither did he. But necessity ruled.

Duchouquette stared from man to man.

The rest of the boatmen did too. "I was afraid of that," he said. "And you are Creoles like ourselves. You would shoot Creoles?"

"But yes," Samson replied. "And then make sure you are properly buried and wept over and your widows notified."

"We number more than you," Fecteau announced.

"Oh yes. And after we shoot, our rifles make fine clubs."

But they wouldn't try that. Not Creole against Creole. "All aboard," Samson said, prodding the opposition forward. He nodded to Bercier who ran ahead and plunged into the cabin, emerging with a handful of rifles, powder horns, and ammunition pouches.

"Is that all?"

"I will check again, Samson."

Bercier vanished into the cabin again, this time emerging with powder flasks and shot flasks for the swivel gun at the bow, along with three knives.

"Now it is an empty nest," Bercier said.

Trudeau marched his prisoners up the plank and into the cabin, and closed the door. None of them protested much. They'd come to no harm; it was fur company war, nothing personal. Nothing to expend lives and blood about, especially the blood of fellow Creoles.

Samson's men gathered their kits, hauled them on board, and stationed themselves on the deck. Two kept their rifles trained on the door, but it wasn't crucial. Samson himself took hold of the tiller and steered the *bateau* into the swift current. Peace reigned, after a fashion. He intended to travel day and night when the moon permitted. He'd stolen a keelboat, the value of which was actually less than the destroyed and stolen livestock. It would have to do.

By keelboat they were only a day and two nights from Wolf Rapids, and they'd make up some of the lost time. Not that he expected Fitzhugh to be there: the packet would be late in this low-water year.

They drifted on into the night, exploiting a quarter-moon until it sank. He let one opposition man at a time emerge, relieve himself, drink some river water, and return. He had nothing to feed them other than what the Chouteau men had on board, which was an emergency parfleche of jerky. They had been making meat as they traveled, needing little else.

When the moon vanished he began steering badly, grinding the keelboat into a gravel bar. His men poled it loose and they

87

drifted in the black current again. Mostly, the river took them where it would, the channel running now to one side and then to the other. He kept two men at the prow with sounding poles as the cool night progressed, and whenever they told him the keelboat was sliding into shallows he veered away. It didn't keep them entirely out of trouble but a keelboat was forgiving, unlike a steam packet.

Samson Trudeau felt no guilt at all, not even for confining his fellow Creoles down there among the bales of robes. They were hungry, no doubt — everyone was — but comfortable, spread out on robes and warm. He sighed. Hard times required hard measures. And he had justice on his side anyway.

At dawn, Brasseau shot a muley doe, and he veered toward the far bank to collect it. Brasseau himself leapt into the river, gasped at its coldness, and then dragged the doe off the shore and floated it toward the *bateau*, where many hands helped him up, and pulled up the doe. Trudeau didn't want to anchor — it would be a temptation for the opposition. They paused long enough to gather firewood and then Trudeau swung the long tiller, steering the keelboat into the relentless current. Swiftly, his men hung the deer from the mast, gutted it, butchered it, and began roasting venison over the small fire crackling in the sandbox that lay aft, the only device for cooking on board.

Around noon they passed a herd of buffalo shaded up along the bank under cottonwoods. No one shot; they didn't stop. His men hadn't slept, nor had he, and the paralyzing weariness of a second day without sleep invaded him. Weariness meant danger. Weariness meant bad judgment. He traded watches at the tiller with each man, and encouraged each man, in turn, to stay alert. He had Corneille Dauphin load the swivel gun at the prow just in case they ran into Indians. This was an oversized blunderbuss with an inch and a half bore, almost a small cannon. It rotated on a swivel pin set in a post. It could fire miniature cannonballs or enormous charges of buckshot.

"Load it with the shot, Corneille," he said, thinking it would be helpful against amassed warriors. But nothing transpired that hot July day. It was the peak of the trading season and most villages were camped around one or another of the posts, exchanging robes for things the tribes prized: axes, hatchets, knives, hoop iron for arrowheads, kettles, skillets, rifles and shot, awls, traps.

Sun blistered the deck making men dizzy with heat and dehydration but still he kept on, rotating the watches at the tiller so that each of his men got a rest in whatever shade he could find, which usually was none at all. The ones in the cabin had the better time of it, he thought. Now there was continuous talk and raillery among them all, the opposition men conversing through the small portholes on either side of the cabin with those on deck, almost as if they weren't prisoners or captors. And the ones in the hold had the better of it: hot as it was in there, it was cool compared to the brutal heat and glare on deck.

Thus they traveled, rotating duties, through the day and into the second night, each fighting exhaustion. Brasseau tied a line to himself and lowered himself into the cold water to shock his body back into life. Others just lay in a stupor, glad of the cool breezes of the night.

By dawn — fortunately, because they needed the light to navigate — they slid into patches of white water, marked by occasional boulders slicked smooth with the abrasions of the current. Wolf Rapids. There wasn't much of a fall, but between the current, the boulders, and the narrowing channel, it stopped the steamboats.

They shot out of the lower end just as sun poked over the northeastern bluffs — and beheld a mountain of trade goods lying nakedly on the shore, and Fitzhugh howling at them.

Wearily, Trudeau eased the long keelboat toward the bank until it touched bottom. His men threw lines to shore. Two or three Creoles Trudeau had never seen before caught the lines and tied them to willows. Fitzhugh stared, first at Trudeau, then at his own men on the deck, and then at a strange face in the porthole of the cabin. "You," he muttered, a crazy joy illumining his face. "All the ol' coons."

Six

In a few minutes Fitzhugh had the whole story. His oxen dead; his mules stolen! A keelboat for a dozen oxen and six mules seemed a fair-enough exchange although Maxim scowled about it. But Maxim was scowling about everything anyway.

"You sure it wasn't just another Blackfeet horse-raidin' bunch?"

"Yes," Trudeau said. "Horse raiders, they come on foot and ride their prizes away. But these came on horseback. Horse raiders, they don' bother with oxen. But these, they hang around and put an arrow into every ox, and steal the mules."

That was all Fitzhugh needed. "I reckon they got a keg o' whiskey for it. What about the wagons?"

"We cached the sheets in the woods near the river. It was all we could do."

He pointed at the boat. "What about them in the cabin?"

"They understand. We tell them the whole story. We're Creoles, they're Cre-

92

oles. They aren't mad."

"I guess you'd better let 'em out."

Moments later, the American Fur engages stood on the riverbank, blinking at the sun.

"What'd you have in mind, Trudeau?" Fitzhugh asked.

Trudeau's gallic shrug said more than words. He pointed at Primeau. "He knows *Anglais.*"

"Unload your bales and then help us load up. We're borrowing this keelboat."

"Stealing it," snapped Maxim.

"I reckon it's repayment, Maxim."

"Two wrongs don't make a right."

Fitzhugh ignored him. "Git your bales out and you can do what you want afterward. We'll leave your powderhorns and duffel, and drop your rifles a mile upstream."

"Monsieur Fitzhugh, I would not wish to leave the robes exposed to the weather."

It angered Brokenleg. "Your outfit didn't care about us leavin' our trade goods out hyar. Luckily there's been no rain — yet."

"I'll give him the sail," Maxim said.

Fitzhugh didn't like it but said nothing. Unless they had a freak easterly wind they wouldn't use the sail. When he didn't object, Maxim stalked sullenly aboard and pulled the sail out of a bin on deck.

Silent Chouteau men hefted the heavy bales up from the hold and handed them down to others on shore. Gradually a carefully built mound of baled robes, fit together like bricks to keep it watertight, rose near the Rocky Mountain Company trade goods. And then under the watchful eye of Fitzhugh's own armed engages the opposition men loaded the boat with Fitzhugh's supplies.

They were sweating freely when it was done although the day's heat had scarcely built up. The Chouteau men spread the sail over the compact load of robes, making it reasonably weathertight while his own men collected their kits and boarded.

Fitzhugh pulled Primeau aside. "You got supplies? Fire steel, and all?"

"I don't know," the man replied.

Brokenleg turned to Samson Trudeau. "Make sure they have what they need. All we want's their boat."

In short order a small heap of provisions lay on the grass, including coffee beans and tobacco, sugar and other staples, camp axes and hatchets, a few knives, and their blankets and robes.

"Primeau. About a mile up, we'll leave your rifles right on the bank close to water.

You wait a while. You come too soon and you'll run into that swivel gun."

Primeau grinned. "We're in no hurry. We'll smoke the *tabac. Merci beaucoup*," he added, half mocking. It wasn't war; it wasn't peace. Fitzhugh grinned back. Fur Company stuff. Maxim scowled again, obviously hating it.

His men swung the keelboat loose. Just to be on the safe side Fitzhugh himself swung the swivel gun around and kept the blunderbuss aimed toward shore. His engages each grabbed a long pole with a knob at one end, and lined themselves along each side. *"A bas les perches,"* cried Trudeau and the voyageurs thrust their poles in unison, the ball in the hollow of their shoulders, walking toward the stern. Sluggishly the boat lumbered forward. *"Levez les perches,"* Trudeau cried, and the Creoles lifted their poles, ready to repeat the operation. Muscling a keelboat upriver was brutal work. Fitzhugh would have poled too but his bum leg prevented it and someone had to steer anyway. He didn't trust Maxim with the job — not with that boy's frame of mind. Dust Devil had scurried into the cool hold.

Less than a mile upstream they found a grassy flat next to the main channel and he steered the boat to it. They left the opposition's rifles there. For good measure, Fitzhugh tied a red ribbon to some nearby brush. In about ten minutes those rifles would be back in the hands of their owners.

His nine engages, six from the post and the new three, poled their way upriver until they hit a place with no bottom, a place where the current shoved the boat hard against the far bank and they'd lost control. As the boat whirled backward and began to turn broadside of the eddy, Fitzhugh steered it brutally into the bank, and at once his engages caught the boat fast with gaff hooks, and dug out the cordelle. This long heavy line they tied to the mast, ran it through a bridle at the bow, and then plunged into the water next to the bank and played out the line until they were several hundred feet ahead of the keelboat. And then they began cordelling the boat forward, a task even more brutal than poling it.

For the next hour they hauled the boat forward, tromping through water, mucking through sloughs, battling brush, detouring around fallen logs, clambering up cutbanks and down rocky grades, the long line biting into their shoulders, the boat a dead whale behind them, resisting every inch, tugging, yanking them backward when currents caught it. In the end the torn muscles of nine men tromping a ragged shore overpowered a sixty-foot wooden boat with eighteen tons in its hold.

They rested through the midday inferno, coiled the endless cordelle and dropped it into its bin, and took up their poles again where the river ran broad over a gravelly bottom. Brokenleg squinted behind, watching sharply for a glimpse of the opposition engages — and saw none.

More and more, though, he fumed at Max, who sat sulking, doing nothing, daring Fitzhugh to make him pole. They were coming to trouble, he and that boy. He was ready to box the boy's ears so soundly that the boy would be governed by fear if nothing else. But something in Brokenleg told him it wouldn't help. Max would not yield. Boxing and tormenting that boy would only produce an angry rebel who'd slip away at the first opportunity. He had to reach Max's mind and soul. And he didn't even know where to start. Max was in trouble with the engages, too, who studied him sullenly, aware that the boy wasn't sharing the toil in spite of a strapping, healthy, seventeen-year-old's body. The time of reckoning had to come soon.

The fourth day they reached the place where the wagons and wagon sheets had been cached. Samson Trudeau steered the keelboat toward the south bank and the engages tied it tightly to stout willow brush. Nearby the carcasses of oxen rotted, filling the meadow with a sweet sickening odor. They'd been half-devoured by coyotes, wolves, hawks, skunks, and raptors. Fitzhugh gagged. Maxim vanished into the hold. Brokenleg had Bercier stay aboard and man the swivel gun against surprise while he limped off with the rest toward the dark cottonwoods that hid the wagons. He hoped they could take the wagons. He'd never see the wagons again if he left them there.

They found the three Pittsburghs untouched and still well-concealed behind walls of brush. Trudeau sent a man to pull the sheets out of the cache while the rest freed the first wagon and dragged it slowly to the riverbank. The keelboat could hold the wagon crosswise, that was plain. Maybe hold all three wagons crosswise — if they could build some sort of stage and muscle them up the steep incline to the deck. He searched restlessly along the bank, looking for higher ground, a low cutbank, and found one two hundred yards back. They unloosed the keelboat and let it slide downstream, and retied it at a place where the bank lay level with the deck. And then they shoved the cumbersome wagon there, hacked through dense brush, eased it over wobbling planks while waves careened the keelboat, and finally aboard. It looked odd and out of place there, a humpbacked camel.

Through the hot afternoon they wrestled the other wagons to the bank. It turned out there was room for two, one aft of the cabin, one ahead of it. Disheartened, Brokenleg helped them drag the third one back to its hiding place and cover it. His leg tortured him all the way, although he'd done nothing compared to the brutal toil of the engages. He stared at the fine freight wagon doubting he'd ever see it whole again. At least he had the three wagon sheets and two freighters, he thought.

They shuffled back to the keelboat and once again the engages began their promenade, this time dodging the wagons, jamming their poles into the river bottom until they bent under the fierce thrust. For boatmen heading upriver toil never ceased.

"Steer," he said to Dust Devil. She took hold of the long sweep hesitantly, and then with an arrogant gleam in her eye guided the keelboat. He grabbed a pole and joined the parade, feeling the toil brutalize his leg. Maxim scowled.

Two days later they approached Fort Cass. Various Indians had spotted them. Crows, he thought. Crows out hunting or root-gathering while they traded. He knew he might have trouble at Cass. Old Isodor Sandoval was the trader but Julius Hervey lingered on as the factor, more vicious than ever, sulking about his damaged hands — hands half-severed by Brokenleg in a brawl a half a year earlier — and looking for revenge. Chouteau men up on the bastions would recognize the boat; recognize the wagons on it, and know exactly what had happened — or at least part of it. The keelboat would pass close to the post and right under the post's six-pounder — which could blow it to bits, kill his men, and destroy the resupply down in the hold. He could run for it — if toiling upriver upon the bent poles of engages could be called running. Or he could stop and tell them the whats and the whys. He knew that if Hervey or Sandoval chose to, they could pick off Fitzhugh's engages easily with rifle shots and just as easily sink the boat or compel Fitzhugh to come to shore. It was something to think about, and Fitzhugh was thinking plenty when they rounded a gentle bend and spotted the gray palisades and bastions of Fort Cass.

Brokenleg steered the keelboat to the Fort Cass levee and his men tied it there amid a growing crowd of Crow Indians.

"Watch 'er," he told his men. "Cut 'er loose if there's trouble."

He limped across an open flat crowded with lodges, heading toward the gate in the log stockade of the American Fur Company post. His flesh crawled, remembering the troubles he'd had there last winter — when Julius Hervey had almost strangled him to death.

Brokenleg knew he'd have to deal with Hervey. The man's sheer force of will dominated the post in spite of the ruin of his hands. He found Sandoval and Hervey awaiting him at the gate, which was good. He didn't want to enter Fort Cass.

"You have my keelboat," said Hervey. The man looked as menacing as ever, pure muscle driven by an untrammeled will.

"You have my mules and you killed my oxen," Brokenleg retorted. "Worth a thousand."

Hervey laughed, that maniacal roar that always sent shivers of dread through Brokenleg — and other listeners. Hervey didn't bother to deny it. There was no point in denying it. Blaming such things on Indians was a great joke among robe traders. "Worth a small keg," he said, grinning. "Mess a' Piegans."

"I'm taking our stuff up to my post," Fitzhugh said.

"What did you do with ours?" Sandoval asked quietly.

"Left it on the bank, along with your men."

"Fifty-five bales," Sandoval said angrily.

"Twelve oxen and six mules," Brokenleg snapped.

"Stiffleg, git your men outa that boat," Hervey said. "If you want them to live."

"I don't think so, Hervey."

"The six-pounder is charged, Stiffleg."

"You'd only blow up your own keelboat. And start a stink that would ruin American Fur."

Sandoval looked worried. "Fitzhugh, go unload that keelboat at your post and float it back here."

Hervey flared. "You gone soft, Sandoval? Some day, some day when I get my hands back — I'll deal with you. Same for you, Stiffleg."

Sandoval met Hervey's mockery with a steady gaze of his own from unblinking brown eyes.

"I ain't returning the keelboat," said Fitzhugh. "You lost it — fair and square."

"Bring it back or we'll come get it," Sandoval said.

"Bring twelve oxen and six mules when you do," Brokenleg said.

"Look, Fitzhugh," said Sandoval overly politely. "You've stolen our boat; put fifty-five bales ashore; put our men ashore — you bring back —"

"Fire the six-pounder," Fitzhugh said. He whirled away and limped back toward the keelboat, Julius Hervey's wild laughter echoing in his ears. He felt his pulse climb as he walked, wondering if he'd take a ball in his back. He shoved through Crow spectators and walked up the plank to the boat even as his men began loosening the lines.

"Are we safe?" asked Trudeau, eyeing the six-pounder and the men around it up in the bastion.

"No," Fitzhugh replied shortly.

"*Sacrebleu,*" the man muttered.

"If Sandoval's in charge we are," Brokenleg added. "But he ain't."

"So you're going to get us killed," Maxim shot at him.

"You got a better way, boy?"

Maxim retreated into sullen silence again. Bercier and Brasseau had finished loosening the lines on shore, and the boat was almost free. A great crowd of Crows stood at the bank watching them. Fitzhugh spotted a chief, Big Robber, and a subchief he didn't know, watching thoughtfully. Salvation, he thought, and maybe trade.

"Whoa up," he said to his men. He clambered off the keelboat and approached the chief, trying to remember enough Crow to address the man.

"Chief Big Robber," he began, supplementing his words with finger-sign. "Have a little ride on the boat — you and whoever you want. We'll give you some good things, powder and ball, ribbons, an awl. Bring your friends."

Big Robber consulted with half a dozen people around him, grinned, and walked up the plank, leading a pack of warriors. No woman braved the vessel but a couple of little Crow boys did, squealing with delight as they examined it.

He heard Dust Devil's muttering from the porthole, a steady stream of soft Cheyenne invective. She hated Crows. It didn't matter. He had safe passage now; a chief, some headmen and warriors, all dressed in festival clothing for the trading, richly beaded and quilled elkskins, headbands, moccasins.

"We want the firewater now," Big Robber signaled.

"I'll pour some in a bit, friend," Brokenleg replied.

His men let the boat drift free and then began poling it forward, foot by foot, under the impotent guns of Fort Cass. Along the shore, Crow women and children kept apace, laughing and waving. Slowly, the keelboat pushed forward, rocking and faltering in the channel current while engages raised sweat jabbing their poles into the riverbed. The chief and headmen watched thoughtfully — to their way of thinking, it was all woman's work.

Fitzhugh didn't even bother to keep an eye on the bastion. They were safe. A single shot from that cannon would ruin Cass's Crow trade and give it all to Fitzhugh's Post. Painfully, the lumbering keelboat slid past the fort and into the broad sweep of gray water that marked the confluence of the Bighorn River. Behind, he heard Julius Hervey's wild laughter rolling down to them from the bastion high above. Fitzhugh squinted up at him. That one enjoyed the deadly game no matter whether he was winner or loser. That's what made him deadlier than a rattler. He loved the murder itself — even his own. Big Robber heard that maniac laughter, too, and watched Hervey thoughtfully.

A while later, when they were well up the Bighorn River, Brokenleg steered the keelboat to shore to debark his guests — and offer them a few trading trinkets and a small jug, which he hoped he could locate in the jumble of casks and crates below.

They were half an hour's walk from Fort Cass and an equal distance from Fitzhugh's own post. He thought of sending Maxim into the hold to find things, but he knew better. Instead, he sent Trudeau and Larue. "Bring plenty o' stuff," he said. "Make this a little celebration."

While he waited, he addressed the Crows. "My chiefs, we will be trading tomorrow. Our prices will be better than those at Fort Cass. We esteem your trade. Bring your people, and we will treat you well indeed, with many gifts."

Big Robber nodded, saying nothing.

When Trudeau and Larue finally emerged laden with gewgaws, Fitzhugh solemnly gifted each man, not forgetting the little boys. An awl, a Wilson butcher knife for each. A one-pound bar of St. Louis shot tower lead, and a cup-measure of powder wrapped in paper for the chief and headmen. The Crows accepted the gifts as their due.

"We want the crazy-water," said Big Robber.

"You come trade, bring robes, and we'll have us a party," Fitzhugh replied. "Lots of the crazy-water when you bring the robes. We'll buy every robe you have. Good Crow robes. You make the best robes."

From down in the hold, Dust Devil snorted.

Big Robber scowled, plainly unhappy. "Maybe not. Maybe not," he muttered. "No robes. No trade."

"You come on over tomorrow after we get the stuff on the shelves, and we'll have us a big trade," Fitzhugh insisted. "Lots o' gifts. We'll mix up a pot o' firewater and ladle her out fast as you git hyar." He'd lapsed into English but they understood anyway, not entirely happy with their gifts. But none of them ever was, he thought.

He left the Crows there, staring at him noncommittally. He hoped they'd trade. At least they'd gotten him and the keelboat past the fangs of Fort Cass. They knew it, too. They'd watched the men up in the bastion thoughtfully all the while the keelboat inched by. They'd know exactly why they'd been invited for a ride. The gifts weren't exactly gifts; they were payment.

His men grew excited as they neared the

small trading house called Fitzhugh's Post, and poled furiously up the Bighorn through a somnolent noon, ignoring the rising heat. And then, at last, the Rocky Mountain Company post on the east bank of the river hove into view, a post built with blood and sweat and impossible labor deep into the winter, against all odds. They cheered. They sang French boatmen's songs. They whistled. And from the post, Fitzhugh's remaining men boiled out — Spoon and Constable and all the rest, fired their pieces and danced around, hoorawing and bellowing like madmen. There wasn't a lodge in sight: every Indian in the area had gone to Cass, which had been resupplied weeks earlier. At Fitzhugh's Post the shelves were empty and forlorn. But soon that'd change.

"A keelboat!" yelled Constable. "We was lookin' for the wagons. Ol' Straus, he dig into his pockets?"

"We stole her," Fitzhugh yelled, as he edged the keelboat into the bank. "And you can bet they'll try to steal her back!"

Seven

Guy Straus wrestled a heavy haversack down the stage and set it on the ground of Bellevue, deep in Indian Territory. Behind him, his guide, Ambrose Chatillon, toted saddles and packs while deckmen freed four horses from their pen at the bow and led them off the *St. Peter*. The packet had made his last run as far as Bellevue on an Indian Bureau contract to supply the agency there. This was as far as Guy could go the easy way; the rest would be grueling for a soft, middle-aged man.

But this is where he would have debarked anyway. And the reason stood before him in the obese person of the Reverend Mr. Foster Gillian, Indian Agent and divine of the Congregational Church. The man stood there, his mournful eyes surveying the debarking passengers from behind heavy jowls and thick muttonchops of graying hair. He wore a black broadcloth suit polished in the seat and elbows from heavy use. Guy recognized the man at once, as much from his expression of pained authority as from his dyspeptic bearing. The man peered at the world with the eyes of the moralist discovering sin everywhere.

Guy knew he was about to present himself as the principal sinner. He also knew that he'd easily acquire the information he wanted: Gillian would burp it out as a matter of superior wisdom. But that could wait. Behind him, his wiry guide tied the packhorses and saddled them, sliding Guy's heavy sack into one pannier of a packsaddle and a sack of equal weight, bearing rations, into the other. The other packhorse would carry more supplies, ammunition, and a small tent. Time was of the essence and he hoped to be off within the hour — if Gillian would consent to interview him at once.

The Indian Agent leaned into a gnarled black walking stick, watching deckmen hoist goods from the hold and swing them ashore where his own men loaded them into drays for the steep climb to the post. Around them all hundreds of Omahas and Otos, largely dressed in white men's clothing, watched thoughtfully.

"Mr. Gillian?" he asked.

The agent turned and studied Guy.

"I'm Guy Straus of St. Louis. A senior partner of the Rocky Mountain Company."

Recognition and something else filled the

face of the agent. He peered more closely now, surveying Straus with squinting eyes. Guy knew what he would see: a man of medium height with wiry blond hair going gray, and brown eyes; a man with a square clean-shaven face, a little soft and overweight, dressed in good cottons and woolens for a plunge into the wilderness.

"I don't suppose I have anything to say to you — or your kind."

Guy had been expecting that, too, and ignored it. "I'd like to ask a few questions about what happened here."

Gillian looked testy. "This is an impossible time. Surely you don't expect me to talk now when we have this unloading to attend to."

"I believe it's attending to itself, sir. I have only a few questions. I wish to know exactly what happened."

"You'll have to wait. See me in a week after we have these goods inventoried and distributed to my, ah, charges."

"I can't wait a week."

"A pity. I must be about my Christian duty now."

Guy stood in the midday sun, a swirl of activity around him, pondering. "We'll wait," he said. "I trust you'll put me up?"

"Put you up?"

"Yes. I'll wait the week. We'll walk up the hill and unload the horses. Perhaps Mrs. Gillian will show us to our quarters."

The Reverend Gillian's face flushed. Guy knew exactly what the man was thinking. Wilderness posts were always hospitable to everyone. Bellevue was also an American Fur Company trading post and there would be no way the reverend could prevent Guy from staying.

"I won't have time in a week. Not ever for the likes of you."

"I'll wait," said Guy, amiably. "I'd like to see how a post operates; meet your Otos and Omahas; talk to the Chouteau men."

"Now see here, Straus. I'm the Indian Agent. I won't have you meddling with my charges. They're like children, you know, easily twisted —"

"Oh, I'll only ask a few questions."

"I forbid it. I'll report everything."

"You already have. In a public document. Accusing my company of certain violations. I suppose I'll have to tell David Mitchell that you wouldn't let me inquire about matters in my defense. I think, sir, he might just call you to St. Louis to answer there — if you don't wish to answer here. Which will it be?" Guy spoke gently but with a certain authority that came from a lifetime of managing a financial enterprise.

The reverend steamed, flushed, paled, and stabbed his walking stick into the clay. And said nothing though orotund words formed and retreated from his quivering lips.

Guy knew at once that he'd won the day. "Mr. Gillian: was there cargo for other companies aboard *The Trapper*?"

"Certainly." The minister's voice had a crackling quality.

"Indeed. And was some of it unloaded here at Bellevue?"

"Certainly."

"Along with passengers. Mr. Gillian, who got off?"

"How would I know?"

"I thought you might. Some Chouteau people no doubt."

"I haven't the foggiest. Deck passengers." Gillian was sounding testy.

"Where was the other cargo destined, sir?"

"I wouldn't remember. See here, Straus —"

Guy smiled gently. "We'll be done swiftly if you cooperate. If not — it'll take a while, and that'd be a pity." He knew he was in command. "How did you determine that the spirits were a part of my company's shipment?"

"Why — the casks were on the Dance, Fitzhugh, and Straus shipping manifest given me by Captain Sire."

"In a different hand?"

"I didn't notice."

"A different hand, sir. In fact we had no spirits aboard."

The reverend snorted and then cackled. "I must say," he wheezed, "I'd expected bald canards. Everyone knows how the companies trade. AFC too. Even here behind my back. Drunken Indians in my chapel, my school, my offices. Come now, Straus. You people do anything for money and don't scruple about it."

Guy ignored that. "Your report says you opened the casks with a bung starter and sniffed. What did you sniff?"

"Spirits!"

"What does two hundred proof grain alcohol smell like, sir?"

"Like whiskey."

"May I report your observations to David Mitchell?"

The man turned wary. "What are you driving at?"

"Pure grain spirits have little smell. What did you do with the evidence?"

"Why — everyone saw what I did."

"You had it poured into the river."

This time the reverend refused to reply.

"What color was the fluid you poured out?"

"Why — clear. Almost like water."

"What color is whiskey?"

"How should I know? I never imbibe. Amber, I suppose."

"Did you keep the casks?"

He nodded.

"May I see them?"

"No you may not. They're locked."

"They are evidence for my defense. The bills of lading —"

"For your defense? Are you mad?"

"For my defense. They were labeled. I wish to see the labels, study the hand. I wish to see what else I can learn — the cooperage, for instance."

"Technicalities! Nonsense! Obfuscation! You'll obscure the truth with smoke. No, I . . . will . . . not . . . show . . . them." He emphasized each word with a pause.

Guy sighed, amiably. "I'll have to inform the commissioner, of course — being denied the right to examine the evidence."

By now Gillian was puffing up like an adder. "I told you I would not — and I won't."

"What if you're wrong — what if we hadn't a drop of spirits in our cargo?"

"Are you done?"

"Almost. Let's agree about this interview — for the commissioner's sake, eh? You did not notice whether Captain Sire's manifests were all done in the same hand. You smelled whiskey in the casks. You poured out a clear white fluid. There was cargo for other companies aboard. You denied me permission to examine the casks. You did not notice who got off here. Agreed?"

Gillian glared. "The devil knows how to lie, sir."

"But never a clergyman. You'll tell Mitchell we agree on this of course."

Foster Gillian nodded.

Guy smiled broadly. "Very well, reverend. I know I can count on you."

He left the reverend stewing, and wandered over to his guide. "Ambrose, I have one more small task and then we'll be off. I wish to pay my respects to Peter Sarpy up at the post."

Chatillon smiled. "No need. He's over there."

Over there indeed stood the veteran trader, AFC veteran, and factor of this trading post — a man Guy had met several times at the Planters House. Sarpy was a relative of the Chouteaus and a company man; one of the best and most levelheaded men in the robe trade. He was, moreover, a man of some integrity. He would have had no part of planting casks in Guy's cargo. He was vulnerable himself — all fur men were. And if he had gotten wind of anything he would have gladly and indignantly shared them with Guy — the brotherhood of traders being more important than company lines. Guy approached, wondering if Sarpy might hold the key.

All that broiling day the engages unloaded the keelboat and toted bales, crates, and rundlets into the trading post. Inside, others shelved the goods in the trading room. Brokenleg helped as much as his bum leg would permit.

"Maxim, you check off them goods," he said.

The youth glared at Brokenleg and vanished into the barracks. Brokenleg had no notion how to deal with him.

The keelboat floated lighter in the water as its bowels emptied, and Brokenleg wondered what to do with it. He didn't want to return it — not when American Fur owed him twelve oxen and six mules. The keelboat had become a sort of collateral.

Better yet, a means to send his robes and pelts down the river and resupply the post. It was better than his livestock; less vulnerable to raids. And it didn't require hay or pasture or constant vigilance.

But neither could it take his goods out to the villages the way a wagon could. That had been part of the strategy: they were going to whip American Fur by wagoning to the villages and trading there. But without livestock his wagons were dead. Which reminded him that he had a Pittsburgh stashed downstream — valuable property to recover if he could.

All winter and spring they'd toiled on the post, and now the original log building sat in the corner of a stockaded yard that formed a corral. Log outbuildings rose at its far side. They'd laid a puncheon floor in the post, which kept it warmer and cleaner. They'd flagstoned outside areas to keep the gumbo at bay. He called the place Rocky Mountain House but no one else did. The name Fitzhugh's Post had stuck. This coming winter they'd live in much greater comfort. Stashed in the keelboat were three good stoves and stovepipe, which would heat better than the fireplaces and save a lot of wood gathering as well. There'd be one in the barracks; another in his own quarters

118

and office; and a third in the trading room. "Fat cow," he muttered, but he didn't mind a bit.

By evening they were ready to trade once again. The shelves glinted with knives and awls and axes, ribbons and kettles. Other shelves held Witney blankets, mostly natural cream with dyed stripes, but some green and red and blue ones also. In the morning they'd run up the flags, fire a volley, and open the trading window once again — if anyone showed up. Not a Crow Indian had come around to watch the keelboat being unloaded, glimpse the foofaraw, work himself into a trading fever. Fitzhugh knew why: American Fur was practically giving its stuff away, selling at a loss, lavishing gifts on headmen, and would continue until it had destroyed the opposition. That's how the giant had whipped the opposition many times. This was Crow country and Fort Cass had the Crows in hand.

Which meant that Fitzhugh needed to reach other tribes. With wagons. In the dusk he called his chief trader, Samson Trudeau, plus Abner Spoon and Zach Constable to him for a little powwow.

"We got the keelboat," he said. "What do we do with 'er?"

"Cache it," said Spoon.

"You got a place to cache a sixty-foot boat?"

Spoon grinned. "We could scuttle it. Bore a hole and sink it right hyar."

"Hate to damage it. We could plug the hole, but it'd be somethin' agin' us if we got into trouble."

"We could jist bucket water into it until she hits bottom," said Zach Constable.

The idea of filling a sixty-foot hold with water using buckets seemed a little dubious to Fitzhugh.

"Roll it onto land?" asked Trudeau.

That's the way Fitzhugh's mind was running. A few logs for rollers and then the muscles of the two remaining saddle horses plus every man on the post. Let her sit on dry land.

"It ain't gonna work," said Zack. "Know why? They'll use the trick you used. Send a whole Crow village hyar to camp betwixt us and the boat; then use them as a screen whiles they roll it back into the drink."

"Roll her clear up to the flat?" asked Abner.

Trudeau frowned. "Eleven Creoles can do almost anything — even drag a keelboat up a fifteen-foot grade. But it will take a day to cut logs and levers."

"Then think about her," Fitzhugh said. He knew what he'd do in the morning: he'd ride over to Cass and negotiate fast — the boat for livestock. He'd cut any deal he could that would save him the job of hiding, scuttling, or drylanding that keelboat.

They ambled back inside, out of the soft summer dusk, and Fitzhugh was momentarily stricken with wonder. Here lay a post where none had been a year before. Here were seasoned traders, old coons, men of the mountains. Here was a pile of goods shining in the wavering light of small fire in the fireplace. He marveled that it had all happened; that they'd fought off the worst that American Fur could throw at them. He was filled with a strange and unaccustomed pride.

The men seemed to be waiting for something. And then he remembered. He'd promised a gill at this moment; a gill each when the post was stocked and back in business.

"Har, we got us a little celebratin' to do," he yelled. "I'm gonna wet my dry."

Men whooped. Several dashed for the alcove in the trading room where the casks of spirits lay out of sight. The rest grabbed tin cups. They wanted their gill straight —

pure grain spirits. Fitzhugh wondered if they'd be fit for the trading tomorrow — or whether he'd be fit. He watched them pull the bung and screw in a brass bung-faucet, and hoist the cask to a counter. They let Trudeau do the honors, knowing his version of a gill was generous. He let the clear fluid fill each cup to the halfway mark, and endured the hoorawing of men who wanted more. Fitzhugh himself felt a mighty thirst abuilding and slid his cup under the faucet, too. No one could drink pure spirits undiluted, though a few sipped and sputtered and gasped, and surrendered to the water dipper.

"Mountain dew," said Constable, grinning.

Brokenleg hunkered down outside the post along with the rest, sipping steadily, ignoring the rumblings of his empty belly. It was better to wet his whistle on an empty gut anyway, he thought. He slapped away a few mosquitos but otherwise the late July night was perfect; the heavens clear, the summer breezes cool. He felt a fine buzz build in his head, the world wobbled, and he thought he had life beavered down.

Until Dust Devil plunked herself down beside him, a cup in her proud little Suhtai hand. "You promised," she said.

He wasn't sure what he'd promised. "You git our rooms cleaned up?"

"You promised. Now we go."

"You sippin' Great-Father's milk?"

"I am all alone. Only woman here. We go get your wives now. Sisters. You made the big vow."

"Sisters. Sisters. *Sisters.*" It was coming to him. He sipped more of the strong water and contemplated it. Three Cheyenne sisters just pinin' for him.

"Aw," he muttered.

"You come get my sisters and make wives or I'll go away."

"Not until mornin' nohow."

"You're not a blanket chief," she said, her face mocking in the moonlight. "Maybe I'll find a real blanket chief."

"Haar." He couldn't think of anything else to say but he was thinking of something to do.

"A real blanket chief would like all sisters, four Suhtai Tsistsista sisters, daughters of a great medicine-maker."

"Haar." He sipped. The water and spirits tasted more like mountain whiskey.

"You make a great oath, make the word, and don't keep it. Bad-tongue. Damn liar," she said. "White men are buncha liars. You biggest liar." She sipped mightily.

"Haar," he said.

"Slaves too. I want some dumb Absaroka slaves. I make them cook and clean."

"Haar."

"Tomorrow we'll go to my father's village and make wives."

"Got to open trade."

"Him, the trader, he can open trade. Lousy Absaroka, they don't tan good robes. I get you good Tsistsista robes and wives."

"Haar!"

He heard the babble near him soften; men listened to Dust Devil and him or drifted to their robes after a brutal day. She tugged at him, her eyes devilish and her mouth smirky. Her hands wandered.

"Haar," he muttered, and drained the rest of the ambrosia. She helped him up, always a painful task because of his stiff leg, and dragged him into the shadows of the post and to the rear, their quarters.

She closed the door and giggled.

"Haar," he roared, the sound rumbling through the post, echoing into the barracks. "Haar . . ."

"Blanket chief," she said, and groaned.

The spirits buzzed.

He slept into the morning, along with the rest except Maxim, who was waiting like a little vulture when he stuck his aching head into the sun.

"It's gone," Maxim said triumphantly. He pointed to where the keelboat had been tied.

Eight

Gone. Hervey and Sandoval had wasted no time grabbing their keelboat back. Brokenleg laughed. He'd have done the same. No doubt it was now on its way down the Yellowstone, heading for Wolf Rapids. But it left him feeling naked. Except for two saddle horses he had no locomotion, no way to take his wagons out to the villages.

Over the winter he could build mackinaws, the flat-bottomed boats that had been the time-honored way to float furs down the rivers. Mackinaws were one-way hulls, abandoned at their destinations. He peered about the sun-gilded flats and saw not a lodge on this opening day of trade. There was his post, bulging with the resupply, its shelves holding an alluring assortment of things tribesmen hankered for. All those Crows camped around Fort Cass knew it but none came. It irked him: five hundred lodges a few miles away; over three thousand Crows from several bands — and not a one toting robes to his trading window.

His humor departed him as he reviewed the whole business. He'd lost twelve oxen and six mules at the hands of those people. The oxen were a dead loss. He couldn't replace them here. Neither could he replace them with horses or mules because he lacked the harness for three wagons. But he did have harness for one; he could put one wagon into use if he could get horses and break them. Breaking mustangs to harness would be slow toil but he could see no other option.

"Well," he muttered to Maxim, "if they ain't comin' here, I'm goin' to them. You're clerkin' today. Go set yourself at the tradin' window. You an' Abner."

"I don't wish to," the youth retorted.

"You got somethin' in your craw. Get it out and get busy."

"You forced me to come here but you won't force me to work."

"Them that don't work don't eat. I'll see to it."

Maxim flushed but held his ground. "It's crooked work. The robe trade is disgusting. We broke the law. We didn't put those spirits on board — but we might as well have. I'll starve."

"Then you'll starve, boy."

It infuriated Brokenleg. The little snot.

But he'd deal with it later. He had more important things to do than cope with a rich man's brat. He limped to the stockaded pen, found his special saddle, the one that accommodated his stiff leg, and threw it over a chestnut, savagely drawing the cinch tight. He lumbered aboard and leaned over to slide his stiff leg into the long stirrup. Then he kicked the horse viciously with his good heel, setting it into a panicked trot up the Bighorn toward Fort Cass. Within a mile he encountered the Crow horse herds, grazing close to Fitzhugh's Post because the grass around Cass had been devoured. It burnt him to think about it. He'd built his post enough miles away from Cass to ensure that he had pasture. He'd by-god like to wring Hervey's neck.

Still — horses were on his mind. He slowed his chestnut to a lazy walk and studied the Crow ponies as he wandered through them — multicolored mustangs, small, mean, boneheaded, roman-nosed, shaggy and tough. They came in every color from spotted Appaloosas to paints to solids, with coyote duns predominating. Most were saddle-broke; none were harness-broke. Some danced away at the sight of Fitzhugh but others, gregarious and curious, followed behind, poking a nose into his chestnut's rump until it squealed and kicked them away.

Herding boys watched him warily. It was their job to prevent theft and each was well armed with a trade rifle. That was fine with Fitzhugh.

Half an hour later he reached Fort Cass and the huge village of Crows surrounding it. Smoke from hundreds of morning cookfires layered over the tan lodges. The fort rose golden and sullen in the early light. At mid-morning — trading followed Indian time — the outer gates would swing open and the shutters of the trading window would swing apart and the exchanges would begin. Cass radiated arrogant power; a force that magnetized several bands of Crows and pinned them there with promises of cheaper goods, better payments for robes — and threats of retaliation if the chiefs drifted to Fitzhugh's Post.

It was a formidable force, Brokenleg knew, the threats of being cut off, charged double, denied gifts, eating even more corrosively into the headmen's thinking than the value of competition. If they'd had any brains they'd play off one post against the other the way trappers played off one beaver outfit against the other. But old Chouteau's grip on these Crow bands was phenomenal.

The whole flat hummed with quiet, early-morning activity. Women vanished into brush for their morning toilet; others carried iron pots or tallow-dressed skin buckets to the Yellowstone for water. Others, the very young and very old, scoured the nearby timber for dry wood, finding none that had been overlooked by a thousand others in previous trading seasons. It baffled him that none of them girdled those cottonwoods and willows for future use, making a common supply of dry wood. But none ever did; none ever looked beyond her immediate needs and as a result they forayed a mile or more just to collect a day's supply of sticks, which they carried over their backs in shawls.

He wandered through the concentric rings of lodges looking for the ones that would be a little larger, a little better decorated, and most importantly, which had the ensigns of office before them: elaborate medicine tripods, feather-bedecked lances thrust into the clay, lodges with several wives busy before them.

He spotted several but kept hunting for one in particular, the home of an old friend from the beaver days, Chief Fat Belly. Brokenleg and Jamie Dance had wintered with that band more than once, back in the sweet, rambling, trapping days. He found Fat Belly's lodge at last, far east of Cass and close to the glinting Yellowstone.

Fat Belly was smoking before his lodge, enjoying the morning sun on his naked chest. He looked up at Brokenleg with recognition forming in his bronzed face.

"Ah! It is my bad leg son!"

The chief scrambled to his feet, beaming. He stood like a barrel on stilts, his hair pinned by a red headband and hanging in two braids, his coup feathers perched jauntily on his head.

"Fat Belly! You're lookin' fit as a fiddle." Brokenleg howdied his old friend, dropped an aromatic twist of dark tobacco in his hands, and settled to the ground, easing his bad leg out.

Brokenleg inquired after wives and children, especially Fat Belly's three sons, each a fine warrior and headman in Fat Belly's band.

"Ah! Bear Medicine — the very boy you used to wrestle with long ago — Bear Medicine, he has two wives and three slaves, a Tsistsista woman, a Siksika girl, and a Siksika boy. He's very rich! He has counted three coups including one of great honor. My other boys, they are fine. Sweet Grass Dreams has a wife but he ignores her and

131

hunts. He loves the hunt. Little Fox is ever the warrior and a master of the stick game. Too much a gambler, I fear. And as for my wives . . ."

Fitzhugh listened, enjoying, remembering them all. Often he'd been a guest in this lodge. A while later — it never did to rush things — Brokenleg got down to the purpose of his visit.

"You up to a little tradin', Fat Belly?"

The chief frowned and sucked on his clay pipe a long while. "You will understand the difficulties, Brokenleg. American Fur is here for all the winters to come. Your company — they come and go. If we go to you — the trading window is shut to us here. They make many threats and give many gifts and tell us how bad you are. I laugh at that but I take the gifts and ask for more."

Fitzhugh knew or surmised all that. American Fur would think nothing of operating Fort Cass as a heavy loss for as long as it took to drive Rocky Mountain Company under. "Well," he said softly, "I come to dicker for horses. Like robes if you got 'em, but I'm a-pecking for some horse flesh."

Fat Belly smiled gently. "So I hear. Siksika. It makes me wonder about the ones in there." He nodded at Fort Cass. "Siksika!"

"I need seven, eight horses. Young stuff. Saddle-broke. Steady ones, calm ones. I got to break them to harness."

Fat Belly puffed, said nothing, peered into the azure heavens, watched his wives mash berries and melt tallow. They were making pemmican. Fitzhugh knew the chief had over a hundred horses including some buffalo runners, several war horses, and a couple of race horses. All the Crow loved a horserace, and gambled wildly on their choices.

"I should consult the medicine-givers," Fat Belly hedged.

"I reckon you can trade hosses if you want."

"It affects the welfare of the village."

"Back at the post I got me a whole rack o' new Leman rifles, fifty-two caliber, good rifled barrels that put a ball plumb center — flint or percussion, whichever you want. A real rifle, a lot finer than them old Nor'wester fusils. I reckon I could spare one for a good pony — I mean a real good hoss, steady, quiet-eyed, halfway friendly, easy to teach drivin'."

The Lemans cost the company twelve-fifty each back in Pennsylvania where they were built. Out here they were worth eighteen or twenty prime robes — a lot of robes.

"A Leman rifle for a good horse," Fat Belly said. He puffed steadily. "Eight rifles for eight horses?"

"I reckon. Help keep them Siksika off your backs."

"I have lots of horses."

"I reckon ye do, and ye might show me a few that got some drivin' instincts in 'em. You up ter taking a hike?"

"There is no need," said Fat Belly. "I will gather my sons and we will meet you at the horse herds. I promised the traders — the one called Hervey — that I would take no robes to you. But a horse is not a robe. The sun must travel a hand's width first. We will show you horses and you will show us Leman rifles, old friend. And we will add another horse for powder, lead, and all the rest."

Before the afternoon faded Brokenleg had traded eight rifles, powder, lead, and bullet molds worth about a hundred fifty robes for nine gentle-eyed mustangs, a mixture of seasoned saddlers and young stuff. He ran them into the fort pen and set to work at once, along with Abner Spoon and Zachary Constable, both of them good with horses. Teaching them to drive would take weeks. They worked into the moonlit night, putting on collars, accustoming them to iron bits in their mouths instead of Indian hackamores, and rubbing them gently. He didn't want a bunch of wild ones, prone to run away with a wagon full of trade goods. They quit deep in the night, scarcely noting that not a lodge had come to trade, not a robe had crossed their counter their opening day.

"Peter Sarpy!"

"Guy Straus!"

The giant trader embraced Guy with a mountain hug which faintly embarrassed the financier. Guy looked the man over, discovering a wilderness dandy dressed in rainbow colors.

"I can imagine why you're here," Sarpy said, glancing at the portly frockcoat-clad presence nearby. "Let's walk up to the post. I don't suppose you've ever seen a trading room."

Guy eyed the steep path doubtfully but followed the giant Creole upslope toward some privacy.

"That *mangeur du lard,* that *vide-poches* has been making life miserable hereabouts. Damned Indian Bureau thought they'd cure corruption and help the tribes by making Indian Agents of ministers. Another stupid idea. These ministers are so busy imposing their white-man morals on the tribes that there's going to be a bloody uprising some day. Know what they do? They tell the Indians they can't have their annuity goods — the stuff the government promised them if they came in to the reservations — can't have their stuff unless they converted, went to church, showed up for lectures and school and what have you. So now we got the biggest bunch of phony Christians you ever did see. And it didn't stop the stealing none. Half those divines get rich selling the government annuities to all and sundry just like all the other crooked agents."

Sarpy led him into a low log building up on a flat above the river and Guy beheld a trading room for the first time. He stood there in the amber light, catching his breath, surveying the orderly shelves of bright blankets, kettles, knives, ribbons, bolts of wool and cotton, and all the rest. Familiar things but somehow magical and mysterious here.

"I see no spirits," Guy said, wryly.

Peter Sarpy laughed, his pleasure booming through the magical room. "You'd like to know what happened. I wasn't there but I heard about it. He found some rundlets down there whiles your boy was showing him around, and had them toted out to the levee. They weren't what they were labeled." He grimaced. "Pretty crude, I'd say. Any old coon would know it was a plant but not this fat divine. No fur company in its right mind would stick casks like that right there, top o' the heap, itching to be discovered. But that didn't stop him none. He got the wrath o' creation built up in him, and thundered and lightninged all over that levee like a good hailstorm, his mind plumb made up."

Guy nodded. "You have any idea how it happened, Peter?"

"No, but I have some notions about how it didn't happen. Look, Guy, this wasn't the work of anyone high up in American Fur. You know why. Company's been burnt a couple of times. It's too vulnerable. You can bet that Pierre le Cadet had nothing to do with it and none of us top men either. You'd better be fishing for smaller fry. Maybe not even a Chouteau man. Someone's got a grudge — against you, or Fitzhugh — whatever."

"How sure are you?"

"Totally, Guy. Here's what can happen. If there's an uproar back east and the reformers take the bit and run, there'd be Indian Bureau and Army swarming every post in the West. And they'd find what they're lookin' for. Believe me, Cadet

Chouteau doesn't want a catastrophe like that. Me, I'd be outa work. Same for all the other company men — Malcolm Clarke, Major Culbertson, Edwin Denig, the Cabannes, the Gratiots — all his cousins, including me. *Mon Dieu!* We're not that lunatic!"

"Who, then?"

Sarpy shrugged. "Who could slip three rundlets aboard and alter the ship's records?"

"A boatman on *The Trapper*. An officer. Maybe a passenger." The widening possibilities seemed grim to Guy. He pulled a folded sheaf of foolscap from his portfolio. He had with him two important documents copied from Captain Sire's records: a list of cabin passengers and a list of the ship's crew. The deck passengers were unknown except for a handful whose passage had been paid by Chouteau and Company. He unfolded them carefully and handed them to Sarpy without a word.

Sarpy dug around for his spectacles and read slowly, his lips forming the names. "There are so many," he muttered.

"Who got off here? Can you name them?"

"Three company men: La Liberté, Germain, Lemoir. All three good men with families. Not very likely . . ."

Guy nodded. "What of the other Chouteau men listed here? Poudrier, Raffin, Dorion, Labone, Dufond?"

Sarpy shrugged. "Didn't get off here — as far as I know. I was tied up with a trade; didn't get down there. But there's this: they're fur men, engages. They'd know how to hurt an outfit if they wanted to. They'd know exactly what to do."

"Their company sent them upriver somewhere?"

"I imagine, Guy."

"Would you question your engages closely for me?"

"I'll do it. Maybe have something for you when you return — you are going upriver, I take it? That's what Chatillon was doing down there?"

"Yes. It's a futile gesture but I'm going."

"Guy, maybe that trouble wasn't aimed at you. Meant for someone else."

That surprised Guy. "Fitzhugh?"

"He's a rough cob, Guy. He's got about as many enemies as friends. And that Little Whirlwind don't help none."

The thought that the blow might have been aimed at Brokenleg rather than the company was a novelty. Guy mulled it over and decided it was worth pursuing.

They exchanged thoughts for another hour and then Sarpy escorted Guy down the hill to the now-empty levee, where Ambrose Chatillon and his horses waited patiently. The *St. Peter* was preparing to return downriver, riding high in the water, its deckmen loading firewood.

Guy clambered aboard the good saddler, feeling his generous buttocks sag into the hard saddle. He knew that in a couple of hours he'd be hurting. But he hoped that by the time they reached his next stop, Fort Pierre, three hundred fifty miles up the river, he'd be hardened to the pain and in much better shape. He'd always wanted to go up the river to the far-flung places where no white men of his sort had ever been.

They rode quietly up the valley of the Missouri through a breezy afternoon. Behind them Bellevue fell away. Ahead lay grassy bottoms with fewer and fewer trees. He felt his horse move under him, its rhythms swaying him gently. Behind, the packhorses followed on a picket line, snorting now and then, snatching grass when Chatillon relaxed his hold on the line.

Guy saw no one. He knew he was unlikely to see anyone for days at a time — and it'd be a blessing. The sunbaked river valley lay in mysterious silence, hiding secrets, shrouding menace. Guy Straus had never penetrated wilderness before and he suddenly felt vulnerable. He eyed Ambrose gratefully, knowing the wiry man could rescue him from most trouble — but not all. A part of him yearned to flee back to Bellevue, back to security and comfort. But not all of him, for Guy Straus was a bold man, relishing this silent valley and new vistas around every bight of the river just as he relished a good and profitable deal.

Late that day they heard a faint roaring upon the breeze, a strange rumble that whispered of demons and rage, pain and blood. It frightened him. But Chatillon merely smiled. "Soon, *Monsieur*," he said softly.

They rode straight toward the roar, which seemed to rise from some place a mile or two forward and around a bluff. The sound arrived coyly, sometimes loud and frightening, sometimes barely evident, depending on the whim of the west winds. It worried the horses. They peered about wildly, ears rotating, steps nimble. Guy felt his saddler gather itself to flee. He couldn't fathom what it might be but gripped his reins with sweaty hands.

Then Chatillon turned toward the grassy bluffs and scaled them, taking his entourage toward a promontory just ahead. Guy felt relief now that they weren't riding toward that ominous growl and clatter. Then, just ahead, the guide reined his horse and waited. Guy rode up cautiously, feeling the wind whip into his shirt and cool him.

Below was a buffalo herd, perhaps a hundred or so, blackening the bottoms. And at its center, several giant black beasts locked horns, snorted, bawled, roared, and gouged at one another viciously, pawing earth, throwing up dust that hazed the area.

"It is the running season, *Monsieur*. The bulls, they are fighting for the cows. They are mad, the bulls. See the blood! They gore each other. They attack anything on sight. If we rode close they would charge into us. It is nature's way, *oui?* The strongest bulls win the cows!"

Guy stared, entranced, seeing a spectacle beyond anything that had been conveyed to him with words spoken over coffee at the Planters House. He understood at once that he was peeking at nature's raw, fierce force as bull crashed into bull with shocks that vibrated the earth under his horse, and thunderous cracks of horn and skull. He marveled that any of them lived through it; that skulls and bones survived; that they had energy left to breed the cows. One bull went to earth, pawing air, half-dazed, while its antagonist gored him relentlessly. Blood and madness. On those sunlit grasslands a savagery boiled that Guy had never grasped before. The wilderness bristled with forces more violent than a thunderstorm. They sat on their horses quietly downwind of the herd while Guy saw at last the sources of his wealth, the animals whose hides would enrich his company. The frightened pack-horses pranced about him but Chatillon checked them. For a long while they watched the ragged battle below; watched the quitters, the weak and wounded, driven from the excited cows.

They are not so different from men, he thought darkly.

Nine

Fitzhugh's Post did a desultory trade through high summer, mostly with Crows who slid away from Fort Cass to sample the wares and prices of the rival post. The village chiefs didn't stop them from coming but neither did any headman bring his village to the post to trade. The threats, bribes, and cajolery issuing from Fort Cass kept the Crow trade from spreading. Even so, through the heat of August the post took in almost four hundred robes which were graded and baled, eleven prime robes and one summer robe to each bale. But the stock of trade goods on the shelves of the trading room scarcely diminished and the post was not paying for itself. It was slowly dying.

Maxim continued to sulk and avoid duty, and Fitzhugh decided simply to let the youth's anger and guilt wear itself out. At least the lad didn't vanish down the river on some reckless lone journey two thousand miles to civilization. Brokenleg knew he had no skills to cope with sulky boys, so he ignored him. He had better things to do. The training of the harness horses occupied every second he could spare. He and Abner and Zach worked the mustangs long hours, driving, harnessing and unharnessing them, deciding which ones were the most reliable. One hot afternoon they hooked a span to one of the wagons and let the pair drag the wagon around the flats. Then they hooked a second span to the empty wagon and let the horses grow accustomed to working in concert. The next day they tried three span, enough horsepower to yank the empty Pittsburgh around with ease, and drove them far up the Bighorn River. A few days later they pronounced the team ready for work. Seven of the nine horses became reliable drays; the other two made decent saddlers although one tended to startle at every imagined danger. He preferred oxen for hauling trade goods but he had no choices. In the wilderness, one made do.

Dust Devil waited impatiently, never failing to remind Brokenleg that he had promises to keep. The thought of them made him faint. But at least part of her notions made a heap of sense: they weren't getting much Crow trade and had better reach out to her Cheyenne or the post would perish.

"All right, all right!" he exclaimed, feeling testy. "Git yourself packed up, and tomorrah we'll go."

"You'll see!" she cried. "Four wives are good. Make you a blanket chief! Big man! And lots of help here!"

"It ain't my goal in life to be a blanket chief, dammit."

"You got to be a blanket chief to be a big-man chief!"

"Who says?"

"I say. Tsistsista say."

It puzzled him. The Cheyenne were the most puritanical of all tribes. Girls kept their maidenhood. Adultery was rare, though divorce was common enough. And yet . . . no tribe was as puritan as white puritans.

"We can use the help," he grumbled. "That's all I want of it. Now what's a proper gift for your pa?"

"A rifle, balls, powder, and blanket for each daughter. Plus lots of tobacco and a bolt of trade cloth for my mother."

"It'll bust the company," he muttered. But he began toting the stuff out of the trading room, not telling Zach or Samson what he was up to. They'd laugh him clear to the Platte River if he confessed. In fact, he intended to tell them he hired some help when he returned with his harem.

He hoisted a load of trade goods into the big freighter, the only one of the three wagons equipped with a seat at the front. He took care to have a good sampling of all his wares, especially the trade rifles, powder, and ball. His men didn't volunteer, and stood grinning at him until he wondered if they knew what sort of trip this would be.

"Git your lazy butts to work," he growled, knowing there was no work. Hardly a dozen Crows showed up on any day and most often that was just before the traders closed the shutters.

They rolled out at dawn, Dust Devil beside him looking smug, a spare saddler tied to the rear of the wagon. He itched to lecture them about running the post, getting work done, getting next winter's firewood cut, building a new shed, scything fields for hay, and all the rest. But he checked himself. Under Samson Trudeau's hand the work would get done, even if slower than he liked. He wanted to sermonize about the trading; about luring tribesmen; about keeping a hawk's eye on the opposition; about getting over to those villages camped at Fort Cass and talking with headmen; about dealing with other tribes that might wander in, Shoshone, Flathead, Sioux . . .

But he clamped his upper molars to his lower and rode off, ashamed of the impulse. Nothing a free mountaineer hated more than a lecture from a boss. Instead, he fumed at Little Whirlwind, letting his sulfurous mood corrode her happiness.

He had a long way to go, at least two hundred miles to get to Little Whirlwind's village, which probably was east of the Bighorn Mountains this time of year. Two hundred trackless miles where no wagon had ever been. He worried plenty about that; about the cutbanks of Crazy Woman Creek and the broken prairie off to the south, with all its dead-ends, low escarpments, and mud-bottomed crossings. And that was only part of it: one could never know what sort of trouble a lone trader and his wife could run into among unfriendly Indians. Or what temptations the wagonload of trade goods were, even to friendly ones. Or which of them would take a notion to steal his three span of horses and the saddler.

Still, the ones he had to watch out for were the Blackfeet, who'd kill him and Dust Devil on sight. And they were rolling steadily away from Blackfeet country as he drove gradually up the Bighorn River valley, between low arid hills. Traders were held in high esteem: traders were the source of the things they coveted most, especially rifles. And what's more, rival traders stood together when it came to trouble. If they troubled Brokenleg, they'd find themselves unwelcome at Cass or Union, or even at Fort William down on the Platte. And they knew it. It was an odd contradiction of the fur business that an unprovoked attack on a trader would shut trading windows everywhere, but at the same time outfits used Indians to raid or harass their opponents.

They rattled through the sweet silence of the prairies, enjoying the soft breezes of morning and evening, while hunkering down during the midday heat. The grass had browned with the passage of the monsoon season, and the clay lay hard under the iron tires making travel easy. The horses settled into their new task, except for one troublemaker named Hail that spooked at everything and itched to run. Brokenleg moved him from leader to swing position so he wouldn't take notions. At swing, he had steadier horses ahead and behind him and was locked in by their quieter conduct.

He showed her how to drive, how to hold six pairs of lines in her small brown hands;

how to gauge the land far ahead, looking for flat, unobstructed passage; how to avoid boulders or soft ground or thickets of sagebrush. He wanted her to learn so he could climb aboard his saddler and scout ahead, choose a road, look out for trouble, and hunt. But she didn't take to it, preferring to gawk, or yanking too hard on the lines until she sored the mouths of the drays. So he drove most of the time, and when he wanted to scout ahead he stopped the wagon and rode his saddler to the next ridge for a look.

She abandoned the driving altogether — that was white men's stuff — and returned to being herself and reminding him of it. It was demeaning for a Suhtai Tsistsista to do the work of slaves, she said. Capture a slave and let him do it.

They rolled through a summer idyll, following the Bighorn River until they reached the Little Bighorn, and then swinging up the tributary to avoid the huge canyon of the Bighorn ahead. They rolled through the country of the greasy grass, a place where verdant valley stayed green from moisture in the soil long after the nearby hills browned. They crossed a low divide and dropped into the drainage of the Tongue River, heading ever southward. The Bighorn Mountains closed in from the west, a blue wall with snow still capping the higher peaks some unfathomable distance upward.

Brokenleg calmed a bit though he was a worrier by nature, and worrying had kept him alive in a land where the most idyllic moment might harbor death. With each passing mile Dust Devil grew cheerier. She was going to see her people. She was going to see her family and acquire three sisters for companions! She deigned to smile at him now and then, and the smile lacked the usual mock in her face. He thought he might yet, someday, lie softly in the robes with her and talk about things he'd never said to her, the hopes and dreams and foolishness locked in his soul, the things that had met only her scorn whenever he'd edged toward them before in the tender moments.

Near the Tongue River they topped a long north-south ridge that ran parallel to the mountains like a wave radiating from a great splash, and spotted a small herd of buffalo half a mile off. They halted the wagon atop the windy bluff and peered into the mass of black animals — brown, actually, but they always appeared black against the sunlit grasses. His mouth watered. Tongue, boudins, humpmeat, boss rib! When he killed a buffler he ate Indian-style, gorging five or six pounds of meat until he couldn't swallow another bite.

"Ah!" hissed Little Whirlwind, breath escaping her as if from a steam pipe. "Ah!"

This would be easy, he thought, clambering off the wagon. The steady southwind put them downwind, and a brushy coulee would let him stalk to within a hundred yards of the somnolent cows. Tongue! Hump! Cow meat! Apparently the rutting season had passed, and this herd had settled into quietude.

"Ah!" she cried, pointing frantically. "Ah!"

He followed the vector of her small finger, and saw it — and felt his heart leap in his chest. He'd never seen a white buffler before, but there it was, a cow, creamy in the sun, visible now that it emerged from behind a distant bull. A white buffler! The source of a thousand legends! One in a hundred thousand, the buffler men claimed.

"You must kill it! You must!" she breathed, scarcely letting the words escape her.

"I reckon I oughter. You know what that's worth? I can git sixty regular robes for it. Heard me a story once of some *Gros Ventre* comin' into a post and itchin' for a

magic white hide the trader had, and offering that much. Heard another story
about how some bunch or other traded fifteen pony-loads o' blankets, guns, and
whatnot, for one o' them white hides."

"No — never! You must not!" she cried.
"It must be given to the spirits. You must! If
you don't, its power won't come. The
Tsistsista tan it and then put it on the pole
for the sky spirits. That is the biggest medicine! It give us everything. They smile at
us!"

"Aw, that's plumb —" he checked himself. He wanted sixty robes. She wanted to
follow her custom, and a fight was brewin'.

"The People know how to do this," she
whispered. "I wish they were here! A warrior who has slain another in battle must
peel the hide. The skin of the head must be
peeled by one who has scalped an enemy.
The hide must be carried on a horse owned
by one who has carried off a captive. It must
be unloaded by one who pulled an enemy
off a horse. It must be carried into the village by one who has slain an enemy in his
own lodge!"

"I reckon I purty-near make it," he said,
grinning.

She glared, sensing disrespect in his tone.
But he slid his old rust-pitted Hawken off

the footboards and checked it, pressing a fresh cap over the nipple. Damned heathen, he thought. He'd shoot the cow, have him a cow roast and a cowhide worth sixty prime robes for the askin'.

"You hush now," he whispered, knowing it was an all-purpose request to her to keep the horses under control. He had to limp his way down that steep coulee, make sure the sentry cows weren't getting restless, and then wait for the albino to present a good broadside shot into that hat-sized spot just behind the shoulders where she'd go down without a struggle.

The hot air raised a sweat on him — or was it the burden that lay on him suddenly? — and he felt a wetness stain his shirt and gather at his neck and brow. The whole damned trip had bitten at him. He was still trying to figure out how he'd gotten himself into marrying her sisters, and now she was telling him he had to sacrifice the white hide to her sky spirits!

He came finally to a place where the coulee debouched onto a flat, and the brush vanished. That was it.

A sentry cow stared at him, and he knew that within seconds the whole herd might bolt. He stood stock-still until she lowered her massive head and snatched some bunchgrass. When she glanced at him again, he'd vanished, settling himself to earth. He pulled his shooting sticks from his kit and poked them into the clay for a benchrest, and dropped the Hawken into the vee. Then he swung the heavy barrel to the right and upslope until it lined up on the white — cream, he corrected himself — creamy cow, which had stopped grazing and stared westward. A beauty! Not a brown patch on her, except for a little on her crown! She stood almost broadside, and he decided not to wait, not even for an instant. He settled the blade sight on the heart-lung area, calmed his own fingers and arms, and then squeezed.

The white cow shuddered, sat down on her haunches, shook her head slowly back and forth, while the throaty boom of the Hawken echoed up the hills, and blue powder-smoke drifted back upon Brokenleg. He loaded quietly, measuring powder from his horn and pouring it down the hot barrel, patching a ball and driving it home with his stick. He found the nipple fouled, picked it clean, and snuggered a new cap over it.

The white buffalo sagged to her side, blood leaking from her mouth. None of the other animals had taken alarm. He knew he should shoot another for meat. If he ate the white cow, he'd never hear the end of it from Dust Devil. He settled on a young heifer that basked in the sun, and shot her. She dropped as if poleaxed. He loaded again and clambered to his feet, letting himself be seen. A sentry cow snorted, and the score or so of remaining animals broke into a sudden gallop.

He squinted up to the crest of the hill where Dust Devil waited with the wagon and waved her down, hoping she'd take the grade slowly. Then he checked the horizons. Where buffalo gathered so did Injuns. But nothing disturbed the breezy morning, and he walked slowly toward the white cow. They arrived at the same moment, Dust Devil hissing and muttering Cheyenne as she slid off the high seat, an excitement and fear upon her.

"I have never seen such a thing!" she whispered. "You must pray to her spirit first! She has given her fortune to you!"

"I don't figure I got to make prayers to dumb animal spirits."

"You must! I will!" She stood before the still body of the white buffalo and sang to it, her arms reaching out to it, saying things Brokenleg couldn't grasp and didn't care about anyway. It was all just Injun stuff. He stood there favoring his bum leg and let her sing, wondering if the cow was really dead or whether she'd rise and fight. Some buffler did. The heifer he'd dropped still lived, or at least she pawed air slowly.

The wagon horses snorted and stomped, not liking the brass smell of blood. At last Dust Devil collected herself from whatever world she'd entered and nodded. He nodded, and began cutting down the brisket, wanting the whole hide. They'd have to turn the white cow over to do it, maybe with the help of the saddler. Dust Devil hissed and muttered, saying incantations known only to herself. Big Medicine. He'd heard queersome things about Injuns and white buffler; now he was seeing some of it.

It took a long while to sever the white head — Dust Devil insisted they take that, too — and peel one side. Then he tied a line to the saddle of their spare horse, and with a lot of grunting and shoving, managed to turn the white cow over. Flies had gathered, and he fought away the green-bellied swarms as he tugged and sliced away the clinging underflesh. But at last he pulled the sacred hide free. He laid it flat and scraped flesh away swiftly, more to keep it from stinking in the back of their wagon than any other reason. He lifted the heavy hide, but she careened away from it, not wanting to profane it. Only a great warrior could handle it, he remembered.

A while later, after he'd cut tongue and humpmeat from the downed heifer, they clambered up to the wagon seat and hawed the horses south, ever south. The sacred hide, stored in the shadow of the wagon sheet behind them, transformed Dust Devil, filling her with utter silence. No longer did she chatter or disapprove; no longer did she scorn whatever he did. Instead, she peered furtively at him as if he were a conqueror, a sky spirit descended to earth. She sighed now and then, with a voice that announced she was in the presence of an ineffable mystery. She wasn't Dust Devil at all.

It bothered him. Where had the spitfire gone? How could a miserable cream-colored buffler hide do that? Were they going to fight about that hide? It was worth sixty robes and he intended to get them for it; make up for all his losses, at least a little. And he'd trade it off right in her village, too, since the Cheyenne were crazier than most when it came to a medicine hide.

They rattled south, up long grades that sweat the horses, and down precipitous ones that pushed the wagon into the breeching of the wheelers and threatened to set them all careening downslope.

"You are a great warrior," she said once, a week later. She'd hardly spoken for days, but kept glancing at him, measuring him for something. A burial shroud, he reckoned.

The Bighorns rose majestically, a wall of mountains to the west arresting the great plains. They forded the Crazy Woman with less trouble than he had supposed and continued southward. The mountains shrank into a towering ridge, less majestic than the lofty peaks to the north, and he knew they were entering Cheyenne country.

"You know where your people be?" he asked one dawn, after they had hugged each other under a robe that kept a heavy dew off them.

"You call it the Powder," she said. "Up the Powder, high, where it is cool."

"You sure?"

"It is always so in the Time When the Cherries Are Ripe."

"How come we haven't seen nobody?"

"It is the sacred robe."

"You figure we got robe-magic?"

She frowned. "I hear you mocking. Be careful. You scorn the greatest power of all. A thousand Absaroka dogs could attack, and not an arrow or bullet would touch us.

159

A great grizzly, full of bear-medicine, could come to us in the night — and touch nothing. But if you laugh at the white cow-spirit she will desert you."

"If you say so," he muttered. He reminded himself to keep his Hawken ready and not listen too long to such folderol. It could git him kilt.

They curled southwestward along with the western mountains, had trouble fording the soft-bottomed north fork of the Powder, and finally struck the Powder out upon arid plains. Some excitement grew in her, as if she intuitively knew they were close to her village. He let her guide him. The Powder ran through such a deep trough, full of obstacles, that he kept the wagon half a mile north to keep from getting hung up. The land had grown harsh and red and arid — not Fitzhugh's favorite terrain — but Little Whirlwind glowed and sighed and peered back into the shadowed wagon box to assure herself that the folded white hide still rested there, the cynosure of a thousand flies.

They rattled westerly for two days, past the recently abandoned sites of villages where grass had vanished and bones lay. "Tsistsista," she said softly.

Then, one afternoon full of puffball clouds and summerbluster, they topped a long rise and peered into a verdant flat of tallgrass, with copses of cottonwoods poking up along the thin, glinting river. At the far end lay a goodly village, over a hundred amber lodges. Brokenleg tugged the lines, letting the sweat-whited horses rest while he and Dust Devil watched the busy valley. Off to the left, herding boys guarded a mass of horses. Along the river, small specks of humanity, squaws, were gathering roots, poking their digging sticks into hard clay.

The Cheyenne policing society, the Dog Soldiers, spotted the wagon and swarmed toward them now, while Dust Devil bounced on the seat, exclaiming, little bird cries rising in her throat. A fiercer bunch he never did see: bronzed warriors, their thick muscles glowing in the hot sun, riding hell-bent toward them, their war cries racketing through the peace.

They pulled up around the wagon, setting the drays into a frenzy, staring at their brother-by-marriage, the Bad Leg, and Little Whirlwind, beautiful daughter of a great medicine chief. She stood on the wagon seat, jabbering in their Cheyenne tongue, and then whirled into the wagon bed and withdrew the medicine hide. Warriors froze at the sight. She unfolded the stiff hide, staggering under it, until she had laid it out before them.

Something changed inside of them and Fitzhugh fathomed this was no longer a family reunion but a victory procession. He hawed the drays, clattered down the soft slope, and into the tawny village where yellow dogs whirled and brown children scampered, and people of all ages lined their route toward the chief's lodge, the visitors announced by the town crier moments before.

It was all so exciting he almost forgot why he'd come — until he spotted Dust Devil's sisters, Hide Skinning Woman, Sweet Smoke, and Elk Tail, dancing about and crying to Dust Devil. And the stern, smiling visage of his father-in-law, One Leg Eagle. Then he discovered he was suffocating.

Ten

Guy marveled at the caution of Ambrose Chatillon. A worn trace followed the river, the indentation of thousands of hoofs and travois poles, but the guide didn't use it. He did not wish to leave the imprint of iron-shod hoofs to tempt anyone. Instead, they pursued a harder route along the base of the bluffs, riding over deltas and spines of land.

"We are less visible here, Monsieur Straus. And in a moment, we can ride up the bluffs, out of the valley, and lose ourselves in a crease of prairie."

It made sense to Guy. His life was in this man's hands. Alone, pilgrim that he was, he wouldn't last long. The Creoles called such a person a *mangeur du lard,* or pork-eater, because such a one ate salt pork and pea soup, and came and went. He smiled at the inappropriateness of it. As the days slid by his rebellious body ceased to torment him; the torture of the saddle lessened — somewhat. But no man who ever lived climbed into his bedroll more eagerly than Guy each dusk.

Through the high summer days they rode from dawn until night trapped them, rotating horses, their progress relentless because Chatillon would have it so. Guy had heard of the vastness of the land, its emptiness, its aching distances that ended at horizons and mysteries, its lurking dangers. But knowing of it from conversation in St. Louis and experiencing it were two different things. Increasingly they spotted antelope, grazing in singles and pairs this time of year. In the winter they would collect into giant herds. Whitetail deer vanished and mule deer replaced them. Once Chatillon pointed quietly toward the shimmering, mysterious river. Guy strained to see, and finally beheld a herd of mustangs, their tails sweeping the ground, most of them duns.

Often the guide rode ahead, or ascended a spine of land that would give him a good vantage to observe what lay ahead. The ninth day out, not far from Fort Pierre, he suddenly dropped his horse down the ridge, staying below the skyline, and motioned to Guy, who spurred his chestnut toward the guide, along with the packhorses. Their picket line jerked him almost out of the saddle.

"A village," Chatillon said, steering them into a long coulee that slashed into the

164

western prairie. They rode up it for a mile or so.

"Who?" Guy asked, when they paused to let the horses blow.

Chatillon shrugged. "When you don't wish to be seen, monsieur, it doesn't matter. Friends or enemies, they are all unpredictable. I would guess Yanton Sioux, or Yanktonai. But they could be Ponca or Pawnee or . . ." He shrugged again.

They followed the watercourse another two miles until it shallowed into a green crease in the browning prairie. Ambrose slid off his horse. "Hold him, monsieur. I will have a look."

Guy took the reins while the guide crawled out of the crease and studied the surrounding country, his head barely above the vee of the swale. Gently he slid back down again.

"The village — it has vedettes, outriders. One is near," he whispered. He slid his rifle from its leather saddle sheath. "But we will not shoot unless we have to. If I must, I will use this." He tapped the grip of the knife sheathed at his belt. "And you, monsieur, must keep the horses silent." He crabbed his way up the low slope again.

Guy didn't know how to do that. He felt his pulse escalate, until his heart hammered in his chest. What folly, coming here! He waited while time crawled.

At last Chatillon slid down to Guy. "The vedette — Ponca I think — he turned toward the river. Perhaps we are safe. He will cross our tracks, though."

He led Guy another mile or so westward across unbroken prairie and then swung north, paralleling the Missouri. Guy felt utterly naked out there, visible for miles. But the sight was breathtaking. Above him rose a bowl of sun-bleached blue, capping incredible distances. The grass here grew short and in bunches, and most of it had cured to a silvery green. They rode quietly across this emptiness, ever northwest, the ditch of the great river sometimes visible, a blue streak in the east or north. He thirsted but they had no water. Chatillon never stopped and skipped the usual nooning. The necks and withers of the horses turned black, and then white with caked sweat and dust.

Not until late in the day, when the sun lingered above the northern horizon, did Chatillon suddenly turn toward the river. Guy didn't sleep at all that night and wrestled with visions of a tomahawk splitting his naked head in two. He remembered the Psalm, "Yea though I walk through the valley of the shadow of death I will fear no evil," and recited it in the fearsome dark. Had he permitted his sons to walk into this? This?

Two days later Chatillon led him into Fort Pierre, a square stockade on the west bank of the Missouri, a key post of Chouteau and Company, trading largely with Sioux. Civilization! His heart gladdened at the sight. They walked quietly through a village, passing brown lodges, smoke-blackened at their tops, most of them with the lodge cover rolled partway up to permit summer breezes to sponge away the heat of midsummer. He eyed the Sioux as curiously as they eyed him, his encyclopedic memory drawing up the thousand images he'd heard in St. Louis. All that talk helped him now. He could identify the medicine tripods before the lodges, with their strange bundles dangling from them; the secret and sacred magic of their owner. He saw buffalo hides staked to earth for scraping, and buffalo meat cut into thin strips and hanging from racks until they became jerky. He saw men with swarthy diamond-shaped faces, wearing notched feathers in their hair, and knew the notches and number of feathers spoke of the coups they'd counted in battle.

At last they rode in, the inner gates

swinging open mysteriously as they approached. And within stood a man he knew, Marcel Charbonne, the bourgeois here.

"I am not seeing this," Charbonne announced.

"You are seeing it," Guy retorted.

"Haw!" Charbonne roared, embracing Guy with an enormous mountain hug.

The beefy bourgeois led Guy and Ambrose toward his quarters while engages scurried to care for the guests' horses. Guy eyed them with a frown, knowing he was more worried than he should be, and a post's hospitality toward the opposition was never violated out here — because mutual survival depended on it.

Marcel poured cognac into three snifters and handed them to his guests. "Dust cutters," he said. Guy coughed as always on the fiery stuff, but acknowledged that the dust was cut indeed.

Guy got down to business as soon as the social amenities permitted. "Marcel," he began, "I imagine you've heard about my misfortune."

Charbonne's openness vanished, and caution filled his eyes. He nodded shortly.

"I'm not blaming the Company," Guy continued. "Peter Sarpy gave me good reasons not to. But I think it's in our mutual interest — your interest, *mon ami* — to solve this mystery. Have you any clues?"

Reluctantly, Charbonne shook his head.

Guy realized the man's attitude had changed swiftly. Sheer wariness had replaced the affable greeting. "Who got off *The Trapper* here, Marcel?"

Charbonne seemed to have trouble remembering, so Guy jogged his memory a bit. "I have Captain Sire's list of American Fur engages on board. Emile Poudrier, Raul Raffin, Pascal Dorion, Louis Labone, and Alexis Dufond."

Charbonne fixed him with a sharp stare, as if to say the question was an impertinence. But Guy never wavered. Long years in the financial world had hardened him to some things and honed his ability to pierce secrets. You didn't lend money to men you didn't trust — or men who weren't candid.

"Sarpy, he would say that," Marcel muttered. "What if it is not so? You are opposed to us, *oui?* Why should I say a thing? This is not a linen-covered table at the Planters House."

Guy waited him out. Marcel hadn't said no. Guy sensed the man had to grumble a while before he acceded. He let the bourgeois grow uncomfortable in the silence.

Charbonne lifted the empty snifter ritually, sucked at a final drop of cognac, and sighed. "Poudrier got off here. He's working for me. So is Dorion. Raffin . . ."

"Raffin wasn't supposed to get off here but he did. He is engaged at Fort Union, to Denig and Culbertson, *oui?*"

"And —"

"Raffin, he gets off — and disappears."

Something pulsed in Guy. Raul Raffin.

"He disappears with a company horse. He signed a three-year engagement again."

"Do you know which direction?"

Charbonne shrugged. "Not a trace. One morning he and a bay horse are gone."

"Surely you inquired of his friends . . ."

"They knew nothing. At least they say they knew nothing. Treachery, Guy. He comes up the river with a new contract — and steals a horse."

"Tell me, did Raffin know Brokenleg?"

"They tell me he did. They were trappers together."

"Any reason for him to hate Brokenleg Fitzhugh?"

Charbonne sighed. "They both wanted Little Whirlwind once."

Another jolt pulsed through Guy.

"Any idea why he might have sabotaged our cargo?"

Charbonne shook his head.

"Marcel, could you guess where he's going?"

The bourgeois stared out the tiny window, one with rare glass in it. "This is where one would leave the *bateau* if one were going to the Cheyenne," he said.

Brokenleg always had a sense of homecoming when he rode into the village of White Wolf. He'd wintered with the band a few times during his trapping days. His pain-law, One Leg Eagle, a great medicine man, and his ma-in-law, Antelope, lived here, their lodge always open to him, except for the taboo: he couldn't say a word, not a blessed word, to Antelope. That was the Cheyenne way and maybe there was some sense in it.

He steered his team toward the chief's lodge for a howdy — the ceremonies couldn't be avoided; a chief's welcome of a guest was a rule in any village. He didn't mind. This time he'd brought a whole load of trade goods, and the way to get started with that was to dole out a gift or two to White Wolf and his headmen. Villagers gaped at the wagon. Most had never seen one before, although a few had rolled over the medicine trail along the Platte River. Children squealed. Women recognized

Little Whirlwind and waved joyously, their hands an invitation for a visit. In a few hours, after a howdy with her family, she'd plumb disappear among those tawny cones of cowhide. Maybe by design, he thought darkly. She'd leave him with her sisters. It parched his throat to think on it, and he intended to wet it with some of those spirits he'd socked away in the wagon bed.

He found White Wolf waiting before his decorated lodge, in proper regalia, bonnet and feather-decked lance, a sort of crown and scepter of the Cheyenne. Fitzhugh clambered to earth, stomped life into his bum leg, and handed the lines to solemn brown boys.

"Ah, Bad Leg, and our own Little Whirlwind," he said in Cheyenne lingo, which Fitzhugh grasped easily. "Come let us smoke."

He saw his pa-in-law there, smiling happily. A throng crowded around the wagon and lodge, including a couple of white men. A black-bearded, barrel-shaped one looked familiar, but the crowds blocked Fitzhugh's view. The man didn't seem eager to present himself. Creole, anyway, Fitzhugh thought.

"But what is this that you've brought? I have heard you shot a white buffalo. It blesses us, this sacred hide."

172

"Back a way, up against the Bighorns."

"Nothing could bring more joy to us." The chief beckoned Brokenleg into the lodge, and several headmen ducked through the oval door and into the lodge, which had its cover rolled up a foot or so above the earth.

"Dust Devil, you mind diggin' me some tobacca?" he said to her.

"I am Little Whirlwind," she retorted in Cheyenne, but she ducked back under the sheet and presently returned with several dark twists, one for each headman. He snatched them and ducked inside, having a bad time with his bum leg, as he always did.

They smoked the chief's long-stemmed calumet quietly, saluting the four directions, the earth mother and the One Above, and eventually old White Wolf got around to welcoming him. The chief didn't ask about the wagon. Politeness forbade it.

"We will give you a new name," White Wolf announced suddenly. You are Man Who Brings the White Cow Hide to the People. Never has a white man done this. Hardly ever has a Tsistsista done this. It is a mark of a great warrior, one favored by Sweet Medicine himself. Ever more, you will be Man Who Brings the White Cow Hide to the People. I will have the crier announce it, and all in the village will be pleased."

"I'm plumb grateful," Brokenleg said, lapsing into his own tongue. Sort of, he thought. He thought he owned that piece of carpet, but apparently it wasn't so.

"One Leg Eagle will follow the customs and we will give it to the sky spirits," the chief continued. "This medicine is greater than the four arrows and the sacred hat."

Brokenleg sat uncomfortably through the long oration, his bum leg poking clear to the cold fire pit. But at last it was his turn to orate a bit.

"I brought a wagonload of trade goods," he announced. "We've built a post up on the Yellowstone — you know that — but we hardly see you there. I came to invite you to trade, just like family. I'm one of you; I'll give good prices for robes, and offer my goods at a better price than any American Fur post."

They smiled at that. He was one of them. But the chief raised a hand. "It is a long way there, Man Who Brings the White Cow Hide to the People. We went there in the Hoop and Stick Game Moon and saw your new post. And our enemies the Absaroka gather there. They are many. We wish you hadn't gone there, but you told us the rivers and the fireboats made it so. We are strong and can always beat the Absaroka People — but there are many there . . . many more than our village."

"I'll bring the goods here in wagons. The Piegans stole our oxen — but I got some horses. I'll meet you two or three times a year on the Tongue, or better yet, the Little Bighorn. How about the Plum Moon, and then the Hard Face Moon, and then the Spring Moon? I'll be there with wagons; you come with your good Tsistsista robes. You come halfway, and I come halfway."

"It is a thing we will talk about in council."

He knew they'd do it; the bonds he had forged with One Leg Eagle and his family made it necessary. No band lightly scorned an alliance with a trader who brought it rifles and knives and pots and powder and blankets.

Finally the chief arose, dismissing them, and Brokenleg limped out, feeling prickles in his bum leg. The chief followed, and then addressed the crowd outside. "Our friend has come to trade his medicine things for robes," he said. "Our friend promises us the best prices for our robes and low prices for his things, as a friend must do. He has brought many good things."

Trade! Fitzhugh rejoiced. "I will visit my family and friends today, and tomorrow I will trade," he said, surveying the crowd. His gaze caught that white man again, and suddenly he knew who it was. Raffin! The Creole trapper from the beaver days with a voice like splintered glass, a man who roared and walked like a black bear, the man he'd beaten for Dust Devil's favors. And even as he stared, startled, at Raul Raffin, the Creole stared back, mockery in his eyes — along with a challenge of some sort. And Fitzhugh knew what that challenge would be . . . But what was he doing here? The man was a veteran engage of American Fur, and far, far from any AFC post.

But One Leg Eagle had collected Brokenleg, along with Little Whirlwind, and was guiding them toward the lodge. In the swirl, Antelope joined them, and then Little Whirlwind's shy sisters. He peered back and saw a swarm of giggling brown boys sitting on the wagon seat snapping lines over the backs of half-trained drays.

"Trust them," said his pap, who himself eyed the rascals. "You go ahead; I'll speak to the boys."

A few moments later he returned, bearing the sacred white hide. His face glowed.

"Only I can touch it. A Suhtai with medicine powers can. A warrior who has done great things can. I will make a sweet-grass prayer. Then Antelope will tan it in a certain way. Then we will give it to the sky spirits. You have brought me the greatest gift of all, and I have gifts to give in return." He smiled, his gapped brown teeth showing.

Brokenleg hadn't been aware of giving him the medicine robe, but he knew what was coming; Fate was closing in, like a tightening noose. Dust Devil grinned at him wickedly. How had he ever gotten into this? Some promise he didn't remember making. Shooting a rare white cow. After that, everything had happened by itself. He eyed Little Whirlwind's sisters furtively, measuring them like beef, for fat and carcass weight, thigh and breast. They looked smug. He could see it, that same blasted Suhtai arrogance, that same Dust-Devil smirky look. He could just git. He could git, ditch it all, hoss 'n beaver, before he was brought to medicine himself. He could lodgepole that wench; that'd do it. Lose him the Cheyenne trade, but git him outa this.

He studied them as they walked along beside him, pretendin' shy when they were all bold as camp-robber jays. Sweet Smoke. Youngest of all, danged near Maxim's age.

177

Sweet Grass Smoke, he corrected himself. Lithe as a snake, her face a bright diamond, with eyes as saucy as a crow's, and wearin' more foofaraw than any decent woman oughter. But she sure was blossoming. Last year she was plumb skinny; now she got a curvy look to her and knew it, wigglin' it all at him.

And Hide Skinning Woman. Plainer than her sisters, big flat nose, older'n Dust Devil, big across the bottom, looks like she could put up a lodge in two minutes. Mean, that's what he saw in her eyes. She had badger eyes, cruel and predatory, and a mouth too wide, like she could suck blood. And that other, Elk Tail, Elk Tail. Now who'd want to marry some old Elk Tail? Who'd hitch up with Hide Skinning Woman? One step older'n Dust Devil, and mad at him, and her pa, for pulling Dust Devil out of the marryin' order. She was a curvy one too — too curvy. Brokenleg began to have visions and sweats. Too curvy for her own good, with a little extry wiggle thrown in. Smoothest skin in the outfit, all dusky peaches, and a mean smile, like a triumphant smile, like she had him at last. She saw him staring furtively, and poked out a pink tongue.

They reached the lodge, where her

brothers awaited, two mean-looking bare-chested muscle-bound stocky types with snakey eyes and scars, and bulgy arms and hands that looked like shotguns to a sooner groom. He couldn't remember their names. Bear Guts or something. Enforcers, that's what. Hangin' around to git this affair done with.

Old One Leg Eagle, he spread the white hide out, wrestling the folds of the untanned pelt gently until it rested on the packed earth before the lodge, and then settled himself exactly behind the rump.

"Ah, my fine son, Man Who Brings White Cow Hide to the People, you have brought me the greatest gift of all. What would I want of rifles, of powder, of blankets, of lead, of pots and knives and awls and blankets, when you have brought me medicine itself? Ah, my own son and friend, I will give you my gifts and good wishes in return." He smiled beatifically. Antelope beamed in a shy way. She was forbidden to look directly at Fitzhugh, and he wasn't supposed to peek much at her. But his mam there was enjoying herself, for sure.

Dust Devil got smirky, and then turned solemn.

Brokenleg hunkered down inside of himself and waited.

Eleven

Oh, Fitzhugh, what have you done? When you was borned, did your Scotch Presbyterian ma ever imagine you'd have four wives — all at once? How are you gonna support four? And if they have a passel of children how are you gonna support them? Maybe ten. Maybe twenty. And how're you gonna take four wives back to St. Louis once a year? Company can't buy all them tickets. And what's ol' Jamie Dance gonna say? Why, you've gone beaver, you've lifted the cache, you've lost your topknot. Then he'd heehaw all over the place. How come you're tying a knot with three strangers. You don't know even one of these dusky maidens.

It was all Dust Devil's doings. She'd caught him in a weak moment. He shoulda called her bluff; let her pull out if she didn't like it. Connivin' woman. How'd she steer him to that white buffler? Her hoodoo spirits, that's how. He shot him an ordinary buffler except it was white, and now he's king o' the heap. At least he didn't have to

lay out a mess o' gifts to the old man —
rifles, powder, and the like. Just a mangy old
hide, not even tanned. Them Injuns are
some peculiar types, all right. At least it
saved him a mess o' trade goods. He'd give
her that. She must o' had some way o'
making that white buffler come. Sendin' up
her spirit-medicine. Her Suhtai magic. Old
man's a shaman; the whole business was
dreamed up over sweet-grass smoke and a
pair o' rattles made from gourds or buffler
bull stones. And that durned Dust Devil,
she knew it all along, and steered him into it
like he was some buffler stampeded over
some cliff.

Half the village had collected around the
lodge, the creased old crones of the village
beaming at him with toothy smiles, and the
children right solemn, and the warriors and
young man half-resentful and back a piece,
not liking to see so many comely girls go to
one white man. Fitzhugh peered about,
wondering what came next. The ladies had
vanished into the lodge, from whence occasional giggles and whispers erupted. How
could a whole village be so quiet? Even the
mutts quit snapping and snarling and grabbing jerky from the racks. Was there going
to be some sorta ceremony? He'd never
heard of any marriage ceremony. They just

did 'er. Gal moved her stuff and parfleches and blankets on over to a new lodge.

That Dust Devil! How come she wanted more wives? Wasn't he good enough for her? Didn't he please her? Didn't they have some fine old times? Why was she pawning him off — gettin' half rid o' him? It was indecent. He never much thought o' decency, not out hyar in the mountains, and the rendezvous. What — what would happen tonight?

He contemplated that awful prospect, a horror building in him, along with a wild thirst. He thought longingly about that rundlet of spirits back in the wagon — ah, just a nip. Enough to pull him through a day and a night. Enough to send him to oblivion until this ordeal passed. He'd rather wrestle a hibernating grizzly sow again and bust his other leg than face this. He'd rather ditch the Rocky Mountain Company, leave old Guy, abandon old Jamie, head into the wilds where no coon would ever find him.

Well, he knew what he'd do. Sweet Smoke — he'd give Sweet Smoke to Maxim. Same age almost. Hide Skinning Woman, why, just right for ol' Trudeau. And Elk Tail, well, she was right pretty. He'd think about that. Maybe two wives wouldn't be so bad. Him and Elk Tail and Dust Devil, a snortin' and hootin' around at night. He'd be willing to try that arrangement. If it was poor doin's, he'd lodgepole her and let Abner or Zach have a crack at her. That's what he'd do . . .

Too late. The young ladies emerged solemnly from the lodge, one by one, each in festival dress, faces glowing. The crowd stirred and whispered. Even old Chief White Wolf stood there, watching the whole mess. Watching a poor defenseless white man git himself hooked like a catfish.

Well, the ladies were plumb purty, he'd allow that. They wore fringed doeskin dresses, each tanned and beaten to velvet, and bleached white. Fine dyed quillwork embroidered the bodice of each, and trade beads blazoned the hems. Each wore high moccasins, similarly embellished with beads and rabbit fur. Each had brushed her blue-tinted jet hair until it shone, and braided it, and tied yellow ribbons to each braid. Each had vermilioned her forehead. Each wore a magical necklace of sacred things, elk teeth, bear fangs, wolf ears, and the like, carefully strung together. Something in him melted. He had to admit he'd never seen such a sight, three dazzling Cheyenne maidens smiling shyly at him, a blush rising on their tawny cheeks, their black eyes bright with happiness.

He suddenly felt grubby. His calico shirt had been soiled by travel; he hadn't been given time to scrub. The red hair of his beard and head lay matted and greasy. His boots were scuffed. His britches were black with grease and dirt. Some outfit to wear at such doings! But no one seemed to notice. He felt touched suddenly: These three were given to him by their father; they had little say in it, although a father usually heeded an unhappy daughter. But none were complaining. Their eyes shone; their faces revealed expectation. They were giving their whole lives to him. It struck him that that was some gift — their lives for a grubby, gimpy old white man. Not so old. He was barely into his thirties. But a year in the mountains aged a man more than five in the cities. He smiled back, worrying about the stink of his armpits and the grime on his flesh.

Dust Devil beamed malevolently, a mock in her eyes. What the devil was going to happen tonight? Did each o' these ladies expect — he broke into a cold sweat. And all together? But he didn't have time to think on these absorbing things. Instead, the ladies ducked into the lodge and brought out their truck. Each had tanned a bridal robe, and each robe was a masterpiece. Somebody — their brothers — had hunted down some cinnamon-colored buffalo, and the young ladies had tanned them until they were soft as velvet. These were gifts to him, and here he was, far from his wagon and not a trinket or foofaraw in hand. But no one minded. They brought their parfleches out, each dyed with geometric designs; each filled with their private things.

And then old One Leg Eagle stood, and addressed the rapt crowd and Brokenleg. "Welcome, son-in-law. Now I have given you all of my daughters. Now you are an honored member of our family and clan, and by marriage, a Suhtai. I hope my daughters will please you. They are fine women. They will lighten your burdens. They will give you many children."

Fitzhugh blushed.

"You have no lodge; only the wagon. So my own Antelope and I will visit brothers this night and you will have our lodge."

His ma-in-law smiled furtively. She wasn't supposed to make eye contact with him.

"You have given our village the greatest gift, the white hide of the sacred buffalo. It will bring joy and fatness, power against our enemies and meat for the cold winters.

Health for all the village. The smiles of the sky spirits. The blessings of Sweet Medicine, and the powers of Mateo, the all-everywhere one. Now I will call upon the great warriors of the village to take the robe away, and the old women to scrape and tan it, and in a few days we will tie it to a pole and give it to the ones above.

"And now we will leave you to your happiness."

"I shore do thank ye," he said, lapsing into English, his throat parched. He wanted some mountain dew right fast.

He watched while four burly, scarred warriors lifted the corners of the white hide and carried it off somewhere. And then the crowd dissipated, the old crones last to go, their eyes knowing as they studied the white man and his brides. Brokenleg broke into a sweat. The lodge stood squarely in the middle of the village, within twenty yards of several other lodges. The ladies eyed him cheerfully, as if this was the fulfillment of design, of lengthy planning and machination. They toted their robes and parfleches inside while he tried to collect his rattled thoughts and do something, anything. He reckoned he ought to collect his wagon and put the horses to pasture, but even as he thought it, his brothers-in-law drove the wagon to the lodge, unharnessed the horses, and led them off to the tribal herd. The saddler went too, he noticed suspiciously. What was he: a Cheyenne prisoner of war? Well then, he'd fetch his Hawken and possibles. But before he limped a step, Hide Skinning Woman had snatched them and was toting them into the lodge. Well then, he'd like some chow, maybe some good buffler. But there was Elk Tail, building the evening fire, and Sweet Smoke preparing to roast some hump ribs that materialized from somewhere. Well then, maybe he ought to check on the cargo in the wagon; make sure it was all in place (and little boys hadn't snatched any of it). But there was his own Dust Devil, drawing him into the lodge, smiling villainously.

He'd been in many lodges over the years, and this one was no different. Its cover had been rolled up. A rudimentary fire pit lay in the center, unused except for light this time of year. Just back of it lay a square patch of naked earth, devoid of debris. It was the altar, the breast of Mother Earth. Upon it, they would occasionally burn sweet grass or sage. The family wealth rested in parfleches around the perimeter. One Leg Eagle's bow and arrows hung from the lodgepole along with a bull's neck shield dyed with the owner's own medicine symbols, a claw and beak. A medicine bundle hung also. Old robes covered the dry turf. Two finely woven reed backrests stood at the rear, in the place where his in-laws would receive guests. The pallets around the perimeter were raised and covered with ground robes, in the Cheyenne and Arapaho tradition. He counted five, the sons having left the lodge. He eyed the pallets suspiciously, wondering what they would hold this night.

Dust Devil motioned him down, and he eased to the earth, his stiff leg paining him as always. She began undoing his shirt, an evil grin on her. He growled. This was all going too fast to suit him. But she insisted, mewing at him to obey, and at last he surrendered. Why, the whole world could peer under that rolled-up lodge cover! By the time they'd wrestled his stained shirt off, the rest of his wives appeared bearing a kettle of hot water and some strange pulverized vegetable matter.

They began at once to wrestle his britches off, and he clung to them as if they were a fig leaf. But then he got the way of it. He was receiving a bath. Outside a lavender twilight settled, and inside it was plumb dark, except for the west side of the lodge, where a soft residual light snaked through the scraped cowhide. By gawd, they were even going to wash his hair. The smiling ladies soaked his head and beard in hot water, rubbed that fiber — he remembered that they used yucca and various roots for soaps — until it lathered, and before he knew it they'd plumb scraped him clean. Most of him anyway. They vanished into the dark suddenly, letting him finish the job.

After that they rubbed his clean flesh with sage and sweet grass, hauled the waterpot out, and wiped him dry.

"Now you smell good," said Dust Devil.

"Now what?" he demanded, not really as irritable as he sounded.

"Now we eat."

The ladies materialized again, this time with bowls of good root stew and succulent chunks of roasted hump meat, dripping fat. He gorged himself and then they wiped his fingers and hands and cleaned his face.

"Here I am, buck naked and your sisters are waitin' on me hand and foot," he growled in English. "Now what?"

"You'll see," she said primly.

He sat in the dark and waited, while that gaggle of women whispered and muttered stuff and cleaned up out in the dusk. He had to admit he was plumb comfortable, leaning into the backrest, his carcass clean and his belly full of hump meat. The pungent smell of sagebrush lingered on his arms and chest. Maybe he could get used to it if he tried hard. But he drove that thought sternly out of his skull. This here excess of wives would be spread among deserving traders and engages.

The women were plain in no hurry, he thought. Maybe they were as shy of this hyar business as he was. But at last, in full darkness, he heard one of them slip into the lodge. Just one. He couldn't make out who.

"Which one are you?" he whispered in Cheyenne.

"I am your woman," whispered a voice back. He heard the rustle of clothing, and the hot presence of someone. And then a wild giggle — Dust Devil's. "They will wait a few suns," she said, sliding to him. "They will not take off the cord tonight."

Ambrose Chatillon led Guy upriver through the summer heat, the days falling behind them like playing cards. Guy realized his clothing no longer fit. He was buckling his belt tighter. His shirts hung loose and his britches bagged. His body still ached at the end of a hard day's ride but no longer tortured him. He'd browned and leaned and muscled up.

The endless transit of the Missouri fascinated him. The abstractions of St. Louis had become reality — and what reality. No man, back in the city, could fathom the length of the river as it sliced through endless prairies that extended some infinitude beyond horizons. The guide seemed uncanny. On two occasions he'd quietly steered Guy away from the river trace to let a passing party of hunters or warriors slide by.

They reached the country of the Arikaras, or Rees, who lived in fortified villages along the river. They'd defeated various fur companies and had even defeated the U.S. Army under Colonel Leavenworth. They had a reputation for treachery; friendliness by day, murder and theft by night. Chatillon did not wish to tackle them and chose instead a dangerous river crossing to evade the villagers. Chatillon advised him to remove his boots and britches and sling them over his back, along with anything in the packs that might be ruined by water. Guy eyed the broad river nervously. It may as well have been a sea, he thought, seeing the far bank a quarter of a mile away.

"Mostly we can walk across here. The river, it is low now, *oui?* See the bar, the ripples, extending so far out. Only a little will the horses swim. Just hang on and let the *cheval* work. Hang on when he crawls up the far side and shakes himself. He will shake you loose if he can."

Chatillon drove the packhorses ahead of him as they splashed along a gravelly bar that transported them almost magically out upon the shimmering, glaring river. The swift water tugged at the horses. Guy could feel it pushing on his saddler. The water crept higher, above the hocks to the belly, where it took on renewed force, pressuring the horse broadside. Guy's feet and ankles and calves hated the chill wetness. Then, ahead, the packhorses plunged off a hidden precipice and began drifting downstream alarmingly. They'd struck the main channel but were two-thirds across. The animals, burdened by their heavy packs, barely kept their heads out of water. But they splashed steadily, suddenly struck solid ground, and leaped to the far bank in a series of lunges. Chatillon followed. Guy felt his own horse lunge, as if diving off a cliff, and felt icy water boil about him. The horse sputtered and then heeled to the right, slowly toppling Guy, who felt himself going over. He hit the water, plunged under, collided with the horse, felt a flailing hoof smack his thigh and again on the small of his back, reached the surface, gasped, inhaled water and air, went under again, felt the horse flail past him, and broke the surface again.

The next moments spun by dizzily, a kaleidoscope of air, water, breathlessness, hurt, and terror. He surfaced again, heard Chatillon bawling at him, saw a rawhide line snake into the water nearby. He lunged for it, caught it, felt its blessed strength as it drew him out of the channel like a hooked catfish. He reached shallows, but was too winded and shaken to stand. Chatillon lifted him bodily and dragged him to the east shore. Guy, on all fours, coughed up water and felt the hot sun pry into the iciness of his clothing. He heard a shrill whickering downstream.

"You are all right. I will fetch the horse," Chatillon said, trotting off.

All right. But his shoes and britches were gone. And his notebooks and the shipping records he'd used. The river had eaten them. He stared at that benign flow of river, half a mile wide, sparkling in the hot sun, and understood its power and terror. Ever since he'd left Bellevue he'd experienced a new world, unpredictable and unsafe, with menace exploding over him at unexpected moments. How could he have fashioned a fur trading company without grasping something so elemental?

Chatillon gathered their kit while the dripping horses dozed and swatted flies. Then he pulled the trigger of his Hawken. The cap snapped but nothing else happened. Using a worm that could be screwed into a rifle ball, he extracted the ball from his rifle and dug wet powder out. He reloaded, and then recharged Guy's rifle as well. Guy found spare britches and some camp moccasins that would have to do until he could have something better cobbled at Fort Clark or Fort Union. They gave the Arikara villages wide berth and rode quietly north. Guy was acquiring mountain vision: he could see the things that city eyes missed, and it added to his confidence. Still, he never doubted that they were helpless and vulnerable in that sea of grass.

Fort Clark, near the Mandan and Hidatsa villages, rose upon them suddenly one twilight, and its factor, American Fur Company veteran James Kipp, welcomed them warmly and immediately put one of his gifted Mandan women to work on a pair of boots for Guy, actually moccasins with buffalo bullhide soles. Smallpox had demolished the Mandans and weakened the Hidatsas, but the post still prospered as a trading center for northern Sioux and their close cousins the Assiniboin.

"I've been expecting you," said Kipp over some real Missouri whiskey that evening. "That's a shame, what happened at Bellevue."

"Expecting me?"

"I got word."

Guy couldn't fathom how Kipp could have gotten word. The resources of the giant company were phenomenal, he thought. "Peter Sarpy persuaded me it wasn't anything the company would do," Guy said, cautiously. "He thought it might be an engage, someone like that."

Kipp poked a finger at Guy and lifted a scottish brow. "I'll say flatly it wasn't the company. That's one area where we let sleeping dogs lie. This whole thing — your license hearings — threatens us, you know."

Guy knew. "I lost my list of AFC engages aboard *The Trapper*, but I know the one I'm interested in. Raffin. Raul Raffin." Guy said no more, letting the name sink into the factor's thoughts.

"Raffin," Kipp muttered. "A good beaver man. Free trapper. Sold his plews to American Fur usually. Got to the last four or five rendezvous over to the Pogo Agie and around there."

That didn't help Guy any. "Our friend at

Fort Pierre, Marcel Charbonne, says he got off there — and vanished."

"So I've heard. He was to go up to Union; Culbertson's man."

"Charbonne tells me Raffin knew Fitzhugh; he and Raffin were rivals for Little Whirlwind. Thinks maybe Raffin headed west, toward the Cheyenne villages from there."

"I've heard the story," Kipp said. "Raffin's a moody one. Big, powerful, dark-spirited. You have any notion why he might have done it?"

Guy didn't, really. "Hurt my partner, I suppose. Drive him out of the upper Missouri. Who knows? Malice? Revenge? Ah, Mr. Kipp — is he capable of planing something so artful as stashing the spirits in the hold and all the rest?"

Kipp nodded. "He's bright. He's cunning. We never trusted him much — he's got some sort of dark life of his own we spotted. We've never given him responsibility, even after all these years as an engage. But Cadet keeps him on."

"What do you make of it, Mr. Kipp?"

"Ambition, Mr. Straus. Ambition."

Twelve

Dust Devil watched knowingly as her man traded everything in his wagon for over three hundred robes. Good Tsistsista robes, too, softly tanned. Hadn't she told him it would be so? Why had he resisted so much? He lacked the wisdom of the People, that's why. She couldn't fathom white men, who had so much things-medicine and yet knew nothing.

In the middle of the day, that other white man in the village, Raffin, strolled up to the wagon where her man was trading.

"I thought I saw you," said Brokenleg between trades.

"I am here," Raffin agreed.

"Workin' for the Company."

"Maybe, maybe not, Brokenleg. I am a free man. I am looking for a good life, *oui?*"

He grinned but the corners of his mouth turned down. She had known him for years; and so had her man. They had trapped beaver, seen each other once a year at the rendezvous. He was a great, square man, like a black bear, with a wiry black beard and sad brown eyes that looked like two wounds. He had come to the village in the days when Brokenleg and Jamie Dance had come, and always with the soft, hungry look in his brown eyes. Hungry for her most of all; she sensed it. But hungry for any Cheyenne maid who wore the rope. The hungry look left his eyes when he gazed at a women with a lodge and man of her own.

She hadn't warmed to him. He had a darkness of soul; his spirit-medicine came from a creature of the earth or the cave. Now he made her uneasy again.

"Odd place to come," Fitzhugh said, shortly. He turned to his trading again, looking over a glossy split robe brought by old Never Run Woman.

Raffin lingered, puffing on a clay pipe, his gaze missing nothing, almost as if he were calculating Fitzhugh's profits. Her man had never liked him much either. No one did. She remembered that this Raffin had often come to the village alone, left alone, his business private and mysterious.

Still, he seemed harmless enough. But she noticed that Fitzhugh peered furtively at Raffin between trades, and sometimes during trades, as if to fathom Raffin's business there in the village of White Wolf. And occasionally Fitzhugh's blue-eyed squint flicked toward her, and she realized Raffin had been studying her.

Later she found out he'd been in the village almost a month, doing ho harm, greeting everyone respectfully, bringing in a lot of game and giving it away. He was a great hunter, people told her. And he spoke the tongue of the People perfectly — much better than Brokenleg, they added slyly. He spoke many tongues of many Peoples, they added. He had made himself welcome, and most of the village women were sure he wanted a Tsistsista wife. They could see it in his furtive glances from those wounded eyes.

Fitzhugh traded away everything by mid-afternoon, and spent the rest of the day sorting robes, folding them and storing them in the big wagon while Raffin watched silently, puffing that pipe. Fitzhugh struck an agreement with Chief White Wolf, too: late in the Moon, When the Water Begins to Freeze on the Streams, he would be at the Greasy Grass with a wagon to trade again; and later, during the winter moons, he would come to their village on the Powder River to trade once more. Raffin listened intently. Wherever her man went, Raffin seemed to appear as if by accident.

She shrugged. It was nothing. This Raffin

was nothing to her. Nothing. She eyed her sisters, who stood about shyly, strangers to the man they'd been wed to. Now that was a triumph, she thought. At last she wouldn't be alone in that post with only white men around, slaving. Her sisters would slave, too, she thought acidly. But at least she'd have company: Suhtai company, speaking the tongue of the People all day. It was good.

By agreement, they played a good Tsistsista joke on him that second night. They all settled into their pallets in the darkness, and none came to him; none took off her rope. He hardly knew what to do, all four wives there in the close dark, and he on his pallet, tossing and turning and muttering and not knowing what to do, or perhaps too embarrassed to do it. When Sun returned at last, and brown light filtered through the cowhide, they rose from their separate pallets, smiled at him, and vanished from the lodge.

She grinned. "See what a great blanket chief you are," she taunted. He stared at her, dark hollows under his eyes, teeth gritted. "Way I want it," he said, unconvincingly. "I hitched up with you."

Maybe, she thought. But that would change when Sweet Smoke or Elk Tail pulled her dress over her shoulders some time soon. She giggled again. It would be fun to torment the white man. Four young, beautiful Suhtai women were more than a match for him. And they'd be merciless.

They rolled north that morning, and the parting filled her with sighs and foreboding, a certain melancholy she always felt when she left the People. Her parents watched them go, a large part of their family leaving with the white man. One Leg Eagle had daubed his face with white clay, a mourning face, but Antelope smiled. The Dog Soldiers gave them honorary escort for several miles down the river and then turned away with a parting shout. Some of them brandished fine new Leman trade rifles, which pleased her. She wanted all the trade rifles to go to her People, to use against their enemies, the Absaroka especially. She hated it when Fitzhugh traded one to the Absarokas. It was like betraying her.

They traveled under a rare summer overcast, unseasonable skies that troubled her. No one else seemed to notice. Her sisters walked beside the wagon or rode shyly and silently beside Fitzhugh, making no talk. It didn't occur to him to teach them English as the wagon creaked and rattled over trackless land. He was acting strange. Instead of being her lion, with hair the color of autumn leaves, he had pulled into himself. She exulted. Four Suhtai wives were too much for any man! Especially three at once!

They made good time because the horses were friskier under the heavy sky, and by dusk they'd gone a long way from her village. Fitzhugh chose a good spot, a tallgrass meadow beside the river with plenty of cottonwoods and brush nearby. While he wrestled collars and hames, bellybands and breeching from six unruly horses, Hide Skinning Woman gathered dry wood, Elk Tail prepared a haunch of cow meat they brought from the village, and Sweet Smoke took a digging stick and walked the riverbank for breadroot, wild onions, and greens. She felt a chill breeze lift in the twilight. The days weren't as long as before, and at night a good soft robe was welcome.

They ate buffalo tongue and root stew, and swiftly cleaned up. They had no lodge but they could crowd into the covered wagon if it rained. Her man looked tired and a little petulant but they would tease him again tonight. Let him wait! Let him lie there, thinking about all four of them! It would be fun. They poured water on the fire until its orange eye dimmed and died and the deep darkness engulfed them. Darkness was good; the hiding time. In darkness lay safety.

But she didn't like the night, a black one because of the overcast. She thought of going to him and climbing into his robe and pressing her loins to his, but she didn't. That would spoil everything. Let him suffer. It was such a good joke that she'd even make a Tsistsista husband suffer. But it was not a good night, and she realized, crossly, that she suffered, too. The night spirits and dead spirits kept her eyes open. She could see them everywhere. She didn't really want to share Brokenleg, not even with her sisters. She thought angrily that Brokenleg should have slaves.

She awoke with a start at dawn and saw at once that it was too late. Hovering in the murky light, hardly visible, were many warriors, twice times the fingers of both hands. She could not imagine who they were or what they might do. Her heart raced; her stomach knotted. Her man sat upright knowing he'd been caught. Her sisters were rousing themselves. She peered hard, trying to see, trying to know who these dogs were. Enemies of the People. So many. Some with drawn bows, others with rifles. They wore little: loincloths, moccasins, medicine bundles at their breast. She did not see war paint. No great chevrons of white or ochre on cheeks.

Her man said nothing, keeping his hands carefully away from the rusted Hawken near his robe. One of the warriors spoke to another, and she knew instantly. Arapaho! Friends of the Tsistsistas! They could understand each other; her tongue and theirs weren't so far apart.

"Friends, we are Tsistsistas," she said.

But none replied. Instead, several sprang into the blackness of the wagon and began pitching out robes. Others trotted away and returned with the picketed drays and the saddler. Two pulled out knives and cut loose the wagon sheet and began hacking at it.

Even as light thickened and color seeped into the world, the Arapahoes loaded prime robes into the wagon sheeting, making packs which they anchored on the horses by using pieces of harness, the bellyband and breeching in particular.

"You reckon on takin' them robes?" Fitzhugh asked in English.

They didn't reply but hastened at their task until they had the robes bundled and spread over the seven horses, burdening them until they could barely stand.

Then a powerfully built warrior, with war

scars puckering his side and arm, stalked toward Brokenleg, picked up the Hawken, pulled the cap off it, and set it down a few yards distant.

"You workin' for the Company?"

The headman's expression didn't change.

"You be working for the Company," Fitzhugh concluded. "I got me a picture of your face in my mind, and I ain't gonna forget it. Someday — maybe tomorrer — I'm coming, I'm coming. I'll bring ye to medicine."

The headman smiled faintly. His rifle never wavered.

Then the Arapahoes trotted off, vanishing in the morning shadows as silently as they came, leading seven burdened horses with them.

"Raffin," he growled. "I shoulda known."

Rage built in Brokenleg. He knew he was in a fix. He couldn't walk clear to the post on the Yellowstone, over two hundred miles on a bum leg. At least not without taking a month. He couldn't buy and train another set of draft horses either — not with the harness pillaged. And he'd have to abandon this wagon, too. The company was whipping him every way he turned. Raffin! Probably hired by old Chouteau hisself back there in St. Louey, to wreck it all. Wreck the Crow trade and see to it that Fitzhugh's Post didn't get any Cheyenne trade either. A smart one, that Raffin. Fitzhugh thought about the Creole. Bile flooded him, and he knew what he'd do if he ever saw Raffin again: he'd kill him. Which was something Raffin would be prepared for.

His women stared at him solemnly in the quiet of the dawn. At last Dust Devil stirred. They'd eat and think on it. The wagon hulked uselessly, as helpless as a beached whale, its naked bows poking the sky. But it still held their chow, their possessions, the bridal gifts of three Suhtai sisters.

"I will go," said Sweet Smoke.

Her sisters nodded. The girl simply began jogging westward at a relaxed pace. It dawned on him that she was running clear back to her village twelve or fifteen miles upriver. She would get help. At that pace she'd be there by noon. By evening . . . he wondered what would happen. Something tickled at the back of his mind: having four Suhtai Cheyenne wives might just be a blessing in ways he hadn't figured.

He watched her go and worried about her. A lone woman, far from her village, would be easy pickings. He scowled, wishing he could protect her, knowing he

206

couldn't. She was rescuing him, and it grated at him.

Three hundred seventeen prime robes, worth five to six dollars in New York if there wasn't a glut, which there often was. Fifteen hundred dollars anyways. At least if them easterners snapped them up for carriage robes, greatcoats, belts for machinery. Buffler wasn't much good for shoe leather; at least no one could make it work well. Fifteen hundred. Part of the reason Chouteau and Company hated opposition so much was that the opposition produced gluts, which dropped the prices for all fur companies. Alone, Chouteau's giant released or withheld bales of robes to control prices. Fitzhugh knew damned well that Raffin was worth any price they paid him; that Raffin's price was nothing compared to the losses American Fur would fetch when Fitzhugh's company horned in. Old Chouteau had probably promised Raffin a thousand — and figured he'd save a hundred thousand by putting the Rocky Mountain Company out of business.

Which didn't help him none. His women had sliced up the rest of the buffler tongue. That's how they ate: buffler for breakfast, and supper. None o' them nooned much. He wolfed down meat angrily, ignoring their piercing glares, and then limped around his prison. He still had his special saddle with one stirrup elongated. Harness — he had collars and hames and bridles and lines. Enough to salvage if he could git it all back to the post and put men to work fashioning bellybands and britching and the like outa buffler. But he didn't know how he'd get that heavy mass of harness up there. That and a heap o' wife-things stuck in parfleches, and a few camp items.

A quiet rage percolated through him. They'd lose all this stuff too, unless she showed up with a dozen ponies and some packsaddles. Behind him he heard the quiet babble of the sisters. Leastwise they had someone to talk to. He didn't. He felt alone. No one on earth, in the whole universe, to talk to. That Maxim sulking up there, not talkin'. Maybe Abner and Zach, ol' coons from the beaver days. But mostly he talked to himself because no one else on earth understood, except maybe Jamie Dance, down hell and gone on the Arkansas River.

He thought he'd better look to their defenses. About all they could do was skedaddle and hide if some outfit showed up. Without muttering a word to the women, he plucked up his battered Hawken and limped to the south bluff, aiming toward a knob there maybe a thousand yards distant. He'd sit up there and roast and keep a mean eye on the horizons.

And that's how the day played out. He sat on his nob sulking and spending his bile on Raffin, thinking on a dozen ways to skewer the Creole. Maybe by God he'd git on down to St. Louey again and skewer old Chouteau hisself in his office on the levee. Cadet spun his webs like a black widder spider down there, hardly caring who got killed out here or why, so long as it prospered his monopoly.

Thus he spent the day. Late in the afternoon he spotted a commotion of dust off the west, and reckoned some Cheyenne were coming. What it would amount to, he didn't know. He glared narrowly at the distant party. Wind whipped up the dust it made and blew it ahead, putting the horsemen at the rear. It had to be his village friends.

He rose, stomped the stiffness out of his leg, and limped down the knoll, arriving at the camp about the time the riders rode in. Cheyenne all right. About twenty Dog Society warriors, the village police; old One Leg Eagle, Sweet Smoke, and four ponies, three with squaw saddles on them.

He let Dust Devil do the talkin' and she was saying a mouthful and a half. He caught words now and then, Arapaho, robes, ponies stolen, and the rest. He didn't hear Raffin none. And didn't see him, for that matter.

At last the shaman turned to Fitzhugh and spoke slow Cheyenne. "We will talk to our friends the Arapaho about this."

"You might start with that Creole Raffin, there in your village."

"He does us no harm. He has honored us with gifts and kindness."

"He would. You better start with him anyway. He's got some answering to do."

One Leg Eagle didn't seem to like Fitzhugh's implications, but let it pass. "I have brought ponies for you and my daughters. I will trade for them when we meet again. A pony will bring good things."

"All right. If we're in business. Losing three hundred robes, horses and a wagon — it puts me at the edge of the cliff."

"If you cannot trade, then bring the ponies back when you can."

"I'll do that."

"I have woman-saddles for them. We will stay with you tonight."

"You mind taking things to the village? Like the rest of the harness? And the things we can't carry?"

"I will. But they will burden Antelope

whenever we move."

"If I can't fetch them soon — moon or two — do what you want with it."

His father-in-law nodded.

That's how the long mean day ended. Except that those Dog Society warriors, tough veterans all, didn't take kindly to him having so much beautiful Cheyenne womanhood doting on him, and stared at him quietly with unfriendly eyes. He could fathom what was percolating in their heads. Their friends and allies the Arapaho had stolen the horses and robes — but that didn't cut ice with them. He was a white man. Still, he'd married into their outfit, and they'd do him no harm, maybe even help a little.

After another restless night, he and his women saddled up the four little ponies, two paints, two coyote duns. His women clambered into the high-backed, high-pommeled rawhide squaw saddles and adjusted their full skirts. He handed them each a parfleche and tied their rolled robes behind their cantles. He salvaged a little kitchen gear, a pot and skillet anyway, tying them onto the saddle of Sweet Smoke, who was the lightest. Then he fixed up his own pony, a mean-eyed dun, and said his goodbyes to his father-in-law, and the five of them walked north, while the Dog Soldiers watched silently.

Fitzhugh cursed. He was a poor man, owing debts even out here. He knew his in-laws had been kind, but it didn't lift his spirits any. They rode north, making good time through a windy dry day, seeing no one. He didn't want to see a soul — not with four vulnerable women and one rust-pitted Hawken. That evening they arrived at a branch of Crazy Woman Creek and camped in a sheltered meadow beside sweet water. He was oblivious of the black-forested mountains vaulting up the western skies, or the game trails through the sweet grasses, or the acrid scent of full-leafed sagebrush, or the gentle labor of his wives, who understood his misery and quietly produced a tasty meal of breadroot, wild onion, jerky, and greens. Neither did he see the brightness of their eyes, the kindness in their wide Cheyenne faces, their eagerness to heal his wounds and balm his spirits by doing everything for him from caring for the ponies to handing him his pipe and tobacco.

That night they made their pallets as usual, and he didn't notice that the women gave him some distance, choosing places many yards away. In the fullness of night, just when he was drifting into oblivion, one of them awakened him. She stood over him in the whiteness of a gibbous moon and slid her full calico skirts down, and pulled the baggy white blouse over her shoulders. Elk Tail. He caught his breath. The moonlight revealed the lovely form of a woman, full-breasted and full-hipped. She untied the sacred cord. It encompassed her waist and was knotted at the front. The two long ends descended down and back to her buttocks, and then each end coiled around a thigh and was tied above her knee. She undid it all in the white light, and slid down beside him, tugging at his shirt.

He forgot his miseries that night, and life became easier and more promising and even joyous all the way back to the post.

Thirteen

Guy had a choice. He could follow the river up to Fort Union and then down the Yellowstone to his own post. Or he could save a hundred miles by cutting overland toward his post on the Yellowstone. The shortcut was tempting but his business was to talk to American Fur Company factors, and those at Fort Union, the company's northern headquarters, were the most important of all. He set aside his yearning to see his son and his post and directed Chatillon to continue upriver.

The late August sun grew sullen and the land parched but at least the evenings were cool. They made steady progress through a land strange to Guy's eye, a desert bristling with cactus and sparse browned bunchgrass, with the yellow bones of the earth poking up everywhere. Some white men would have called it a wasteland but he knew better. It supported some of the greatest buffalo herds on the continent — and those who preyed on them. One day they hid on a wooded river island while a vast Sioux village dusted by. Hunkpapa, Chatillon thought. Guy was too busy holding horses and keeping them from whinnying to notice.

The next day they encountered a buffalo herd crossing the river. On the far shore the herd snaked into the river, following some ancient trace and some ingrained wisdom, and proceeded to walk out upon a long hard-bottomed shallows in forty or fifty columns. He'd never seen so many buffalo, and not all the descriptions of the vast herds allayed his astonishment at the black river of animals, most of them larger than cattle, many of them bellowing and bawling until the crossing raised a low thunder that he found frightening. Chatillon held the packhorses nervously. Guy was aware that a herd like this sucked up horses as cleverly as a night raid by warriors. The herd snaking down the far shore never ceased, and eventually Chatillon gave up.

"It will cross for days, Monsieur Straus," he said. He backtracked downriver to an island that would hold the horses and keep them out of the way of the herd, and made camp there in the middle of the day. Above them, the herd continued to thunder its way across the Missouri. Gray wolves gathered on the eastern bank, and some few swam the river as well, staying with the herd. Several dead buffalo drifted by the island, drowning victims, dark and slick in the roiling current. Chatillon waited for a young cow to slide by, and then waded into the river and snared it with a rawhide line. They would have delicious humproast and tongue that evening without firing a shot.

The thunder of the crossing rolled down upon them through the twilight and into the night, slowly unnerving Guy. It was as if a violent storm had settled over them and would not budge or abate. He could not shut the herd out of his ears; it invaded his head, his mind, his body. The whole river below the crossing had turned brown with mud and the feces of tens of thousands of animals, and the air swarmed with flies and fleas and the armies of parasites that lived upon the herd. Guy didn't dare drink the river water and knew he'd be fighting insects all night.

And still they came in numbers unimaginable, robbing him of sleep or even rest. That incessant roar eroded his serenity; drove him half-mad.

"I do not see many like this," Chatillon said. It seemed an understatement to Guy.

Guy crawled under a good Witney

blanket hoping to think about other things than nature gone berserk, but he couldn't. The roar became a throbbing pain, a headache, and the night stretched out endlessly. At dawn they were still snaking down the bluffs and across the river. Countless corpses still rolled by. Wolves and coyotes still lined the riverbanks, bright-eyed spectators. Guy rose along with a quarter-moon, and fought his way through brush to the upstream tip of the island where he could sense the motion of hundreds of thousands of the beasts. This had become a matter of theology, and he bowed his head and asked God questions: why had he made so many? How could nature be so improvident? He found no answers.

A little after dawn of the third day a silence settled on the Missouri; the water cleared to its usual opaque green, the dust settled, and the emptiness returned to that aching land. Guy's headache lingered, and along with it an odd fear crabbing at his soul. He'd seen something too extravagant to be explained with words or counted with numbers. He had witnessed something more frightening than grand, that savaged his soul in ways he couldn't fathom. He wondered if Chatillon had felt it, this prodigality of nature and God. He studied the guide for evidences of torment like his own, not wanting to say anything about his private terrors. But Chatillon was matter-of-factly saddling and bridling horses and breaking camp. Guy fought a powerful urge to turn around, go back to the world he knew and grasped.

"We must be careful, monsieur. Where the buffalo are, so are the hunters."

They splashed across a hundred yards of gravel shallows and then out upon the riverbank. The smell of the herd lingered. Guy thought it would linger a thousand years. Fifty generations from now mortals would smell the herd there. They pushed upstream again, seeing nothing. The land lay dead, as if the herd had sucked into its maw every sparrow and mouse and snake. They made swift time, and with every mile from that place of psychic terror Guy's soul eased. He would not describe this to anyone; not even Yvonne in the middle of the night amidst their nakedness. He could not bear to whittle what he had seen into miserable words.

The river turned west and south, and they saw only emptiness. Game grew scarce and Chatillon had a hard time making meat. One night they had nothing. The guide dug up roots known to Indians, and boiled them. They filled Guy's belly at least.

Then they reached the confluence of the Yellowstone, a place where the varicolored waters threaded and mingled, a place as wide as a shallow sea, glinting in late afternoon light.

"This evening, Fort Union," Chatillon said.

Eagerness consumed Guy. At last he'd see the place he'd heard of all these years, the crown jewel of American Fur, with luxuries unimaginable, carried clear up the river. They reached the post in the last of the sunlight. The long light burnt the top of the cottonwood stockade as if the post were ablaze. He saw nothing but a high gray wall with stone bastions at opposite corners, the post sitting on an uneven flat well above the diminished flow of the Missouri. A scatter of lodges surrounded it, Indians camped on raw earth where not a blade of grass and not a tree offered shade or firewood. The place was so hard-used, he thought, that the fort must have to import hay and firewood from vast distances.

The massive gates had long since been closed but now one of them mysteriously swung open to admit them, and Guy knew that the cyclops eye of the post never ceased to observe the traffic, no doubt through a spyglass. He and Chatillon rode into a village surrounding the yard. A village. Homes and shops crowded the walls; engages, some smoking clay pipes, emerged from barracks to see the newcomers. Chatillon hailed them in French; these were old comrades of the wilds, men he knew.

Striding toward him, down the porch steps of that famous factor's house where the emperors of the North resided, was an old friends, and partner in the Chouteau company, Alexander Culbertson.

"Guy Straus!"

"Alec!"

"I heard you were coming. Come in, come in, Natawista is just clearing the table, but there's plenty left."

"Alec, this is Ambrose Chatillon —"

"Of course, of course. Put up your kit and come in, Ambrose."

The guide nodded.

In minutes, Guy found himself at a linen-covered table with Alec and Natawista, describing their adventures up the river. Ambrose, who knew little English, excused himself and headed for the barracks and a familiar tongue.

Culbertson, a lean, dark-bearded Scot, listened attentively, saying little. Natawista, a petite and beautiful daughter of a Blood chief, understood everything but didn't venture the English tongue. She wore a bright red calico, the color that had made her famous up and down the river.

"But Guy," Alec said, "you haven't told us what demons drive you two thousand miles up the river late in the season."

"You already know."

Alec smiled. "Our expresses are fast."

"Tell me about Raffin."

"Raffin?" Culbertson was puzzled. "Whoa up, Guy. Let's start at Bellevue — and the kind attentions of the Reverend Mister Foster Gillian. Not a Presbyterian, thank God."

Guy led them through it all, from the confrontation with Gillian to the talks with Sarpy, Charbonne, and Kipp. "Raffin was due here on *The Trapper*; he's your man. He jumped off at Fort Pierre and no one has seen him since."

Alec stared into a wineglass. "We gave him a three-year renewal. He's a good man, but with limits. Not an easy man to get along with. He's always off somewhere."

"I think he planted those casks of spirits and altered the ship's records. Just why, I don't know."

"If he did, it was something he did on his own. The company wouldn't stand for it,

Guy. For obvious reasons."

"That's what all of you have been telling me."

"We're as vulnerable as anyone else."

"So you all say."

"There'd be no profit in it for us."

Guy pushed back annoyance. "That's debatable, Alec."

"Of course. *Ecrasez tout opposition.* You're the first serious opponent we've had in several years. But Guy, we'll do it other ways. Gifts and price-cutting."

Guy smiled coldly. "Perhaps you could supply me with a motive then?"

Major Culbertson drummed the linen with thick fingers, apparently debating what to say to the powerful rival at his table. "I think your partner is — abrasive. I find him so. Raffin — he's rather like Fitzhugh, in a way, something raw-edged about the man."

"Motive?"

"Little Whirlwind. Not so long ago."

"I've heard it. That puzzles me. Why wreck our company for that? It doesn't make sense. Why buy three casks — a pretty penny for an engage, even a senior one like Raffin — three casks that incriminate my company — but not Fitzhugh in any way that Raffin could benefit from. Eh?"

"I can't read minds, Guy. You don't even

know Raffin did it."

"No — I don't. Perhaps the company did it. Perhaps Pierre Chouteau had it done."

"He didn't."

"We're real opposition, Alec. With a purse."

Alec poured more French Bordeaux from the bottle transported two thousand miles from St. Louis on an annual steamboat. "I can't answer your mysteries for you, Guy. But take my word for it. Pierre *le cadet* would be mad to do that. He didn't try."

"So you all say. But Raffin makes no sense."

"Maybe he wants to pick up the pieces, Guy."

"How?" Guy shook his head. No ordinary engage, no matter how ambitious and unscrupled, would go to such lengths. It wasn't in their Creole nature, he thought. And what would he get out of it? He wouldn't hurt Brokenleg much. The Rocky Mountain Company, indeed. But not an old rival for a Cheyenne girl. "Alec, whoever planted those casks was aiming to hurt me, not my partners."

They both stared into their wineglasses in the amber of a single candle.

Guy laughed. "Well, that's that. I've never had the chance to thank you and Joe

LaBarge for sending me news last year. Starting up a fur post against your outfit was — well, reckless. But we'll see, we'll see."

"May the deepest pockets survive," said Alec Culbertson, making a wry toast of it.

"Four wives and no robes. I think we will make you an honorary Creole," said Samson Trudeau, surveying the collection of Cheyenne beauties Fitzhugh brought with him.

Abner Spoon took a long look at the sisters and turned sulky. Zachary Constable started to make ribald observations but Brokenleg silenced him with a glare.

Assorted Creoles eyed the shy wives with an assortment of expressions, none of them disinterest.

"You must be awfully tired," persisted Zach.

"Cut it out."

"Do you keep them all happy at once?"

"Cut it out."

"Maybe they are just honorary wives."

"Cut it out."

"Do you share the wealth?"

"We got work to do."

"We trade robes, not lie in them," said Samson Trudeau, solemnly.

Brokenleg turned hot and choked back a

retort. "How many robes did we take in?"

Trudeau shrugged. "Since you left? Over two hundred. But of course that's nothing compared to three more wives. Three wives are worth a thousand robes, St. Louis prices."

Fitzhugh knew they weren't going to let him alone so he ignored them. "Who from — the robes?"

"A few Crow. Some Gros Ventres — the Atsina, not the Hidatsa — a band came in and traded, monsieur. They have no allegiances, *oui?*"

"Good robes?"

Trudeau shrugged. "Some, some not."

That's what Fitzhugh figured. The Atsina were a wandering band of moochers. They did no more work than they could get away with. But even the robes of moochers would bring something. "They complained a lot about prices, vowed eternal friendship, and tried to steal anything not nailed down."

Trudeau grinned.

"Better'n nothing," Fitzhugh added.

"Indeed, monsieur. I am thinking I have nothing and you have four wives. One to hold your cup while you sip spirits. One to spoon food into you, one to dress and undress you —"

"Dammit, Trudeau, we got things to do.

Another wagon stole; harness and a whole team. No way to get robes or trade goods in and outa hyar —"

"Four wives to tote robes, monsieur."

"Go to hell."

"Some men are lucky in love; others born to suffer." He sighed. "Why am I so ugly, so humble, so poor, so lame with words, that I cannot have four wives?"

"I'll cure you. Starting today, we're going to build a pair of pirogues and a mackinaw. By Gawd, I'll sweat yer smart mouth outa you."

"Very good, monsieur. Perhaps the wives will assist. I am sure all your legs are broken."

Fitzhugh roared, bulled toward the man, but the post's factor danced away easily, wheezing with joy.

Dust Devil followed all this and translated wickedly to her sisters, until they stood tittering like a limbful of crows.

"Maybe Fitzhugh will share, Trudeau," she said. "You work hard. I tell him to get slaves, lots of Absaroka women, but he likes wives."

"You stay outa this!" Brokenleg roared.

Hide Skinning Woman muttered something in Cheyenne, and Dust Devil translated. "She says you are the blanket chief;

this Creole is just a boy."

Trudeau gaped, first at Hide Skinning Woman, then at Fitzhugh. Hide Skinning Woman smiled sweetly, her black eyes shining. She looked plumb gorgeous, Fitzhugh thought. She still wore her bridal festival dress of whited doeskin, fringed at the hem and sleeves and brightly quilled. They all looked ravishing. In fact, his life had changed radically in the space of a few days, and the anger brewing deep within him had drained away.

"Whar's that boy?" he asked abruptly.

"Maxim? He reads in the barracks all day."

"He still sulkin'?"

"*Oui . . .*"

"I've a mind to send him down the river after all."

"Now that you have four wives, his labor is not necessary, monsieur. In fact —"

"Trudeau!"

The Creole looked wounded.

"Git busy!"

Slowly, the raffish crowd that had gathered in the stockaded pen next to the post to witness this peculiar homecoming dissipated. Fitzhugh left the horses to the engages while his wives toted parfleches and his possibles to their quarters. Dust Devil

227

had turned bossy, steering her sisters with a firm hand. Well, she was his sits-beside-him wife now; the senior one, who occupied the place of honor among Injun wives. He followed them into the rectangular post, past the trading room and robe warehouse, past the barracks room to his own quarters. His and four wives, he thought, suddenly alarmed. It had been divided into his office, a sitting room, and bedroom. That bed — a narrow pallet of woven rawhide tied to a frame, with a narrow tick on it — he'd have to change that. He'd have to turn the whole damned bedroom into a pallet, or stack female bodies . . . aw, hell, he'd let Dust Devil see to it. They'd do it their danged Suhtai Tsistsista way, and he was just along for the ride.

He found them whispering and giggling, and thought they needed — he wasn't sure what they needed. He glared at them all, or tried to. It was hard to glare at honey-fleshed smooth-skinned curvy wives, all of them wild as hares. He had known he'd be in for it when he got back, but he hadn't expected — "Aw, hell," he muttered and limped out.

He found Trudeau in the trading room, no doubt comparing wives and curves and dimples with Abner and Zach. They ceased their bawdy palaver when he wheeled in, at any rate. He glared at them, too. Glare was the only weapon he had against such formidable gossips.

"Can you lissen a piece?"

"Shore, pore old Brokenleg."

The mockery didn't escape him. "Dammit, we've purt' near gone beaver and you sit thar —"

"It's not everyday the post is so radically improved, Monsieur Fitzhugh. Where once there were only hairy beasts ugly as apes, now there is grace . . ."

"Trudeau. We're makin' boats. I want you to git any of them that was voyageurs. Larue, Bercier, Brasseau, Dauphin, Provost — you know. This hyar outfit's gonna have us a chantier, a boatyard like them Chouteau posts. We'll start with the pirogues, a pair of big 'uns hollered out of cottonwood. We got trees a yard and a half thick yonder. I want the pirogues hollowed out and a deck acrost the pair and a mast and a square-rigged sail. That'll git us a load of goods up the Bighorn and Little Bighorn to the Greasy Grass. We're meetin' Dust Devil's people there for some robe tradin' in October."

Trudeau, suddenly serious, nodded. "It takes four men four or five days to cut out a pirogue. And the rest . . . We can make it easily."

"I'm glad we can do something easy around hyar. I suppose they'll steal the pirogues from us, too, like they got the robes and wagons and hosses and oxen."

Trudeau said nothing.

"You git that done and you start on a mackinaw so's we can float robes down next spring. That'll take doin'."

A mackinaw would be a large project, he knew. As much as any fur post could do in wilderness. The long, flat-bottomed boats could carry fifteen tons safely downriver. They lacked means to pole, cordelle, or sail back upstream, but more and more the fur companies were hauling them back upriver on the steamboats. Building one would be an ordeal. First logs had to be squared, and hoisted up on a scaffold. Then pairs of sawmen, one above and one below, had to hand-saw the planks. These had to be shaped into a flat bottom with thick cross pieces and pegged together because they had no nails or screws. The plank sides had to be attached to elbowlike supports, and watertight bulkheads fore and aft built to protect the cargo in the center. The gunnels stood a couple of feet above water at the middle of the fifty-foot vessel, but rose at either end. Finally a mast and sail and oars and oarlocks had to be added, along with a rudder and a platform for the steersman so he could see ahead.

It'd be a winter's work. But a properly built mackinaw operated by five or six voyageurs could take the entire returns of Fitzhugh's Post to market. The packs of robes would lie secure and dry under old lodge covers tied to cleats on the gunnels. It was the only option Fitzhugh had now, with his overland transportation demolished. But it had always been the way the fur companies brought the robes to market.

He watched Trudeau explain all that to his engages. And he knew that the lazy days were over for them all, and not even four Cheyenne ladies cooking and gathering firewood and keeping house would make things easier. But that was how it'd been from the beginning. In the wilderness one made do. But it wasn't enough. The Chouteau outfit had harassed and boxed him, demolished his equipment, rendered him helpless. He'd have to do something about that or the Rocky Mountain Company would go beaver, like all the rest of the opposition companies. But what?

Fourteen

American Fur engages ferried Guy and Chatillon and their horses across the Missouri in a mackinaw. From the Missouri, Chatillon headed south across a nose of land until they struck the Yellowstone. Guy paused, staring at the river of his fortunes, studying its cool waters as they roiled between arid bluffs. Cottonwoods dotted the bottoms.

"We have a long way to go, monsieur. And we must find a ford. Your post is on the south bank."

Chatillon led them cautiously upriver, avoiding the traces, hewing closer to the shoreline and the cover of brush and cottonwoods even though that route was longer and filled with obstacles.

"This is a great artery," Chatillon explained when they rested one noon of a cool September day. "Here we are in the country of the Sioux, Assiniboin, Blackfeet, Cree, Gros Ventres, and River Crow."

"These River Crow — they are separate from the others?"

"*Oui*. These River Crow live along the Yellowstone and Missouri. The Mountain Crow live on the upper Yellowstone, the Bighorn, and in the valleys of the Stony Mountains. They are friendly — with the weapons they get from white men they are a match for the Blackfeet, a much larger tribe. But they are great horse thieves. Famous thieves. And white men's horses — ah, monsieur, we will have to be very careful now."

"You mean the Rocky Mountains?"

"Names change, *oui?*"

They ghosted ever south and west, ducking painted war parties, hunting parties, and once a whole village traveling along the south bank. With each passing day excitement built in Guy. This was not the Yellowstone so much as Fortune River! Somewhere ahead were his partner, his son, and numerous engages. Ahead was a post filled with a fortune in trade goods, paid out of his own pocket and last year's returns. Back in St. Louis all these things were figures added in columns on foolscap, but here two thousand river miles away these things were palpable. He observed the passing landscape keenly; wondering if the brown grasslands above the bluffs would support life as white men knew it; wondering if these rich Yellowstone bottoms would support farms. Or whether, as seemed more likely, these vast steppes would forever be the dominion of wild Indians, buffalo, and mustangs.

They awoke one morning under a grim dark overcast, and felt an icy breeze out of the northwest cutting into their robes. All day they rode through it while the temperature plummeted. By evening Guy's bones ached. How could this come upon them in early September? But to ask the question was to answer it: they were far north. Fort Union lay at forty-eight degrees north, just one degree south of the British possessions. That evening the air smelled of snow, and moist gusts slid around his canvas bedsheeting. Sometime in the miserable night he felt flakes of snow sting his cheeks. He burrowed under his blankets and canvas but it didn't help, and he lay shivering in the icy black. The winds rose, driving icy granules of snow over him. He dug into his kit for an old wool shirt to wrap around his head but that didn't help.

He rose and walked around, wrapping the blanket close to him, trying to stamp feeling into numb limbs.

"It is bad, *oui?* But a fire, it is no good in this gale. We will have to suffer."

Chatillon's observation didn't help any.

After the longest night of his life, a grudging dawn grayed the world, and Guy discovered an inch or two of snow caught in grass, covering cottonwood and willow leaves, and clinging to the northwest side of trees. Only a gray light penetrated to the earth from the low overcast.

"We will walk. We can't make coffee now. Maybe I'll find a little nook in rock somewhere. But walking, Monsieur Straus, it is the salvation of cold men."

They walked, leading the horses, and Guy had to admit there was something to it. Briskly they walked upriver, covering the miles even faster than if they'd been riding, and the exertion warmed his body and drained the pain from his muscles. He felt grateful that he'd been hardened by these weeks of wilderness travel. But how would he ever get back to St. Louis in comfort? He felt the northern winter lurking just beyond the horizon like a hoary gray robber peering over a wall, ready to pounce.

But the next day summer returned; the last patches of snow vanished by mid-morning and the only difference between this summer and the summer before the storm was a coolness rising from the bones of the earth. They passed the confluence of

235

the Powder and a few days later the Tongue, which cut out of the south from a country of odd spikes and wind-sculpted stone dotted with jack pine.

Above the Tongue, Chatillon studied a wide place where the Yellowstone braided through several gravelly islands. Sign abounded of a ford. A buffalo trace ran to the bank and was visible across an island, and evident on the south bank.

The guide sat his horse for ten minutes studying the surrounding hills, the wood flats across the shimmering water, the country behind him. At last he led Guy down to the riverbank and across a vast gravel flat that was actually river bottom when the flow ran higher. The water never stopped the pasterns of their horses en route to the island.

Chatillon pointed, and Guy saw the darker water of the channel beyond. The guide nudged his reluctant horse into the river again, finding good footing on more gravel. The channel dropped off swiftly. One moment the horses were hock deep; the next they were swimming, but they found bottom within seconds, and bounded in great leaps toward the south shore. It had been an easy crossing. The guide didn't let the horses stop and shake; he kicked savagely until they had all reached a copse of cottonwoods, and there he let the dripping horses spray water.

They hugged the brushy shore, staying away from the worn trace that ran closer to the south bluffs. Late that day they crossed a grassy park that horseshoed into the river, and discovered a ruin in the timber beyond. A wagon.

Guy stared, recognition coming to him. One of his own Pittsburghs! It had been well concealed here, but not well enough. Tribesmen had stripped it of every bit of metal. They'd pulled the heavy iron tires off, leaving loose felloes and spokes on the ground. They'd stripped away the metal furniture, the hounds, the bolts that held the doubletree to the tongue.

The guide studied the wreck. "The iron, it makes good lance points and arrowheads. It makes awls and knives. It makes hatchets and axes. They have watched the smiths work the forges at the posts. They know how to heat and hammer and make things."

Guy nodded. The Pittsburgh had cost a hundred fifty dollars. He wondered how it had ended up here, abandoned. Whether men had been killed here. The ruin filled him with dread. Was Maxim all right?

"Let's hurry," he said, tautly.

"We can risk the trace, I think," said the guide. "Crows here. Mostly we are safe."

They made swift time along the trace. The guide sensed Guy's urgency and they raced ever south and west, passing stray Absaroka hunters once or twice, not pausing to parley with the curious tribesmen.

Then at last they plunged out upon a vast flat, a square mile of land dotted with innumerable lodges and scores of Indians, dogs, ponies, racing little boys, brush arbors — and beyond, the gray palisades and bastions of Fort Cass.

"Don't stop," muttered Guy.

"Are you sure? Here we pause at the posts. They have already seen us." He pointed to a watchman up on the near bastion. The man's brass spyglass glinted in the morning sun.

Guy studied the solid post, the silvery cottonwood logs, the Chouteau ensign flying over the gates, the hum of life around the post. He estimated a hundred Crow lodges there — at six or seven to a lodge, a formidable village. This is where the Rocky Mountain Company had intended to trade! This is where Brokenleg had planned to come! But Pierre Chouteau had gotten wind of it and had refurbished and re-opened the abandoned post — and had captured the whole Crow trade before Brokenleg even had a chance to open up a trading window.

"We'll go on," he said. "I want to get to my place."

They rode past Fort Cass, even though a welcoming shot — or was it? — rattled through the valley. West of the post they found innumerable ponies grazing under the eye of Crow boys. They struck the Bighorn River near the confluence, and swung upstream. Excitement built in Guy. He kicked his saddler into a jog and yanked the picket line of the packhorse that followed behind.

For two miles they pushed through dense cottonwood timber that lined the Bighorn River. The trees thinned into grassy parks. This valley was broad, but not so broad as the mile-wide trench of the Yellowstone. Guy felt he was riding through the center of something, a crossroads perhaps, or a place of meeting and gathering for many tribes heading up or down the two rivers. A good place for a post!

Chatillon smiled. "Almost. Around the bend there."

Guy hurried his saddler along, cutting the trace toward a point where the western bluff projected close to the river. Then at last he rounded the bend, beheld a broad open flat not unlike the one around Cass, and saw a low, rectangular building of graying cottonwood logs. A low, peaked earthen roof rose over the logs. The building formed the northeast corner of a stockade of cottonwood poles.

On a staff above the doors an ensign lazed in the slight breeze — their own ensign, with a gold RMC embroidered on a blue ground. A dozen lodges rose nearby — different somehow from the lodges around Cass.

Fitzhugh's Post!

Maxim Straus had discovered sin. In all of his seventeen years he hadn't thought much about it. But the events at Bellevue and Sergeant Bluff had changed that forever.

He brooded through the summer, his mind locked on the realities of an evil world, the evil staining his own family and himself. The evil surrounded him there at the post: it resided in the breast of Fitzhugh and the rest. The robe trade itself was evil to its core, a sin against God and man. Maxim knew he could atone forever and not wash away the evil he and his father had gotten into.

They had come to his father, these rough

trappers, and bent his father away from the honorable business of Straus et Fils, a firm unstained through generations of Strauses. But there on the levee at Bellevue, the Indian Agent and Christian minister had stained him and the company forever, branding himself and the Rocky Mountain Company as lawbreakers and corrupters of red men.

He felt the guilt upon him and knew it was deserved. It didn't matter that the casks in that hold didn't belong to the company; a few dozen miles upstream the packet boarded even more casks of spirits that did belong to the company, and that broke the law of the Republic. His father seemed to approve. His father had fallen in with vicious men, in a business with dirty hands.

Straus et Fils had financed the fur trade, beaver, and now buffalo, but had never been a part of it, of the scandalous business of defying law and pouring spirits into savages to cheat them out of their robes and pelts. Maxim had felt, at first, a numbness, along with a terror that he would be caught and jailed by the authorities. But that had given way to a rancorous contempt of Fitzhugh and a raging anger toward his father for succumbing to these wilderness criminals, for betraying him, for violating the ancient standards of his forefathers.

He had taken to scrubbing his face and hands, pricking himself to offer a blood atonement, and refusing to do anything whatsoever to advance the enterprise, but it wasn't enough. It was nothing. The weight of guilt hung on him like irons until he couldn't bear to see the sun and couldn't bear to sleep, and couldn't bear the presence of these beasts and criminals and sinners against God and man.

The wrath of God was on him. Nothing would ever make life worth living again. He sighed, knowing he had been doomed at seventeen to a life of hell. He wished he could die, and crawl to the farthest darkness where he could hide from the divine light. But he couldn't. He couldn't go back, either. He'd been dragooned off the packet, kept a prisoner by a man who had no right to lay his bloodstained hands on him.

And so the summer had dwindled away, and Maxim Straus lived in a world without gladness under a cast-iron cloud of guilt and rage. At least Brokenleg had let him alone. If Brokenleg had made him labor in that corrupt enterprise, record each ugly transaction in the ledger, Maxim had intended to walk away. If some tribesman pierced his chest with an arrow as he walked down the river, all the better, for that is what life had come to. Let him die and rot away until not even his bones scourged the earth.

Thus he had endured, silent, a fierce glare in his eye, avoiding meals with the rest, loathing them all and Brokenleg especially — even more now that he was squandering his lusts upon four wives. Maxim had won his small battles, too. None could oppose his fierce glare. Even Fitzhugh's blue eyes slid away, unable to meet Maxim's unblinking ones.

Maxim was out sitting on the riverbank watching the clean river when two white men rode up; men he'd never seen before, no doubt as corrupt as the rest. And then, slowly, it dawned on him that his father was dismounting — Guy Straus! Tanned, thinned, muscled, hardened, but his father! And a guide, of course. Chatillon, the one who'd come upriver last winter. His father here!

Guy's attention was riveted to the post, the visible manifestation of a heavy investment, and he didn't see Maxim rise, panicked, not knowing whether to flee, whether to shout condemnation at his father — or whether to run to him, hug him, and weep. All those impulses fought within Maxim, tearing him to bits. In the end, he chose to do none of them. He would acknowledge his father, but coolly, from some vast distance across a moral chasm, and they would eye each other as utter strangers.

"Maxim! Son!" Guy's keen eyes caught Maxim's slow progress toward him, and the love in those words tortured the youth.

"Maxim, I've come!"

"So you have."

"You look well, Maxim. We're blessed by God. You're safe. I never fathomed — in spite of all the talk, I never grasped how it is here, so far . . ."

"I'm not your son; you're not my father."

Guy pulled back as if smitten by a whip. He paused, collecting his wit. "But Maxim —"

"Nothing you do will change that," Maxim continued.

"But what have I — what has happened?"

"You know as well as anyone. But you don't listen to your conscience or atone before God."

"I'm so happy to see you, son. You can't know how a father rejoices to see a son looking fine and strong, transformed from boy to man . . ." Guy stopped, his words falling helplessly to earth before Maxim's stony stare.

Maxim stood still, rooted to the soil like a

bitter shrub, unyielding.

"Har! Guy!" From the door of the post Brokenleg Fitzhugh erupted, limping wildly, laughing and bawling. He grasped Guy in arms of iron, bawling like a buffalo calf.

"I came," muttered Guy.

"Har!"

"I had to see it."

"Solid as rock hyar. We're making some headway."

Maxim wanted to call it a lie. They weren't making headway. The wrath of God lay on the post. But Maxim pressed his lips together.

Guy turned to Maxim, his eyes penetrating right through the youth. "Come along inside, son. Show me everything. Show me the trading room and your ledgers and our goods and robes. We'll tour, and then I want to hear all about your life — everything."

Never had an invitation tortured Maxim more. Involuntarily he rushed forward to meet this paternal love, only to halt suddenly. "Go ahead," he muttered.

"He ain't been happy," Brokenleg muttered. "Hyar now, come meet my wives." Some vast wickedness built up in Brokenleg's face.

Guy looked startled.

"Got four. Haw! Work like beavers, too. This post's plumb comfortable now."

Guy grinned. "Ah, you wild men. You had me believing it there for a moment."

"Haw!" Fitzhugh hooted and danced around, right on his gimpy leg. "Haw!"

In spite of himself, Maxim tagged along. He could watch. He didn't have to participate. He didn't have to approve. They all swept inside, into the familiar gloom of a post with few and tiny unglassed windows that were open to weather and flies and mosquitos in summer and shuttered in the winter.

"I ain't asked you how come you come clear up hyar, Guy," Fitzhugh was saying.

"Show me the post."

"I guess it has to do with them spirits. Are we shut down?"

"Not yet. Let me see the trading room. I've studied every trading room I could coming up the river."

"You're comin' with bad news. No reason to come half acrost a continent otherwise."

"No, that's not why. I came to find out who wanted to damage us and why. And to let you know what I found out. I can point the finger, though I lack details."

Fitzhugh grunted.

"And to see our post. And my good, strong boy."

Maxim listened, tagging along, hanging back, pretending to be invisible, like an angry ghost. But his father's bright curious gaze caught him again and again as they toured the trading room, warehouse, barracks, and offices. Guy met Spoon and Constable for the first time and renewed his acquaintance with the rest of the employees. He was escorted into the stockaded yard — where the sole wagon sagged, ox yokes lay in a mound, and four horses stood in shade, their tails lashing at deerflies.

"You've had some difficulties," Guy said softly. "I saw one of the Pittsburghs in ruins on the Yellowstone."

"Chouteau's doin's."

"We'll tell our stories now. We have serious matters to talk about. Your office will be a suitable place . . . Are you coming, Maxim?"

"No," said Maxim.

"After I talk to Brokenleg I wish to talk to you."

"There's nothing to say," Maxim snapped. But there was a lot to say if he could steel himself to say it to his own father. And his father wouldn't like to hear it.

Fifteen

Brokenleg listened quietly as Guy Straus described his visit to David Mitchell and his arduous trip into the wilderness. The senior partner had changed. The wiry blond hair and hawkish nose set in a square face remained but the trip had hardened and tanned him, stripped away the softness of St. Louis.

A new iron permeated his tone as well. Guy Straus was fighting for his financial life and everything he said was imbued with urgency and anger. The case had already rocked Washington City, and had reached the ear of President Tyler. Eastern reformers were howling. Senator Benton was howling back against those who wanted to yank the licenses of every robe-trading outfit.

"We stopped at every post. Not a factor among them, from Culbertson to Sarpy. Thought the company had caused it. I suppose it's so. It was Raffin. Acting on his own. I . . . hear he had some differences with you."

Differences. How them damned easterners put it. Raffin'd been in White Wolf's
village and was eyeing Little Whirlwind for
himself — but he lost her, Brokenleg
thought. She never cared a hoot or a holler
for him. "I reckon there's that, only it don't
make sense what he's doin' now. If he's
doin' it. It don't make no sense to me at all."

"I didn't come all this way to worry about
motives. If he did it we've got to prove it —
or lose our license. You know what that
means. Shut down. Sell off the trade goods
at a loss — cheaper than hauling them down
the river. Pay off our men."

"We'll maybe go beaver anyway, Guy.
Raffin, Hervey, and them, they fixed us
good. No oxen. One wagon. Lost more
horses and mules than I can count. I'm
building pirogues. We'll put us a mackinaw
together to git down the river with. But
we're being cut to pieces. Them Crows are
being bribed and bought by Hervey; Raffin
— if he's the one — he's keepin' us from
reaching the Cheyenne."

Straus nodded. He studied the ledger
again under the buttery light of the oil lamp.
"We've lost a quarter of our trade goods and
have three hundred seventeen robes." He
pushed the books away. "You've hardly
touched the ardent spirits, though," he

added. "Five and a half casks out of the six. Made into trade whiskey, worth what — three, four thousand robes?"

Maxim, who lingered at the door, scowled.

"Before we git our license lifted for bringin' spirits up the river," Brokenleg muttered. He found himself guffawing harshly. "Some joke," he muttered. "Spirits all we got goin', whiles down there they're nailing us for it."

Guy stared into the glassed flame. "Why is this Raffin in the Cheyenne village? You know him; I don't."

"Well, one thing he's not doin' is stirrin' em up agin me, least not the headmen. Not with me married in, and my pa a medicine chief. Naw. He's in thar to spoil it, is all. Like he fixed it to steal our horses and robes after the trading. 'Rapaho bunch."

"That's not what a rival for a Cheyenne girl would do — is it?"

"No. It's comp'ny work."

"Every factor on the river told me the company had nothing to do with it. They were sincere, Brokenleg."

Fitzhugh grunted. "Guess we got to ask Raffin."

Guy laughed shortly. "They told me he's ambitious — and he's been thwarted by the

250

company. No one quite trusts him, at least the factors don't. He's away a lot, running errands it seems."

"What's that supposed to mean?"

"He wants to get rich — at our expense. Get us into licensing trouble, destroy our livestock and wagons, pick up the pieces."

"He's taken orders too long. Someone's telling him do this, do that, paying him."

"You'll have to find that out, Brokenleg. Our license depends on it. I can't stay here. It's all up to you."

"You come a long way to find out. Chatillon, he's some guide."

"The only factor I haven't talked to is Julius Hervey. I'm riding over there and do it."

"No you ain't. He'd as soon cut yer throat as look at ye."

"I'm going."

"You ain't. You might be some senior man, but it don't matter to him. All blood's red and he likes to spill it. He's meaner'n ever since I whacked my knife acrost his hands last winter. He's a hater and he'd like nothin' better than to git ahold of the top men in the Rocky Mountain Company and work a little surgery. You ain't going."

"Brokenleg — I'm going. And I want a translator. I plan to talk to the Crows there."

Brokenleg glowered into silence. A senior partner would do whatever he felt like doing. "All right go," he snarled.

Guy smiled wryly. "When a man yells, he's sincere," Guy said.

"Now I got to go and protect you," Brokenleg grumbled.

"I'll go alone, thank you."

The meeting had degenerated. Brokenleg lifted himself out of his wooden chair, favoring his bum leg. "Let's git outa hyar," he muttered.

Guy stayed him. "Where's Little Whirlwind? I wish to pay my respects. And meet — her sisters is it?"

"Her sisters. Sweet Smoke — she's the youngest. Hide Skinning Woman — she's the oldest. And Elk Tail. She's the, ah, best looking. Sweet Smoke, she's not much older'n Maxim."

"And they've come to help. Are they on the rolls of the company?"

"Ah, naw. Dust Devil, she wanted some one to talk to. Gets herself all lonely around hyar. She's after me to buy some slaves — good Crow women she wants. Pay some trade goods, git some slaves she can boss around. Me, I'm again' slavery." Too late, he remembered that Guy owned five or six blacks back in St. Louis. "Anyway, we went down to her village to trade and git her some sisters to talk with. They're handy — helpin' around the post a heap and don't cost the company none. They even git us greens and roots against the scurvy."

That wasn't the whole of it but maybe it'd do. He steered Straus back to his quarters and found the ladies there.

"Ah, Little Whirlwind!" exclaimed Guy.

She abandoned her moccasin-making and stood. "You come long way," she said. "We see you ride in. These are my sisters."

She introduced them while Brokenleg stared daggers at her.

"Lotsa wives, hey? Suhtai wives. Like a big chief."

Guy looked nonplussed. "Wives?"

"Him. My father, he give us all to him."

Guy Straus looked stricken. He peered at the beaming Cheyenne women and at Brokenleg, who felt his cheeks flush and hated it. He'd never blushed in his life. Not even as a little snot had he ever blushed. But now he felt blood in his face, itching his flesh.

"He married them all," said Maxim wearily. "He is not a temperate man."

"You shut up," growled Brokenleg.

"You see?" Maxim smirked.

"Wives? You have four wives?"

"Like a chief. Like that trapper one, Jim Bridger. Blanket Chief. Fitzhugh's a Blanket Chief."

"I see."

"He can do it. He makes us all happy." Dust Devil beamed maliciously. She knew white men. She'd been to St. Louis and understood things. And she was enjoying every second of all this. "We take turns," she said. "Me, I'm the sits-beside-him wife. I tell my sisters what to do."

Fitzhugh blushed.

"The red is becoming, Brokenleg. I'd be red, too," said Guy. "This changes my opinion of you. I never dreamed I'd have a partner with four Cheyenne princesses for wives."

"It's some better'n slaves!"

"Oh, I don't know. With slaves things are — simple."

"It wasn't my idea!"

Sweet Smoke giggled. She'd been picking up English fast. Danged if she didn't look pert when she giggled. Hide Skinning Woman stood, stocky and dignified and expressionless. Elk Tail rose from the floor, her face showing curiosity.

"It is Elk Tail's turn tonight," said Dust Devil. "But Brokenleg doesn't deserve her. She's Suhtai. She should have been given to a great warrior — not a stiff leg."

Guy sighed. "This affects the company, Brokenleg. We can't afford to transport all these lovely ladies back to St. Louis each year —"

"I ain't bringing no one. I quit. Take your company. I'm out. I ain't no partner. You find someone else. I'm takin' me away from hyar."

But Guy wasn't deterred. "St. Louis is a long way, you know. A man and four beautiful Cheyenne girls. We'll see, we'll see. You might bring them to the licensing hearings."

"It's not funny, father." Maxim stared dourly at them all.

Guy Straus turned, his gaze boring into his son. "Take me to a private place, Maxim. We're going to talk." He turned to the rest. "We have family matters to discuss; excuse us."

Brokenleg watched them retreat, bile building in him. Let that little snot complain, he thought. Let him talk high and mighty about licenses and spirits and wives and getting yanked off the packet by mean ol' Brokenleg. If Guy didn't like it none, he could run this hyar post by himself.

Guy steered his sullen son down to the

255

river and along a trace there, no doubt an ancient Indian trail. He didn't press the boy. He'd learned the value of walking, of silent presence, of communion without words. The summer heat had vanished and the day was idyllic. They scared up some magpies but nothing else traduced the sunny peace.

He guessed what was seething inside of Maxim's head; it wasn't hard to fathom. Actually, he was proud of the boy's moral and spiritual sense: it resided in himself as well as his father and grandfathers, and he considered it a mark of his people. Maxim had discovered his soul and there was nothing wrong with that, even if the lad overreacted and made life miserable for every mortal about him. Seventeen was a hard age even for someone without Maxim's sensitivities.

Guy discovered a place where meadow swept out to the water's edge forming a sort of grassy point, and steered the boy there.

"It's good to see you again, son. You're strong and healthy, and I rejoice."

Maxim said nothing although his gaze darted furiously from one thing to another.

"You'd like to express your disapproval, I imagine. Of the company. Of my partner. Of me, no doubt."

Maxim stared bleakly at Guy. "I don't want to talk."

"Of course you don't. But you ought to. Do you want to go home? Go back with me?"

"Not with you."

"You do not like to see the Straus family in this business and you blame me for it."

The boy remained mute but he was listening.

"It is a hard business and I've had many regrets. Many more regrets than just our troubles with licensing and spirits. There is something in me that was not in my father."

Maxim started to say something and checked himself. Guy knew it would have been accusatory, maybe even brutal. Maxim looked miserable, holding in all those accusations seething inside of him.

"I'd prefer to do the robe business without resorting to ardent spirits."

"Then why don't you?" Maxim shouted. Then, more quietly, "It's too late."

"There'd be no business. No robes. No profits. None of the tribesmen would show up — few, anyway."

"So you sold out!"

Guy paused, forming his thoughts. "I confess I hadn't thought about it much. Not until that bad news came. Not until our trading license was threatened. It was simply a part of the business. And universal. Every post peddled spirits. Every trader used spirits as a gift and a lure. And you know something? General Clark knew it and tolerated it. His unspoken attitude was, just don't get caught. That had been mine too — until this summer."

"We're breaking the law."

Guy had no answer to that.

"You're —" The lad swallowed back his accusations.

"You'd like me to get out of this. You think it's too late. You think you're dishonored; we're all dishonored. You think I've betrayed our people."

"That's not all."

"You think we're harming the Indians."

"We are!"

Guy mulled a response to that. No question about the fur trade was more vexing. "Suppose we didn't offer spirits, but the other things they want: blankets, trade rifles, powder, axes, knives, kettles . . . Would they come to our post?"

This time Maxim didn't reply immediately. A kingfisher slapped into the water and rose again with a silvery minnow. "If none of the other companies offered spirits — we'd have trade."

"But that's not the real world. That's the ideal world, isn't it?"

"That doesn't excuse it!"

"No . . . it doesn't. But we live in an imperfect world." Guy knew that young idealists never accepted that tack. There was only good and evil, right and wrong."

"Don't tell me it's their own choice. They can't deal with spirits. They've never had spirits. Not until traders came."

"Well, son, what do you propose."

"Nothing! Leave me alone!"

"Do you want to go home?"

"Not with you!"

"If you stay here I trust you'll earn your keep. A post can't afford —" Guy was going to say a parasite and troublemaker, but checked himself.

"I was hauled off the boat," Maxim returned, a withering sound in his voice. "Dragged off. What choice had I? Like some prisoner."

Guy was prepared for that one. "It might have been a mistake. Brokenleg has rough ways. On the other hand you haven't reached your majority. He had a — a parental right."

"I don't want to stay here. I want nothing to do with the robe trade. I'll go to St. Louis with you, but not home. It's not my home anymore. Never!"

Tears leaked from Maxim's tortured face.

"Very well, son. We'll go back together and —"

"Don't call me son!"

That hurt. Guy peered into the swift flow of the Bighorn, rushing by like the river of life. "Would you prefer to go down with the returns in the spring?"

"I don't know."

"Would you feel the same way if Brokenleg and I found who put those casks on *The Trapper* and freed the company of blame?"

"Yes."

"Do you blame yourself? For not being alert when you checked inventory in the hold?"

"Yes."

"Nobody blames you but yourself."

"And the Indian Bureau! And the commissioner! They'll put me in jail!"

"No. They might lift our license to trade with these tribes. Look, Maxim. I'm sorry as can be about this. I wish I'd given it more thought before we formed the buffalo robe company. We can't get out easily. I have contracts with partners to honor. Shall I break my word?"

Maxim looked miserable again and studied the river sullenly, avoiding Guy's eyes.

"Do you think your grandfather, father and I should not have capitalized the fur trade? Capitalized the Chouteaus? Did we stain ourselves by lending?"

"Yes!"

The violence of Maxim's response told Guy a lot. He knew suddenly that reason and compromise would not do here; that his son would be estranged for as long as he failed to view the world with any charity or love or — sense of reality.

"All right." Guy turned to walk back to the post. Maxim hung on there, preferring his own company. Guy knew he had lost a son. This business, this company, had cost him his own flesh and blood. The realization lay heavier in him with each step back to Fitzhugh's Post. What would he tell Yvonne? She'd opposed it from the beginning, a cassandra who'd warned and begged. Guy felt a weariness in his bones, his soul. The company seemed doomed; his enormous investment lost; his youngest child harsh and unforgiving, believing his father to be . . . not honorable. Guy twisted his bleak thoughts away and choked back his own pent-up love for the fine young man he'd sired and raised. He wondered if he'd ever see Maxim again.

He had to make some decisions and not

least was whether to fold things up. This post had acquired few robes and was bleeding away his investment each day. American Fun had whipped him badly — he had to acknowledge it. He stared at the empty flats, devoid now even of the few Gros Ventre lodges that had been there the previous day. From a boatyard to the south came the ring of axes and mallets.

He found Brokenleg in the shadowed trading room. "I'm going to Fort Cass. I'd like you to accompany me."

"It ain't wise."

"I wish to go anyway. Will you come? I'd like it, but I won't press you."

Fitzhugh muttered, his eyes blazing, his gaze piercing and retreating.

"I'll make your decision for you. In the light of what happened last winter — when Hervey almost killed you — I'll go alone."

"It ain't —" Fitzhugh flopped an arm helplessly.

"It's a risk I'll bear, Brokenleg. I'm the managing partner. I wish to discuss their conduct with them. Hervey especially."

"Your funeral," Brokenleg retorted. "I'll git your saddler for you. If you ain't back by this evening I'm goin' after you — and all them in there."

"That won't be necessary," Guy said.

Sixteen

Guy Straus sat his horse before Fort Cass wrestling with fear. The log palisade rose before him like a feudal castle possessed by a lord who knew no law but his own. Back in St. Louis they spoke of Julius Hervey with a certain quietness that suggested dread. The man who ran Fort Cass was a favorite of Pierre Chouteau even though he'd hurt American Fur badly at times. Some called Hervey mad but that wasn't accurate at all. He'd simply turned wild, as wild as the sea of wilderness he lived in. Every restraint had vanished from his head.

When they spoke of Hervey back there at the Planters House, they spoke of horror, in whispered conversation. Odd how the very mention of the man had always changed the tone, how fur and robe men turned solemn, sipped hard at their bourbons, and wondered — but never out loud — why a man so murderous enjoyed Pierre *le cadet*'s patronage. Hadn't he murdered more red men than one could count? Ruined trade with whole villages? Stolen the wives of engages and free trappers and dared them to take the women back? Those few who did try ended up feeding fish in the river, lying in shallow graves, or as cripples, deaf and blind. Hadn't Hervey ruined every rival outfit by any means, ranging from theft and murder to bribery and stirring up tribal passions. Hervey sober was bad enough; Hervey drunk was a creature from Hell.

Only months ago Hervey had nearly stolen everything the Rocky Mountain Company brought up the river; nearly killed Brokenleg; and did steal Little Whirlwind, using her and abandoning her to a wintry doom. And now with the new year and new trading season, Hervey had been stirring up the tribes again, destroying the Rocky Mountain Company's livestock.

The man had to be dealt with. Guy had a few weapons of his own, he thought grimly. The kind of weapons that could bring Julius Hervey to justice. Guy touched heels to his saddler and threaded his way through the vast Crow encampment surrounding Fort Cass. Whatever else Hervey had done, he'd succeeded in bringing almost the whole Crow nation to his trading window. One band after another came in to exchange beautifully tanned robes — none other were as fine as Crow robes — for all the foofaraw, whiskey and trade goods Pierre Chouteau and his cohorts had shipped upriver to entice red men.

The day was not peaceful. Black-bellied clouds scudded low, bringing sudden chill and stirring up blasts of wintry air, only to yield to sunlit moments when the fading summer sun warmed flesh and soul. The winds flapped the American Fur Company ensign above the gates. It fit Guy's mood. He passed numerous women fleshing fresh hides staked to the earth, their labor patient and familiar so they could gossip with each other as they created the wealth that brought them ribbons or a good drunk.

He paused at the maw of the post feeling the heaviness of the silvery cottonwood logs that imprisoned all that lay within. The outer gates were open; the inner ones closed. But mysteriously they swung open as he rode close and he felt himself riding through a gullet and into the belly of the whale. Engages closed the giant gates behind him. Standing before him in the cluttered yard was a muscular, dark-haired man with a mocking look, and Guy knew at once he was seeing Hervey.

"You came to sell out," Hervey said, without greeting or welcome.

Guy sighed and dismounted. He tied the saddler to a post. Then, as quietly as his roaring soul permitted, he turned to Hervey. "I am Guy Straus of St. Louis. I'm the senior partner in the new Rocky Mountain Company."

"You were," said Hervey, his eyes dancing. "Now you're here."

"You are the factor, Julius Hervey. We have business."

"None that I know of." Hervey nodded at an engage. The man untied Guy's horse and led it toward a stock pen at the rear of the crowded yard.

"I'd just as soon you leave the saddler here," Guy said.

"You won't need it," Hervey said. "You just sold it to us."

Hervey's taunt worried Guy. He peered about the small fort. Log rooms surrounded the yard. Beyond, the palisade towered over them. A brown mountain of graded and baled buffalo robes stood in an open warehouse. Several engages were grading and baling more at a press in the yard. The smell of manure, cooking meat, and human sweat lingered in the close confines. Cass was a rough place with none of the amenities of Union, or Clark, or Pierre.

"If you won't invite me to your offices, I'll

invite myself," Guy said. He'd spotted them next to the factor's log quarters. He walked that direction until Hervey's powerful hand caught Guy's arm. Guy looked at that hand. It bore deep scars across its back where bone and muscle had been severed. But it seemed functional enough.

"Very well," said Guy. "We'll do our business here."

Hervey laughed easily, his eyes mocking. "We have no business." Hervey's massive hand whirled Guy around as if he were a doll.

Guy was beginning to think Hervey was right: they had no business. "Then I will leave," he said. "But not before cautioning you about certain conduct."

Something wild, like twin blue flames, danced in Hervey's eyes. Hervey's wounded hands formed into giant fists which he lifted and clenched before Straus. "Fitzhugh should have killed me. See? My hands work." Slowly he flexed his fingers, clamped and unclamped his fists, the hands Fitzhugh had slashed to bits while Hervey was strangling him last winter. "I can choke an animal better than ever."

Guy felt a dread tighten in his chest but he pushed it aside. "You have caused us great loss. You set the Blackfeet on us — killed our oxen and stole our mules. I'll bill Pierre Chouteau for it and for the wagon as well."

Hervey smiled.

"Mister Hervey, there are limits. Even in the fur trade, there are limits. Even for you, there are limits. You are a long way from a court and a judge but that doesn't mean you are exempt."

"You lost."

The response mystified Guy. "Mister Hervey. There are boundaries. Undercut us on prices if you will. Bribe chiefs and headmen. Race to get your resupply in first. Manipulate prices in the wholesale markets — in New York. Glut the market with robes to hurt us if you must. Pressure your suppliers if you please. I expect all that from a combine the size of American Fur. But there are lines, sir. I will draw lines and you will heed them: I will draw them at murder, theft, willful destruction, mayhem, inciting the tribes to violence. Those things will not be tolerated."

"You forgot some. Getting you into license trouble by planting spirits. Getting some friendly 'Rapaho to steal robes and horses from Stiffleg. Capture. I favor capture myself. I capture everything I can lay my butchered hands on." That blue flame danced in his eyes again. "It is profit."

"Is Raul Raffin your man?"

"Who knows?"

"Every American Fur factor up the river said the company wasn't involved. Only Raffin. Perhaps you and Raffin?"

Hervey nodded. "Me and Raffin."

Guy decided it was time to go. And leave a gentle warning behind him: "I've drawn a line, Mr. Hervey. I am not without resources." Hervey froze, looking amused. It was as if he was waiting for whatever would happen next. "I'll be leaving now. Thank you for your hospitality, Mr. Hervey."

Guy left the factor standing there in the windy yard, and hunted for his saddler. It'd vanished. He had the sinking feeling that the horse and saddle had been stolen, too. He found a gate leading to a pen and found a pair of burly Creoles guarding it. He tried to slide by only to have a muscular arm block his path.

"This too, then," he muttered. The saddler had brought him clear from Bellevue. He turned toward that mocking figure standing in the yard. "I'll be talking to Pierre Chouteau," he said, heading for the towering plank gates. Two huge engages stood at them barring the way, their gaze upon Hervey. Neither Creole looked comfortable. He knew, suddenly, that his liberty had been taken from him and perhaps that would be only the beginning.

He spotted the door to the trading room and found another giant lounging before it. He pushed in anyway, only to find himself thrown back. He staggered and tumbled into the grime of the yard. He picked himself up and dusted off his black broadcloth coat and britches under Hervey's amused gaze. His frock coat showed manure stains along the right sleeve.

"Come," said Hervey. Guy paused, wondering, and then followed him toward a room with a door opening on the yard. An office? Hervey paused beside the open door. Beyond lay a naked log-walled cubicle with a clay floor and not a stick of furniture. It stank of urine. "I just bought you out," said Hervey.

"No, that is not what you've done."

The windowless room looked like a rat's hole to Guy. He suddenly wondered what other mortals had been penned there, desperate and hungry or cold, awaiting the fate Hervey fashioned for them. A swift shove careened Guy into it, and the door slammed. Something metallic clicked. Small pricks of light worked through the planks of the door along with the glow of liberty at the transom and the threshold. He heard Hervey humming to himself outside. "Yankee Doodle."

"Sign it over, Straus," Hervey said. "Or don't if you don't want to. It makes no difference." Nothing more.

Agony gripped Guy Straus. He peered about him in the dim light that leaked like quicksilver from the doorway. Massive log walls, uneven clay floor that reeked acrid odors. A ceiling of handsawed plank so low he could touch it, so oppressive it seemed to crush him. A storage room that had stored living mortals before.

Perhaps it was a joke. Guy set his shoulder into the door and pushed. It rattled slightly and held. No joke. Julius Hervey had imprisoned him. Guy felt his pulse rising, some terror too deep to fathom shrieking through his body. He didn't know what he was afraid of; only that the walls and ceiling and floor threatened him. He discovered cold sweat on his brow and felt it collect on his chest.

He paced. The cubicle was scarcely ten feet square but it permitted him to walk a tight circle while he tried to bring his crazed body under control. Calm had vanished; his body acted as if it were about to be pushed off a cliff. He couldn't think; his mind had ceased to function and thought had been replaced by a white hum, pure animal instinct. He paused at the door, pressed an ear to it, and heard little. Scraps of French from the Creoles out in the yard. He wanted to shout and roar.

Instead, he paced, hoping this rude jest would end but knowing Hervey didn't jest. He discovered a terrible thirst in him and then a vicious hunger, and knew he had lost the freedom to feed himself or find water to slake his thirst. They became urgent to him: he needed water at once, at once! The very necessaries of life, water and food, lay beyond his means. Air! He needed air! He'd suffocate! Indeed, the air was rank. He gulped it in, exhaled it slowly, and wondered how long it'd last.

A terrible helplessness slid into him. He had never been familiar with helplessness. He'd never experienced confinement. He'd never had to wait on the whim of another — a madman at that — for sustenance. Never in the quiet comfort of his life in St. Louis had he known anything even remotely like this. The only time he'd ever thought about confinement and helplessness was when his father had had the stroke, a few months before his father died. Guy remembered how his father had lain helpless and desperate, a prisoner in his own body, his will thwarted and humbled, his eyes wild with an anguish he couldn't voice.

Guy stretched his hands, pumped his arms and legs. His body worked. Soon Hervey would free him! If Hervey didn't the Creoles in the post would help, even if in the middle of the night. The thought comforted Guy. An end would come to this. That thought calmed him a little. He peered about, looking for weakness and seeing none. He'd worn his black suit as he always did on banking and business occasions when formality was required. His finely tailored business clothing carried its own messages to the beholder. Now he regretted it. If he'd worn his trail clothing he would have his penknife which he'd used so often to shave bits of tinder to start the campfires, along with flint and steel and charcloth. With a penknife he could begin to cut his way free from his wooden cage — to whittle away the planking around the door latch.

But that was idle yearning. He had nothing. He was here, caged by a madman after traversing two thousand river miles of open country with scarcely a building upon it, much less a jail. It struck him as odd and paradoxical to be confined here. *Here!* His throat felt parched; his stomach rumbled, though he'd felt no need only minutes before. He ignored the howling of body and soul, or tried to.

Time stopped. He imagined he'd been confined scarcely fifteen minutes. How could he endure an hour, a day, a month? He knew he had to stop his fevered mind from racing, and stop his fevered body from straining at his bonds, or he couldn't endure. Calm, sleep, naps. These might help. He settled himself down upon the filthy clay, repelled by the sinister odors that lifted to him. He closed his eyes, shutting out even the vagrant light from the door. But all he felt was helplessness. He no longer possessed the simplest things. He could not control whether he lived or died, whether he was cold or hot, hungry or full, thirsty or satiated.

He let his vision slide past log walls and dark plank ceilings, out, out upon a sunnier landscape not of the world and its finite horizons but beyond, where love shone like a hundred suns, and the scent of goodness was an incense. He summoned up psalms, which came to him in rusted fragments, drawn from some deep well of sweetest water.

"Blessed is the man whom thou chastenest, O Lord, and teachest him out of thy law;

"That thou mayest give him rest from the days of adversity, until the pit be digged for the wicked."

Thus he occupied himself, dredging up bits and pieces of a lost Talmudic education. There had been no other Hebrews in frontier St. Louis, no temple. When he was twelve his parents had sent him down the river to New Orleans for a season to learn at the hand of a rabbi. But there'd been nothing since. Even his wife was a gentile and his children were not actually Hebrews, though David and Maxim both sought knowledge of their heritage from him. Clothilde had followed her mother and become a Catholic. He chided himself for his neglect of the sacred things.

And he prayed, feeling the weight of his own iniquities and worldliness at first. But as he stumbled through his supplication he felt his spirits soar and his sense of unworthiness depart like a heavy weight off his shoulders. And he marveled. White light shone sweetly in the midst of this dark dungeon. He had been lax but had never abandoned his faith, and now it flooded through him.

A calm permeated him at last. It had come with surrender, and the acceptance of his straitened world. He would not rattle the door in anguish or lament the lost minutes or cry out against oppression, but would spend his time here renewing his peace day by day.

He forgot himself at last. His own misery no longer occupied his mind or drove him into despair. Instead, his mind turned to his captor, Julius Hervey — a man such as Guy had never encountered before. Nothing, utterly nothing, stayed Hervey's will. His sojourn in these wilds had stripped him of every vestige of restraint and honor. A man devoid of civilizing impulse could only be mad, or nearly so. He remembered the wild flame in Hervey's eyes, and saw in it the dance of darkness.

What did Hervey want? Why had Hervey thrown him into this hole? What did he hope to gain from it? The more Guy pondered these questions the more they mystified him. Hervey was not without restraints, even here in a sea of lawless land. Alec Culbertson was set over him. And Hervey was responsible to Pierre Chouteau as well. In fact Chouteau doted on him, called him his mad dog, resorted to him when he needed something done that wouldn't look good in daylight, and boasted of him among fur men in St. Louis — in part to scare off opposition companies. Julius Hervey had never failed to make a large profit even when other factors failed. Hervey was American Fur's mad dog.

What did Hervey want? An agreement to shut down Fitzhugh's Post and get out of the business? Some piece of paper to that effect? A forced sale of Rocky Mountain Company property for a pittance? No. All these things Guy would swiftly repudiate back in St. Louis. The whole world would know of the duress. No. Hervey wasn't that naive or dumb. The captivity of the principal partner of the Rocky Mountain Company would only cause scandal that would reverberate clear back to John Tyler in the White House. What then?

Nothing that Guy could think of — until he realized that reasons didn't have to be rational. Madness had its own reasons. Guy felt the stirring of anguish again. A madman could discover pleasures in humiliating — or torturing — a man in Guy's position, a financier, a power to be reckoned with in the city called the gateway to the West. A madman might delight in starving or dehydrating a man like Guy . . . The helplessness flooded through Guy again. His sojourn in the darkened room might be paradise compared to what Julius Hervey might do to him, bound hand and foot to the robe press out in the yard.

But that didn't make sense. Hervey didn't make sense.

The light changed and Guy guessed the day was fading. He had no way of knowing except to tell day from night. No one came. Hunger and thirst goaded him now. And that is what Hervey wanted. To let Guy experience the crying of his own body and to beg, to surrender himself to Hervey's will, do anything for a scrap of food, a sip of water. Power. Hervey was mad for power.

Guy knew then he had a weapon after all, a weapon that would have its effect even upon a half-mad man. He had a weapon that would drive Hervey to some sort of defeat — if Guy could endure it — and he wasn't sure he could. Guy knew what he would do: he would refuse all food. From now until his release he would not swallow a bite. Hervey might demand, might torture, might command, but Guy would swallow nothing . . . if he could find the courage and subdue the madness of his own body. He might die of hunger. But that would be the last thing that Julius Hervey wanted, the one thing that would ruin the man forever. Guy felt the torture of his empty belly and prepared himself to endure.

Seventeen

Guy Straus had thought about death a great deal, as many middle-aged men do. And the contemplation of his end had helped him understand the living of his life. He had hoped for a good death; all men do. But he had never imagined, back there in St. Louis, that it might pounce upon him at a northern fur post, in a reeking little dungeon, at the hands of a man without scruple.

Night poured through his soul like a vat of India ink, his mood perfectly matching the blackness of his cell. He was denied even the hope of stars, the pinpricks of light that promised a tomorrow. His body tormented him, revealing hurts and discomforts as he slouched against a hard log wall. Thirst was the worst: he'd been confined since yesterday morning without a drop of water. A hundred yards away a great torrent of it raced by en route to the Gulf of Mexico.

He dreaded a death from thirst. Of the agonizing way to die it was one of the worst. Hervey knew that and was using it. Guy wished he could subdue his tortured body the way some men did, transporting their souls to some distant shore until they scarcely noticed their own mortality. But he couldn't. The ache of his empty stomach intruded upon his thoughts; his desperation for water became simply an obsession burning in his mind like a forge.

He could not think but his will collected and hardened, and when the whirl of time brought a faint light to the threshold he had prepared himself. He would use his sole weapon, if given the chance: he would use his death. Oddly, he had not spent the night mourning, or yearning for Yvonne or his children, or the comforts of his brick home. Instead, he had honed down his will into a sharp blade that would cut even Julius Hervey. Through some mysterious process he'd gotten to know Hervey through the endless dark; almost as if Hervey had sat down across from him and bared the working of his soul. Almost as if Julius Hervey's spirit had confessed and Guy was his confessor.

Hervey's spirit knew nothing of love and didn't understand it. Hervey's spirit was possessive. Hervey wanted to own men even more than he wanted to own anything else. Men and women. There were only two ways to possess another mortal: with love, or with the threat of death and pain. As Guy listened to Hervey's spirit that night, Guy knew what he had to do to resist. He had to die. It alone would defeat Julius Hervey.

Guy waited as the light thickened in the pinholes around the door, knowing that Julius Hervey would soon come to torture him. He was not mistaken. He heard the clank of metal and the door swung open suddenly, revealing Julius Hervey in aching light. Guy blinked at the whiteness.

"The great capitalist," said Hervey.

Guy smiled.

Hervey waved a glass carafe filled with clear, sweet water, and chortled. "Come out and have a drink," he said. "Breakfast. You'll want breakfast."

Guy didn't move.

"Your rescuers didn't show up, Straus. Ol' Fitzhugh, I was rather hoping he'd poke around. Or the boy. I like the boy. I ain't seen hide nor hair. I thought mebbe you'd all be here together by now."

Guy smiled and slouched into the log wall. He could scarcely keep from staring at the carafe of cool water.

"You ready to deal? Any time you want to deal, we'll deal, Mister Moneybags."

Guy smiled.

"Mebbe you aren't hungry?"

"Oh, I'm that," said Guy. "But last night, Mr. Hervey, I realized the end had come for me and I've made my peace with God. Perhaps you should make peace with God."

For once, puzzlement replaced the smirk on the man's heavy face. Hervey peered into the gloom of the dungeon as if looking for something — like a cache of food and water smuggled in by an engage. He found nothing. Guy saw that several Creoles stood out in the yard watching all this, and listening.

"You coming out or do I drag you out?"

"I'm quite comfortable, thank you, Mr. Hervey."

"You ain't ready to come to medicine."

"I've made my peace with God," Guy said, knowing his spirit had but his body hadn't. The promise of water and food set off wild spasms through his body.

"Well, croak then," said Hervey. The smirk had returned. He swung the door shut and latched it. Guy repressed the need to scream at him, to say yes, yes to anything, only give him water. Instead, he slumped back into the wall, closed his eyes, and began reciting the fragments of psalms he remembered. He found other fragments returning to him as if freed from the bottom of some sea, rising to his awareness but encased in barnacles. He spoke them out loud, feeling giddy with need.

Guy knew he'd won the first round, triumphed not so much over Hervey as over his own body. But he didn't know how long that would last before his body betrayed his will.

He dozed for the first time, and awoke surprised that he had dozed. The thread of light along the threshold glowed bright, and he guessed it was midday. His throat felt parched, and he could hardly muster the saliva to wet his lips. But as long as he stayed quiet he seemed to dominate the roaring lion of his own body. No one came. He'd passed a full twenty-four hours there and had plunged into the second day. He tried to doze again but that blessed estate eluded him. Several times he heard men just outside, often whispering in French. The engages did not like this; but none of them dared to thwart Julius Hervey.

The day wore on and Guy's spirits grew ragged. Was he simply committing suicide? Why resist Hervey? What did Guy live for, hope for, dream of? Guy couldn't even answer those painful questions. He was doing what he was doing because — he had to. He knew he was severely dehydrated now. His heart raced for no reason. His body cried for water. The hunger he could endure but not this.

Hervey showed up late in the afternoon. The door swung open again and the rushing light blinded Guy. The muscular factor with bulging eyes — Guy had never noticed the bulging brown eyes before — wasn't smirking this time. He peered at Guy. "You gonna eat?"

Guy smiled.

"If you don't I'll pour this down your gullet." He held a black kettle full of hot buffalo stew.

The fragrance intoxicated Guy. "Why?" he asked.

The question surprised Hervey. "Eat!" he yelled.

"I will have water. No food."

"Eat or I'll stuff it in!"

"Do as you will."

Hervey squatted, dipped an iron spoon into the warm stew, and lifted it to Guy's lips. Guy somehow kept them shut, defying his own howling body even more than he was defying Hervey. The factor held the spoon there and then dashed the stew into Guy's face. Guy sputtered.

"I'll pry your jaws apart."

"You seem most eager to feed me."

Hervey didn't answer. Instead, he lifted another spoonful to Guy's lips and met the same obdurate resistance. Guy waited for Hervey to fulfill his threat and pry Guy's jaw open, but it didn't happen.

"I'll leave this here. You'll come around," he said.

Guy shook his head. "I wish to die in peace. You may leave now."

"Why?"

Guy suddenly felt he had become the master and Hervey the servant, though he couldn't say why or point to anything that had happened. "It defeats you," Guy replied softly. "You have no power over a man who welcomes death."

Hervey laughed. "You're trapped in this hellhole. You can walk out any time you want —"

"Oh, no. I can't do that. Walk out."

Hervey peered into Guy's eyes, and Guy saw the blue flame of madness dancing in Hervey's face. "I own you. I have you here. No one can rescue you here. We are a thousand miles from anywhere. I have you like a canary in a cage. I can feed or starve you. Not all the capital in St. Louis can rescue you."

"Ah, Hervey. I don't need rescuing. I've made my peace —"

"Shut up!" Hervey stood and booted Guy. The boot caught Guy's hipbone sending waves of pain down his leg and up into his belly. "Shut up!"

"You may bring me water," said Guy. "I'll accept water."

"You'll eat the stew!"

Guy shrugged.

Hervey lifted the pot and dashed its contents over Guy. The fragrance maddened Guy. He felt the liquids drip down his waistcoat, soaking his shirt with slime.

"You may bring me water," Guy said. He would permit himself water, but not a bit of nourishment.

Hervey stalked out into the blinding light, leaving the door open. Guy gazed into a sunlit and glorious world. Then Hervey returned and slapped the kettle to the gummy clay. The water in it shimmered.

Guy smiled as Hervey slammed the door and locked it again. Guy knew he had won.

Even before the day waned Brokenleg knew that Fort Cass had swallowed Guy Straus. He also knew there wasn't a thing he could do about it. Julius Hervey did what he chose, protected by a high stockade and an army of Creoles. Hervey would do whatever he felt like doing, including murder if it suited him. In the past murder had often suited him.

There was the possibility, of course, that Guy Straus was simply negotiating something or other over there, a respected guest and powerful rival. But Brokenleg knew better than that. He knew Hervey. And he knew Guy was in trouble. Brokenleg reviewed his options and found them bleak. He had no way to break into Fort Cass and rescue Guy.

He found Maxim sulking in the barracks, as usual. "Your pa's been caught. I told him not to go but he wasn't listening."

Maxim peered back with an owly look on his face. "I don't care," he muttered.

"I think you do. He's your pa. Even if you don't approve o' him he's your flesh and blood."

"I told you I don't care."

"Hervey, he could be hurtin' your pa."

"That's what happens in the fur business."

"Forcin' your pa to sell out, close us up."

"Then I'm on Hervey's side."

Brokenleg couldn't believe his ears. "After what Hervey done to us?"

Maxim nodded defiantly. "Leave me alone."

Brokenleg did. He hunted up Chatillon,

who was out on the streambank. "Straus is stuck at Cass. Hervey's got him. Probably got him sittin' there until he says he'll quit the Yellowstone. That's what ol' Hervey wants. He's jist been waitin' for something like this. You got any notions how to git Guy out?"

"Surely they won't harm a man like Guy Straus. Pierre Chouteau — he tolerates a lot, but not that. Mon Dieu! Guy Straus lends him money when American Fur needs it!"

"You know Hervey. He'd shoot God if it suited him."

"We could ride over and talk, *oui?*"

"We could. But I ain't."

"It could be fatal."

"Ambrose, you come a far piece with him, set around a lot o' fires at night. Did Straus, did he mention — did he say he had any business with Hervey? Like shuttin' down this post and sellin' out?"

"*Non,* none that he told me about."

"People git to talkin' on the trail. He say anything about Hervey?"

Chatillon shook his head.

"Well, I'm not goin' over there. Hervey, he's jist waitin' for me to ride over and walk right into it. Then ol' Hervey'd have the pair of us. If he wants me he'll send for me.

Or he'll ride hyar."

The next day dragged by like a lame man. Brokenleg careened around, looking for ways to cause trouble. He stomped over to the *chantier*, the shipyard, where the Creoles were cutting the second pirogue with two round adzes. The first of the big dugout canoes gleamed white in the sun. A giant cottonwood had been whittled into a sharp-prowed little boat, and hollowed out except for two bulkheads. The dry center area between the bulkheads would store cargo; the men paddling the pirogue would sit fore and aft.

"Hurry it up," he growled, and stomped off to badger his four wives. He couldn't find a one. Off in the woods berrying. He'd got a whole damned Cheyenne village to care for. He didn't need four wives. Grudgingly he admitted they made themselves useful, bringing comfort, better food, and ease to the post. But right now he was tired of responsibilities, and four wives were three too many. Maybe four too many. He had an itch to stuff the whole post into Maxim's hands and ride off for the high trails and the whispering pines — alone. He and Jamie Dance had done all right out in the high country; they could do it again even if beaver plews weren't worth nothing.

But a rider approached, and the rider was

Julius Hervey sitting comfortably on a scrawny saddler. Brokenleg wished he had his Hawken. He'd have shot Hervey right out of his saddle. Put a fifty-three caliber ball right between his eyes and wipe that smirk off his ugly mug. But he didn't. So he stood his ground before the gates of his post and waited, clenching and unclenching his fists. He was no match for Julius Hervey, not with his bum leg, but he made up for it some by hotting up every time he took sight of the factor of Fort Cass.

Hervey stopped a little over a good knife-throw away, a cautious gesture if not a respectful one. "I got Straus," he announced. The smirk plastered his big square face.

That was no news to Fitzhugh. He nodded. He studied Hervey's calico shirt, deciding to aim his knife at the man's heart. He could do it faster than Hervey could pull that big pistol out of its saddle sheath.

"You're closin' down, Stiffleg. We come to a little agreement, old Straus and me."

That was no news either. "No I'm not."

Hervey smiled that mad blue-flame smile of his. "It doesn't matter what you do. It's Straus's company."

"Bring him here," Brokenleg said.

"He won't like that. Trouble from you."

"I'm a partner."

"A sixth. He's got control. He and I came to a little agreement. Rocky Mountain, it's merging with American Fur. I'm takin' your stuff. All the shelf goods, all the robes, and the post. Any of your engages that want to switch, too. But not you. You're gettin' out."

Brokenleg didn't believe a word of it. "Forget it, Hervey. I'm stayin' put. He can tell me in person. Until he does I'm trading robes and running the business and watchin' out for you. You got my mules, you got a wagon. You got my oxen kilt. But you got more ta lose, Hervey. Jist remember it."

"He won't like that — you fighting him."

"That's your problem, Hervey. How's your hands?"

Hervey held one up. The gashes that Brokenleg had carved in them had healed pink. "How's your throat, Stiffleg?"

"It ain't forgot your fingers."

Hervey laughed. "You got until tomorrow. You clear out. You and all them sluts you got. And walk. I got the horses. Leave the shelf goods. Leave the robes, too. Old Guy, he was glad to gimme them robes. Where's his boy? He wants his boy."

"Like hell he does, Hervey."

"I'll go," said Maxim. Brokenleg whirled.

Maxim stood beside him. And arrayed beyond were most of his engages and Dust Devil. He'd been so absorbed with Hervey he hadn't seen them. They all looked solemn. Especially Spoon and Constable who understood English better than the Creoles.

Maxim held a poke. "You'll stay," rasped Brokenleg.

"You'll have to make me — the way you always do."

"He'll come," said Hervey, smirking.

Maxim dashed away, reaching Hervey in a moment. Brokenleg let him go. Spoiled little parasite, he thought.

Hervey chortled. "He don't like you none, Stiffleg."

"He don't like the business."

"I don't like you," echoed Maxim.

Brokenleg ignored him. It wasn't news anyway. "Hervey. I'm not shutting down. You come around here again and someone gets hurt."

"Straus."

Maxim glanced sharply at Hervey. "What did my father agree to?" he asked.

"Come along and find out."

"I asked you what my father agreed to." An imperious tone crept into Maxim's voice.

"He agreed to a drink of water." Hervey thought that was pretty funny but it eluded Brokenleg.

Maxim wasn't mollified. "I asked you an honest question and I want an honest answer."

"That's a good question, Hervey. What did he agree to?"

"Whatever I tell him, Stiffleg."

Brokenleg tried to make sense of it. Had the senior partner of the Rocky Mountain Company agreed to anything? And why? Guy Straus was a tough bird, equal to any occasion. Not one to sell out or betray a partner — unless he was in worse trouble than Fitzhugh had imagined.

"You tell him I'm hyar to stay. I'm trading. I'm shipping robes next spring. You're not his messenger, Hervey. If he wants to bust up the company he can come hyar and tell me."

"You lose," Hervey said. He turned the saddler and prodded Maxim ahead of him, not giving the boy a chance to reconsider. The boy turned back, something terrible on his face. For a fleeting moment he looked about to weep. He lifted a hand — an imploring hand. But Hervey maneuvered his horse between Maxim and the post, harrying him along as if he was a calf.

"Good bye, Brokenleg!" Maxim shouted. It wasn't unkind. And the tone seemed regretful.

Brokenleg watched them go, something fiery building in him. If Straus sold him out, if Straus quit, if Straus couldn't resist Hervey's mad cunning — then by God, that was it. No Rocky Mountain Company. A vision of mountain brooks and lazy days flashed through him.

Fuming, he watched the most unpredictable man in the northern country ride off with another hostage.

Eighteen

The sudden light blinded Guy but he could see that it wasn't Hervey standing in the bright doorway; it was Maxim. Hervey stood behind him.

"Here's your pa, boy." Hervey shoved and Maxim careened into the darkness, staggered to the far wall, and tumbled to the clay.

"Maxim!" exclaimed Guy.

Maxim collected himself and sat up. "You wanted me," he muttered.

"No, Maxim — I don't want you at all. Not here."

Maxim stared accusingly at Hervey, awareness building in him. "You invited me," he whispered.

Hervey loomed in the doorway enjoying himself. "Welcome to Fort Cass. Big and little Straus. You ready to talk?"

Guy shook his head.

"Pilgrims," Hervey said. "City boys. Long way from home."

"This won't escape the attention of

authorities in St. Louis," Guy said.

"Where's that? I never heard of St. Louis. Here is here."

"An agreement made under duress is not recognized anywhere, Monsieur Hervey."

The bourgeois laughed again. "It doesn't have to be."

"Out there, Monsieur Hervey" — Guy pointed into the yard of the post — "are forty men. Eighty eyes and ears. Including your chief trader, Isodore Sandoval. Men talk. Here at Fort Union and at every post down the river."

"I'll give you a few minutes to think it over."

Maxim stood shakily. "I'm leaving here," he mumbled. He picked up his poke and headed for the doorway which was blocked by Hervey. The man's square-toed boot caught Maxim in the groin, driving him back into the far wall. Maxim gasped, shrieked, and sobbed.

Guy sprang up, dizzy with hunger. Weakness hit him. Then Hervey's fist hit him, a sledgehammer knocking him into the clay again. Amazing pain lanced outward from his shoulder. He groaned.

Hervey lounged against the doorframe again, enjoying himself. "Ten minutes to think it over, Straus."

"Think what over?"

"Whether the boy gets hurt or not."

"He's already hurt, Monsieur Hervey."

Hervey addressed the gasping boy. "Dummy. You pilgrims are all alike."

Maxim wept, rocking back and forth in pain, not listening. But Guy was listening.

"What is it you want, Monsieur Hervey?" Guy asked.

"You and me, we're going back to your place and you're telling Fitzhugh you sold out. Maxim, he stays right here just to make sure you behave yourself."

"And what is the sell-out price you're offering?"

"Free trip down the river."

Nothing. Not a sale, but theft. "I think not, *mon ami.*"

"I think so, Straus. The boy needs a whipping."

"When they hear of this in St. Louis —"

"Where's St. Louis did you say?"

Hervey was right. Where indeed was St. Louis. By the time the story got whispered down the river there would be a hundred versions, many of them favorable to Julius Hervey. And Pierre Chouteau would reward Hervey for breaking up the opposition on the Yellowstone.

Guy peered angrily at Maxim. The boy

had cost him his victory. Maxim had curled up into a ball on the slimy clay and lay groaning. As long as Guy had only himself to worry about he would have outlasted Hervey. Not even Julius Hervey could twist the arm of a man resigned to death. But now . . . an unfamiliar bitterness welled in Guy as he examined his moralizing son. But Guy knew he had no choice at all; he could let his own boy be tortured to death, or he could surrender.

"Monsieur Hervey, I wish to talk privately to my son for a few minutes."

Hervey shrugged. A shrug of triumph, Guy thought. A moment later Hervey vanished from the doorframe. The light from the yard still blinded Guy after almost two days of blackness. Across the yard engages stared and whispered as they slowly folded robes and placed them in the robe press for baling.

Guy wanted to accuse but knew he never would. No father could accuse his own son of something so terrible. The boy didn't gasp any more, but Guy waited anyway, watching blue-bellied flies buzz and hum. The summer had ended and the flies of summer were doomed even if they didn't know it.

Maxim stirred and looked up at Guy, pain radiating from his begrimed face.

"You won, Maxim. I will do what you

wish. We'll be closing the post on the Yellowstone. We will lose a lot." That was as close as Guy would come to an accusation.

Maxim swallowed hard and listened.

"Mr. Hervey has his ways, doesn't he? You knew that, though."

Maxim nodded, rubbing the tears away from his eyes. "I don't like this business. It's illegal. We shouldn't have expanded."

Guy cut him off sharply. "Maxim! I'm going back to Fitzhugh's Post to tell our partner. You'll be kept here."

"Brokenleg won't like that."

"No, he won't. I don't like it either. I must do it because —" he stopped short. Because if he didn't Hervey would begin torturing Maxim.

"Because of me."

Guy nodded. "Because of you."

"You can tell Brokenleg but he won't do it."

"He has only a sixth of the company, Maxim —"

"Papa! You came all the way up the river on the *bateau,* and on horseback, and you don't know how it is here. *There is no St. Louis.*"

Guy sighed. Brokenleg wouldn't do it. Long ago he'd formed the company with Fitzhugh and Dance because he knew they never caved in. Maxim was right. "Maxim — son — our time together may be short. I want you to know I'm proud of you. I'm especially proud of your . . . moral courage. I want to tell you also . . . that I love you. Whatever happens now — and it may be terrible for us both — I want you to know that."

His son's tears welled up again.

"What would you like me to do, Maxim?"

"Don't go, papa."

"Hervey will hurt you. That's his way of coercing me. And Brokenleg."

Maxim groaned, hating it. "I shouldn't have come. I knew what he's like. I was so angry with Brokenleg — with you . . ."

"That's the past."

Maxim stared into the bright light of the yard, his face a mask. Guy watched his son change, as if the finger of God were touching him. Maxim turned at last. "I'm not as strong as Brokenleg. I wanted to be but I never will be. Maybe we owe him something. Owe ourselves something. Let's tell Hervey no. You won't go. You won't tell Brokenleg anything."

Guy clambered to his feet and clasped his son by the shoulder. "You might be hurt, Maxim."

"I know."

Guy found himself staring out upon the brightness of the day. "Evil is weak even if it roars and threatens. Evil things are done in darkness — not in light, light like this. Brokenleg has his own ways of fighting . . . and we have our own, Maxim. Do you follow me?"

Maxim nodded.

"All right then. Hervey may carry me bodily back there but he can't make me say what he wants me to say to Fitzhugh. In fact I'll say just the opposite. I'll tell him to hang on — no matter what. Evil's weak, I believe. I was praying when the door opened and I saw you. If I am taken away, never cease . . . and if I never see you again . . ."

Guy couldn't finish the thought. Maxim smiled. Smiled for the first time since Guy had arrived at Fitzhugh's Post. The young man settled down against the wall. Guy, dizzy with hunger, poked his head out into the blinding light and summoned Hervey, who stood near the robe press.

The bourgeois trotted across the sunny yard, a malign joy upon his face. "I'll get horses saddled, Straus."

"There's no need. I'm not going."

Hervey looked startled. "Not going?" He chortled. "You're going."

"I will not say to my partner what you want me to say. And he will not heed me in any case."

Hervey grinned, something feral and dangerous in his muscular form. His big fist sailed out of nowhere. Guy felt something like a steel bar slam into his nose. He felt blood gush from his nostrils even as a shock of pain exploded in his skull. He felt himself toppling to earth, gasping for air through red-hot nostrils. He felt himself being lifted easily and dragged out of the sunlight and into the blackness. He heard Maxim shout and the door slam shut. He saw only darkness, heard only weeping, and tasted blood in his mouth.

One by one, Brokenleg considered and discarded plans. Each seemed dumber than the last. He gave up on the idea of sneaking into Fort Cass somehow and rescuing Guy. He didn't think much of sending an express rider up to Fort Union nearly three hundred river miles away to get help from Alec Culbertson — who might or might not tame his mad dog Hervey. He loathed the idea of knavery — pretending to agree to Hervey's terms as a way to spring Guy and Maxim, and then welshing. He saw no gain from stirring up the Indians; that was always a double-edged sword. The more he reached for answers, the more will-o'-the-wisp they all seemed.

He ran a callused hand across his balding head and into the fiery red hair sprouting from its rear. He had come up with nothing. He cussed Straus for coming up into country he didn't know, with people who didn't act the way people do in places like St. Louis. Why didn't Straus stay put and leave the running of a wilderness post to someone who knew something? He sighed. It didn't do any good to cuss Straus. Junior or Senior Straus. He wished by God they'd stayed downriver where they belonged.

The cussing and wishing didn't help him either. He gimped about his quarters so angrily that none of his ladies dared say a word to him — not even Dust Devil. There was no telling what Hervey might do. The one sure thing about Julius Hervey was that he'd do what he wanted and no other soul on earth could predict what that might be, or even supply a reason for it.

He got tired of scheming — he wasn't good at it anyway. It was Straus's mess, not his. Straus had been warned not to ride over to Fort Cass — but he'd ignored the warning. Young Straus — he'd made his own choices, too. Brokenleg felt like leaving them to the fate they'd arranged for themselves — but couldn't. Guy was his partner. And unless Guy sold out, turned over the fort and trade goods — everything Brokenleg had struggled to build — Brokenleg figured it was his problem.

He stalked out of his rooms glaring at three Cheyenne wives, and stomped into his trading room where he found Zach Constable and Abner Spoon dealing with a stray Crow woman who'd slid away from Cass with a robe or two, looking for a better price.

"I'm goin' over to Cass for a parley. If I don't come back, don't you cave in — you understand? If Hervey comes around hyar and says we caved in don't you believe it. Shoot him if ye can, and shoot anyone trying to take over. You tell it to Samson, too. By gawd I'm not quittin'. Even if them Strauses go under I'm not quittin'. We built this post outa nothing but our own raw need to git it built; we stocked it; we come out even last season. I'm not cavin'. If Guy Straus wants to git out I'll find a new partner — Robert Campbell maybe. He loves to git in his licks against Chouteau. You understandin' me?"

Abner said, "We ought to go with ye."

"That'd jist start some killin'. No. This

coon's goin' to talk to Hervey or kill him, one or the other or both."

Zach said, "He don't have a bum leg, and his hands are good again. We oughter come along."

But Fitzhugh wouldn't listen. "You send an express if I don't come back. One to Campbell — he's got some money in this hyar outfit — and one to Jamie Dance." He glared at them for emphasis. "You quit on me and I'll come outa my grave and strangle you."

Zach grinned.

Fitzhugh stomped out, found Ambrose Chatillon in the barracks, and repeated the whole thing. Chatillon would be the express rider. Then he hunted down Trudeau, found him at the forge holding a horse being shod by Bercier, and hauled him off to a private corner. The chief trader listened behind a masked expression, and shook his head sadly.

"All three of you caught by Hervey — all the owners. *Non,* it is madness."

Brokenleg growled at him, limped out to the pen, threw his saddle over a gaunt Cheyenne pony, and rode out, his rusty Hawken a rod of iron across his lap. He reached Cass in an hour, noting the lively trade it was doing with several sprawling villages of

Crows. He threaded through the lodges, past staring old women and curious children, until he reached the opened gates. There he tied his horse to a hitch rail, daring any Crow in sight to swipe it. Hawken in hand, he stomped to the trading window, which opened on the passage between the inner and outer gates, the common place for it in fur posts.

A seamed old crone barely tall enough to see over the counter was trading there, her worn split robe lying before her while the clerks examined it. Sandoval, in fact. Good, he thought. Isodor Sandoval was second in command behind Hervey and actually one of the few in the company Fitzhugh liked.

"I want to see Hervey," he snapped over the head of the old woman.

"Take your turn," Sandoval retorted. He deliberately slowed down the trading, listening intently to the old woman's wishes — red ribbons, a fire steel, and a cup of sugar. Sandoval leisurely scratched the transaction into the ledger while a clerk gathered the items from the shelves and poured a cup of sugar, ritually keeping his thumb in the measure.

The little woman, frightened by the brooding presence behind her, gathered her things and fled.

"Get me Hervey," he rasped before Sandoval said a word.

"He said to tell you he's not talking unless you're ready to deal."

"Where's Guy Straus?"

Sandoval shrugged uneasily. The man's gaze darted away.

"I said where's Straus?"

"Brokenleg —"

"Where's the boy?"

Sandoval sighed. "Hervey has them."

"Are they hurt?"

Sandoval clammed up. Brokenleg took it for a yes.

"What does Hervey want?"

Sandoval shrugged. "He always wants whatever there is to want, Brokenleg."

"He isn't goin' to git it. Go fetch him."

"Not while you have that Hawken pointing through the window, Fitzhugh."

"That's where she's going to point."

"You set it down and I'll send for him."

But he didn't have to. Behind Fitzhugh, one of the inner gates creaked open and Hervey emerged, his fist swallowing a little pepperbox with six barrels and the hammer on full cock. Brokenleg's thumb snicked back the hammer of his Hawken.

"Stiffleg! How good of you to come!"

Hervey slid around Fitzhugh heading

toward the outer gates.

"I guess if you feel like shuttin' them gates on me, Hervey, we'll both be dyin' in a minute."

Hervey's black eyes danced fire but he halted. "I have Straus. Do you want him?" he asked.

"I'm not hyar to dicker, Hervey. I'm hyar to tell ye a thing."

Hervey shrugged. "Stiffleg, I thought you'd want to know about big and little Straus."

"Nope. They made their own medicine. I come to give ye the word, and the word is, no deal. That post o' mine is goin' to keep on a-goin', and nothing that happens hyar is goin' to change that. I'm gittin' robes and I'm gittin' goods up the river, and if I don't have them Strauses for partners I'll have a few others. So you may as well spring 'em loose 'cause you can't make medicine."

"Spring 'em loose! How you carry on, Stiffleg. They're guests, quite comfortable, dickering about the final details of the sale. Quite profitable for all. You ought to set down that old piece and jine us."

"This old piece'll put a ball through yer heart before it gits set down, Hervey. My finger's itchin' and my throat's remembering them hands o' yours."

Julius Hervey laughed easily. "Almost, Stiffleg. Almost. Next time maybe."

"That's all I got to say to you, Hervey."

"Straus, he won't like that none. He's got two-thirds and the say, Stiffleg."

"I got the post and the goods. Tell him that."

"Sounds like a little rift in Dance, Fitzhugh and Straus, Stiffleg."

"You call it how you want. I got my message to you. Now — am I gonna git past you and ride away or do we have us a tussle?"

Hervey eyed the fifty-three caliber bore of the Hawken pointing just to his left, and glanced swiftly at the thirty-two caliber bores of his pepperbox, and nodded. "A nice social visit, Stiffleg. I'll tell old Straus. You come visit anytime."

But Brokenleg wasn't listening to banter. He backed his way through the outer gates, his cocked Hawken never wavering. Hervey vanished from sight as Brokenleg rounded the corner. Brokenleg waited there for Hervey to peer around the corner and start firing that little popgun, but Hervey was too wily for that.

Brokenleg clambered up, having the usual bad time getting aboard a pony, and then squinted around murderously, ready to shoot. But Hervey let him go.

"I lost me a partner maybe," he muttered, actually believing the opposite.

Nineteen

The dayglow faded around the old plank door and Guy knew night had arrived once again. His nose tortured him. His face had swollen and never stopped aching but at least his headache had subsided grudgingly. He and Maxim sat in utter darkness, as if a great abyss separated them from the living. Cast into hell, he thought. His hunger ceased to torture him the way it had and he found his mind keener than he'd ever imagined it could be.

Maxim sat across from him, stoic and silent. Guy knew he was condemning himself for coming. It was the nature of sensitive seventeen-year-olds to condemn themselves and the whole world around them. But there'd been something else between them, too, unspoken but present. Love. Guy knew his son's soul was in turmoil. Life's brutalities didn't dovetail with his ideals, and he didn't feel so noble after all when confronting the hungers of his body. They'd been brought no food.

For some reason Hervey hadn't bothered them again. For hours Guy had dreaded the moment that Hervey opened the door intending to commit some sort of mayhem or torture on Maxim as a way of breaking down Guy's will. Guy probed himself, wondering what he'd do if that happened, and he knew he couldn't bear it; he'd do whatever Hervey wanted. But the minutes, and then the hours, whirled by. It puzzled Guy: Hervey was capable of anything.

The night grew chill; autumn had slid across the land outside of their prison. He and Maxim had no robes. Guy stood in the inkiness, unable even to see the oppressive walls.

"I'm going to walk to stir my blood," he said to the boy. "I might run into you."

"I'll walk too."

They found each other, clasped hands, and toured their ten-foot-square universe for what must have been half an hour. It felt good but it stirred up Guy's hunger and dizziness again.

They settled into the clay again, needing to talk. Guy sensed it in Maxim. A few hours in this sort of confinement was like a lifetime for a young man, harder for Maxim than for Guy.

"Evil is weak," Guy said. "Have I told you

why I have refused food?"

"No."

"It is my sole weapon. Hervey has power only over those who want life and liberty. When I don't eat he has no power over me. It's a way of telling him that I accept death."

"He has the power of pain, papa."

"*Oui,* he does. And he's hurt me. Hurt us."

"I deserve it."

"Ah, *cher* Maxim, you torture yourself more than Hervey ever could."

"You say evil's weak. We're evil!" Maxim's young voice cracked with emotion. "We violate the law!"

The question of the spirits again. That episode down in Bellevue had scorched Maxim's mind and fevered his imagination. "We are not alone, Maxim," Guy replied.

"Two wrongs don't make a right! Just because they debauch the Indians doesn't mean we should! It doesn't make it right for us to do it!"

"It's a hard world isn't it?"

"We didn't have to get into this business with those — criminals."

Maxim's accusations whirled out of the darkness like the voice of the burning bush confronting Moses, unsettling Guy. He had no very good reply. "Maxim. For decades

Straus et Fils has capitalized the fur trade. Each year the money we lent to the Chouteaus — or to the opposition — went into spirits taken up the river, or loaded into cannisters and carried out the Platte River road to the rendezvous on the Green River or the Popo Agie or Pierre's Hole. Your grandfather, my father, and I always knew that."

"Then we share the guilt." Maxim's voice seemed harsh.

"Are you sure you should feel guilty?"

"Yes! The spirits ruin the tribes. If they didn't squander their robes on spirits they could buy useful things from us! Tools, harness, traps, saws, axes, plows, cloth, seed . . . They could make something of themselves!"

"Like white men?"

"Yes!"

The darkness lay thick. He couldn't see Maxim although the lad was a few feet away. "Perhaps the tribes trade for what is useful after all, Maxim. A lot of our things they have no use for. You'll not find a man among them who'll harness a draft horse and plow and harrow and plant seed and harvest a crop."

"That's what we should trade to them, so they have no choice."

"No choice. Maxim, Maxim, what is liberty all about?"

"But these are savages, papa. They don't know that spirits hurt them. They've never had spirits."

"They like spirits, Maxim. So much that no post can survive without spirits."

"It doesn't matter what they like! They shouldn't have spirits. That's why Congress passed a law —"

"Several laws. Prompted by Eastern reformers. Who were right in a way."

"I know what you're telling me. You're telling me that life is real, and I don't appreciate that in business one has to bend a little. Just as Straus et Fils bent a little. But I won't bend. What's right is right! And I'm cursed with it."

Guy sighed. In every age that he knew something about there'd always been a few like Maxim, the few so principled that they'd rather starve than survive because all getting and spending seemed filthy to them. He admired them, to a point. They were reformers. They became monks and ascetics rebuking the world, saints and martyrs generating the hatreds of others. Was Maxim becoming one of those or was he expressing the absolutes of a seventeen-year-old? Guy didn't know. Those ascetics and reformers and men with burning souls so often took to burning others. The Spanish Inquisition came to Guy's mind, a process that tortured, tormented his own Sephardic people.

A sudden sadness sifted into Guy; a foreboding that he was losing a son. Especially when he said what he was about to say. "There are two implications for you, Maxim. One is that you should resign from a business you detest . . . and the other . . ."

"What other?"

"The other is that you should make your own way in the world now and not depend on Straus family money for your comforts. If it's tainted, Maxim, then you'll not want to spend it. At least if you wish to live by your principles."

"Papa —"

"It's something for you to think about. If we ever escape here. The prophets wore skins and ate honey and locusts and rebuked Israel. Some of them, anyway. The price."

"The prophets were right!"

Guy didn't answer. The sadness deepened in him and he felt a weariness upon him, a weariness of soul, of wrestling with life and its awful choices. He felt as if all wisdom had vanished from him and he was nothing more than an animal. They had wrestled with something that had no answer — unless the answer was God's mercy upon all sinners who fumbled through life.

Neither spoke the rest of the night although Guy sensed that Maxim wanted to. Guy had led the youth to the ultimate realities. He wondered whether, come dawn, the son who shared this dungeon with him would be a stranger to him. He had not driven Maxim out, but he feared Maxim would drive him, and all the generations of Strauses, out of his soul.

With the dawn his hunger returned, and the emptiness of his belly clawed unbearably at him. They drank the last of their water and waited. Maxim wouldn't look at him. Whatever the bond of the night, it was lost in the bleak glow of another day. Guy closed his eyes, trying to drive away the torment of his belly and the ache across his nose and face. He was beyond communing with the Divine except to mutter a simple plea for help.

He heard noises, the rattle of metal, and the door swung open along with his dread. But the man standing there wasn't Hervey; it was Isodoro Sandoval. Guy blinked. The streaming sunlight had a way of torturing his eyes at first.

"Come," said Sandoval. "You are free.

Senor Hervey says it."

"Free?" It amazed Guy. He'd been steeling himself for indescribable torments. "Why?"

Isodoro shrugged uneasily.

"Why?" asked Guy, insistently.

"Senor Fitzhugh came. He says to Hervey . . ."

"Yes?"

"He says, it doesn't matter what the bourgeois does to you and Maxim; he's not selling out."

"He said that?"

Isodoro seemed indignant. "You have no friend at all, this Fitzhugh. He cast you to the dogs. He says he'll keep the post going even if you both die."

"See, papa? Now you know how he is! He didn't care about us!"

But something else was blossoming in Guy's mind. "So Hervey gave up. It did him no good at all to hold us. And we are free."

"He had no principles!" Maxim snarled.

But Guy started laughing, wheezing, and bellowing, dizzy from hunger.

"I don't know why you're laughing, papa."

"That's something you'll have to find out for yourself, Maxim." He turned to Sandoval.

"You'll bring my horse and saddle around."

Sandoval eyed the clay. "Senor Hervey says to put you out of the gates on foot."

"Stealing my horse, is he? As well as our other horses and mules? No, Senor Sandoval. I'm going to sit in there and starve myself to death until he returns our property to us."

"Senor Straus — you must leave at once."

But Guy didn't listen. He settled back into the clay and propped himself up against the log wall. "I will stay here until he returns all stolen property. Tell him that."

Sandoval shrugged and wandered off to consult with Hervey.

"Papa! Come. Let's get out of here now! Before he hurts us more!"

Guy smiled. "Maxim, you have your principles and I have mine. Staying here and starving is my principle — and my sole weapon; the power of the weak against the strong, *oui?*"

"Papa! You must come now!" Maxim sounded frantic. He dove into the dark room again and tugged. "Come!"

"I am stubborn, Maxim."

"But don't you see? We're free!"

"Then go! What's stopping you?"

Maxim paused, confused. "I don't know. Oh, papa . . ."

"You'll do what you must, son, and I'll do what I must. Hervey has my horse. This post has a lot of my livestock, mules, horses. We'll take it back. Enough to pull wagons and carry hunters and give us all transportation. *Oui,* Maxim?"

"But you're so foolish! He's so evil. He'll —"

Guy laughed, his dizziness making him wobbly.

Sandoval returned, his gaze averted. And along with him three burly Creole engages. "Señor Hervey, he says no. He's keeping everything he got. He says if you don't walk out we must carry you out."

The Creoles and Sandoval looked uncomfortable but ready to execute their orders.

"Very well, Señor Sandoval. Let them carry me out."

"Papa, we'll walk. I don't want their filthy hands on me."

"You may walk, Maxim. I will be carried."

Sandoval sighed and nodded. One Creole clasped Guy's feet, the other slid his hands under Guy's shoulders. They lifted him up just high enough off the earth to keep his rear from dragging across the yard as they proceeded toward the open gates.

Guy knew two things: his position was undignified to all those engages who gaped at the spectacle. And his soul and spirit were visible to them all, including Hervey, who stood at the door of the factor's house and watched them carry Guy through the gates and deposit him on the naked clay in front of Fort Cass.

Maxim marveled at his father. Guy hadn't eaten in two days, yet he was walking the four miles back to Fitzhugh's Post without faltering, his body erect, his jaw jutting, his legs moving as rhythmically as steam pistons. They left Cass behind them and paced through a windy autumnal morning along the trace. Maxim was seeing something in his father he didn't know was there — an iron will governed by principle. His father had refused to leave his prison! His own father, Guy Straus! Hervey hadn't returned the livestock, of course, but somehow Guy had won.

What's more, Maxim felt his own shame. When they were given their freedom, the sole thought in Maxim's head was escape from Hervey's clutches. But his father turned out to be the more principled of them, accepting the terror and helplessness and darkness of that hole to make a point while Maxim had thought only of his own liberty. Furtively, Maxim peered at the father he'd never known before, seeing traits in the elder Straus that he wished he could emulate. And only hours before he'd been lecturing his father about principles! Maxim burned with shame, knowing that he'd been the compromiser and trimmer after all.

Was he wrong about trading illegal spirits for robes? No, he thought, he wasn't wrong. That sort of trading would continue no matter what laws were passed, because spirits were a commodity the tribes insisted on having. The real world would never acquiesce to his ideals. Robe traders did what they had to: some supplied the spirits reluctantly; others didn't care what effect they had on the tribes.

Neither of them spoke during that long hike. Maxim worried when Guy slowed down, obviously at the limits of his energy in his half-starved state. But Maxim said nothing. Instead, he admired the man plodding grimly beside him. Maxim knew, suddenly, he'd come into his own maturity this day. He'd discovered he had his own weaknesses and he had no right to condemn others, condemn his father, for anything at all.

They raised Fitzhugh's Post by mid-morning and discovered a few lodges there.

"Can you tell me what tribe they are, son?"

"I don't know. Not Crow, though."

They trudged past seamed old women and curious children and on into Fitzhugh's Post, where engages gaped.

"*Mon Dieu!*" exclaimed Samson Trudeau. He looked shocked, and Maxim realized how bad his father looked with his swollen nose and face, yellow and black and blue, and his stew-stained black suit and grimy flesh.

"I am hungry," said Guy.

Little Whirlwind snapped something to her sisters, who ran back to Fitzhugh's quarters.

Abner Spoon helped Guy into the barracks and sat him down on a bunk while many of the rest crowded around silently, absorbing the sight of a brutalized man. They stared at Maxim, too, but not with the same sympathy. Maxim shrank under their gaze: in their eyes he had been a traitor and a harsh critic. Someone handed Guy a tumbler of water which he drank greedily.

Brokenleg pushed into the room and stared at them both, his gaze raking Maxim cruelly and then settling gently on his partner. "Guy, Guy," he muttered. "You're hyar and in one piece I reckon."

Guy smiled wanly.

Maxim spotted Ambrose Chatillon pushing through the crowd of giant Creoles surrounding Guy. Chatillon surveyed Guy and smiled gently. "Monsieur, you have survived a fate worse than the wilderness."

Maxim discovered a vast, silent esteem flowing between the guide and his father, a bond forged from weeks on the long upriver trail. More than esteem, he realized. Mutual respect. The wiry guide plainly admired his father. The realization renewed Maxim's shame.

"Robert Fitzhugh," said Guy, and Maxim held his breath. It was the first time he'd heard his father address Brokenleg by his given name. "Is it true that you told Hervey you'd never cave in — no matter what Hervey did to Maxim and me?"

Fitzhugh nodded, scowling.

"You told him you wouldn't heed my instructions?"

"Sorta. I told him I wasn't doin' nothin' until you were both free." Fitzhugh met Guy's direct stare with a bright glare of his own.

"You went so far as to tell him you'd seek out new partners, new financing, if Hervey destroyed my son and me?"

Maxim dreaded what was coming. He recognized the muted thunder in his father's voice, and knew its lash. But then his father's voice softened. "I was tempted to cave in — anything, anything to escape that hellhole. But I overcame that. I refused to eat."

That puzzled everyone there except Maxim. Guy peered about at all of them, smiling gently. "When I accepted death he no longer had any power over me. When I refused to touch food he raged at me, poured a pot of stew over me — and walked out helplessly. He could not terrorize a man ready to die and starving himself day by day. I knew I'd won — until Maxim came. Then he had a new way of terrorizing me . . . but we survived that, my son and I." Maxim caught the proud glance of his father's eye.

"But we were still prisoners, Mr. Fitzhugh. And then you freed us."

Something released in Brokenleg's taut features. "I thought as how it might," he muttered. "I thought as how that devil might give up seein' as how it'd do no good to be poundin' and starvin' and holdin' you — and might git him into a heap o' trouble with Culbertson and Chouteau and them."

Guy sighed. "You'd never quit. Strauses

might come and go; partners might live or die — but you'd never quit. That's why I went into business with you and Jamie Dance, Brokenleg — that's what I saw."

Brokenleg scowled. He didn't like being assessed, being weighed, not by Guy Straus, not by any mortal. Maxim could see that. "I'll handle the post; you can handle the rest of 'er back in St. Louis," he muttered. It was a rebuke to Guy for coming up the river, for ignoring Fitzhugh's cautions, for being a *mangeur du lard,* the Creoles' word for tenderfoot.

But Guy was laughing easily. It made Maxim wonder: his father enjoyed this bristling porcupine of a man.

"Haw!" roared Fitzhugh.

The whole exchange bewildered Maxim.

Little Whirlwind pushed her way through the Creoles carrying a platter of sliced, cold buffalo tongue.

"Buffler!" roared Fitzhugh. "It's a strong meat — puts strength in a man."

Maxim and his father ate. Maxim wolfed down meat as fast as he could swallow but Guy took his time, telling the story of their ordeal to the assemblage in between bites. Or part of the story. Guy slid past the beating he'd received. And said almost nothing about the spiritual struggle that had led him to accept death. Or the discovery that not even Julius Hervey could break the will of a man ready to die. But even though he said little, the engages seemed to grasp the things Guy hinted at as Guy toyed with his meat. His father didn't eat a lot, and it worried Maxim.

"I've been the cause of some difficulties and worry here, gentlemen," Guy concluded. "I certainly apologize. In the morning Monsieur Chatillon and I will be leaving you. And leaving you with admiration. I think I know what sort of man it takes to run a fur post. I esteem you all."

"But papa — you've hardly been here —"

"Our business awaits me, Maxim. I've been away too long. You'll join us, I trust?"

Suddenly Maxim found himself the cynosure of all eyes. He did not see a friendly face among the engages. Brokenleg paused, glaring. Maxim knew Brokenleg wanted him to go. A few hours ago Maxim had wanted nothing more badly. But that was before he'd allowed Julius Hervey to herd him to Fort Cass. Everything had changed. Maxim glanced at Guy, who waited patiently for a response. He saw a man of steel and principle and felt a sudden rush of pride well through him.

They all wanted him to leave. He glanced

furtively at the engages, reading the contempt in their faces; the scorn in the eyes of Little Whirlwind; the flat antagonism in Brokenleg's glare. He felt small inside. He'd judged them ruthlessly for months, scorning the business, presuming it was corrupt and its participants were barbaric. They itched for him to say *au revoir* and head south.

He didn't know what to say at first. Or even whom to address. He chose his father. "I owe you and your confreres an apology. I owe Monsieur Fitzhugh an apology." He turned to look into Fitzhugh's glare, which struck him with the force of anvils. "I have learned that I was wrong; that you do the best you can in a world that — that you didn't create."

Brokenleg's glare didn't soften a bit.

"I am sorry, Brokenleg."

Nothing changed, except that Maxim wanted to crawl away from there. He'd lost the respect of these men.

"I want to stay and work hard and do my duties — if you'll have me."

He desperately wanted Brokenleg to say yes, stay, it'll be fine, all's forgotten and forgiven. Instead Brokenleg glared, his gaze boring in Maxim until Maxim wished the earth would swallow him up.

"I'll go with my father," he muttered miserably.

"Reckon there's no need. I need me a clerk."

"I'll make the best clerk I know how!" Maxim cried.

Twenty

The new pirogue bounced on its tether at the riverbank in front of Fitzhugh's Post. Like countless other pirogues built by traders and trappers to get themselves and their furs back to St. Louis, this one had been made from two giant cottonwood logs hewn into the shape of long canoes. These had square sterns and were carefully hollowed out until about two inches of wood remained, along with watertight bulkheads every few feet. Connecting the two canoes was a deck of hand-sawed plank which would store cargo. A mast projected upward from the front of the deck; a tiller from the rear. Two hand-hewn paddles, *avirons* the Creoles called them, awaited strong arms.

A pirogue could be handled by a single man but two or three were better: one on the rudder, the others paddling or setting the square-rigged sail. They could carry tons of cargo, such as beaver packs or baled buffalo robes, along with all the gear necessary to survive on the two-thousand-mile trip down the rivers.

Brokenleg knew he'd never see this one again. Building it had occupied his engages for several weeks. He had intended to use it to carry trade goods up the Bighorn for the rendezvous with the Cheyenne. But that had changed with Julius Hervey's theft of Guy's horse and saddle. The post had no spare horses for Guy, and no saddle either. Hervey and American Fur managed to make off with everything the post had, Brokenleg thought angrily. The pirogue would take Guy and Ambrose Chatillon safely down the river along with the four hundred baled robes the post had traded for so far. Guy had no other means of getting home other than hoofing it — with proper boots — the whole distance.

It irked Brokenleg. He could hardly get through a week without losing horses or mules or oxen — and now a needed pirogue. At least he got to keep Chatillon's saddle horse and a pair of packhorses, Brokenleg thought. Now he would have nothing to carry his outfit to White Wolf's village except for what could be carried on two pack animals.

But that's how it had always been in the mountains. There never was enough of anything, and resourceful mountain men learned to make do or do without. He had manpower, round adzes and axes — the entire makings of another pirogue. After his men built the mackinaw.

Brokenleg hated goodbyes and was ready to bolt. Around him stood every soul connected with the post; his men, his wives, and Maxim. A small crowd of Salish, out from their western valleys to hang buffalo and to trade, watched with avid curiosity.

"Well, Brokenleg," said Guy, kindly. "It's up to you now. The hearing is in January. We'll lose our license after this season or not. The key is Raffin, I think. Raul Raffin. That's the only clue I got from talking to every trader on the river. I don't know what you can do about it — we need a confession or a witness." He sighed. "Do what you can. This may be our last year. Unless a miracle happens, Mitchell will stop us. Stop us down on the Arkansas, too."

"I'll find Raffin," Brokenleg muttered. "Some way, I'll shake it out o' him."

"Frankly, I don't know how."

"I got my ways."

Guy smiled faintly. "I know you do. Everything's riding on you. We survive or go under. We profit, or we . . . don't."

"I'll see you in June," Brokenleg said, cutting it off. He hated this.

Out in the pirogue Chatillon was checking cargo, lashing down the tarpaulin over the mound on the deck. The square-rigged sail flapped and fluttered over him, ready to fill its belly with wind.

"Maxim," Guy said, his voice brimming with a sudden tenderness. "*Au revoir.* I'm proud of you . . . Be sure to —" Guy cut himself off. No admonitions this time. Guy was talking to an adult, not a boy.

"Papa —" Maxim left the rest unsaid. Brokenleg sensed that father and son had not only come to some profound reconciliation, but had bared their souls to each other in their long walks. There wasn't anything that needed saying now. "Shalom," Maxim added.

Guy, wearing his newly washed black frock coat and britches, shook hands with each of the engages, pausing to pat Samson Trudeau on the shoulder. Then — his face frozen peculiarly — he shook hands with Little Whirlwind, Hide Skinning Woman, Sweet Smoke, and Elk Tail, and finally with Brokenleg. Then, quietly, he clambered aboard, picked up a paddle from the near hull, and settled himself in its forward compartment.

From the riverbank engages tossed the loosened line into Chatillon's hands, and the swift current tugged the pirogue out and away. It drifted into the main channel and picked up speed and then swept around a broad bend and out of sight. The world seemed emptier suddenly. Brokenleg hadn't expected to feel loss; all the while Guy was present in the post Brokenleg had felt Guy's authority and power looming over him, judging, weighing, impeding him. He'd expected relief when the senior man in the company left — but instead, he felt a hollowness. He sighed, staring at the silent mob on the shore. Maxim looked stricken.

"We got work to do," he growled. He glared irritably at Maxim, neither liking nor trusting the young man.

Engages drifted toward the *chantier* to continue work on the mackinaw. Abner and Zach and Maxim headed back to the trading room to dicker some more with the visiting Salish people. His wives vanished in four directions to hunt roots and berries, gather wood, soft-tan some elkhide they were working on. He had to admit the four Cheyenne women had transformed the post, freed up his engages, improved their meals. Dust Devil had even kept her tongue quiet about the visiting Salish — who weren't ancient enemies of the Cheyenne.

He stared at his post without joy, feeling the brutal hand of the Chouteau company on it. In its yard lurked a wagon and ox yokes he couldn't use. Nearly every horse he'd brought or bartered for had vanished, along with a wagonload of good robes. It maddened him. Back in his free trapping days, he'd have picked up his Hawken and started hunting down his tormentors. But now — he was wrestling with the business of doing business. Everything he did these days had repercussions. He glared about him, thinking he'd never been cut out to be a storekeeper. He'd been the son of a New York State innkeeper and had fled that settled life — only to be some sort of storekeeper anyway. He'd never stop chafing, no matter how well he did.

Still . . . maybe he'd just quit being a storekeeper a while — long enough to git him what he needed, and maybe take the war back to Chouteau. He'd been toying with a notion for a day or two — nothing he'd try with Guy Straus lookin' over his shoulder. Or Maxim, he thought dourly. But ol' Guy was drifting past Fort Cass about now and out of Brokenleg's life.

He limped back to the post and into the yard looking for a horse. He didn't know what he had left. He recognized the small dun mustang Chatillon had ridden clear from Bellevue and decided that one would do. He poked a heavy iron bit into the gelding's mouth and buckled the bridle. Then he found his special saddle and an old blanket, and threw them over the dun and drew up the cinch.

Moments later he steered the surefooted little mustang up the trace toward Cass, intending to have him a little look-see. A mile below the confluence of the rivers he swung away from the river trace and poked through cottonwood timber toward the bluffs of the Yellowstone, and steered the dun up a grassy coulee toward the broken prairies above. Juniper and jack pine dotted the grassy slopes, giving him cover as he rode cautiously eastward. He kicked the dun up a hogback and peered cautiously over the top, discovering what he was looking for. The Fort Cass horse and mule herd grazed peacefully, under the watchful eye of two well-armed, mounted engages. Seventeen horses and mules, including the bay stolen from Guy. Brokenleg suspected most of the mules were his own though he couldn't prove it.

Each morning the fort's herdsmen drove the livestock out to pasture; each twilight the herdsmen brought the herd back and penned it inside of Fort Cass for the night, safe from Crow or Blackfeet pillagers.

He knew this wasn't the whole herd. The four or five post hunters would have saddlers and a cart or two for hauling in the buffalo carcasses. For Cass probably had twenty-five horses and mules. Brokenleg stared at the grazing animals, wanting them all. He wanted every animal Fort Cass possessed.

"I'll git ye," he muttered. "Ye owe me. I've lost a dozen oxen to your arrers — them Injuns ye hired. Ye owe me six mules, a few saddlers, and the Cheyenne ones that got stole. Ye owe every critter ye've got and then some. Plus some wagons. Plus a few hundred robes."

But that was only part of it. He wanted to put Hervey's hunters afoot just as Hervey had starved Fitzhugh's Post by stealing or killing livestock. Let them starve for a change! Let them go hunting on their own two feet. By gar, it wouldn't even up the score none, but it'd help a little!

A couple of the horses had picked up his scent on the westwinds and stared at the ridge. Brokenleg backed away and headed downslope fast. A few horses staring in his direction would be all the sign a herdsman needed to investigate. He kicked his dun toward a thick grove of juniper, raced around the back, and clambered awkwardly out of the saddle. Then he poked through the brittle dark limbs until he could observe the ridge. No one appeared. He waited a while more, waiting for a herdsman to show up, but none did. It pleased him. They weren't suspecting trouble. Few men, red or white, ever dreamed of bringing American Fur Company's own type of warfare to an American Fur post. But Brokenleg had just such a thing in mind. He wanted a dozen or so horses and mules and knew where to find them. The only difficulty was the broad daylight. There'd be no cover, and the act would be naked, made swiftly known to Hervey, to Culbertson, and down the river to old Pierre Chouteau himself.

But maybe that was good, not bad. Brokenleg's old trapper instincts rose within him. If they wanted a fight he'd give 'em a fight. If they snatched his horses he'd snatch their horses, and he wouldn't use bought Injuns to do it either. He'd been too cautious, or maybe bein' a partner in a big fur operation had put a crimp in him. This hyar struggle had been one-sided too long.

Feeling good, Brokenleg steered his dun back to Fitzhugh's Post and began running his hand over his balding head and red mane, something he never knew he did when he puzzled things out.

It wasn't something to rush into. Hervey had twenty-five or thirty men at his disposal; Brokenleg could scarcely muster a dozen. And Brokenleg had an ordinary log house with a stockaded pen attached to it — not a regular fur company fort with bastions. If he snatched their livestock they'd come running, and they'd find ways to break into the yard and take the animals back. Neither could Brokenleg graze his new herd without putting up a bloody fight day after day. Worse, Hervey could probably put his Crows to work, harrying Fitzhugh's Post, killing men and stock. If Fitzhugh started a war it'd be one with long odds.

He couldn't hide the horses either. The odd thing about wilderness was there it didn't conceal anything. He could spirit the livestock off to some prairie drainage and Hervey's Crows would discover it within hours. Livestock had to water at least once a day. Neither could Fitzhugh spirit that many horses out of the country without leaving plenty of sign. Still, it was that prospect that excited him. If he had twenty or thirty pack animals with packsaddles and panniers, he could haul a whole trading outfit to the Cheyenne villages, trade through the winter, and return with robes packed on the stock. And Hervey could do nothing but stew and rage.

One slow autumnal afternoon when only he and Zach Constable and Abner Spoon manned the trading room, he brought it up. He trusted their judgment. They'd waded the creeks and skinned plews and fought Bug's Boys as free trappers like himself.

"I'm thinkin' ol' Hervey's got a mess of horses and mules, and we hardly got enough to do our huntin'. What Hervey's got is mostly ours and I'm fixin' to do somethin' about it."

Abner's face lit up, but Zach peered warily at him.

"You be diggin' us some graves. And yerself," Zach muttered. "Next day there'll be about five hunnert Crows firin' their pieces through every chink and diggin' through the stockade to git the horses back. And ol' Hervey and his outfit'll be right hyar helpin' out. And then they'll burn us or starve us for good measure."

"How you gonna do it, Brokenleg?" Abner asked.

"Git clear out," Brokenleg said. "Throw packsaddles over their back, load up an outfit, and git on down to the Cheyenne for a winter of trading. All before they even hear about it over to Fort Cass."

"They'd come after ye anyway," Constable said.

"I aim to git their hunting stock, too. The whole herd."

"They'd git more fast enough — trade with the Crows."

"By that time I reckon I'll be clean out, headin' for Powder River."

Zach looked skeptical if not worried, but Abner listened intently.

"First thing Hervey'll do is git him some huntin' horses. That's how he hurt us last winter — keepin' us from making meat. After that maybe he'll be fixin' to make trouble. Send some of his Crows hyar to worry us a bit."

"Kill us and burn it down."

"There's that. And they got the men to do it."

"Fire, it burns where the wind takes it," Abner said. "Fire burns Fort Cass wood faster than our wood — it's older. I guess ol' Hervey knows that."

"Hervey don't care," Fitzhugh said. "He'll burn us if he's a mind for it. Kill us, too."

"I don't want any part of it," muttered Zach.

"You figure it's always one way? We take it and take it from Hervey and never deal out a little thunder? Is that it, Zach?"

Zach stared into the crackling fire, saying nothing.

"Remember old Sublette and Jim Bridger and them — the Rocky Mountain Fur Company? They pretty near whupped Astor jist by buildin' posts and keepin' American Fur busy in its own back yard. Like buildin' Fort Williams right thar beside Fort Union."

"Pretty near," Zach agreed. "But they didn't have no one like Julius Hervey callin' the shots then."

That was true. Brokenleg knew it made all the difference. Julius Hervey didn't care what got wrecked and who got killed. He didn't even care if old Chouteau took a loss for a few years if that's what it took to erase the opposition. Reluctantly, he admitted to himself that the thing he proposed could result in the death of his engages, the burning of his post, the theft of his trade goods and robes . . . and big trouble for Maxim.

"Who you gonna take with you down to the villages — if you do this hyar?"

"Me and my ladies."

"With twenty, thirty packhorses to pack and unpack and picket and water and guard?"

342

"Well, I was sorta seein' how the stick floated. You want to come? I thought to leave the post to Samson Trudeau and Maxim. I ain't sharin' wives, but maybe they'll introduce ye to some likely Cheyenne girls if'n you got the itch needs scratching."

That met with silence. He didn't expect a response, really. He was pleased that neither one argued that it couldn't be done. That alone made up his mind for him: these two coons not laughin' at him or sayin' it was impossible.

"I got to corral them Creoles and start buildin' packsaddles and halters and bridles, I guess," he said. "That's a heap of crosstrees and rawhide and all. And we got to make up a mess of panniers too if we got hides around. Should be some."

He knew they'd go. It'd take a few days for them to come around to it, though. He knew his good, solid chief trader, Samson Trudeau, would object and see only doom in it — doom for the post and its men; murder and mayhem and fire and war. He worried about Maxim, too. The lad had dug in, said little, done more than a day's work each day, wanting to recover what he'd lost. Brokenleg wanted to leave Maxim here as clerk and trader. The young man had picked up a lot of Crow and some Gros Ventre and some other tongues. But — he was the first thing Hervey'd go after. A hostage. Brokenleg wondered what he'd do if Hervey snatched the boy and threatened to kill him. Brokenleg thought about that and answered the question in his own mind.

Through a chill, overcast fall, well-built packsaddles multiplied in the warehouse, along with braided rawhide halters and bridles, picket lines and cowhide panniers. Brokenleg would have preferred lighter duck cloth, sewn and riveted into panniers, but they had none. His ladies filled in, turning each buffalo hide the hunters brought in into parfleches. They converted the worst of the trade robes into apishamores to keep the pack animals from galling. By the time the cottonwoods turned golden and the aspen yellow, Fitzhugh's Post had a pack outfit for thirty animals — but not the animals.

With the arrival of *Hikomini,* Freezing Moon, a young Cheyenne slid quietly into the post one evening, all but invisible to the nearby Crows.

"Aaiee!" cried Little Whirlwind, who jabbered Cheyenne with the young man and then remembered to introduce him to Brokenleg. "It is my cousin Bear Claws.

Chief White Wolf has sent him to you."

The chief wanted to know whether Brokenleg planned to trade at the Greasy Grass during the Freezing Moon as planned. They'd heard in the Cheyenne villages that Fitzhugh had no horses for his wagons.

"Bear Claws, you've come a long way," Brokenleg muttered in his poor Cheyenne. "You need a rest. I'm glad you came. I can't make it to the Greasy Grass to trade but you tell White Wolf that I'm coming with a whole outfit to the Powder to trade with his village all winter. I'll be there soon, in the Big Freezing Moon, *Makhikomini*."

"You are coming with the daughters of One Leg Eagle?"

"Yes, the daughters of One Leg Eagle, and two others to help with the packhorses. I'll have a whole trading outfit — enough to trade all winter. Trade rifles, blankets, knives, powder and lead, axes — everything."

"White Wolf is eager to trade. The Tsistsista need many things and have many robes. It was a good fall; we killed many buffalo and our parfleches burst with pemmican. And now the women have fine robes. He said to bring all the rifles and not to trade a one to the dogs."

"We'll do it."

Bear Claws peered about the post seeing only a few horses in the yard. "I do not see this string of packhorses, Brokenleg."

"I'm getting it. I'm about ready for it. A week maybe."

The youth waited for more, skeptically.

"Don't you worry. We had a lot of stock taken from us and I am going to take it back."

Bear Claws smiled. "I wish I could be along. I love to capture horses."

"I think maybe you'd better get our news back to Chief White Wolf. Where'll you be on the Powder?"

"Where Crazy Woman Creek joins it. It is the perfect place for a winter village. Before *Hikomini* has passed."

"One more thing, Bear Claws. Is the white man Raul Raffin still in your village?"

"He is."

"What's he doing?"

Bear Claws hesitated. "He likes to sit in the councils of the headmen. He listens much. He has taken a widow and cares for her. He knows White Wolf sent me to you."

Fitzhugh nodded. "Bear Claws. This is important. Whatever you do, don't let Raffin know we're coming. He's no friend of the Tsistsistas. He's there to keep me from trading. Tell all that to Chief White

Wolf. Ask the chief not to say a word — not to any headman, not to any medicine man, not to his wives."

"I will tell him."

The runner ate and rested, and trotted away from the post within the hour. Fitzhugh watched him go, wondering what Raffin would do.

Twenty-one

Everything was as ready as Brokenleg could make it. In the yard lay twenty-five packsaddles and all the necessary tack. A whole trading outfit had been snugged into panniers, along with whatever household things his wives would need. His wives' high-cantled squaw saddles were ready along with the hackamores the Cheyenne women used. If all went well the whole outfit would be loaded onto pack animals in the space of an hour. If all went well.

He and his men had saddled by the light of a torch. There were only six animals at the post including Spoon's and Constable's personal mounts. Brokenleg had commandeered them all. They had to pierce through the black vaults of night and be in place before dawn. Brokenleg nodded and the six horsemen steered their mounts through the gate, rode past a few dark lodges and up the eastern bluff. The night lay frosty over them but not bitter. No inky cloud hid the crystalline winter stars. This would be a cold business in every way.

Brokenleg pulled his beaver-fur cap tighter over his balding head to armor himself and ignored the cold fingering up his sleeves and around his neck, and along his calves. He'd spent his life in the mountains and had learned to endure discomfort. As they heeled the reluctant horses eastward he reviewed everything: the outfit was ready, his wives were ready. He knew where the Fort Cass hunters and herdsmen would go this early December day. For several days the hunters had ridden out to a small buffalo herd ten miles east. And the herders had been taking the Fort Cass livestock in the same general direction, enjoying the company of the hunters for part of the day.

This morning was going to be one the Fort Cass herders and hunters remembered a long time. Fitzhugh worried the possibility of resistance around in his mind. The last thing he wanted was war, injury, death — to his men or the Cass engages. He had no quarrel with the Creoles working for American Fur; only with the mad dog Hervey, who'd stolen or slaughtered Fitzhugh's stock as fast as it could be replaced. Now it was in the hands of Fate. One reckless move by some engage and someone would die. Fitzhugh wondered whether Guy would approve and decided Guy might. Guy would be far down the river now, maybe back in St. Louis — if he and Chatillon had escaped the endless perils of the river.

They rode into a graying dawn. The fugitive sun rose grudgingly in the southeast in this winter solstice time, shed no warmth, and hastened into exile after a brief appearance. It had been an open winter so far and they were leaving no tracks across an earth frozen as hard as an anvil. He could see the steam of the horses' breath as they carried the nightriders toward their rendezvous. At a certain broad coulee southeast of Fort Cass they halted. There'd be a long wait here. The Cass herdsmen rarely left the post until mid-morning. This coulee, which ascended to the high plains from the Yellowstone bottoms, had been the makeshift road of the Cass engages for weeks. No juniper or jack pine dotted its grassy slopes — except at one place near the top, where thick juniper carpeted a side drainage. Brokenleg had considered that lone concealment with delight.

His men dismounted in the tender light and stomped life back into their limbs. The horses snatched at brown grass. The engages pulled their saddle horses back into the juniper — and waited. The cold bit at them all. Brokenleg pulled off his mitten and stuffed a numb hand into his coat and finally under his armpit where the cold fingers enraged his flesh but absorbed its warmth. He wished they could have a fire. Men with numb fingers could scarcely load and shoot. Of course the Cass herders would be just as numb by the time they arrived here.

Trudeau said nothing and Brokenleg knew he didn't approve of this, especially since he would be lowering his cold rifle against fellow Creoles. But Samson Trudeau was loyal; his soul was given to his company. Abner and Zach would enjoy it; they had a wild, joyous streak that pointed them toward any convenient brawl. They'd all wrestled and roared through the rendezvous in the beaver days, and those who had been formed by the mountains carried those things with them out of the mountains.

When the sun was making a serious show of lighting the world, Abner signaled from his lookout up on a ridge. The men pulled their frosted rifles from their saddle sheaths, wincing at the cold of the steel in their hands. They checked caps and loads, shook their powder horns, and fumbled in their possibles for balls and greased patches. Men muttered. No one wanted to shoot, but shooting was a part of it. Brokenleg knew that these men would try to wound, not kill, if they were forced to fire at all.

The Creoles, Abner and Zach hid themselves in the juniper, each finding a bench rest for his rifle. Samson joined Brokenleg, and both of them mounted their cold animals and held them there, standing in plain sight of anyone coming up the coulee. They heard the herd and huntsmen before they saw them, the soft sounds carrying on the hard winter air. The Fort Cass herd appeared first — and stopped uncertainly at the sight of Trudeau and Fitzhugh. Brokenleg steered his horse to one side to let the Cass herd pass.

"I make it nineteen," he muttered.

"I counted twenty."

"Enough anyhow."

The mounted herdsmen spotted them, studied them a moment, saw two opposition men sitting harmlessly on their horses, and proceeded. Behind the herders came the Cass hunters on horseback, except for one driving a cart drawn by two dray horses.

Good. Together. Fitzhugh felt his pulse lift. These things could go bad in an instant.

"Bien, bien," said a herder. And then, seeing Brokenleg, switched to English. "The opposition. You are seeing where we

make the buffalo, *oui?*"

"You see any buffler?"

The herdsman grinned broadly. He turned to the hunters. "They want to know where the buffalo hide themselves." He shrugged. "We cannot keep you from following us, *oui?* It's a cold day."

The hunters pulled up. Three this morning, and two herdsmen. The hunters' rifles lay in the cart wrapped in robes, along with a few supplies.

The hunters and Samson exchanged things in French that Brokenleg couldn't get a handle on, but it didn't matter. They were all jabbering and smiling and having a fine time that cold morning, their breaths pluming with every word.

Until Larue, Dauphin, Spoon, and Constable emerged from the juniper thickets, their four rifles lowered.

Recognition pierced through the Cass contingent. "Ah!" cried the herdsman who seemed to be in charge. *"Sacrebleu!"*

A hunter eased toward the cart.

"Non," snapped Larue.

The man stopped.

Brokenleg, grinning, slid his rifle from its sheath. That made five rifles against five engages.

"Tell him these hyar horses and mules,

they belong to us."

Samson did. The hunters and herdsmen responded, and Fitzhugh waited for a translation.

Trudeau shrugged. "They say the cart horses don't belong to us, and the saddlers they're riding. But they admit the rest do."

"Tell 'em we're takin' 'em all and not arguin' about it. Old Hervey, he killed a dozen of our oxen and stole a bunch of Cheyenne ponies — you know. And then let's get this palaverin' over with."

Trudeau addressed the prisoners and in a moment all of them slid down from their mounts. The cart man clambered down with a longing glance at the rifles and robes.

"Tell 'em they got a long cold wait."

But that was already obvious to the Cass engages who were being herded back to the juniper thickets at gunpoint. Spoon unhitched the two drays from the cart shaft and collected the Cass saddlers.

"Leave them saddles on?" he asked.

Fitzhugh sighed. "Yes. And keep the harness on them drays, too. Hervey and them, they got Guy's saddle. And Raffin's bunch of Arapaho got all our harness and robes." He eyed the horse herd, which was drifting apart. "Let's git."

Back in the junipers Trudeau and his Creoles were tying legs and wrists with rawhide thong even as they joked with their opposites from Fort Cass. It'd be a cold wait but not a bad one, Fitzhugh thought.

He and Abner and Zach didn't waste another moment. They turned the livestock toward Fitzhugh's Post and drove the horses and mules slowly, not wanting them to get heated up and unmanageable. A half hour later they rumbled down the long grade into the Bighorn valley, threaded through naked cottonwood timber, and out upon the flat. A few of his engages whistled. The stock trotted easily into the stockaded yard and the gates closed behind them all.

"Let's git loaded and git going," he muttered. But he didn't need to instruct them. Engages caught animals, haltered them, slapped packsaddles over them, and hoisted the heavy panniers. His wives scurried about loading ponies with their truck.

"Anyone hurt?" Maxim asked. He looked troubled. Fitzhugh shook his head. Maxim grinned and saddled mules.

"They gonna have them an all-day visit, them Creoles. Have them a little fire to keep warm and do a little frenchie talkin' until the sun sets. Then ol' Trudeau and Larue and Dauphin'll ride on in."

"And Hervey's men'll have a three or four mile walk."

"Keep 'em warm."

Maxim sighed, wrestling with all of this.

Late in the morning a large pack outfit trotted out of the gates of Fitzhugh's Post with seven riders guiding it. Four Cheyenne women and three men. The remaining engages watched and cheered. By sundown that evening — when Trudeau released the Fort Cass herders and hunters — they were twenty-three miles up the Bighorn, and not stopping for nightfall.

Maxim watched the lone horseman with dread. Even from where he stood in the open door of Fitzhugh's Post he knew he was seeing Julius Hervey riding toward him on a chestnut. So Cass had a few horses after all. Most posts kept a horse or two in their pens at all times.

Maxim held the company's two-barreled fowling piece in the crook of his arm. It was charged with buckshot but it gave him no comfort. Julius Hervey could walk straight through two blasts of buckshot, grinning, murder in his eye. Julius Hervey could paralyze a man with his mocking stare; paralyze Maxim so badly he couldn't lift his piece, aim it, pull the hammers back, and squeeze the trigger. Hervey was like that.

Maxim peered about him. Samson Trudeau stood behind him in the post, also armed. Other engages crowded about, staring at the bourgeois of Fort Cass as he rode steadily, a horseman of the apocalypse. The doorway was the only place anyone could see out: the glassless windows had well-scraped rawhide over them, affording an amber light within. Maxim felt his own fear crawl through his gut and knew the rest felt the same terror clawing at them. Hervey rode alone and that somehow made it worse, as if this sole rider was more than a match for all the post's defenses.

On came Julius Hervey, his gaze taking in everything — Maxim and his piece, the engages standing behind watching his every move. Hervey smiled slightly and kept on. He reined at last before the doors, surveying the quiet post, the half-dozen Salish lodges nearby, the trampled clay and fresh horse sign around the high gates through the stockade. Then, with an invisible instruction to his horse, he turned it and rode slowly along the perimeter of the post, pausing on horseback at one point to peer through cracks in the wall of logs. Maxim knew he'd see no horses within. Brokenleg had most of them; the remaining three, two saddlers and a pack mule, were out with the post hunters.

Then Hervey vanished around the corner. Behind Maxim the engages ran through the post and out into the yard to keep track of the lone horseman, fearing fire or mayhem or murder.

"Perhaps he means no harm," said Samson Trudeau, obviously not believing a word. "He's alone."

Maxim shook his head. He didn't feel like saying anything. They waited at the door beside the trading window wondering if Hervey would return. A few moments later Hervey rounded the other corner and walked his chestnut straight toward them. Maxim's pulse catapulted. Hervey seemed unarmed save for a sheathed rifle, but Maxim knew better. Hervey always had a little six-barreled pepperbox and a vicious Arkansas toothpick. Maxim felt his terror rise as Hervey approached. He hated his own fear.

At last Hervey reined up before them, not twenty feet away.

"Stiffleg — he's gone."

It wasn't really a question. Maxim nodded.

Hervey laughed easily. "You're in charge, little Straus."

Maxim shook his head and mustered

some words which rushed out in a squeak. "Samson Trudeau is — our chief trader."

"You're in charge, little Straus. Why don't you come with me? I'll get you down the river to your old pap safely."

Was Hervey going to capture him — again? Maxim felt an odd tug, the call of obedience. His wobbling legs wanted to walk out toward Hervey of their own volition, as if the man had a magical stranglehold on Maxim's will. "No!" he cried. He lifted the fowling piece and felt the tremble in his arms. He snugged it in his shoulder and thumbed back the two hammers. They made loud clicks in the morning quiet. Beyond Hervey, Salish people scattered.

Hervey laughed softly and the laughter reduced Maxim to nothingness. He lowered the piece, not knowing why he lowered it. It was almost as if the buckshot would turn around and pierce him if he pulled the triggers.

Behind Maxim, Trudeau spoke up. "Go now. You have seen what you wanted to see."

"I saw what I wanted to see," said Julius Hervey.

"Fitzhugh evened it up, Monsieur Hervey. But it is not enough yet. You owe more still."

"It's all mine," said Hervey. He dismounted lithely, his eyes alert, and walked straight toward them. Maxim watched him looming up, terrified.

"I'll shoot!" he cried.

Hervey laughed and kept on coming. "I am going to see," he said. He walked straight by Maxim and Maxim swore his fingers had been paralyzed on the triggers. Engages toppled back to let him pass. Hervey walked easily into the trading room while engages fumbled in behind him, gaping. Hervey wandered along the shelves, examining goods, poking and probing, eyeing the shafts of Osage orange bow wood brought up the Missouri — a trade item American Fur didn't have.

"Stiffleg took most of it," Hervey said to no one in particular. Maxim sensed that Hervey knew the count on every item, knew what Brokenleg had taken, what he'd left behind.

Casually Hervey wandered from the trading room into the adjoining warehouse and eyed the heaped robes and bales. There weren't many. Most had gone down the river with Guy Straus and Ambrose Chatillon. Engages tumbled along behind him like the crowds that gathered for a guillotining. No one had the will to oppose this demonic man.

At last Hervey stepped outside and clambered onto his chestnut again, the mockery still upon him. "Better come along, little Straus."

Maxim lifted his scattergun again for an answer. He was taking heart now that Hervey was leaving. And then Hervey trotted off toward Fort Cass, leaving an odd vacuum behind him.

That was all. Maxim's dread eased through the rest of the quiet December day. The Salish traded a few more robes and lounged about, enjoying the visit. But the feeling never left Maxim that Hervey wasn't done; that he would strike back in his own way at his own time. He'd said as much.

That twilight the post's hunters returned carrying a doe and an antelope. No one had molested them. They unloaded the horses, fed them cottonwood bark, and hung the meat in the cold yard where it would freeze and keep.

Next morning, after the tardy sun began its low arc across the December sky, the hunters rode out for more meat. A few minutes later the Crows arrived. Maxim stood at the door of the post once again, seeing a whole village ride majestically onto the flat before the post, countless ponies dragging travois with lodges packed on them; men and women wrapped in creamy blankets, their breath pluming the air; starved curs slinking along. And warriors, too, flanking the village on their ponies, all of them wearing their coup feathers, their bonnets, and carrying their gleaming rifles and strong bows.

They were painted. Maxim stared at one and another, discovering white or black chevrons on their cheeks, vermilion on their brows, handprints on their medicine horses. On they came, a large village, several hundred men, women, and children.

Painted. A sudden chill swept through Maxim.

"You see that?" he cried to Trudeau.

The chief trader nodded and turned to his engages. "Prepare to fight," he said. Terrified engages dashed for their rifles, and stationed themselves at the windows. Fitzhugh's Post was no fortress with bastions at the corners. It was an oblong log building set in the corner of a stockaded yard.

But nothing much happened. The headmen approached the Salish, their hereditary friends and allies, and palavered there for a while. Then the Salish women began dismantling the Salish lodges and packing while the Salish warriors gathered their ponies. In a little while the Salish pulled out, even as the Crows were raising their own village well away from Fitzhugh's Post — a rifleshot away, Maxim thought.

By noon a great Crow village arced around Fitzhugh's Post, guarding its front flanks and the post gates. The warriors did not remove their paint, and even though cold winds drove most of them into their lodges, a few remained, watching, riding back and forth around Fitzhugh's Post.

"*Sacrebleu,*" muttered Trudeau. "We are prisoners."

Maxim didn't know for sure, but a dread had seeped into him.

Late that afternoon the post hunters — Brasseau and LeBrun — returned with a part of a slain elk. The pack mule carried two quarters; the hunters carried a little more. They rode unsuspectingly through the great encampment, past lodges belching cottonwood smoke, past the peaceful cones that shed light through their translucent covers.

Within the post engages ran to open the stockade gates. But the Crow warriors sprang into action. They grouped together and lifted their rifles and bows, some of them pointed toward the oncoming hunters, others covering the engages who had opened the gates. Brasseau and LeBrun halted, awareness flooding through them. Time stopped.

A powerful-looking headman with a great scar across his cheek motioned. Reluctantly the hunters dismounted. Paul LeBrun looked like a man about to die. Maxim caught his breath, horrified. He stood at the cracked-open post door watching. Crow warriors grabbed the bridles of the horses and then pointed. LeBrun and Brasseau realized they were being told to go into the post. Both ran swiftly toward Maxim's cracked door and stumbled in, panting. Neither stopped. They raced into the trading room to replace the rifles and powder and shot they'd just lost.

Maxim slammed the door and bolted it. He heard the stockade gates slamming shut — and something else. The smack of arrows striking the door he'd just shut.

Prisoners! Hervey's Crows had surrounded them. Hervey's Crows were violating the traditional neutrality of the post. Hervey's Crows would starve them all to death and keep other villages or tribesmen from trading — or helping. Hervey had struck back.

Twenty-two

They raced ever south and east, as if trying to escape from Winter Man. But he had them in his clutches and he blew upon their backs, sending icy air across their necks. Sometimes he spat snow at them, swift mad flurries from earth-scraping black clouds. But so far the snow didn't stick to the breast of Earth Mother. Winter Man blew, and scraped the iron earth dry, and piled up the snow in ditches and timbered slopes.

They made good time, harried along by the breath of Winter behind them whipping through their capotes and buffalo coats. Little Whirlwind drew the hood of her scarlet capote over her hair and laughed. She didn't mind. Winter Man was driving her toward the People. She and her man and her sisters would spend the whole winter trading with the Tsistsistas just as she'd always wanted.

No one pursued them. For a while her man and Abner Spoon and Zach Constable had watched behind, ready to fight, ready to run harder. But Julius Hervey never came, and only Winter Man deviled them. Ah, how it pleased her to see the captured horses and mules trotting along, as eager to flee Winter Man as their owners. She loved to watch the long string of them, twenty carrying what her man called the trading outfit; five more carrying their camp supplies. Wealth! She felt incredibly wealthy.

And more. At last her man had made himself a warrior. He had captured all those horses from the enemy and now he could wear two notched eagle feathers in his hair and show her village that he too was a fighting man, even with his wounded leg. That was worth more to her than all the wealth of the packtrain. Brokenleg was a true warrior! They would give him a new name soon. She would go to the shamans with a gift and ask them what Brokenleg's medicine name would be. She favored Many Stolen Horses but she knew it would be up to the grandfathers to decide. She peered over the pack animals at her man and liked that name. Many Stolen Horses. The shame she'd always felt about him lifted from her.

How swiftly the pack animals raced ahead! It gladdened her that they took no wagons. Wagons were almost useless. Every little while the white men had to stop, get out with an axe or a spade, and cut through brush or dig a ramp down a cutbank. Wagons took forever. She thought they were clever — who of her people had ever seen a wheel? — but almost worthless. She loved these horses and mules that were trotting along with Winter Man breathing on their rumps, each carrying a heavy burden. They didn't stop for ditches or cutbanks and they wove through sagebrush and juniper easily and splashed across creeks. They were traveling forty white man's miles each day, Brokenleg told her. Fast.

The Tongue River stymied them. Clear ice skimmed over its top, too weak to support man or horse. They could see black water gurgling ominously underneath. Brokenleg kicked his horse to the bank intending to break ice, but the chestnut balked. The more Brokenleg kicked and cursed, the more the horse dug in. Finally it whirled away and refused to budge. Spoon and Constable had no better luck, and neither did Hide Skinning Woman, Elk Tail, and Sweet Smoke. Twenty-five pack animals milled on the bank, scattering at every effort to force passage. Angrily Brokenleg dismounted, dug an axe out of camp supplies, and began hacking some long limbs off of a box elder. The others watched, puzzled.

"Watch our back trail," Fitzhugh growled at Spoon.

After he had cut and limbed four poles, he lashed them together into a crude raft. He slid it out onto the quaking ice and gently lowered himself onto it, having trouble with his bum leg. When he was prone he pulled out his camp hatchet.

"I'll probably git me a cold bath," he growled. "Gimme a line."

Then he pushed out, using his hatchet to claw ice and pull himself and his raft forward. The ice complained and threatened and once popped ominously, but the long poles spread Fitzhugh's weight. The Tongue ran narrow, perhaps fifteen yards, and at the far bank where an inch of water lay over the ice, Fitzhugh wormed his way off, getting wet and cursing. But he had his woven rawhide line in hand — and it stretched back across the river.

"Tie it to my hoss," he yelled.

Constable did, making sure the knot was firm.

Fitzhugh tugged and Constable whipped, and between them they forced the wild-eyed horse into the river. Its hooves flailed ice, shattering it into floes that slid beneath the surface sheet. Fitzhugh winched the chestnut along, sweating and muttering. The horse was soon out of Constable's reach, and only Fitzhugh's constant tension on the bridle drew it forward. It crashed through ice and then balked.

"Yell a little," Fitzhugh commanded.

Constable yelled and cracked his whip. The horse clawed forward again, up to its belly in icy water. It peered around and discovered Fitzhugh's shore was closer than the one it had just left. It shrieked and bounded forward, crashing through ice, cutting its pasterns and cannons as it lifted its legs out of the ice-traps, and finally bolted out of the water. It shook itself violently, spraying stinging-cold water over Brokenleg.

The results weren't good. The horse had opened a water passage partway but left the ice intact the rest of the way, except where hooves had broken through. Wearily, Fitzhugh prepared to drag another horse across. But he couldn't undo the clammy knot that anchored his braided line to the bridle. Water and pressure had shrunk it beyond the clawing of his numb fingers. Angrily he cut it off and then pitched the weighted line across the river.

The next horse came even harder than the

first, balking at every step. It peered wild-eyed at Fitzhugh, reared back, and crow-hopped, spraying its hooves in every direction. But at least its violent flailing loosened enough ice to open a water passage. After that they tied the line to a pack string and Fitzhugh reeled six unhappy packhorses across. Spray soaked the panniers, and she hoped nothing had been ruined. Little Whirlwind couldn't make her mare ford the cold river and finally Zachary tied the line to it.

"She's gonna buck," he said. "If ye get bucked in, stand up proper. River's waist high at the worst. Don't git sucked under that ice — or that'll be the last o' you."

Little Whirlwind nodded and clamped her high-pommeled squaw saddle. From the far bank Brokenleg coaxed the mare outward. Little Whirlwind felt the mare's back hump under the saddle and watched the mare's ears flatten back. The mare minced forward, hating the icy water. In the middle it halted. Water swirled around its legs, teasing its belly, touching Little Whirlwind's moccasins. Brokenleg tugged again. The mare bucked and Little Whirlwind clung. But the high water had taken the buck out of the little horse. It suddenly plunged forward, almost unseating Little

Whirlwind. The mare clawed up the far bank and shook, while Little Whirlwind hung on, gratefully.

Her sisters forded more easily. Abner Spoon, who'd been watching their back trail, was last and his passage was easiest. It had taken the rest of that day, and they camped there on the south bank of the Tongue out of the northwind.

They had two small tents, but Brokenleg had never used them as they were intended. Instead, he and Abner and Zach had made two half-shelters of them cornering around a fire. They plugged the ends of the open-sided lean-tos with pack panniers, making windproof shelters open to the fire, a much warmer arrangement than crawling into the cold tents. As long as someone fed the fires through the night they slept tolerably well in their robes even when the nights grew bitter. Her man talked of zero, but she didn't understand that, and when the white men talked of below zero, she laughed. How could there be anything below zero?

She supposed she and her sisters and Brokenleg would crowd into her parents' lodge but she didn't know what the other white men would do. They had to stay somewhere, and there was also a lot of trade goods to protect from Winter Man.

From the Tongue they swung east, racing over humped prairie with vast slopes pocked by drifts of snow. But only rarely did they have to fight through snow or break a trail. Winter Man's icy breath had swept most of the broken prairies clean, giving them passage and brown grasses for the ponies to eat.

Late one afternoon they stood on a wind-whipped ridge staring down upon a great river basin black with naked trees. A certain lavender light lay over the prairies, a light she never saw in the summer, a light subdued by an odd blue haze in the air. Her heart lifted. Off to the northwest she saw a pall of gray smoke hanging in a sheltered place. A village! Maybe her village!

"The Powder and the Crazy Woman?" she asked her man.

He nodded. "You reckon that's White Wolf's village?"

"Let's find out!" She heeled her mare, sent it racing downslope, upsetting the packhorses. She heard cussing behind her but she didn't care. Not even the icy air stinging her cheeks and biting her ears bothered her. They still had a long way to go, several white-man's miles, but she wouldn't stop now, so close to the Tsistsistas!

Beneath her the iron-hard earth jolted the

hooves of her mare but she never slowed. She felt wild and reckless, crazy as a magpie. She knew it might not be her village. It might be Lakota or Arapaho — or some enemy of the People. But recklessness engulfed her. She heard Fitzhugh yelling behind her but she didn't feel like stopping. Instead, she smoothed the mare into a canter that ate up the ground and sent the clatter of her hooves echoing across the frozen prairies. She descended a gentle bluff into the Powder valley, and felt the wind surrender.

She threaded through naked cottonwood timber, never slowing, the branches black against the lavender sky. She got lost, struck the bank of the Powder and retreated, pushing north and east through woods pocked with drifts. Then suddenly, even as the light faded, she burst onto an open flat and beheld a village, amber light radiating from each of the tawny lodges. She wasn't sure at first: she saw no people because they were all huddled around their hearth fires. But then the little things spoke to her; the way the wind flaps of the lodges had been fashioned; the way brush had been piled around some lodges to cut the wind; the way the village lay in concentric half-circles facing the river. And the way some lodges had been painted. Lodges she knew!

"Aiee!" she cried, delighted that she had caught the whole village napping. No dog soldiers had stopped her; no town crier raced among the lodges to announce her. She steered her heaving mare through the village streets, heading for the chief's lodge, something buoyant and joyous lifting in her breast, her heartbeat as fast as the mare's.

She found White Wolf's great lodge, and sprang down even as a woman's hands pulled the door flap aside and someone stared. She waited impatiently until she was summoned in, and then plunged into the sudden warmth and light.

White Wolf sat in his proper place at the rear with the hearth fire between him and the door, eyeing her curiously. And next to him, in the honored-guest place, sat Raul Raffin.

With growing relief Guy watched Ambrose Chatillon steer the pirogue through the bewildering ocean where the Missouri debouched into the Mississippi. The levee of St. Louis lay ahead. For eight weeks they'd sailed down the endless river, buoyed along on the current and driven by the tailing winds billowing out the square-rigged sail. A cast-iron overcast and icy winds marked this late November day, but they had escaped the bitter weather, sliding south just ahead of winter.

Excitement and sadness jostled in Guy's head. He'd come home safely across a vast and hostile wilderness he'd come to love in some mysterious and poetic way. Whenever he thought about what he had seen his soul wanted to compose songs or write epic verse. Chatillon had steered the double-hulled craft deep into the nights, using moonlight when they had a little, to carry him ever southward. Guy had come to love the sturdy pirogue with its giant hollowed-out canoe hulls that had forty bales of buffalo robes in their bellies. Evenings, as they drifted downriver, Chatillon had cut poles and built a tiny cabin on the crossdeck, which he roofed over with the duck cloth that had pinned their gear to the naked deck. They'd anchored safely at islands when they could, shot game along the banks in the lavender twilights, and slept in snug quarters on the rocking deck.

Guy watched the familiar city rise upward from the river under those lowering clouds, and joy built in him. In an hour he'd see Yvonne and Clothilde! Return to his gilded salons to tackle a mountain of delayed business. And have two long talks — one with

Pierre Chouteau *le cadet,* and the other with Indian Commissioner David Mitchell. He sighed. This long journey had been a failure. He had a name but no evidence.

"It makes snow," Chatillon said, pointing to a few flakes driven before the brisk breeze.

"But we're here," Guy said. "Just in time!"

Even as they spoke Chatillon swung the tiller and drove the pirogue toward the levee directly below the great Chouteau warehouse where the bales were destined to go. Expertly, Chatillon swung the craft close to the bank until a hull scraped. Not a soul stood on the levee that wind-whipped gray day. Chatillon leapt to land and secured the pirogue with braided rawhide lines to posts there. Guy felt a sudden sadness. This craft, hewn from wilderness logs, had been his home and a good one. He could hardly bear to give it up. He clambered down to the moist clay of St. Louis and peered around, dumbstruck by what he had achieved in four months. He, a sedentary financier, had traveled two thousand miles into a vast wilderness and back again. And not a soul waited on the bank to welcome him. It was as if he'd gone to the North Pole, or sailed a bark to unknown South Pacific atolls.

He and Chatillon stared at one another uneasily. They'd shared hardship, danger, and adventure, and now it was coming to an end. No barriers of class or wealth had ever separated them, and they'd often talked in rapid French long into the evenings.

Ambrose Chatillon shrugged deferentially, as if to say that St. Louis and polite society made things different. "Ah, Monsieur Straus. I'll get the clerks and warehouse men to unload. I'll have a dray bring your things to Chestnut Street, *oui?*"

"Get a receipt for the bales," Guy said, concealing his feelings with business matters.

"Indeed. I'm ready for some grog."

"You'll be wanting the rest of your fee, ah, Monsieur Chatillon." Against his will, formality had crept into his words. "You'll find me in my salon, or my house."

Chatillon shrugged again. "I will sample some grog first. My throat is parched and the grog shops *là-haut* — he waved his hand at the dives along Front Street — have pretty serving wenches." He smiled woefully. "I will come visit you later, *oui?* After a day or two."

"We'll say *au revoir* then," Guy said, relieved. He was no good at partings.

He stood silently while his wiry friend

walked to the Chouteau warehouse to rouse some clerks and stevedores. When at last Chatillon, a pasty-faced clerk — how white-fleshed they looked here in St. Louis! — and two slaves emerged from a dark doorway, Guy stirred.

Half a continent and back! He studied the gloomy offices of Chouteau and Company there on the riverfront, and a nearby building that housed David Mitchell and his Indian Bureau, and decided to see both men later. His family awaited him. He walked lithely up the steep slope to town, a slope he'd puffed his way up before the wilderness had hardened him. He wondered if they'd recognize him in his rough clothes, gray woolen britches and elkskin jacket and low-crowned beaver felt hat. He wore a deep tan, too, the product of months of blistering sun and unchecked wind. He felt faintly disappointed, wending his sole way up Chestnut Street after such a journey. But what had he expected? A brass band and bunting and speeches? Ah!

Gregoire admitted him, staring blankly at the stranger before him for a moment until recognition flooded into his bituminous face. "Monsieur Straus!" he whispered. "Monsieur Straus! I never expected, ah —" The slave fumbled for words. "I will fetch the madame," he muttered and fled.

Guy laughed and pursued Gregoire back toward the conservatory where the glottal sound of a harpsichord echoed. He found her there, bolting up from her stool.

"Guy!" she cried, staring at the stranger. "Guy!" Yvonne stood, her figure garlanded in severe black, and closed upon him. He swept her into his embrace, feeling her rigid body slowly melt as she hugged.

"I made it," he muttered into her silky hair. "All the way. Maxim is well."

"Oh, Guy."

She sounded so distraught that Guy gently pried himself free to look at her, noting the black. "Has something happened?" he asked, dread geysering up in him.

"Why — why do you ask?"

"You are in mourning."

"But —" She laughed hysterically. "For you. I just knew I'd never see you again. I had Madame make me . . . mourning dresses."

Guy roared. He couldn't help himself. Yvonne had always been the pessimist, seeing the worst possible conclusion to everything. Seeing doom before doom came visiting.

"My little Cassandra," he said, between wheezes.

"But Guy — I just knew . . ." Tears welled up in her bright eyes and she clung to him desperately. "I just knew," she muttered into his shoulder. "I'd never see you again. It's so far and so — so terrible . . ."

"It's not my ghost you're hugging," he said. From the corner of his eye he spotted his servants peering into the conservatory.

"Gregoire! Fresh coffee!"

They fled.

"And Clothilde is well?" he asked.

"Of course. But she won't listen to me. She wears summer frocks in this . . . this . . ."

"You are beautiful in black. You are beautiful in anything — or nothing."

"Oh, Guy!"

He had much to tell her and some things to conceal because she couldn't bear them. He had decided not to say anything about his imprisonment by Hervey, his lonely vigil in that cubicle in which he came face to face with his own mortality and understood death and life for the first time. And he wondered, too, what to say about Maxim and Maxim's scruples. He'd tell her that, he thought, but not just yet. In the dark, during their communion of souls and bodies, when they lay beside each other. Then he would talk about Maxim's anguish of soul and the bitter compromises that life imposed on all mortals, including himself. Actually, Guy was proud of his son, proud of Maxim's stringent scruples, proud that the young man's restless soul sought those things that were right, and tried to make the world right.

For now it was enough to assure his dear Yvonne that all was well — and not well. Fitzhugh had traded for only a few robes and had lost several hundred he'd traded from the Cheyenne, along with two freight wagons and all his stock. He'd been checked and defeated by American Fur at every hand. But that wasn't the worst of it either. It occurred to him that his gargantuan effort had failed. They'd lose their license; they might have to pay a fine or see their robe returns confiscated, depending on what the Indian Bureau chose to do.

"There is this sadness," he said to her later as they sat on the settee and sipped the chicoried coffee. "I stopped at all the posts and talked to the traders. I did find out some things. I have a name and even a motive. One named Raul Raffin — an engage of Pierre *le cadet* for many years. Everything points to him. None among the bourgeois at the posts thinks the company did such a thing. Putting those casks aboard among our dunnage. But Raffin, ah, madame. He was a rival of Brokenleg long ago for the affections of Little Whirlwind."

"I wish they'd both failed," she replied tartly.

He nodded. "And I can't prove a thing. I have the name, the man — and nothing to present to David Mitchell. I will tell him what I know — and he will shake his head and remind me that rumors and scapegoats won't rescue the Rocky Mountain Company. I fear we'll lose our license after all."

"I knew it would fail," she said. "I wear my mourning clothes for Straus et Fils."

Twenty-three

Nothing in Pierre Chouteau Jr.'s riverfront office spoke of power except the man himself. He welcomed Guy with a small Gallic pucker of the lip and then settled himself behind his battered desk among his dusty Indian artifacts and fossils. But Guy knew that this dark-haired man with the sardonic smile was the lord of half a continent. No one, not the United States Government and its agents and armies, exerted as much dominion over a territory that extended from the Mississippi River westward to the Mexican possessions and the disputed Oregon country.

"Ah, my friend Straus, you're safely back in St. Louis. I trust your business goes well?"

"Couldn't be better," Guy responded.

They both chuckled. Like God, Pierre Chouteau knew the flight of every sparrow.

"That's good and bad. Too many robes. The market can't absorb them all. Why, Ramsey Crooks and I have just agreed to hold some back to keep the prices up."

"Sorry to bring them down again."

Chouteau shrugged. "Four hundred robes."

Fencing. One never talked with Pierre Chouteau forthrightly, cards on the table, Guy thought. It was always a trade-off — a peek at something in exchange for a peek at something else. And Chouteau played his games as well. Like telling Guy how many robes Guy had brought down the river in his double pirogue. This banter was the only kind of business negotiation that Chouteau understood. And it took a quick mind to understand it and counter it. Anyone who didn't understand Pierre *le cadet* would suppose it was banter over steaming tea.

"You have an engage named Raul Raffin."

Chouteau looked puzzled and pursed his lips. His eyes gleamed. "Why, the name is unfamiliar. What post is he at?"

"Wherever you assign him, Cadet."

"Ah, my poor tired brain. *Oui,* I recollect. We have such a man. They come and go, the Creoles."

Guy smiled. Raffin had been with American Fur for years. "He interests me. Do you know his whereabouts?"

"I suppose you wish to steal him from us.

Ah, the opposition. We put up with many trials from the opposition."

More banter, Guy thought. "He failed to show up at his post last summer."

"Ah, I hadn't heard. And which post was that?"

"You'd know better than I, Cadet. I suppose you've removed him from your rolls. A deserter."

"We don't like deserters, Guy. Let a man abandon his contract with us for no reason, and he never works for Chouteau and Company again. I'll check." He rang a small silver bell and a ruddy clerk in a shabby black suit materialized.

"Have we a Raffin on our roster, Hieronyme? Be swift, if you please."

The clerk backed away and Guy swore he left dust floating in the sunbeams.

"Now we will know for sure. I trust this man has behaved himself?"

Fishing, Guy thought. Chouteau revealed nothing and sought everything. "No, he has not. He probably damaged my company."

Chouteau arched an eyebrow. "Men have their foibles. Perhaps it was a love rivalry. I always ascribe rash conduct to love, to rejection by a beautiful woman. Ah, women! How they govern the affairs of the world!"

Chouteau knew a lot, Guy thought. He

probably knew everything his own factors and traders had told Guy upriver. He obviously knew that Brokenleg and this Raffin had once competed for Little Whirlwind. Maybe it was true. Maybe Raffin had some longstanding grudge against Brokenleg. It made a good story. The sort of story that could conceal darker purposes.

Guy smiled gently. "An engage would have to spend more than a year's salary to buy three casks of spirits. How could he live, eh? An engage spends his annual salary and more at the posts. No, Cadet. There's more."

The faint smirk returned to Chouteau's face again. "Ah, logic," he said. "The downfall of accountants. Men with passions act — no matter the costs! Especially the French!"

Hieronyme returned bearing a battered ledger and set it before Chouteau.

"Why, he's engaged — this year and the next two. But if he's abandoned his contract, why, we'll scratch him off. We've hired our share of loafers and scoundrels — and discharged them. We want good men up the river. I must look into this Raffin." He handed the ledger to the clerk. "Hieronyme, find out what you can about this Raffin. Monsieur Straus believes we have an unruly engage who has fled his post."

"Bien," said the clerk, dusting his way out of the office.

It was a charade, Guy knew. Something about Cadet Chouteau led Guy to believe that none of this was news. Every conversation Guy had had with the American Fur factors and traders up the river had been duly reported, in minute detail, to this man across from him. In a way, though, the whole interview had helped. Cadet Chouteau would not be fencing so much if he had nothing to conceal. He might even be helpful. Neither of them had broached the subject of the three planted casks of spirits in the cargo of *The Trapper* — and Cadet's lack of curiosity said a lot.

Guy stood abruptly and gathered his walking stick and cape. "I must be off, Pierre. You've been most gracious, as always."

"But you've barely arrived —"

"I found out what I needed to know," Guy said roughly.

For a second, Cadet's gaze froze, only to melt again into his purse-lipped mockery. *"A bientôt!"*

It had been a typical session with Cadet, Guy thought as he pushed into a biting wind toward that other place on the waterfront he wished to visit. Not a candid word; everything buried in veils of wit and deception. Not lies, really. He'd never discover Cadet in a naked lie. But simply layers of innuendo and deceit that concealed truth.

He found the Indian Bureau's superintendent, David Mitchell, shoveling sticks of wood into his potbellied office stove. No polite minions guarded his door even though this complex of offices in a waterfront building was a bureaucratic empire rather than a commercial one.

"Guy!" cried the commissioner. "I'd heard you got back yesterday with forty bales. Back your tail up to the seat and tell me."

Word of his return seemed to have whipped through St. Louis, Guy thought, remembering their lonely docking on a silent levee.

With Davey Mitchell there'd be no pussyfooting around the thing that interested them both. And even the upriver gossip would wait. "I have the name of a man," Guy began without preliminaries. "An engage named Raul Raffin. He'd been with AFC for a decade or so."

"I remember him. Big dark Creole."

"That's what they told me. He went up on

The Trapper with several other engages — beginning his new term. And abandoned the company at Fort Pierre, striking west. He's living with the Cheyenne in White Wolf's village."

"What does this have to do with — anything?"

"He's the one."

"You don't know that."

"No, but he's the one."

"That's not going to help you a bit."

Guy sighed. "That's the trouble. I don't have a thing to tell you."

"How do you know? I mean, Guy — you have a name. What else?"

"Every American Fur trader and factor along the river — Sarpy, Chardonne, Kipp, even Culbertson, thought it was the act of a lone man, not a company thing. I'm not so sure, Davey. How would an engage without a *centime* afford three rundlets of pure ardent spirits? Why would he? They all suggested he had a grudge against Brokenleg, but . . . that's not the way a man with a grudge acts. No. Raffin had a silent partner or two, and this was directed at my company."

A wry smile lit David Mitchell's face. "If it was your company's spirits that Gillian poured into the Missouri then you must be dry up there on the Yellowstone. But if you've spirits up there, then those rundlets were planted. All you have to do, Guy, is swear you have your own spirits on hand, the casks you probably loaded at Sergeant Bluff or somewhere near there . . . But now you'll tell me you haven't a drop of contraband at Fitzhugh's Post."

Guy didn't answer. He couldn't answer.

Mitchell laughed raucously. He hawked and spat at the stove, and the gob popped into steam. "Let's go back to Raffin. How d'you know?"

"He's there with the Cheyenne. Brokenleg traded for a lot of robes and some horses while Raffin hung around — and when Brokenleg started back, he was robbed of everything, including the horses."

"By?"

"Arapaho."

Mitchell shook his head. "What does that prove?"

"Why — that Raffin is destroying our Cheyenne trade. His marriage is the one advantage we have over American Fur. Someone — maybe even Cadet — pulled him off his regular duties, bought the rundlets of spirits, had Raffin plant them and alter the cargo manifest — and then head out to the Cheyenne to keep on making trouble with us."

"Guy, can Raffin read and write?"

"I didn't ask."

"If, as you say, someone added those casks to Captain Sire's cargo manifests — that someone had to read and write. Maybe you'd better find something written in Raffin's hand. I've got Sire's cargo manifests right here — they're evidence. Get a sample of Raffin's hand and you might have a case, eh?"

Guy felt dumbfounded. He'd missed the obvious.

"Cadet might have something written by Raffin — if you can get it," Mitchell said. "Which you won't. He's not dumb. But you haven't much time, Guy. I postponed the hearings until January second to give you a chance up the river. I have half the reformers in the East on my back — saying I'm kowtowing to the corrupt fur lobbies. Maybe they're right. I can't hang on, Guy. You'll have to be here — or your counsel — on the second."

"What will happen?" Guy asked.

"Three affidavits from Bellevue. Foster Gillian's, his wife's, and one from his factotum, a young divinity student with fire in his eye named Marshall Landreth. They can't leave Bellevue — not with river ice, in winter. But Captain Sire is here and'll testify. And several others who saw it."

"It's a trial?"

"Nope. Indian Bureau hearing. All we need to pull a license. But we follow ordinary rules of evidence. By several acts of Congress spirits aren't allowed in the Indian Territory, except for boatmen's rations. The law's been broken — by someone. We — I mean myself and whoever they send out from Washington City — if we find it against you, we'll pull your trading license end of this robe season."

"The southern post, too?"

"Both. Same company. I'm sorry, Guy."

"But Dance's in Mexico."

"Trading with our tribes. Sendin' robes back over our territory."

"And what do I need for a defense, David?"

Mitchell shrugged. "Not for me to say, really. None of this is for me to say. But you need to prove someone else did it — it wasn't your stuff. Maybe you could prove it by swearing you've got your own stuff up there." A quirky grin slid onto Mitchell's face and stuck there. Guy wanted to laugh with him, but it hurt too much.

Fitzhugh's Post was dying. A great Crow encampment clamped the post like an eagle's talon, letting nothing in and nothing out. It formed a great arc, pinning the post from all sides except the river.

Maxim knew the end was near. But he didn't know what end or what to do. They'd run out of firewood, and now they huddled under robes against the brutal December air. They'd run out of meat; the hunters couldn't leave. When they tried, they'd been driven back by volleys of arrows. In the yard, the two remaining saddlehorses and the pack mule starved. The woodcutters couldn't get out to cut cottonwoods and strip the logs of good green bark, which made a winter feed for livestock.

They were running out of water. Brokenleg had meant to dig a well but it hadn't been done. Instead, he had filled several kegs with river water and stored them against emergencies. Most of that foul-tasting water was gone and the remaining keg was frozen solid. The stock hadn't been watered but the engages had chipped ice from one keg and melted it over kindling made from butchering a bunk — and quenched their raging thirst.

"We can slaughter the mule," Trudeau said. He and Maxim stood in the yard, staring disconsolately at the animals.

Maxim nodded. They could do that. "We

could try to dig a well. We're only fifteen feet above the river," he said.

Trudeau laughed. "Starving men digging a well?"

"There'd be mule meat."

"Ah, young Maxim, where would it lead us?"

"Brokenleg never gave up. He said in the mountains you never give up."

Samson slid into silence, staring at the cottonwood palisade around the yard. "They haven't fought us. They could overwhelm us easily. A few engages against so many. Maybe we could try the white flag again — try to parley again."

Maxim thought they might try, but he knew they'd be driven back. This village and its headmen were under the thumb of Julius Hervey and would do nothing that was not Hervey's design. "What'll we offer them?" he asked.

Trudeau shrugged. "It's for them to say — if they'll parley."

"I think they'd let us go — if we left everything behind. Walk out," Maxim said. "That's what Hervey wants. For us to walk out and leave the spoils."

"We could fight," Samson said.

They'd considered that a hundred times, with every growl of their hungry bellies. The

Crows had pitched their lodges out of effective rifle shot. A naked plain, whited with packed snow, surrounded the post. For six days and nights the engages had peered over the stockade and counted the lodges and debated war. This Crow village could field somewhere between a hundred fifty and two hundred warriors, most of them armed with trade rifles.

"I don't want to if I can help it," Maxim muttered.

Samson Trudeau became very gentle. "Ah, young Maxim. All the ones who've been in the mountains, the beaver men, they've been in corners as tight as this. Against the Pieds Noirs mostly. Fate — Fate sometimes decrees a victory if brave men seize it."

Maxim blinked. "We can escape with our lives — if we walk out. That's what Hervey wants." A wave of anger engulfed him. "And that's what he'll get tomorrow. Time's running out."

"There's one thing, Maxim. I am many years in the mountains and this I know. Indians don't like sieges. They're impatient. They love another kind of war — swift attack and ambush on horses. But they are not made for this, *non*. Maybe tomorrow they will pack up and leave."

Maxim laughed bitterly, and yet Samson had given him a thread of hope. "Let's try, Samson. Fitzhugh would try. We can tear down that shed for firewood. We can slaughter the mule for meat. And we can start on a well — if we can chop through the frozen ground."

A wry twist of a smile built on Trudeau's lips. "All because we hope to wear them out. Very well, young Monsieur Straus. We will do this."

That gray morning, under Samson's direction cold-numbed engages began chopping down the commodious shed in the yard, where harness and saddles and prairie hay and cottonwood fodder had been kept. It had a sod roof over logs, and would give them a lot of heat. Jeannot Provost and Gaspard Larue slaughtered the bleating mule, letting its hot blood gout from its throat. The engages watched hungrily. The rest tackled the new well. Lebrun and Grevy hacked at the frozen clay with axes and discovered the frost went down only a foot. The rest found shovels and spuds and began loosening and pulverizing the resisting clay. It gave them something to do and they became cheerful.

"We dig a grave for us all, *oui?*" joked Bercier.

Gallows humor.

Several times they spotted Crow warriors peering at them through the chinks in the stockade. Maxim clambered up to the shed roof where he could see out, and found the Crow camp in some sort of excitement, blanket-clad warriors eyeing the post. Some of them hastened north — to tell Hervey of these things: engages digging a well; a mule being cut into usable pieces before it froze solid; smoke from the post chimney.

They toiled all that brutal day, driving the six-foot diameter well down four feet, hoisting out rock and clay, and hammering one boulder to pieces. They devoured stringy mule meat as fast as it could be boiled and softened, and eyed the remaining horses expectantly. Night fell along with the temperatures, but still they hacked and chopped and snatched pitiful bits of icy clay out of the deepening hole. The starving horses nickered and bleated, wanting water and food. The anemic white moon quit them before midnight, and the engages piled angrily under their mountains of buffalo robes, shaking with cold.

At dawn the next morning Julius Hervey sat his dun horse before the post. "Little Straus," he yelled.

No one had seen Hervey ride in. He was

simply there as the day brightened, his breath pluming the hazy dawn. Maxim peered through a crack: Hervey waited alone. His Crow allies stayed well back — out of rifle range.

Maxim opened the door a bit, saying nothing. His scattergun felt comfortable in the crook of his arm.

"Ah, little Straus. You can leave safely, you know. On down the river."

Maxim shook his head.

"You'll die, little Straus."

"And you'll be out of American Fur — the scandal will be too much."

"Where's St. Louis did you say?"

"Then we'll die." Maxim didn't feel like dying but he said it because Fitzhugh would say it.

"The Kicked-in-the-Bellies are great friends of mine, little Straus. They know where to trade."

"I'm through talking," Maxim said. Some fiery impulse flooded him. He lifted the fowling piece, aimed it, and squeezed the icy trigger. The explosion rocked the piece into his shoulder. Buckshot hit the dun, which screeched and began bucking. Hervey flew off, catapulted slowly to the frozen earth, bounced, tumbled, and lay still.

Maxim stared, shocked at his own act. Had he murdered a man?

Slowly, Hervey sat up, shaking his head, recovering his wind. The horse sagged to earth, its lifeblood spilling from a dozen holes in its chest and withers.

Julius Hervey stood, shakily, and the wild look in his eye terrorized Maxim.

"You're dead little Straus," was all he said.

Maxim slammed the post door, just as several lead balls from Hervey's pepperbox smacked into it.

Twenty-four

Something bright and predatory kindled in Raul Raffin's eyes. Little Whirlwind noticed it as she settled herself in the woman's place and undid her red capote. The heat felt delicious. Chief White Wolf waited patiently for her to settle herself. Unlike white men the People were never in a hurry.

"Our daughter of the village has returned to us," he said at last. "Is your man with you?"

"He's coming. I saw the village from the bluffs and put heels to my pony."

"Is he alone, Little Whirlwind?"

She knew the question contained a lot of questions. "No, my chief. He brings his wives, my sisters, and a whole trading outfit — many pack loads — and two other white men to help."

Raffin listened with bright curiosity and she saw something like triumph flare in his eyes, which left her uneasy. He'd said nothing and yet his eyes had spoken to her already: they roved over her face and figure, caressing her, possessing her. And they revealed amusement, too. She hadn't liked him winters ago when he and Brokenleg both courted her, she liked him less now.

"They are coming, then. I'll summon the wolves to help them." He rose slowly and walked around the sacred altar and the central fire, which billowed smoke in his wake. He vanished into the twilight and she knew he would send the village police, the dog soldiers, out to escort Brokenleg.

"Ah, Little Whirlwind," said Raffin. "I've waited for this moment." He spoke in accented Cheyenne.

"You'll have to keep on waiting."

He laughed. "I will have you," he said. "Stiffleg never was a match."

She formed a sharp retort but White Wolf clambered through the oval entry and closed the door flap behind him. He settled against his reed backrest in the place reserved for him exactly opposite the lodge door. His rheumy eyes peered at each of them, as if he'd sensed that an exchange had occurred in his absence.

"My daughter, I will hold you only a moment. You are eager to fly to the lodge of One Leg Eagle and Antelope. They will welcome you with joy. Our village rejoices that you and the Badleg have come . . ." He nodded toward the white man sitting in the place of honor. "You know this one, I am sure. We have welcomed him here many winters."

"I do."

"Tell me, will the Badleg and his men need a lodge?"

"I think they do, my chief. They have two little cloth tents that have no warmth in them."

"It will be done, then. The widow, Makes the Doe Come, has a great warm lodge. I will invite her to stay here. She'll be happy to have someone to talk to. My wives will make good company."

"The white men will be grateful, my chief. They are called Abner Spoon and Zachary Constable."

Raffin laughed shortly.

White Wolf turned to Raffin. "You know these men?"

"Ah, *oui*," Raffin said, lapsing into French. "In the mountains."

The chief said nothing for a moment, as was the way of the Tsistsista. Then he addressed Little Whirlwind. "Monsieur Raffin has heard that you and Badleg were coming to winter with us. He came this very day to tell me that those he is with, American Fur, will bring a trading outfit of their own to our village. He tells me they will offer us twice as much for a robe as Badleg. No matter what Badleg offers — they will double it. And the price of their trade goods will be exactly Badleg's price. This he told me before Sun vanished. And I told him, yes, that is tempting and my People would benefit — for a winter. But it would put Badleg out of the trading business. And then American Fur would have no rivals and would make its prices high again. I told him that, and I also said that Badleg is an adopted son of this village, one of our People by ceremony."

Raffin followed all that, the gleam never leaving his restless eyes. "I know when I am defeated," he said, but the way he said it made her wonder. A foreboding filled her. Would Brokenleg trade all winter only to lose his robes and horses again — to that scheming treacherous Raffin?

"You took our robes and horses from us before," she said.

White Wolf raised his hand. "We will not hear such things," he said sharply.

"The Arapaho dogs. He set the Arapaho on us."

"Little Whirlwind. You have not lost your contempt of other Peoples," said White Wolf. "Go now to visit your own lodge. I hear the People stirring anyway."

Dismissed. She pulled her capote back on and crawled into the winter night just as her man and the long string of laden pack animals wended through the village, illumined by the amber glow of the warm lodges. Something joyous welled up in her. All her dreams had become real. Here she was in her own village, and here was her man bringing treasures to the People — fine rifles, blankets, axes, kettles, awls . . . everything the People could want for their comfort and safety. She looked for her sisters and didn't see them. They'd gone to the lodge of her parents.

Brokenleg steered the great procession of horses straight toward the chief's lodge for the welcoming, even as blanket-clad Tsistsista People poured from the warm lodges to see this great event. "Hyar, Dust Devil," he called, cheerily as he reined up. Breath plumed from his mouth and the horse's nostrils in the deepening cold. She gathered her own pony and held its reins, postponing the moment when she would greet her parents because everything she was witnessing was so grand, and she was the sits-beside-him woman of this great trader. She felt the envious gaze of all the women in the village upon her.

She turned and discovered White Wolf emerging from the lodge, grasping a thick blanket tightly about him. And Raffin followed. They, too, would not miss such a sight.

Brokenleg staggered to the ground. He could never dismount the way others could because that stiffened leg prevented it. But he landed and stomped as he always did while Spoon and Constable herded the neighing pack animals into the open area before the chief's lodge. She caught the sour scent of cottonwood smoke on the air, and the scent of cooking — the meat of *Pte,* the sacred buffalo. The People had found many this winter.

"Har, Chief White Wolf. I come. I got me an outfit." He stopped suddenly, staring at the bearded white man standing beside the chief. "Unless you got other plans," he added, tersely.

Her man had forgotten to speak in the tongue of the People, but White Wolf didn't seem to mind.

"Son of the People, you are welcome. We will trade when Sun returns. We all welcome you to our fires. Our daughter of the village tells us that a lodge would be welcome and I have arranged it. If you need another I will arrange it. Winter Man bites at our cheeks and fingers and yours also. Let the People welcome you. Let the sons of the village help you unload your ponies, and the daughters of the village gather firewood and bring you buffalo tongue. Then, when you are settled, and before the horned moon rises, come smoke the sacred pipe and we will talk of things in council, with my headmen."

"I got me a whole load, chief. Rifles and ball and powder; kettles and axes and knives and blankets . . ."

"In the morning we will begin," White Wolf said. He turned to Little Whirlwind. "My daughter, take your man to the lodge of Makes the Doe Come, and bring the widow here."

She did as she was bid, leading her man down village streets through the concentric circles of glowing lodges, feeling the magic and goodness of this place of the People. The last of the daylight purpled the sky, silhouetting the forest of black lodgepoles above her. Her village was more beautiful in dusk than even the streets of St. Louis, where lanterns cast their amber glow from glassed windows.

A great crowd of the People followed, chattering and whispering and eyeing the packs on the horses, wondering what magic and medicine lay within each. And among them she spotted Raffin, striding wolfishly along, his brown eyes missing nothing. Fitzhugh spotted him, too, and watched coldly, the coldness in his eye something she had rarely seen in him.

They arrived at the lodge of Makes the Doe Come, and the young woman awaited them joyously. Her man had died a great death stealing horses from the Blackfeet dogs, and left her an eighteen-skin lodge and many good things. Soon she would be married, but she chose to grieve for a few moons more.

"I am honored to offer my lodge to the Son of our People," she murmured shyly.

Fitzhugh thanked her and immediately presented her with some gifts — an awl and a knife and some red ribbon he'd stuck in his elkskin coat. Then the widow, carrying a small bundle, hastened off to the comfort of the lodge of her chief.

Magically, many hands slid the heavy packs off horses and mules and led them off to the village herd where they'd make a good living gnawing at cottonwood brush and pawing up grass from under the thin shell of snow. Smiling women brought cooked tongue, the smell of it dizzy on the frosty air. Others carried whole bundles of good dry squaw wood. Pretty girls wrapped in blankets smiled at Spoon and Constable, and Little Whirlwind wished she could flirt, too. Maybe she would. Maybe she'd flirt with Raffin a little, just to make Brokenleg more ardent in the robes. She laughed softly.

"Hyar now, it beats Fitzhugh's Post," said Abner Spoon.

"I ain't used to gittin' waited on hand and foot," said Zach.

A mountain of loaded packs rose before the lodge but she didn't worry about their safety. Not the smallest thing belonging to a guest of the village was ever taken . . . But she saw Raffin studying that heap; the brightness of his eyes, and she worried.

She tugged at her man's sleeve. "I think you should put the packs inside — if they'll fit," she said. He paused, seeing the solemnity of her face and the reason for it standing nearby, grinning.

He pulled loose of her and limped on over to Raffin until he stood before the Creole. The excited crowd quieted. "Raffin," Brokenleg said in English. "This time, we're going to settle some business."

"No!" cried Little Whirlwind.

Her man turned to her, puzzled by her sharpness, and then she saw understanding in his eyes. He had not yet smoked the pipe with Chief White Wolf. He could not get into a murderous fight, or even some shouting, without disturbing the peace of this village. It would scandalize the Tsistsista and they might not trade with him.

Not now. Some other time.

He turned to Raffin. "We'll settle it. You and me, we're going to settle some scores. You're workin' for Chouteau, tryin' to bust up my business. You put them 'Rapaho on me last summer. You came up on *The Trapper* a ways. Long enough to slide them kegs into our goods and fool with Sire's manifest. Lots o' passengers then, lower river. Easy to keep outa my sight. You're workin' direct for Cadet, maybe Hervey, and the rest of them out at the posts don't know nothin'. But I'm tellin' you, Raffin. You ain't workin' any more. You touch this outfit and I'll come after you. And so will these folk that want to trade. You touch our robes and I'll come after you. You touch Little Whirlwind and you won't live to tell it in the grog shops at St. Louis. I can't make you leave this hyar village — it ain't mine to make you. But I'll be watchin' and waitin'."

"Ah, sad things happen, do they not, Stiffleg? You get caught with spirits and

409

blame me! The Arapaho strike, and you blame me! Sad things. Maybe you'll lose your whole outfit here — and blame me! Or your wife — and blame me!" Raffin laughed suddenly, a raucous, defiant laughter that announced that it was all a grand joke.

The people of the village could not follow the English but Little Whirlwind knew they understood most of it anyway, and she worried about the scandal. And Raffin's threats. She wondered whether her man, or Raffin, would leave her village alive.

Raul Raffin floated around the trading lodge like a gray owl, missing nothing. Brokenleg wondered how the man could endure the cold. He had the feeling Raffin recorded each transaction, as if his brain was the company ledger. But Brokenleg didn't have time to worry it. The trade went better than he had imagined and he didn't have a spare moment. The Cheyenne had an endless supply of robes and were hauling away everything he'd brought.

Patiently they queued to enter the trading lodge, bringing soft-tanned buffalo robes with them and leaving with Leman rifles, powder and shot, fine Witney blankets, knives, kettles, hatchets, or yards of trade cloth.

There wasn't room in the lodge for the three tons of trade goods brought from Fitzhugh's Post plus the growing pile of traded robes, plus a small display area, and room for Spoon and Constable to live, and room for one Cheyenne at a time to squat near the door and bargain. Brokenleg pitched his little tents and stored traded robes in them. He left the parfleches full of trade goods outside. But when a snowstorm dumped a foot and a half of soft powder on the village and the following chinook turned everything around his lodge into a mire, he knew he would need more shelter.

He traded a Leman rifle and sixty loads to a young widower for a good lodge, seventeen hides, and pitched it beside his trading lodge. After that he had room not only for the parfleches and panniers he'd packed, but for some robes which he stowed in a great circle inside, back from the smoke hole above. The new lodge had cost plenty — the rifle and loads had been worth twenty-five robes or so — but he had the warehouse he needed and room to trade and display goods in the other lodge.

December slid by, and with it Christmas. But he'd plumb forgotten about Christmas, and all that seemed strange to him anyway, like some distant echo from a forgotten past. They entered what these people called *Ok sey e shi his,* Hoop and Stick Game Moon, or January. They called February the Big Hoop and Stick Game Moon, and he didn't know why. But he knew it'd turned bitter cold. Arctic air eddied out of the north, biting the cheeks and fingers of anyone who dared step outside. Trading slowed. It was better to huddle around the lodge fires.

Still, the mountain of pungent robes grew in his warehouse lodge, and his trading outfit dwindled. He eyed the dark piles of robes and wondered whether his pack animals could carry them all back, or whether he'd have to rig travois. And he worried about Raffin. The man hung around the trading lodge, boldly watching, counting, poking his head into the warehouse lodge, and laughing every time Fitzhugh caught him. Raffin was waiting for something; waiting for trading to end. Waiting to pounce when Fitzhugh left the village with all his robes.

The village elders and dog soldiers watched Raffin, too, aware that this man from the other company might try to disturb the trade which benefited them so much. The whole village sported new blankets, new trade-cloth shirts, gleaming rifles, and

412

shining knives. But Raffin did nothing — at least as far as Fitzhugh could tell. Each day, Brokenleg and Abner or Zach went out to check the packhorses and cut cottonwood limbs for them to gnaw on. The coats on all the village stock as well as his had grown so shaggy he could scarcely tell one from another except for his mules and a few that he could recognize other ways. It worried him. Raffin would know that, and might be pilfering the pack animals one by one.

"You reckon we got 'em all?" he asked Abner one day.

"Damned if I know. I don't even know how all them Cheyenne can tell one from another, wearin' coats like that."

"The village boys are watchin'. Leastwise by daylight. I don't see much night-herdin' this kind o' weather."

"Them injuns, they don't raid none in January unless one or another's got a big mad goin'. They sit around keepin' warm and playin' the stick game and makin' little Cheyennes all night and gossipin' and tellin' tall tales."

Brokenleg sighed. "That's why I don't like it. Raffin, he could walk off with horses now — nothing but a boy or two keepin' an eye on them."

"He's jist bidin' his time, Brokenleg. He

413

ain't gonna touch us hyar in the village. Git him into trouble with the headmen so bad he'd never git out of it. Them Cheyenne, they're mean when they wanta be. You ever seen one of them dried-up finger necklaces they wear, or dried-up ear necklaces?"

"Yup. It could be my ears if they took a notion."

During the long bitter stretches when village life died, Fitzhugh worried a lot of things around in his mind. Like those license hearings down to St. Louis. By now, he might be a partner in a dead outfit. Brokenleg had busted his brain trying to find some way to prove Raffin planted those casks, but he knew in his gut that getting a confession out of Raffin that would save the Rocky Mountain Company was impossible. Brokenleg had brought a small ceramic jug of pure ardent spirits along, and it lay in the bottom of a parfleche like gold. He'd thought to use it on Raffin to loosen his tongue, but gave up on that. Brokenleg knew his own tongue would loosen first. A drunken admission wouldn't help. And anyway, that little jug, meager enough for a long winter, was hoarded treasure that Brokenleg didn't intend to share with anyone, not even Abner and Zach. Which reminded him, he was getting plumb dry.

He'd been wintering in the lodge of One Leg Eagle and Antelope along with their four daughters, and it'd driven him into a big dry. Too many wives and in-laws in there to suit him. It occurred to him that Hide Scraping Woman had a bulge to her belly he hadn't seen before — she was pregnant, and had never said a blasted word to him. Probably the rest were, too. Visions of three or four squalling brats dizzied him. He squinted narrowly at Dust Devil and Sweet Smoke, and they smiled back, saying nothing. And he couldn't speak to his mother-in-law, neither. Some old taboo. Not a bad one, he thought. His wives had slid into his robes night after night in the blackness but he'd pushed them away. He couldn't even think of it in the lodge with a dozen ears listening in the space of ten feet. One Leg Eagle was plumb cheerful and told bawdy jokes he said he got from the Crows one time, while antelope smiled at him, understanding and enjoying his discomfort. It'd turned into some damned joke, and he was the butt of it. Maybe them Cheyenne weren't so puritan after all.

Dust Devil turned sulky and went on long walks, even in the bitter air. She liked to traipse past Raffin's little lodge, too. Brokenleg had spotted her doing it, and knew it was to annoy him and get even for ignoring her in the robes. And she'd succeeded. Which was why he was building up to a Big Dry. Raffin had spotted it, too, and made a point of stopping Dust Devil and visiting with her whenever he could — especially when Brokenleg was in sight.

Brokenleg endured, but he didn't know how long he could before something snapped inside. It was worse than bein' in St. Louis with all them dudes on the streets starin' at him. His thoughts turned to murder. He took to wrapping himself in a scarlet blanket and stalking past Raffin's lodge, listening for the sounds of talk inside, or the sounds of mating. Itching to climb in there and hunt around for something, anything, that would pin Raffin to the casks of spirits that probably had cost the company its trading license.

He'd shoot Raffin if he could. He'd stick his Green River right between Raffin's ribs. He'd by god string Raffin up by his thumbs and make him squeal. But all that was empty dreaming. He knew that. Raffin stayed close to his lodge; never left the village; never — as far as Brokenleg could tell — even bothered to check on his own horses out in the cottonwoods. Instead, Raffin seemed to anticipate Brokenleg's every act, showing up to watch every big trade, ogling Brokenleg's wives whenever he was in sight of Brokenleg, a mean mock on his black-bearded face.

At the beginning of the Big Hoop and Stick Game Moon, Brokenleg couldn't stand it any more. He slipped into the trading lodge and uncovered a parfleche buried near the rear, worried that his prize might have been discovered by Zach and Abner. But it was there. He slid his hand into the dark corner of the rawhide and felt its icy hardness and its weight. He lifted it gently, his eyes filled with love, and slid it under his blanket, away from their prying eyes. Then he walked into the vicious night. He peered down the village street toward the glowing lodge of his in-laws and rejected it. Instead, he stepped briskly over squeaking snow toward the small lodge on the outer edge of the village, where Raffin whiled away his life.

He paused at the flap, and then scratched it softly, the Indian way. It parted, emitting dim light from the tiny fire within.

Raffin stared into the blackness, seeing Brokenleg there, and noting the gray porcelain jug.

"This hyar's pure spirits."

"You have come to drink, *oui?*"

"I reckon if I sip enough I'll be ready to kill ye."

Raffin laughed, and pulled the flap aside. "Come in and let us kill," he said.

Twenty-five

Raul Raffin studied the porcelain jug happily. "We will drink, and den we will kill, *oui?*"

Fitzhugh lowered himself against some duffel piled to one side of the compact lodge. "Sounds about right, 'cept it ain't we, it's I."

Raffin laughed softly. His eyes glowed. "She is pure spirits, *oui?* I'll get the waters. Pure spirits, dey torture the throat and make me weep. How can I kill you when I'm crying?"

He plucked an iron pot from the hearth and vanished through the door flap. Brokenleg eyed the man's possessions. Raffin did not live austerely. The flicker of the small fire revealed an array of curios hanging from the lodgepoles — a grotesque necklace of human ears he'd traded for; a human skull with an arrow piercing it through the temples. The arrowhead had broken off. A ceremonial lance with a pitted iron point and a dozen scalps dangling from its shaft. One of the scalps was brown; the rest blue-black.

Raffin pierced through the door, the iron pot in his hand brimming with water. He settled himself happily against a backrest at the rear of the small lodge. "I have only one," he said, reaching for a tin cup. "We will share, *oui?*"

He lifted the porcelain jug and twisted its cork free, anticipation shining from him. "You want it cut a lot or a little?" he asked. "You're the guest. You choose. After you die, I'll drink the rest my way — very petite the water."

"Just a dash in 'er. Like at the rendezvous," Brokenleg said. His leg hurt him. It always did when he was trying to sit up in lodges and the thing poked straight out.

"Ah, the rendezvous! Someone always die at the rendezvous! We'll have one, Brokenleg. For the old times, for the beaver days. And den we'll fight."

"Didn't come to fight, unless you want to git killed. I come to squeeze a confession out of ye after I git yer tongue loosened up."

"Ah! A confession! Like the sacrament. Confession and absolution before the priest Fitzhugh. Ah!" He emptied the entire cup of spirits, and hiccoughed. "Ah! He wants a confession! Dat will be easy, Fitzhugh. I will confess before I kill you."

He poured a slug of spirits into the empty cup and carefully corked the jug again. He would not risk spilling a drop. Then he splashed water into it and handed it to Brokenleg.

He watched, grinning, while Brokenleg sipped warily and then deeply. Brokenleg sighed, knowing that soon the ache in his leg would vanish.

"The bad leg, soon she doesn't hurt! Ah, Brokenleg, how slowly you sip. I drink fast and kill fast. You drink slow because you are afraid of me."

"You put them casks on *The Trapper*," he said.

Raffin laughed easily, sipped, wheezed, and wept as the fiery stuff tortured his throat. "You are a bad priest, Brokenleg. You should wait for confession."

"You put them 'Rapaho on me last summer. That took my stock and my robes."

Raffin belched and gulped, draining the tin cup. He mixed another cupful. "It is atrocious, the taste. Ardent spirits and water from Crazy Woman Creek. But ah . . ." He belched happily and licked his lips. "Ah . . . I'm getting ready for sacraments. Tonight we have two — confession and murder."

"You're workin' private for Cadet

Chouteau. The others, they don't know nothin'. You put them casks on somewhere and come up the river, keepin' outa my sight. You got off at Fort Pierre where you weren't supposed to, and come out hyar to mess up my Cheyenne trade."

"More than that, Brokenleg. I kill you and catch Little Whirlwind. She likes me some; she's scared of me, too. Dat's perfect, *oui?* I make her happy and scare her out of her wits."

Brokenleg ignored that. The spirits had taken hold, pushing pain farther and farther away and heating up his belly. "When you git up to killin' you go right ahead." He grinned back, feeling pretty good. It seemed almost like a rendezvous on the Popo Agie. The fire-licked Creole across from him had waded the creeks and pulled the beaver out and made the plews. Brokenleg felt a vast affection for him, a living relic of the wild days. "Ah, Raffin, mind you the time, rendezvous o' eighteen and maybe thirty-four, when that coon got hisself knifed, and they used his carcass for a card table, playin' euchre?"

"Oh, I see dat, I see dat. You, Brokenleg, you're too skinny to make a good table. But I'll try it. Solitaire."

"You haven't got a deck."

Raffin shrugged and sipped and coughed. "*Merde!* Dis water and spirits, it scrapes the skin off my throat!"

"You never were much of a drinker, Raffin. You Creoles."

"Ah! I kill you sooner than later."

"You ready to confess yet? You got yer tongue loosened up proper?"

"Ah, Brokenleg. For you, *mon ami*, I will confess everything. From the beginning. Like a river dat flows out of my heart into a puddle on the ground."

"Well, git to it!" Fitzhugh's body was afire. A fine hum rose within him, the throbbing of his own blood, and he felt it float him until he could soar anywhere, out the lodge door, over the village, up into the sky.

"I am rich," said Raffin.

"You're dead is what you mean."

"Ah, non, *mon ami*. Chouteau Cadet, he calls me in one night, after the clerks are gone. I go in dere, big old brick building down on the river, and he's waiting with a lamp lit. 'Ah, Raffin, I've been thinking about you,' says he. Well, I won't describe all dat. He just tells me this Rocky Mountain Company and my old *ami* Brokenleg, dey are the first competition in many years he's worrying about. Because of the Straus money, and because you and Dance, you

423

are . . . it don' matter what he say.

"No one knows of my visit. I go to Independence, and a man meets me with three casks. I go to Westport and wait for the *bateau*. It comes, and dey load in your outfit. It is simple. Dere on the levee at Westport under the bluffs, I carry the casks and put them with your things. Pretty soon the stevedores carry them in just like the rest of your outfit. I see the second mate at the gangway, and I say, add two casks of vinegar and one of lamp oil because I just deliver dem from Independence for Rocky Mountain Company. He says he's got no pen and ink so I go on board and climb up to the empty pilothouse and look, and there is a stoppered bottle of ink and a quill right beside the log book, and I bring it down. He hands me the cargo list and I write it in and hand it back to him."

"You musta figgered the army'd catch it at Leavenworth."

Raffin spat into the fire, making it pop. "Ah! Stupid army. Dey come into the hold and look around and don't see the casks, and I am thinking, American Fur, it just gave Rocky Mountain Company three extra casks of spirits. Dey don't look very hard, dem lieutenants."

"Then what?"

Raffin chortled. "You want more, eh? The whole confession. Everywhere I sin, *oui?* No, I can't say to you, Father, I fornicate seventeen times. You got to hear about all seventeen and describe the girls, each one."

"What'd Cadet pay you?"

"A year's extra to do it, another year's wage if I succeed, *oui?*"

Three hundred dollars, Fitzhugh thought. Three hundred dollars to tear apart a venture worth two hundred times that.

"He give me the first year in gold; I get my regular pay, too. He give me the second after your company is dead."

"Guy Straus told me that Culbertson and the rest think you deserted — you're off the rolls."

"Cadet — he take care of dat."

Brokenleg felt sleepy. He wrestled with himself to stay alert. He watched the Creole push fresh sticks into the dying fire and huff at it until it blazed up, driving back the sinister shadows.

Raffin watched the blaze and sipped steadily, refilling the battered tin cup again. He thrust it toward Fitzhugh. "You want?"

Fitzhugh took it — he'd never turned down a sip in his life. He felt the fire slide into his belly again, and sighed.

"How come you don' ask me about the rest?"

"Because I know. Cadet sent you out hyar to the villages to make trouble for me. I got the Cheyenne trade sewed up so it's no good him sendin' an outfit. I'm kin and they'll trade with me. You made it look like you deserted — got off the boat at Pierre — to keep the company out of it. You got out hyar and waited and made friends some, and figgered how to do it 'nother way, like puttin' them 'Rapaho on me after I traded last summer. Them stealin' my stock and gittin' the robes. Did they bring them robes to you?"

Raffin shrugged. "*Non, non.* They trade the robes at Laramie. All that matters, we take dem from you. Big loss for you. And stop your wagons."

"You done that all right . . . You been in touch with Cadet? You send some express down tellin' him?"

"Naw. I work it out. He don' want me sendin' express or showin' up in St. Louis."

"You an' Hervey, you almost licked me, Raffin."

"Almost! Almost! You wait. Raffin, he's not done yet."

Brokenleg nodded. He felt fine. Now he

426

knew everything. For the first time in months his bum leg stopped aching.

"You going to sleep, Stiffleg?"

"Naw. Let's do the killin'."

"Now?"

"Right now."

Raffin laughed, a fine raucous howl that sounded like the bark of a wolf.

Maxim watched Fitzhugh's Post die. His engages had lost both will and strength, and now worked listlessly at the well, stymied by a stratum of river cobbles that had to be pried loose. Their mule-meat diet had allayed hunger a little but the carcass had been stripped to the bone. The remaining horses bawled pitifully for food and water. A light snowfall rescued them for a day or two: the animals licked up every flake that fell in the yard. Engages salvaged a few quarts of water by scraping the three inches of white off roofs.

Arctic air crowded in after that forcing them to keep the barracks stove burning. Day by day the firewood from the demolished shed dwindled. Men eyed him accusingly, knowing that he could save them simply by surrendering. Their stomachs spoke through their eyes and with their angry silence.

Tomorrow they would have to butcher a horse. It'd be a futile gesture, especially if they didn't strike water. He opened a shutter and peered out upon the solemn white flat. The great arc of brown lodges stood like a wall, all of them leaking gray smoke. Their captors enjoyed every comfort, he thought. They could outlast him.

He didn't know what to do. This was his second winter in the mountains and he'd reached the ripe age of seventeen. Responsibility had fallen on him too soon and he resented it. More and more he sought out Samson Trudeau, but the veteran of many a trapping brigade had no suggestions.

"You think we could parley with the headmen?" he asked.

Trudeau shrugged. His shrug was a Gallic expression of defeat. "Ah, Maxim, I don't know the tongue. A little of the hand-language. I never learned much. The partisans who led us, they knew the finger signs."

Maxim sighed. He couldn't even communicate with his captors. "Maybe they know English or French. Lots of trappers wintered with them."

Trudeau shrugged. "I think she is over. Soon we have disease, scurvy. The water, it doesn't come. The shed gives up its last firewood. Why do we wait?"

"Brokenleg would." He said it stubbornly.

"Brokenleg, he's got magic. He goes and talks to them. He makes things different."

"And I don't."

Samson glanced away.

"My father taught me something. When Hervey held him in a dark storeroom he fought back by surrendering life itself. He told Hervey that he would choose death."

"Ah, *oui*, Maxim. He chose that for himself. He didn't choose it for you. He didn't choose death for the engages. We are loyal — every one of us. But are you going to choose death for us? A bad death from thirst and disease and empty bellies?"

Responsibility again. It crushed Maxim's young shoulders. He stared bitterly into the wintry distances seeing blanket-wrapped Crows amble from one lodge to another. "You can go. All of you can go. They know the white flag. Take a white flag and go — go to Hervey, go on down the river. Take the rifles and some shot."

Trudeau grunted. "They might kill us if they don't see you surrendering."

"I'm staying. My family has tens of thousands tied up here."

"It'd be a great scandal in St. Louis."

"What do you mean?"

"Why, Maxim, not even rival fur companies can do such a thing — starving out the opposition with a siege."

"American Fur would just blame the Crows. Hervey would say he tried to stop it, and it'd die away. A scandal in St. Louis won't help us any."

Trudeau joined him at the unshuttered window. "I'll tell the engages," he said. "Some may go. I think all will go."

"Bien."

"Give them each a gill of spirits to bolster them, eh?"

Maxim didn't want to. But he sighed and nodded. Better to give the engages a gill than to give the spirits to Hervey.

Trudeau left him at the glassless window and went to inform the men out in the yard. Maxim was letting icy air into the barracks but he didn't care. It was over. He leaned into the window, brooding, watching the Crow village. There'd been no sign of Hervey ever since Maxim had shot his horse, but Maxim knew the man's purposes had influenced these Crows; that Hervey hulked out there in spirit if not in person. Maxim thought about murder, and it shocked him that he could even imagine shooting Julius Hervey on sight. He knew that Hervey would shoot him on sight now

— no matter whose son he was.

One by one the weary engages wandered into the gloomy barracks, warmed their numbers fingers over the grudging fire in the stove, and glanced furtively at Maxim. It didn't take Trudeau long to collect them. At last they were all present: Trudeau, Larue, Bercier, Brasseau, Courvet, Dauphin, Guerette, Provost, and the three new ones, Lebrun, Grevy, and Poinsett. All good men and true. All etched with fatigue and despair.

Maxim couldn't find words. He stared helplessly at them, the bitterness lumping in his gullet. "You can go. I'm releasing you."

They stared.

"You can go! Pack your kits. Take your rifles. Take whatever stores you need."

No one said a word.

Trudeau cleared his throat. "Monsieur Straus is releasing you. He's staying here. He tells me he will not surrender the post. If it is taken it will be captured, not surrendered. He tells me that you each may have a gill of spirits now. We have enough water left to cut the spirits a little. It's his way of saying *bon voyage.*"

Oddly, the engages did not seem to jump at the offer. They glanced at one another nervously, uncertain. At last Gaspard Larue spoke up. "They might kill us if we walk out."

"Take a white flag," Maxim replied.

"You are not surrendering?" asked Lebrun.

"It's my family's property. And the partners' property."

"Ah, Monsieur Straus, they'll kill you. Hervey —"

"Have a gill."

"That is a good idea," said Corneille Dauphin. "I can't think on an empty stomach."

No one laughed.

"We are far from water. Five feet down and solid cobbles," muttered Jeannot Provost. "*Oui,* I'm thirsty. Spirits and snow."

Five of the six thirty-gallon casks sat in the storeroom. The sixth, tapped by a faucet and half empty, lay hidden in a corner of the trading room. Courvet wandered off to fetch it. Brasseau gathered tin cups. Grevy lifted the kettle of precious snow-melt from the stove.

Solemnly, Courvet poured a gill into outstretched cups and Grevy ladled ice water until they all were served. All except Maxim who didn't touch spirits. They peered nervously at one another, oddly afraid to touch their lips to the spirits, as if doing so would seal the fate of the post. But this was a wake anyway, and Maxim eyed them impatiently.

At last Trudeau broke the spell. "To our employers," he said and sipped. The rest muttered something. They all sipped silently, wheezing as the fiery spirits burnt their throats. But no one spoke. This business had a funeral quality to it and the spirits would do nothing but ease the pain. It was midday, an odd time for this anyway. The January sun hung low in the south but fired the snow into brilliance that would blind a traveler.

Maxim watched them moodily, wondering where they would go. To Hervey? Up to Fort Union? None of them had spoken of salary. He could give them chits if they asked. They could trade for supplies here or at any post. But the subject of wages seemed out of bounds and not a man brought it up.

Maxim squinted out upon the brilliant flat again and spotted something. Three blanketed Crows approached, headmen from the look of their headdresses. One carried a white rag on a stick. The surrender party. How uncanny was their knowledge, he thought. Not so uncanny, though. Crows had often peered through the cracks in the stockade walls, missing nothing.

"They're coming," he said.

Engages crowded to the window to watch

the threesome walk across the snow-pocked flat, but no one said a word.

Maxim left them and walked to the front gate next to the trading window, opened it, and waited. He recognized the three: two war chiefs and a shaman. He knew their rank but not their names. They weren't armed — as far as he could see. Blanketed Indians were famous for hiding rifles under cover.

They paused at the door, surveying Maxim. He peered back, half afraid, half angry.

"You will surrender?" asked one in clear English.

They could communicate. Maxim waved them inside without answering, and steered them into the barracks. His engages peered over their cups at the Crows, and the Crows peered back, studying the cups, the cask with its brass bung faucet, and the cold room.

That's when the devil took Maxim Straus.

Twenty-six

The potbellied coal stove in the Federal Annex held January at bay. The three supervisors up on the dais looked like ravens on a limb hunting for scraps of meat. Guy sensed that one of the two out from Washington city, Superintendent Philander P. Roscoe, had missed his calling: he should have been a hangman by trade. He had those wounded glistening eyes, set in a cadaverous face beside a nose sharp enough to cut glass, of a fanatic. He occupied the center chair as chairman, a bad omen. The other man who'd made the arduous trip, Major J. Broderick Eastwood, USA Ret., looked merely venal and Whig, a Tyler appointee fattening at the public trough. He sat to Roscoe's right; Davey Mitchell to the left.

In spite of the blistering heat boiling out of the stove, Roscoe wore a silky scarf around his scrawny neck, and a thick woolen waistcoat underneath his frock coat. Fever leaked from him like the heat of righteousness. He dabbed at reddened nostrils with a slimy handkerchief, sniffed and honked.

Worse yet, the Reverend Mr. Foster Gillian had skated down the wintry river after all and now rested his corpulent funeral-clad person on an oaken witness bench alongside the natty Captain Sire. The pink-cheeked divine looked positively triumphant, as if this were the climax of his earthly sojourn and upon the completion of his testimony the heavens would open, a shaft of golden light would pierce down, and cherubim and seraphim would escort the man to this reward. Guy hoped he wouldn't rattle on too long.

Guy himself wouldn't testify though he had abundant things to say. He did not wish to be asked embarrassing questions about the liquor traffic in the Indian territories. He noted that Cadet Chouteau had likewise made himself scarce and for the same reasons, though Chouteau would have dearly loved to witness the demise of his rival. But Robert Campbell was present behind Guy, a mountain of moral support if nothing else. He wished Yvonne were beside him as well but his little Cassandra couldn't bear it. Guy himself would entrust his case to his counselor, Hiliodore Billedeaux, a man of flowing white mane and vast simplicity.

"It's past the hour and we shall begin," said Roscoe in a voice surprisingly mellifluous. "This is not a court trial. It's a licensing hearing and will be decided administratively by the Indian Bureau. However, normal rules of evidence shall obtain. The superintendents themselves will call forth testimony and evidence. We are gathered to determine the suitability of a certain Rocky Mountain Company, also known as Dance, Fitzhugh and Straus, to conduct a trading business in the Indian territories. Our business here is licensing — but we may turn over evidence of criminal acts to federal prosecutors for further action."

A hanging then, Guy thought. Davey Mitchell looked uncomfortable; the other ravens positively rapturous. Eastwood picked his nose surreptitiously, his fig-leaf fingers covering the boring of his thumb.

"We'll begin with the Reverend Mr. Foster Gillian, and remind all witnesses that your testimony will be sworn and subject to prosecution for perjury. Mr. Gillian, do you swear to tell the truth, the whole truth, and nothing else, so help you God?"

"Oh I do, I do, I certainly do, before Almighty God."

"Are you the appointed Indian Agent for

the Otos and Omahas, located at Bellevue?"

"Indeed, sir. They are my blessed charges, my sheep, my little ones."

"We have before us three affidavits prepared by you, your wife, and one Marshall Landress, your assistant I believe?" He handed the copies to the reverend. "Is one yours and do you know for a fact that the others were prepared by those whose signatures they bear?"

"I do, sir. These are the very documents we drafted."

"Would you tell us what happened upon the occasion of the arrival of a packet named *The Trapper* last summer — the second trip, I believe?"

Foster Gillian did. This was his moment of glory and he hoarded every second of it. His jowly face turned holy; his gaze direct and bright; his spirit lofty, radiating sublime joy upon the assemblage. Little by little, leaving no nuance unplowed, no stone unturned, he wove his tale of discovery, there in the dark hold of the packet, of nefarious spirits being smuggled upriver by a notorious combine of grafters out to debauch poor savages.

He had a tongue, thought Guy. A lot of Sundays in the pulpit had given him the golden voice and the mesmerizing glow.

The three ravens watched and listened and nodded and scratched notes with Josiah Mason steel nibs. When the reverend finished, like a thunderstorm receding into twilight, the heavens didn't part.

"Counsel may examine," said Roscoe, dabbing at his flaming nostrils.

Hiliodore rose, smiled benignly, introduced himself to the ravens, complimented Gillian on his elocution, admired Gillian's exact recollection of passages from the Psalms, St. Mark, St. Luke, and Second Corinthians, and asked the reverend what whiskey looked and smelled like.

"Why, I know what you're driving at. Straus pestered me with it. Pure grain spirits have little odor and are transparent. Still, I had no trouble — no trouble at all — discerning the contents of the casks." He dug into his commodious coat and extracted a phial. "Here! I have brought some, taken from one of those casks." He turned to the commissioners. "See whether it's vinegar or lamp oil!"

The commissioners tasted and smelled. Hiliodore did, too.

"I think," said Roscoe, "that we are satisfied that these are pure grain spirits. We'll turn this over to a chemist for analysis if you wish, Counsel Billedeaux."

"That won't be necessary."

"I have a phial taken from each cask," announced the reverend. "Here. This was labeled vinegar; the other lamp oil." He passed two more to the commissioners, with the same result.

Trumped by Gillian, Hiliodore Billedeaux turned to the other pivotal question. "Mr. Gillian, how do you know that these casks were the property of my clients?"

"Why! They were there, right there, on top of crates of firearms — right in the middle of Dance, Fitzhugh, and Straus dunnage. And of course we all know how these nefarious companies debauch —"

"Stick to the question, Mr. Gillian."

Foster Gillian let himself deflate a moment, and smiled. "It was right there on the ship's cargo list — the list for Dance, Fitzhugh, and Straus."

"At the very bottom, was it?"

"Indeed, right there, the last item. They'd made it last hoping it'd be ignored."

"You're speculating, Mr. Gillian. But tell me, my friend — was this in the same hand as the rest?"

"I didn't notice."

"It is in a different hand. Have a look." He plucked up the cargo manifest from the pile of papers before the commissioners, and handed it to Gillian. "Is this the list you looked at, and is the last entry in a different hand?"

Gillian nodded.

"Let the record show that the witness nodded affirmatively," said Hiliodore. "Have you any evidence — any evidence at all — that this contraband was owned by my clients, or that they were aware of its presence?"

"Why, that boy, the Straus boy, he knew it. He told me he'd seen it after they left Westport, and added it to his own company copy."

"He also told you he had thought it was vinegar and lamp oil, did he not?"

Gillian laughed pleasantly. "He wasn't a very good liar. I can read faces, you know. I know the face of a sinner, sir, and this, this Straus —"

"The lad isn't here to defend himself, Mr. Gillian."

The reverend didn't like being interrupted. "Mr. Billedeaux," he said, a weary patience in his tone. "We all know that anything boarded at Westport would be, ah, discovered by the regular inspectors at Fort Leavenworth. Therefore, the boy lied. These nefarious spirits would have been slid

441

aboard at some place after Fort Leavenworth and before Bellevue."

"Ah, reverend. More suppositions. Con-
fine yourself to what you know, please."

"I know that boy lied."

Guy's temper climbed and he squirmed
on the hard wooden bench. But there was
little he could do. Hiliodore was taking a
beating . . . and so was he.

The retired major, J. Broderick Eastwood, intervened. "The Leavenworth inspections are thorough, sirs. There's no
possibility that casks with such labels upon
them would have escaped the attention of
the army."

But they had, thought Guy. The
Leavenworth inspections were erratic;
sometimes exhaustive, sometimes cursory.

Hiliodore smiled. "Thank you, sir. It's
something to consider. I'm sure whoever
put those casks in the hold intended that
they should be discovered at Leavenworth,
just as you suggest."

"That's a fancy theory," said Eastwood.
A small titter rose in the overheated room.
The coal stove spat.

"Ah, gentlemen, if it makes no sense for a
fur company to slip contraband aboard
below Leavenworth, then it makes no sense
for a fur company to slip contraband aboard

below the next inspection point at Bellevue."

Gillian said, "The fur companies do as they will — a godless lot, making themselves lords of the wild. They buy and bribe their way —"

"Are you suggesting, Mr. Gillian, that you are bribeable? Have you been approached?"

"They bribe the venal army at Leavenworth."

Major J. Broderick Eastwood stiffened slightly.

"You didn't answer my question, Mr. Gillian."

"I serve a higher calling. Does that answer it?"

Hiliodore sighed. Guy sighed. It was going badly even though the reverend was an ass. He had hoped things would go better than this. The entire case, Hiliodore had told him, rested on the question of ownership of those casks. He couldn't prove the company didn't own them — but he felt that the Indian Bureau couldn't prove the company did own them.

They sparred through the rest of the morning, making small points that would have no effect. Guy smelled doom in the air, along with the occasional whiff of coal smoke from the potbelly. They adjourned for lunch and resumed at two, with Captain Sire the next witness.

"Is it unusual," Roscoe asked the captain, "for your ship's cargo manifest to be drafted in more than one hand?"

"It's commonplace."

"Did this last entry in a different hand mean anything to you?"

"No. I didn't see it, actually. My mate handles the cargo. He lets me know if we're carrying hazardous substances. He told me about the casks of powder Dance, Fitzhugh and Straus had aboard. I made sure they were properly stowed and isolated."

"Did your mate make that entry, perhaps?"

"No. It's not his hand. He keeps our log on occasion and I'm familiar with his hand."

"Whose hand wrote the rest of the manifest?"

"Young Mr. Straus. He gave me our copy and kept his own."

"How do you know that?"

"He told me at Westport. He'd been made responsible for checking off the company cargo as it was boarded. And he gave our copy to me, and I gave it to my mate and had him check off the dunnage as it was boarded also."

"Captain," said David Mitchell. "I have a question."

Here it comes, thought Guy. Mitchell alone among the commissioners knew enough about fur company practices to ask the right question: such as, did you take aboard contraband spirits above Bellevue? Captain Sire's answer would destroy Guy — if he wasn't already destroyed.

"Captain Sire, did you board any contraband, or suspect you did, at any place — a wooding lot for instance — between Leavenworth and Bellevue?"

Ah, Davey, ah, Davey, Guy thought.

"None to my knowledge. I would have known about it, I'm sure. I believe Maxim Straus was correct when he told Mr. Gillian the casks had been boarded at Westport."

Guy waited for Roscoe to ask the next question, but Roscoe was honking phlegm into his slimy handkerchief. Slowly, Guy eased into the hardwood bench.

"Somebody's not telling the truth!" thundered Gillian from his spectator bench.

"Mr. Gillian — please. This may not be a courtroom but we shall have decorum," said Roscoe.

"The reverend is suggesting I'm not telling the truth," said Captain Sire. "I will stand on my statement. The casks in question were loaded at Westport." The captain sat patiently in his chair, his natural authority speaking for him.

"Why there? If they'd only be discovered by the army at Leavenworth?" asked Mitchell.

Sire smiled. "I cannot guess at intentions, commissioner."

Roscoe said, "The contraband was on board at Bellevue. There's no dispute there, is there Captain Sire?"

"I saw the reverend pour clear fluid into the river, sir. It could have been water. I can say only that the casks were aboard, but I have no knowledge that they contained spirits. They didn't contain whiskey, I'm sure of that."

"Do you segregate cargo by owner?"

"As far as possible, sir. It makes unloading easier."

"These casks were with other Rocky Mountain Company dunnage?"

"I have no idea."

"Does cargo get mixed up?"

"Once in a while — when we shift it to get over a sandbar."

"Had you encountered any sandbars below Bellevue?"

"None."

"Then the cargo didn't get mixed up."

"I don't know, sir. I didn't enter the hold."

"I'm trying to make the point, captain, that in all likelihood the contraband didn't arrive there — in the Dance, Fitzhugh and Straus goods — accidentally."

The hangman, Guy thought. Making a case.

"It's unlikely, sir," said Sire.

Hiliodore rose. "That is our contention, sir. No accident at all. The casks were planted in my client's goods during the loading at Westport for nefarious and sinister reasons. To cost my clients their license."

Philander P. Roscoe smiled slightly, a faint twitch in his cadaverous face that vanished instantly. "Come now, Mr. Billedeaux. We need more than theory and scapegoats. You must prove it."

"Nay, sirs. It's the opposite. We needn't prove it. You need to prove that the contraband belonged to my clients. If you have the slightest doubts about it, you may not withdraw the license. The Constitution provides that the accused must be considered innocent until —"

"We are quite familiar with it, counsel," said Eastwood.

"Then you know the burden of proof's on

you. Have you heard a thing today tying the contraband to my client? Not a word! Have you found the link? Nothing! Can any of you say, within your esteemed selves, that you know for sure? Of course not! Would you deny a large and valued trading company its license on the most circumstantial and vague sort of evidence? Isn't some competition against the Chouteau interests a good thing — for the tribes?"

"This is an Indian Bureau administrative hearing, counsel," droned Roscoe. "Not a court. We adjudge the evidence before us on its merits. It's within our power to weigh probabilities."

Guy had heartened at Hiliodore's sally, only to lose hope with Roscoe's retort. Hiliodore's main argument — that nothing the commissioners had heard tied the contraband to the company — had died in Roscoe's reply.

That white-maned bulldog Billedeaux turned to new things. "Sirs, my client, Mr. Straus, believes the casks were planted by a certain Chouteau employee named Raul Raffin. This Raffin had nursed an ancient grudge against one of the partners, Robert Fitzhugh, over, ah, an affair of the heart. Mr. Straus went upriver at great expense last fall to get to the bottom of these matters, and learned that this Raffin had been on *The Trapper* and got off at Fort Pierre — deserted the company, rather. He was to continue on to Fort Union where he was engaged by Major Culbertson for a new three-year term with the company. My client tells me that this man now resides in a Cheyenne village and makes it his business to ruin the trade of Dance, Fitzhugh and Straus."

"Theories again, counsel." Eastwood said it and began reaming his nostril. He sounded skeptical and bored. The hearing had consumed a day, and had slid into tedium and triviality.

"Ah! Not theories. The finger points! We know a few things about him. He can read and write. He has kept ledgers at the posts. We are endeavoring to obtain a sample of his hand and believe that Major Culbertson will supply it. Now, sirs, what about this hand? Will it match the mysterious hand found at the bottom of Captain Sire's cargo manifest? We believe it will. And we respectfully request that your decision be postponed until this vital piece of evidence is available to you. Only then will you be able to act with assurance."

"And when would that be?" asked Roscoe.

"We don't know. Before the end of this

trading season surely."

"We don't know either — and we can't postpone that long, especially for an ephemeral bit of handwriting that may or may not have anything to do with this case. No, counsel. I'm sure I speak for my colleagues when I say we can't delay for anything like that."

"Well now, whoa up, sir," said David Mitchell. "If they can prove this Raffin planted those casks and added a line to the manifest in his own hand, I think that's important. Let's leave it this way: we'll reopen it and reconsider if such evidence materializes. And make our present decision conditional."

"It's been a long day, Superintendent Mitchell," Roscoe said.

Guy couldn't make anything out of a reply like that.

Roscoe stood. "This concludes the hearing. My colleagues and I will weigh the material before us in the morning and make our decision known before noon tomorrow."

Guy bundled into his buffalo greatcoat and pushed toward the double doors at the rear. Hiliodore caught up with him as they pierced into the wintry dusk of the riverfront.

"I don't have a good feeling about it, Guy.

Not when they ignore customary burden of proof. It's up to them, not us."

"You did what you could," said Guy.

He slept soundly that night, much to his surprise. There was no suspense dogging him. At noon the next day he stood before the ravens once again.

"The Indian Bureau hereby withdraws the trading license of Dance, Fitzhugh and Straus effective at the end of the present trading season, July 1. The aforesaid shall abandon all trading with all tribes on or before that date. The superintendents find that the aforesaid company attempted to smuggle contraband spirits to its Yellowstone post, against U.S. codes prohibiting it." Philander P. Roscoe droned on, reviewing the evidence or lack of it, dismissing the entire Raffin question as unsubstantiated, and reminding other fur companies that a similar fate awaited them if they debauched the tribes.

Hiliodore slumped.

Guy sighed. Old Cadet Chouteau had whipped him. Even now, Chouteau's minions raced out of the hearing room with the news that would warm Cadet's heart. . . . The commissioners had been right — but on the wrong evidence. The peculiarity of his position didn't elude Guy. Perhaps he could return the favor to Cadet — one way or another.

Guy guessed he'd walk up the hill and tell Yvonne. She would start talking about selling the house.

Twenty-seven

Raffin sipped steadily and stared into the guttering flame. He sighed as if the world were weighting his shoulders. Fitzhugh watched and waited.

"I'll let you live a while," Raffin said. "You want some?"

Brokenleg shook his head. Raffin poured more from the jug and added a splash of water.

"In ancient days I come here to winter — I was a free trapper den. Like you, *mon ami*. And Chief White Wolf, he is my old ami. I help him sometimes. Powder and lead; I get it for him. I get a lodge, me and another Creole. And one day I see this *jeune fille* — this girl, and dere's no one in this village like her. She's almost skinny. She's got shiny hair in braids and bright eyes and pouty lips. She's maybe fourteen and stuck up. She don't even look at me. Well, she looks at me but I'm just a white man. She's a Suhtai, and looks down her petite nose at everyone, the rest of them Cheyenne included.

"Da next winter I go back and she's still not taken but the boys, dey are playing the love flute outside her lodge. I think, I'll make the bride offer to her pa, One Leg Eagle. But I'll give her some foofaraw first so she likes me and says to her pa, take the gifts. I do dat. I give her the red ribbons and the yeller ribbons, and she smiles and her eyes glow. I get her name this time: it's Little Whirlwind, and dat's a good name for her all right, only the whirlwind's not so little. She's a tempest. I am thinking, I give any bride-gift he wants and then the old medicine man give me the girl. I got a couple spare horses and a spare rifle for him, a Hawken with a flintlock.

"Den you ride in, you and Dance. And you see her, too, dis Cheyenne girl with sun streaming outa her eyes, dis little snot dat's above everyone. Like some Indian princess. You ride in and I see her peeking at dat red hair of yours, peeking and pretending she don't see it none and it don't interest her."

Raffin sighed and sipped a long draught. He wheezed. He hadn't watered it much. "Whew!" he gasped. "Dis stuff. I drink dis stuff maybe one time a year."

Fitzhugh listened and fought sleep. He'd had plenty of it himself. It had loosened Raffin's tongue and more. Raffin's face had

454

turned melancholy.

"Den you are dere, sniffing around the lodge of One Leg Eagle, and I see her looking sideways at you, watching you but not showing it, and I know I've lost her. You get her. I go back to my little lodge. One Creole heart busted up. All busted up. Dere goes my dream. I was gonna maybe trade robes somewhere at a little post, me and Little Whirlwind, the two of us at some place near her village. Maybe for American Fur. She made me dream, dis Little Whirlwind. Den you come along."

Raffin stared into the flame and slid sticks into it. Tears oozed from his dark eyes, startling Brokenleg. "She likes red hair," he muttered. "I don't have a busted leg, no limp. I'm no cripple. I am strong as a bull. But it don't count. You come along and I see the disdain. The more she disdains you, the more she likes you. And dis Creole, he thinks dis world is too damn cold."

"I never knew that — how you felt, Raul."

"You took the only ding I ever want away, and my life isn't so good. After the beaver quit I work day after day and month after month for Cadet Chouteau. I have a few Indian girls but dey aren't Little Whirlwind. Creoles got soft hearts. Creoles, if love goes bad we weep."

"These country marriages, they don't last. Mosta of the trappers I know dat take an Injun wife, they lodgepole her after a year or two. Git tired o' her. Sometimes they run off, git tired o' him."

Raffin nodded and sipped. "You damn Enklish, you don' know about love. You're a northern race — cold and mean. Love, it got wasted on you. Little Whirlwind, she's wasted on you. Brokenleg, you don't know what you got. You got — a princess. You got a beauty. You got sunshine, like light pourin' from da Virgin. You don't know that."

He wept again, sipping spirits and leaking tears from his brown eyes. They stained his cheeks and vanished into his bushy beard.

Brokenleg felt a bilious humor swell in him like stomach gas. A maudlin drunken Creole. It'd soured a good night. "So you got your revenge," he said harshly.

Raffin stared. Shrugged. "I do everything Cadet wants. I wreck you good. I got a whole year pay for it. Maybe two. But it don't do me no good. It don't make me happy." He stared moodily into the embers. "You know what I am? I'm Cadet Chouteau's wolf. I'm on the rolls at Fort Union but I don't spend no time there. I'm a gray wolf prowling around, makin' trouble

when he wants me to. I go stir up villages —
I know most of the tongues. I go around, fix
the opposition. Fix you good. He don't like
me around St. Louis none but he sends me
messages. In French. He never signs them.
They come up on the expresses, addressed
to me, sealed. He writes careful, not sayin'
much, but I always figure it out. Dat way he
talks to his wolf. I can read and write — dat
makes me different from the rest. And I
don't need friends and comforts. My Creole
heart's broken, so I am the gray wolf
slinking along the ridges. You see me now
and then — mostly you don't see me at all.
But I'm dere. I'm everywhere."

He sipped again, and then sat up straight.
"Now you know everything about Raul
Raffin. But you don't come here with a jug
for making talk, eh? You got business. All
night I wait for you to tell me your business.
I already know, but you got to tell me."

Raffin was right. Business hung over all
this like a snow mass waiting to avalanche.
"You tired o' bein' Chouteau's gray wolf?"

Raffin laughed. "*Merde!* You ask dumb
questions."

"You could get out, you know. Do something else. Beats me how a man can enjoy
skulking around out hyar all alone."

Raffin's face darkened. "It suits me fine. I

457

lose the one thing I care about so I do dis. You got something I want; I got something you want. Are we gonna do business or not?"

"I ain't followin' you."

"You're followin' plenty good. You just aren't admitting it yet. *Là-bas,* behind you. That parfleche you're leaning on. Give it to me."

Brokenleg lifted himself and turned warily, wondering if he'd be knifed. Carefully, he edged the heavy parfleche out from behind him and shoved it across the lodge, past the fire. Raffin yanked it the rest of the way and untied the flap. He rummaged within and then pulled out something flat, carefully wrapped in oilcloth, and undid the cloth. Within was a soft leather pouch, from which he extracted papers.

"Dis one here, I write it a few days ago. I get out the quill and the ink. I think maybe I am leaving here soon. But I still got some business with you maybe. So I wait." He handed the sheet to Brokenleg. "It's what you want, eh?"

Fitzhugh studied the sheet. Dense, thick script covered half of it, blotted several times. It carried a January 1843 date. Raffin's signature had been scrawled below the text, which was in English. He read with amazement a brief account of Raffin's private work for Chouteau. And a detailed account of Raffin's successful effort to plant three casks of contraband spirits in the Rocky Mountain Company cargo. He said he had acted on Chouteau's private instructions.

Fitzhugh stared at the document, scarcely believing his eyes. Scarcely believing it was in his hands. He could probably plunge out the door flap with it.

Raffin laughed. "It don't do you no good. You take dat down to St. Louis and them Indian superintendents, dey look at it and laugh. Dey say, dis here is a forgery. Oh, dey compare it with the handwriting on the cargo manifest, what I wrote dere, and it's the same, but dey say no, Dance, Fitzhugh and Straus, dey just hire a forger. You need dese too."

He handed five sheets to Brokenleg. Each contained a brief message in French. They were dated — the years ran from 1837 to 1842 — but not signed. Something commanding and elegant lay in the script. There were no blots.

"I can't read French."

Raffin wheezed happily. "Dat's why he wrote dem like dat. He send dem to me. He don't want Culbertson or Denig or Kipp to

459

know. And dose Creoles, dey can't read anyway."

"These are from Cadet Chouteau? Instructions to you?"

Raffin nodded. "Dey tell me what to do, what he wants. One dere tells me to erase the opposition — dat's you — by any means. Dat's his way of saying, kill you if I have to."

Brokenleg stared at these documents dumbfounded. "How do I know? I can't read French."

Raffin laughed. "I can read dem. But see — I take good care of dem. Oilcloth to keep the water out. Leather pouch, and den inside a good waterproof parfleche too. My petite letter and dese here, dey go together. You need everyt'ing."

"I could duck out with these."

Raffin laughed again. "Try it, eh?"

He held a throwing knife in his hand.

Business. "Raffin, what do you want for these? My robes hyar?"

"Robes?" Raffin didn't say any more, but mirth played over his sallow features. "Robes? What're you gonna do with dese robes? I get word dat your post — it don't exist no more. Dem Creoles, dey are either dead or walking down the river. Your robes, what'll you do with dem? You and Spoon and Constable, eh? Naw, Brokenleg, you don't want to think about what I want for dem letters."

His post gone? A whirl of dread whipped through Brokenleg. His men killed by Hervey — or Hervey's Crows? Trudeau? Maxim? All the rest? Some sort of brutal assault?

"How do I know that?" he asked, half-choked.

"You don't. You can go look. You got time. Middle of *l'hiver*, eh? I get word from Hervey. Him and me, we get word. He know where you are always. Few days ago I get the word."

Fitzhugh had the bad feeling that it was all true. And he knew what Raffin's bargain was.

"You want Little Whirlwind."

Raffin's eyes lit up. "Ah, *mon ami*, now you get around to it. You gimme Little Whirlwind, and I give you dose papers."

Little Whirlwind. A Devil's bargain if ever there was one. Not so hard to do, either. Trappers unloaded their squaws all the time; traded them off. Just moved their truck out of the lodge — that was all it took. They got the idea. Sometimes the squaws did it to the trapper — moved his truck out. Then he got the idea. It wouldn't bother the

Cheyenne none. The warriors struck deals like that all the time. "You want Little Whirlwind," he muttered.

Raffin chuckled pleasantly. "I'll quit old Chouteau. I get Little Whirlwind and I don't care what he thinks. I'll lose a year's salary, one hundred fifty — but it don't come to so much for a poor engage. I got more; I got gold in my parfleches. I'll never go back to St. Louis again. Maybe down to Bent's Fort — dey got lots of Southern Cheyenne dere, make Little Whirlwind happy. She obeys, *oui*. Good squaw does. She looks down her nose at me, disdains me, tells me she's a Suhtai and don't forget it, *oui?* I take here dere — or maybe Fort Hall. Hudson's Bay. Maybe Oregon. Who knows?" He shrugged. "She'll be happy. Dey get used to it and dat's it. She don't act good, maybe I'll lodgepole. Day are used to dat, too. *Oui?*"

A Devil's bargain. Brokenleg stared into the flame, dizzy. A confession and some supporting documents. Enough to rescue the company — maybe. If the post on the Yellowstone remained. And his men were alive and trading.

"I oughta go on up there and have a look," he muttered.

"No time, no time. Dose papers, you

don't get dem later. You come to do business tonight. I been waiting for weeks for dat. You do business tonight, or no business never."

"All right, Raffin. You git Dust Devil," he said.

The one who spoke English smiled faintly at the sight of the engages sipping spirits. He surveyed the shelves of the trading room, finding them stacked with untraded merchandise. He wandered into the warehouse, discovering crates and barrels containing more trade goods along with a pile of robes, most of them baled. His two colleagues trailed along, plus Maxim. He walked into the yard and studied that, his gaze halting at the half-destroyed shed being used for firewood; at the gaunt, desperate horses with their heads hanging; at the well-pit with round cobbles rather than water at its bottom.

He turned to Maxim. "The men are having a final drink."

"Yes. Some will leave. But I'm not surrendering. All this belongs to my family and our partners."

The headman laughed softly. "Then you will die."

"Maybe not. If your friend Julius Hervey

wanted you to take the post by force and kill us, you would have done it long ago. But that would anger the grandfathers."

The headman shrugged. "Maybe you will die of thirst or cold first."

"Maybe. Maybe Brokenleg Fitzhugh will return with the Cheyenne first and drive you away."

The headman shook his head. "No. Your men would stay and wait. But they are leaving. Only you will stay."

They wandered back into the trading room where the engages sipped silently. Maxim turned to his guests. "I don't know your names," he said.

"I am in your tongue, Big Robber, chief of the Absarokas."

It startled Maxim. Big Robber was a great chief of the Crows. The man before him looked formidable, a giant built of slabs of muscular flesh. He was a legendary chief who knew numerous white men. He had been friendly to them all, and a steady, thoughtful leader. It heartened Maxim slightly.

"This is Whistling Deer, head man of the Kit Fox Society, and Badger, a sacred man of our people."

"I am Maxim Straus."

"We know that."

"Would you care for some spirits?"

"Surrender first, young one, and then we will have spirits."

"Where's Hervey?"

"He awaits word."

He's not here then, Maxim thought. "Samson, a gill for these friends if you please."

"No, we will wait," said Big Robber. "When you go away we will have a party."

"I am not going — and I have a whole cask for your village." He nodded to Trudeau, who vanished into the storeroom and returned hefting a heavy cask. Without being bidden to, Trudeau screwed a brass bung faucet into it while Big Robber watched, frowning.

"Not now," said Big Robber peremptorily.

Samson Trudeau glanced at Maxim, who nodded slightly. The chief trader hefted the cask again and carried it past the three Crows and out the door. Big Robber watched Trudeau walk across the brilliant white flat, a thundercloud building in his face, but he did not prevent it. The other headmen watched sharply, saying nothing. Out at the edge of the village blanketed people flooded out to Trudeau. He set the cask into the snow, made some sign talk,

465

and then walked slowly back, unmolested. At the village, people scattered toward the lodges to grab cups or drinking horns.

"It's not cut. The little cask will make a grand party for your village," said Maxim, the Devil prompting him again.

Courvet handed each of the headmen a tin cup brimming with slightly cut spirits. They accepted. Big Robber grimaced slightly, a man tempted against his better judgment. Crow chiefs had always resisted the white man's vice.

"It makes no difference," he said at last. "You will surrender anyway."

Out at the village a mob collected around the keg and some warrior splashed the spirits into cups. Women elbowed their way ahead of the men, and many got to the spirits first. One warrior guzzled, cried, and spat, dancing around, clutching at his throat. Whoops and howls echoed across the flats.

Swiftly the afternoon mellowed. The three Crow leaders sat down beside the engages and sipped. Big Robber told bawdy stories — the Crow were famous for them — translated, and enjoyed himself. Outside, Crows gathered into knots to talk and joke. Wintry air didn't prevent them from having a party.

Maxim eyed them all soberly, pushing aside thoughts he didn't want to think. At last he nodded to Trudeau, who had stopped sipping, and they gathered buckets and headed for the river. No one stopped them but many eyes watched. They replenished the water casks in the post, led the two desperate horses out to water and then let them graze on picket lines. They grabbed axes and cut firewood and hauled armloads of it into the post.

The pair labored steadily for two hours gathering water and firewood and then cottonwood bark as fodder for the starved horses. Several times grinning warriors approached, cup in hand, their faces friendly. But Maxim never slowed down; he was driven by some terrible force within himself to do what he could before the siege lowered over the post again.

"I think they are out of spirits," said Samson. Off at the village some men had lifted the cask and tilted it to extract the last drop.

Without a word Maxim and Samson returned to the post, hefted another cask of two hundred proof spirits, and carried it out to the village. Happy crowds swarmed around them, laughing and pointing. They set it down beside the empty cask, drilled the bung faucet into it, and presented it to the Crows, who cheered. If Maxim could have spoken the tongue, he'd have made a speech.

"Bring the old cask," he said to Trudeau. "We'll fill it at the river."

Together they filled the cask with water and hefted it into the post. Hunger weakened him but he ignored it. The sun shone over Fitzhugh's Post for the smallest moment and he had much to do. He didn't know how this would end: he only knew what he had to do.

The coy January sun was already sliding toward its hiding place when an old Crow woman approached the trading window carrying a split robe. She smiled and pushed it across. Within, the chiefs and engages watched cheerfully.

"She makes a trade," said Big Robber. "Our friends will treat her good. Give much."

Trudeau spotted it and dashed in. He examined the worn robe, which wasn't worth much. Maxim watched, sudden hope swelling in him. "Give her a lot," he whispered.

Trudeau gave the seamed old woman her heart's desire: a yard of red trade cloth, a knife, and yellow ribbon. She beamed at him and at her chiefs, and limped off clutching her booty.

That's when trading started in earnest. Maxim, almost speechless, found himself recording transactions in the ledger while Trudeau pulled good robes proffered by laughing Crows, mostly women, across the counter and pushed trade goods out the window.

"You make bigger than Fort Cass," said Big Robber. "Now we are friends."

Some shrewd young Crows began shoving meat across the window — even a rear quarter of an elk. Trudeau surrendered sixty loads for it. It took three unsteady engages to drag it out to the yard and hang it.

The trading — along with a lot of whooping and howling — lasted deep into the evening, done by lantern light. And when at last Trudeau and Maxim closed the trading window half the engages were asleep, along with Big Robber, Whistling Deer, and Badger. A hundred fifty-seven new robes lay in the warehouse — costly robes when the price of two precious barrels of spirits were added in. But cheap, all in all — considering what had happened. No engage had left or showed any sign of wanting to go. The post had a month's supply of frozen meat hanging. Water brimmed from every container.

Maxim gathered his horses and brought them in after a day of grazing. No Crow had molested them. Then, as the post quieted, and the hilarious village slid into sleep, he walked out into the yard and peered up at cold glaring stars, the eyes of God. And there, in the icy blackness, he let the thing he'd pushed aside all that strange day slide into his mind. He wept with a bitterness he'd never experienced in his young life. The Devil had won.

Twenty-eight

Fitzhugh wanted a drink. He told himself if he didn't have a drink first he couldn't do it. But he had to do it, and there wasn't a drop in the village. He'd crawled into One Leg Eagle's lodge last night feeling like a burglar, but no one had noticed. He hadn't slept much either in spite of all the spirits he'd downed in Raffin's dubious company.

One thing haunted him: was it worth it? Ditching Dust Devil to save the company? *Maybe* save the company. Maybe those papers wouldn't change the Indian Bureau's mind. Maybe the Indian Bureau had been bought by Pierre Chouteau — who seemed to own everything else. Maybe that confession of Raffin's was no confession at all. Maybe the hand wouldn't match the hand on Captain Sire's cargo manifest. Maybe those weren't Chouteau's private notes. Maybe Raffin was gulling him, toying with him . . . But as he lay in the midnight dark of the lodge, he knew Raffin's papers were good. Raffin wanted Dust Devil badly enough to do it. And he still had some sort of future in the southwest, far away from the dominions of Chouteau and Company.

He didn't even know how to do it. Divorce Indian-style was easy and common. All they did was pitch their spouse's truck out of the lodge. That was the signal. No quarrels, no miserable harangues — usually — and no guilt. Even the Cheyenne, more puritanical than other tribes, didn't take marriage as seriously as white men. Lots of women in this very village had been married to several husbands. And those husbands had traded them to others. And a lot of marriages were plural. White Wolf himself had three wives.

Brokenleg knew he had to do it somehow. And he knew Dust Devil would come clawing at him when he told her. He had to tell her. He couldn't just pitch her stuff out of her parents' lodge. It wasn't his lodge and, anyway, her stuff was all mixed up with that of her sisters. And he somehow had to lead her over to Raffin and give her to him. Not until he did would Raffin hand over those papers.

His head ached. He spotted wintry stars through the smokehole and wished for spring. He wished for any time but tomorrow. Maybe it was all for nothing. Maybe he didn't have a post up there on the

Yellowstone. Maybe it was a burnt-out hulk. Raffin's news had chilled him. All his men, Maxim, scattered or dead; all the trade goods and robes and furnishings in Julius Hervey's hands. Why didn't he just tell Raffin to go to hell?

He sighed, wide awake.

"Why don't you sleep?" whispered Dust Devil.

"Leave me alone," he muttered.

He thrashed and pummeled his robes. His leg hurt again and the hard ground rose up and smote him.

"You're keeping us awake!" she hissed.

He clambered up, found his beaver-skin cap and a robe, and crawled through the door into the night. A new moon made the snow glow slightly. He caught the scent of sour cottonwood smoke ebbing through the village. Not the slightest breeze drilled the cold air into him.

He pulled the robe tight around him. He wore it skin out, hair in, but it didn't keep winter at bay very well. He had as much winter inside of himself as outside, and found himself wishing for summer. The heavens opened up to him and he sensed the distances above him. He wished he could be up there somewhere, peering down on all this, getting some perspective. From up there everything must look like the crawling of ants, and was even less important, he thought. What did he want? To rescue his partners, Jamie Dance and Guy Straus, and get rich trading for robes — or Little Whirlwind? She of the apricot flesh and scornful eye and Suhtai heart?

He reproached her in his heart. She hadn't been much of a wife. She'd scorned him, mocked him, and insulted white men and other tribesmen from the start. She'd humbled him, demanded slaves and riches and he didn't know what-all, nagging all the while. And hardly a tender moment between them. She'd told him he wasn't half the man that any Tsistsista warrior was. She'd told him to count coup and make war — that's what she wanted for a man.

"I'll by god get shut of her," he growled into the silence. "She was no damn good. I've got me three more, sweeter'n her, and not mean and clawin' at my soul all the time. Even her pa and ma get mad at her for disdainin' everyone and bein' mean."

But even as he said it, love clawed at him just as hard. That beautiful tempest of a woman was alive in every fiber, brimming with passion and joy and anger; seething with feeling, her life a rhapsody of being and doing.

"Ah, hell, they trade wives all the time. It don't mean nothin'," he grumbled. He knew he'd have no trouble with her family. It would be his perfect right to give her to Raffin. He wouldn't have any trouble with anyone else, either. Most of the Creoles he knew made a "country marriage" as they called it, kept the Indian girls until they got tired of them, lodgepoled them and got another. No one would rebuke him — except himself.

"You're mad at me," said Dust Devil, startling him. She emerged from the darkness wearing her scarlet capote with the hood up, bewitching even in a bitter winter night. She was fully dressed, in her calf-high rabbit-trimmed winter moccasins and fringed doeskin shirt.

"Yeah I am," he snarled.

"I can tell."

"I'm divorcin' you. Splittin' the blankets."

She absorbed that a moment, then growled, some odd muttering down at the bottom of her throat, half laughter and half anger.

"Me and all my sisters?"

"Jist you."

"You like them better than me." It was a statement.

"They aren't so proud."

She laughed softly again, but it sounded odd, as if it really was a snarl. "You're too smelly anyway. Tsistsista wash every day — even now."

That relieved him. If she'd sobbed and begged to stay with him, his soul would have shattered like glass. He peered about him — how could he be doing this? Saying these things? He could stop — he could retreat. They hadn't tumbled over the cliff — not yet.

"You takin' it bad?"

She hissed. That's all she did. He'd turned her into an enemy with a few words.

"I'm givin' you to Raffin," he snapped. But the words choked out.

She registered that a moment. "I am not free?"

"Naw."

"I cannot go to a Tsistsista man now?"

"I told you. I'm givin' you to Raul Raffin. He always wanted you from the time you were fourteen."

"Maybe I don't want him."

"You're Cheyenne. It ain't yours to say."

She hissed again and it sounded like river ice scraping against itself. "He has wounded eyes," she muttered. "He looks like an elk that's dying."

"Well, he's got you."

She squinted at him in the dark. He saw that lovely flat-planed face framed by the red hood. Her eyes studied him, gleaning more understanding from the way he stood and gestured and grimaced than from his words. "He give you something for me," she said. "Maybe the talking signs that tell the grandfathers about who put the spirits on the boat. Yes?"

"Yes. He'll gimme that for you."

"Ah! Like a bride price. Better than many horses and guns and blankets before your lodge! It's a big gift, these papers. More than you gave my father for me!"

"Lots more. Raffin, he can't work for Chouteau no more."

"Is this the biggest gift any white man ever give for a woman?"

"Mebbeso. I don't know."

"Am I worth a lot of money?"

"Yeah. You're worth mebbe fifty thousand dollars."

"How much is that?"

"Everything the company ever bought, and all them robes too."

"Ahhhhh!" Then she looked crestfallen. "But he takes me from here. Yes?"

"I don't know. That's up to him. He said maybe he'd go on down to the Bent's Fort area — away from Chouteau."

"Bent's Fort? Ah. Charles Bent will be there with Owl Woman?"

"Her and all the southern Cheyenne, in and out o' there all the time."

"They have the four sacred arrows," she said. "But not many Suhtai. Mostly Omissis."

"Guess you'll have to look down your nose at them, too."

She smiled. "I like this. We will go to Raffin now? I like him better than you anyway."

Suddenly it was reversed. He wanted to cry out to her, tell her he loved her, tell her she had been his princess — but he bit it off. "Let's go git him up. Git it over with," he muttered, stunned by loss.

The lodge had chilled but One Leg Eagle scarcely seemed to notice. He sat before the dying coals, lost in another world. He had fed sweet grass to the waning fire and then dried sage leaves carefully hoarded from summer. Little Whirlwind had thrust herself into the pungent smoke until it clung to her and permeated her scarlet capote.

She sat across from him, waiting patiently. Her mother and sisters had discreetly vanished. Brokenleg had gone to check on his horses. She pulled her capote tighter to ward off the chill, and waited for her father to make his medicine. Was he not the greatest shaman of the Suhtai, and keeper of the Medicine Hat? She trusted him utterly.

His eyes remained closed and he seemed to be listening to voices she had not heard, nodding occasionally, waiting for the sky spirits and the wind spirits and the spirits of those who crawled across the breast of earth mother to impart their sacred wisdom to him — and her. For soon she would leave her family — perhaps forever. The old medicine had been broken and One Leg Eagle listened and waited for the new.

The news had brought tears welling up in Antelope's eyes, and cries from her sisters, but her father had nodded calmly, closed his eyes, and peered inward upon worlds known only to him. "It is time to find new medicine," he'd told her.

No one questioned Brokenleg's right. He had only done what was his privilege, the privilege of any man among her people. And he remained the son-in-law of One Leg Eagle and Antelope three times over. He would spend many more moons in this lodge.

"I have always thought that this might

be," he said at last, returning from his dreamland. "It is a sorrow for us, but it is the way the life-dream unfolds." He eyed her, as if wondering whether to say what filled his mind. "The medicine of Little Whirlwind was strong," he said gently. "The whirlwind whipped up dust and threw it in people's eyes. The whirlwind would sting a man, a husband. It is good that the old medicine was broken. It is good that you have come to sit here this last time and receive all that the spirits can give you. I am only the Listener."

She would receive new medicine then, and a new name. She wondered if Raffin would call her by the broken name. She would insist that he use her new one because that is who she would soon be — if her father's listening gave her one.

She discovered a faint rebuke in his words and that was strange in her ear. He had gently told her that she had stung and hurt Robert Fitzhugh. She let that slide from her mind. Not even her father could say that to her.

"Southwind and Sun have made a great conceit out of the whirlwind," he said.

She didn't like that, either. Was he rebuking her? She knelt uncomfortably in the sharpening cold. He slid back into his private world again, nodding and rocking, while she waited and thought about Raffin and how he might treat her. His wounded eyes made her uneasy. She was carrying Fitzhugh's child, but neither Fitzhugh nor Raffin knew that. Her time to stay in the women's lodge had come and gone, and she knew that at last she would bear a child. Antelope had suspected it and had eyed her with questions in her warm eyes, but Little Whirlwind had chosen to say nothing. Now she wondered if Raffin would be angry with her for that.

Her father stiffened, and gazed sadly at her. "I have no name for you," he said. "The spirits do not speak to me. I see only the sky with nothing in it and the earth with nothing on it. I have listened and waited. Perhaps some day your medicine spirit will come upon you. You must fast and seek the vision. If you should live among the southern People, one of them might guide you. But I have nothing to give you now."

A great sadness fell upon them both.

"I may never see my father or my mother, or my brothers and sisters, or the grandfathers and grandmothers again," she said, fear clutching her.

He nodded. "It is like death. Having no name is like death, too."

481

It terrified her, having no name. "I will keep my old one," she replied with an edge to her voice. When she left this lodge no one of her family would speak her name, and she would be like the dead to them unless the spirits gave her a new name.

She didn't thank him. She'd grown numb in the cold lodge, and stood.

"It is time," he said, rising slowly. He found a blanket and steered her out into glaring sunlight. They waked quietly toward Raffin's lodge and she was grateful that village gossip had not yet caught up with her. She stared at her village, her people, the familiar lodges whose inhabitants she knew so well, and her heart ached. But her heart had ached when Fitzhugh had taken her away. This was nothing new. And surely Raffin was a great man among the whites, and had no limp either.

They found laden horses tied before Raffin's lodge, including one with a high-backed woman's saddle on it. She and her father reached the lodge door and he scratched at it softly. She peered around, hoping no one was in sight. No one was. Her mother and sisters were visiting somewhere. The door flap slid aside and Raffin beckoned them in. She found a warm lodge with nothing in it — except Brokenleg, who stood solemnly, looking truculent and uncomfortable. Their gazes dodged each other.

"Ah, Little Whirlwind, you have come. Welcome to my lodge. And you as well, One Leg Eagle. I am honored," said Raul Raffin gracefully. She looked him over with dread.

"Ever since I saw you, when you were a maiden, I loved you and wanted you," said Raffin in good Cheyenne. "My heart died when I lost you. You know little of me but I know everything about you, for never a day has passed that I didn't think of you or ask about you. No woman of the Tsistsistas is more beautiful."

He smiled, a curious joy in his pain-laden eyes. His great beard fascinated her. It was made of black wires.

"I have a bride-gift for you," he said. He reached into his capote and withdrew a long soft-tanned leather pouch and handed it to her. It felt velvety in her hands. She undid the soft thong and withdrew a medicine pipe that seemed to glow in her fingers. Its bowl had been carved from the red pipestone that came from the quarry far to the east, and its long hardwood shaft had been smoothed and rubbed until it shone. No amulets or feathers adorned it. She felt afraid to hold it because its pipe-spirits spoke to her.

"It's a Cree pipe I traded for once. Its owner, a headman of the Crees called Walks on Water, says it is a great medicine pipe."

"This is for me?"

"You'll keep the pipe. I don't know why, but I thought this is the very thing for you."

"But a woman —"

"I see a medicine woman of the Tsistsistas before me."

"I have no medicine." She turned to her father, a question in her eyes.

He nodded.

"I am the pipe-keeping woman then," she said. The pipe leapt in her fingers, and felt silky in her hand. This was confusing and she didn't know what to say. "I have nothing for you," she said.

"You are everything I want."

"I will keep the sacred pipe," she said, sliding it back into the velvety pouch.

Fitzhugh glared, but she didn't mind. What a morning was this!

"All right, Raffin," he muttered. "I done my part of it."

Raffin laughed softly. "Now we kill each other, eh?"

That frightened her, but both white men laughed. How could they laugh and talk of killing? Still, Brokenleg looked like he was about ready to do it. He'd become a familiar stranger there, someone who'd vanish from her thoughts soon. Had she ever made love with that man? She'd never have to go to St. Louis again! Never have to ride the fireboats again!

"Ah! Maybe Raffin should kill you!" she cried.

But Raffin was digging into his blue capote, and this time he withdrew a flat packet wrapped in yellow oilcloth and handed it to Fitzhugh. She yearned to know its contents. Was this her bride-price? She hoped she was worth a lot. Any Tsistsista woman as pretty as she should be worth a lot.

He carefully unwrapped the folded oilcloth until he bared several sheets of paper with the white men's talking signs on them. He studied each one, squinting furiously at them, as if the talking signs baffled him.

"Damned French," he muttered. "If this hyar's a joke, Raffin —"

Raffin shrugged. "I think you make your part, and I make my part of the bargain, *oui?* Dey are the papers. Dere's my name, *oui?* And I write in Enklish."

"If this hyar's a joke, watch your back trail because I'm a-comin'."

Brokenleg folded the oilcloth over the

papers again and tucked the bundle into his coat. Little Whirlwind itched to know what these papers were, and tonight she would ask Raffin. She had a good idea, though. These talking papers would save the company. She was worth the price of the company!

She turned to her father. "I am worth a lot."

He nodded, not really understanding.

Brokenleg growled something and limped out. The parting of the door flap shot dazzling light into the little lodge. His red hair flamed in the sun as if he was on fire. The flap fell back, leaving her in shadow. Utterly against her will, she sobbed once. And then choked down the shards of her soul.

Raffin turned to her. "We have a long way to go, Little Whirlwind. But soon we will be far to the south. Are you ready?"

The moment had come. She hugged her father and was glad her sisters and brothers and mother were not there because she couldn't bear it.

"I am your daughter," she whispered.

"You are my daughter, Keeper of the Pipe."

Raffin helped her into the saddle, which felt icy under her full skirts. He clambered into his own saddle, holding the picket line.

He addressed One Leg Eagle. "I will be good to her," he said.

Her father stood as silent as rock, weeping.

She wiped away tears as Raffin led her up the Powder River, and her village slid behind naked cottonwoods and vanished behind her, like a dream upon awakening.

Twenty-nine

The day after the great party Fitzhugh's Post did the biggest robe business in its brief history. Cheerful Crows, remembering a legendary bacchanal, piled fine buffalo robes into the trading window and walked away with mountains of goods, all of them traded at normal prices. Wizened women, young men, even children, waited patiently for their chance to trade a robe or a pelt for some foofaraw. Some of them traded the robes off their backs, the very robes that had warmed them as they waited. Samson Trudeau examined the robes and pelts and kept two clerks hopping among the shelves and two more engages hauling the harvest into the warehouse. The post acquired a sizeable collection of elk hides, wolf pelts, otter and mink, which all found ready markets back in the States.

But Maxim watched it all darkly. Was this how the world worked? Debauch the Indians with illegal spirits and reap the harvest? He alone was responsible. Did good come from evil? These questions rattled through his mind, swaying him one way and another. One moment he truculently justified his conduct; the next he sagged into despair. He knew, vaguely, that this was a rite of passage; that he was leaving behind him the ideals and dreams of youth and innocence, and plunging into the harsh realities of adult life. And he mourned his lost innocence. But his very eyes told him that before the sun set there would be five or six hundred new robes in the warehouse, and countless other furs that would buoy his family's venture and even turn a profit.

But he couldn't reconcile it, and his anguish put him in a bad temper. He'd neglected everything until Samson Trudeau gently took command and set his remaining engages to work, some cutting firewood along the river, while others tackled the half-dug well with renewed vigor. The memory of thirst, cold, and starvation goaded them all into furious labor. They all vowed never to be trapped again. By mid-afternoon the well-diggers had struck moist clay, and the woodcutters had dragged a dozen cords of long limbs out of the timber and into the yard. By late afternoon the well-diggers were bucketing water out of the new well and lining it with the cobbles they'd pried from the earth.

They laughed while they worked, sang bawdy French ditties, and devoured meat — while Maxim scowled and wrestled with his conscience.

The post imprisoned him. For days it had been his jail and fortress. Now, suddenly, he needed to flee it. He wandered out upon the flat, meandered through Big Robber's village, where women toiled around outdoor fires and men gossiped and gambled on the stick game, and hefted the new rifles they'd just acquired. They grinned at him as he passed but said nothing because he could not talk their tongue. Sixty gallons of raw spirits had turned these people into friends. A debauch had wrested them from the American Fur Company and Fort Cass.

Life had become a mystery to him. He ached to find something to hang on to, to justify all this before the dwindling sun of this day vanished. He wanted answers before winter night came, and found none. He reached the river and stared into it. Ice stretched out from the banks, but open water rippled in the lavender twilight where the main channel ran. This very water would eventually flow past St. Louis, far away. St. Louis, where his family lived. This very water. It was as if his deeds would be carried on the breast of the rivers, the

Bighorn, the Yellowstone, the Missouri, the Mississippi, into the ears of law-givers and judges and juries.

In the end, theology rescued him. A mortal, dealing with the realities of the world, could hardly get through life without sinning, he thought, the inkling of his salvation coming to him in the dusk. All mortals were sinners. None was perfect, or ever could be. But there was Yahweh, God, loving mankind and wanting the love of mankind, ever forgiving transgressions of the law, ever loving mortals like himself who'd trimmed and compromised — and failed the ultimate tests.

"Ah, it's you, little Straus. I've been looking."

Maxim whirled, finding Julius Hervey on horseback and closing. Julius Hervey, trotting relentlessly toward him, the dusk not hiding the wild fires in his eyes, or the mesmerizing evil of the man.

Theology vanished before the terror of that man. Maxim peered wildly about looking for succor. The post lay an infinity away. Not even any Crows wandered near. He was alone — alone with a madman who would kill him. Bitterly he recollected shooting Hervey's horse from the safety of the post, and Hervey's mocking threats.

491

"Why, little Straus. You've stolen my Crows."

Maxim couldn't speak. Terror welled up in him. He backed away, edging toward the ice even as Julius Hervey edged his horse closer and closer, strange fires flaring in him.

"How delightful to find you alone. Are you a man, little Straus?"

"What — what do you want?"

Hervey laughed, a maniacal howl on the icy night wind. "I want my Crows. I want you."

Maxim's limbs wouldn't work. He wanted to find a stick, a rock, anything. A sling and a pebble against Goliath. But nothing lay at hand, just grass leading into river brush and beyond that, black ice. His pulse began to lift, and his body convulsed. He'd have to run, run for his life, run a half a mile, run faster than a galloping horse.

Words came. "I've done nothing you wouldn't do."

Hervey laughed. "Where is St. Louis?" he asked, mysteriously. "Where is St. Louis?"

"Take your Crows. We have a Cheyenne trade."

"No, you don't. We've made sure you don't. Where's old Stiffleg, eh? He gonna come rescue little Straus?" He chuckled easily.

"I'll fight my own fights," Maxim said, feeling his body tense. Hervey kept edging the dark horse closer, crowding Maxim, forcing him back. A sheathed knife hung from his belt. His own voice mocked him. Julius Hervey outweighed him by fifty pounds, and his strength had always been a legend of the north.

"How does it feel, little Straus? You ready for this?"

Maxim backed into the brush and stumbled. Easily, Hervey slid off the horse. Maxim saw his chance and ran, dodging the horse just as Hervey landed on his feet. Maxim felt icy air burn his throat and scorch his lungs, felt his legs pound the frozen earth. And felt a giant force claw him to a stop and whirl him around.

Julius Hervey wasn't even breathing hard. "Where you going, little Straus?"

"St. Louis!" he cried.

Hervey's gloved hand gripped the wool of Maxim's mackinaw coat, imprisoning him. "I'm St. Louis," he said. "I'm Washington City. I'm God."

Maxim punched. He smacked his fist into Hervey's face, some frantic animal instinct driving it. He felt it connect and rock the man. Hervey quaked and his laughter slid into a snarl. He shoved, and Maxim found himself careening backward, stumbling, toppling to the cast-iron earth.

Hervey's boot smacked his ribs. Maxim felt arrows of fire pierce his body. The boot hit again and pain geysered through his chest. He couldn't breathe. He writhed sideways just as Hervey's boot caught him again, this time into his hip, numbing his side.

Maxim gasped and rolled but Hervey landed on him like a cat, straddling him, gloved fists, hard as anvils, cracking his nose and jaw, boxing his ears. White fire laced through Maxim, shrieking pain he'd never known or imagined. Blood welled from his nose and gums. Teeth rattled in their sockets. Sledgehammers slammed down, one after another, never ceasing no matter how Maxim twisted and dodged and writhed and shrieked.

And all the while, Hervey laughed and taunted and joked. "How's that, little Straus? Had enough? Not enough yet — you're still bawling! How about an arm? Let's bust an arm!"

An awesome blow bludgeoned Maxim's left arm and he felt something snap, felt his fingers numb and his hands spasm helplessly. Heard laughter high and mad and mean. "No arm. Little Straus lost an arm!"

And still the blows showered over him, rocking his head, convulsing his body. But they seemed fainter and fainter, even though his body tossed and bobbed, fainter and fainter until the blows disappeared behind a great black curtain of velvet laughter.

Some eternity later he awoke to pain, which inhabited his whole body, overflowing like bile. He awakened to nausea, too, and the throbbing of a headache beyond fathoming. Someone was sliding him onto something but his eyes wouldn't open and he didn't care. The only reality was pain. Voices drifted into the tiny corner of his mind that knew life, voices in a strange tongue. He felt himself being carried, each movement lancing pain through a helpless arm, carried, swaying, rocking, hurting. He knew somehow he was being carried to Fort Cass, and his rescuers were Crows.

Brokenleg waited restlessly. His Cheyenne winter had ended. He was out of trade goods. He'd acquired over two thousand robes which were nestled in three lodges, one of them Raffin's, and two tents. These had come not only from White Wolf's village, but three other Cheyenne bands wintering along the Powder. He itched to return to the post, but winter pinioned him there. He worried about his post and its fate, remembering Raffin's words. He itched to go there and find out but great ridges of snow and brutal cold foiled him. He desperately wanted to take his precious papers down the river. He'd do it personally as soon as he could. But not until winter eased its grip. The papers were everything: wealth, profit, a future.

Other things plagued him also. His horses were gaunted and winter-weak, and yet he would be asking them to shoulder enormous loads. He needed more, and intended to trade his three lodges for them. He and Abner and Zach spent the better days building travois, one after another, to carry the mountain of robes. They constructed twenty and then devoted their free days to peeling cottonwood bark from green limbs and feeding it to their ribby horses. Village people watched curiously, amazed at the industry of the traders. This time of year most Cheyennes huddled around their hearth fires, visiting, gossiping, spinning the tribal legends, hunting, and making love. Among the Cheyenne, along with all the northern plains tribes, every autumn was the great birthing time.

In the lodge of One Leg Eagle and Antelope life continued placidly, undamaged by Little Whirlwind's departure. If anything, Hide Skinning Woman, Elk Tail, and Sweet Smoke outdid themselves to please him, making quilled and beaded winter moccasins lined with rabbit fur, cooking succulent buffalo hump rib or tongue, and pleasuring him with bright-eyed joy as if to tell him that they understood everything. The loss of one-quarter of his wives had caused scarcely a ripple.

He wondered if he missed her. Sometimes he did; other times he barely noticed. He didn't miss her vitriolic tongue or her contempt of others, but he missed her mockery and merriment. But she was gone and even the memory of her faded as the sun returned to the land of the Cheyenne, and nibbled holes in the snow.

Upon the arrival of *Po o tan e ishi*, the Buffalo-and-Horses-Begin-to-Fill-Out-Moon, Brokenleg decided to go even though great ridges of crusted snow barred his way. He gathered his numerous ponies, traded his lodges for more, loaded his travois with mountains of robes, smoked the pipe with his friends throughout the village, gave White Wolf a parting gift of tobacco, feasted with his family, smoked quietly with One

Leg Eagle to renew the family bond, and departed on a bright March morning, deceptively warm. He hoped he wasn't too late. If the river ice broke he could be trapped.

His women, gorgeously attired in blanket capotes made from blue and green and cream Witney blankets he'd given them, boarded their ponies along with Zach and Abner, and they took off, escorted for a while by the Dog Soldiers, many of them happily hefting good Leman rifles they'd bought from him.

They clung to the windward side of ridges where the snow was lightest and brown grass poked through to support the horses, but now and then they hit terrible pockets of crusted snow that bloodied pasterns and tipped the travois. They slogged through an empty world, devoid of bird song. Not much game was evident, though they spotted tracks.

They reached the Tongue and found the ice creaking and rubbery, so they crossed one animal at a time while the gray ice growled and complained. But it held. That was the last great water barrier. Fitzhugh rejoiced although he worried the horizons with constant glances, awaiting the late blizzard that could trap or destroy them. They lost a horse on the Little Bighorn. It died in the night from unknown causes. They lost another on the east bank of the Bighorn, this one gaunted and winter-sickened. In each case they had to adjust the loads, burdening the others all the more.

Beside them the Bighorn River groaned and sighed, and finally broke its icy cap and sent the shards whirling north, with a great clamor. At one point the giant slabs formed a thundering dam, driving water out of the riverbed and forcing them to detour.

And then they were nearly home. Worry clawed at Brokenleg. Would he find — nothing? His post an abandoned ruin? Or find a siege? He was tempted to reconnoiter lest he walk into grave trouble, but some urgency crabbed at him and he drove his party harder than ever into the icy night, taking advantage of a frosty half-moon. They'd arrive well after dark, which would be good if there was trouble at hand.

They broke out of the naked cottonwoods and beheld the silent flat, washed with pale light. No lodges clustered around the post but it stood darkly, intact.

"She's there," muttered Abner.

"Looks dead," added Zach.

Brokenleg studied the gray hulk and then slid his Hawken from its sheath and fired it.

The boom startled the peace. He kicked his horse and tugged at his picket line, and his weary parade coiled out of the latticework of branches and into the nakedness of the flats. Brokenleg reloaded as they walked, wondering if he'd shortly see the cold glint of rifle barrels poking from unshuttered windows.

Instead, he heard a shout. "Is that you? Brokenleg?" Samson's voice. Rejoicing, he hollered back, and moments later the yard gate creaked open and the post swallowed thirty laden horses.

Fitzhugh's Post lived. Its engages lived.

"You be here, old coon," bawled Fitzhugh.

"*Sacrebleu!* So it seems!"

Fitzhugh clambered off his weary horse. His leg collapsed but he caught the saddle fender and righted himself. Then he caught Samson in a mountain hug while around him men bawled greetings and barked at the moon.

"You all right?" he asked anxiously.

"Ah, mostly."

"You traded any?"

"Three thousand almost."

The number dizzied Fitzhugh. "So many?"

"Got some Crow trade. I see you got the Cheyenne."

500

"Twenty-one hundred, and some pelts."

"Ah . . . And is there other news? The company — does it live?"

"It lives, I reckon. Tell you about it later. Got me some papers from Raul Raffin — he done it. He done it and confessed it."

"Raffin? Him it was?" Samson looked troubled. "Did you beat him to a pulp? Why would he admit to such a thing?"

"Cost me some," Fitzhugh said.

Around him, half-dressed engages unhooked travois and dragged the heavy loads into the warehouse. Others led the weary horses to a pen and bucketed water from a well Fitzhugh had never seen before. "Ye got some talkin' to do," he muttered.

"So do you, *mon ami.*"

He headed toward the warmth of the post, his three wives ahead of him, Trudeau uncomfortable at his side. "Where's Maxim? He sulkin' again, Samson?"

Samson stopped, looking miserable. "He's — dead."

"Dead? Dead?" The enormity of it rushed through him. "Maxim?"

"It's a long story. But I will tell the ending. Julius Hervey caught him alone near the river and beat him. He lingered for four days and died. Something inside of him all torn up. He's buried over there."

Samson waved at some place outside the post.

"Hervey murdered him!"

Trudeau nodded.

Brokenleg's gorge rose but he choked it back. Maxim, Maxim . . . He limped across the yard and through the gates into the snowy wilderness. He rounded a corner of the post, heading in the direction Trudeau had pointed. The grave lay there, scarcely twenty yards from the stockade, cold stone heaped over it abundantly, an act of love from those who'd clawed away the frozen clay and laid him there. "Boy, boy," he muttered. "Hope ye be with God." He tarried there until the cold bit him.

He limped back, his leg torturing him, his thoughts torturing him, and found Trudeau in the warm trading room beside a radiant stove.

"Tell me everything," he said.

Trudeau nodded. "I will, but answer a question first, eh? Where's Little Whirlwind?"

"I gave her to Raffin."

Trudeau sucked breath and then exhaled slowly. "I ask one question and get answers to the others. Ah, *mon ami*, the boy, Maxim, he saved us. And I will tell you how, eh?"

Trudeau talked swiftly, punctuating his

narrative with Creole gestures, and bit by bit Brokenleg learned of the siege, the desperation, the starvation, the brink of doom . . . and of Maxim's remedy — two casks of the spirits he hated so much. And of the toll it took on the youth, who'd wept the next day and was wandering alone along the river when the angel of death visited him.

"Boy, boy," Brokenleg muttered. "You growed up and died the same day." He sighed. "Hervey. Forty-year-old giant in his prime, mountain-strong, kickin' a boy to death." He sighed. "You got witnesses? We got anything?"

"I have made a record, Brokenleg. The whole story — what I learned, what the Crows said, and some of Maxim's rambling thoughts as he died. Take it to St. Louis, take it."

"Where's St. Louis? Don't know where it is," Brokenleg muttered. "There's only hyar."

But the next day he left for St. Louis.

Thirty

Yvonne clung to Guy through the service, and Guy knew that behind her veil she wept. Her priest, Father Desmoulins, droned on, trying to comfort them as best he could as they sat in the chapel of the cathedral church. It wasn't easy for the priest, who was comforting a Catholic mother and Jewish father grieving over the loss of a son who hadn't made any choices in his brief life. Still, the promises and hopes of the psalms lifted some of the darkness out of Guy. On one side of them sat their beautiful Clothilde. On the other, Robert Fitzhugh, his stiff leg poking under the pew ahead, looking bizarre in a hastily tailored black suit. Beyond Brokenleg sat Hiliodore Billedeaux, Guy's counselor. Guy didn't know who sat behind other than his friend and lender Robert Campbell, but there were several.

The priest concluded a prayer and a benediction, and this part of it was done. The service did little to mend the ache over a life snuffed out at seventeen on the twenty-seventh day of January, eighteen forty-two, two thousand river miles away. But it was something to mark the event, make it dark and sacred in their thoughts. When Yvonne had received the news she'd sighed and wept, and remarkably, had refrained from telling him she had known it would happen all along. He escorted his silent wife and daughter to a waiting black chaise driven by his slave Gregoire and saw them off, the chaise rattling through spring sunlight to their home. He had other things to do that could not wait.

So much more to do. Grimly, he and Brokenleg followed Hiliodore to his carriage and were transported through balmy air to Hiliodore's chambers. There the attorney collected a sheaf of papers, some of them brought a great distance, and added to them an affidavit of Robert Fitzhugh describing a confession made to him by one Raul Raffin. Not a word had been spoken. Nothing was worth saying. Billedeaux drove them down the steep grade to the levee and the federal offices where David D. Mitchell, Superintendent of Indian Affairs, Central Division, ran the vast western territories. Mitchell was expecting them, and wore black.

"Gentlemen, be seated," he said.

Billedeaux extracted the papers and laid them before the superintendent who perused them carefully, reading them twice while his visitors waited silently. He rose, withdrew a folder, and extracted from it a cargo manifest, and turned to its last entry, nodding.

"The same hand as far as I can tell," he said. "And these are Cadet's notes. I know that hand better than my own. And Trudeau's account of the murder. Mr. Fitzhugh, do you vouch to me that the events described in your affidavit are correct?"

"I swore it, didn't I?" Brokenleg snapped.

Mitchell let it pass. He drummed thick fingers on the oak top of his desk and then reached for his quill and ink bottle. He scratched something on paper, blotted, and handed it to Hiliodore. "That's a conditional permit to trade as you had been. Conditional because it must be approved by my colleagues in Washington City. I'll forward these as soon as I have copies made. This should suffice. I think you can complete your plans to resupply your posts."

Guy nodded.

"Monsieur Mitchell, we thank you," said Hiliodore. "Is there anything else you desire of us?"

"A word with Guy, please," Mitchell said.

506

The attorney and Brokenleg filed out, leaving Guy with Davey Mitchell.

"Guy, Guy, I'm sorry. You know American Fur."

"I'm sorry, too."

"They stop at nothing. Old Cadet tolerates it. Are you doing something about Hervey?"

"Hiliodore has obtained a warrant. For murdering Maxim. For imprisoning me. And we are suing Cadet."

Mitchell nodded. "You on your way there?"

Guy nodded.

"I'm so sorry Guy. You know their motto: *ecrasez tout opposition.* You knew that when you formed your company. Only no one imagined the monopoly would murder your son."

"No, I didn't imagine it. I should have."

"The chances of pulling Hervey out of that wilderness to stand trial are pretty —"

"Slim. It's a step that has to be taken."

Mitchell nodded. "You have returns coming?"

"A mackinaw with five thousand robes and pelts."

Mitchell whistled. "No wonder Hervey . . ." He stopped abruptly. "You licked them."

"The price was too great," said Guy.

"I was going to ask you whether it was worth it, but you've told me. God keep you, Guy," said David Mitchell.

"In one way . . . it was worth it," said Guy. "Maxim had a vision of the world — and died a man."

Moments later they walked along Front Street, the great river shimmering nearby, and into the grubby offices of Chouteau and Company. A clerk admitted them to Pierre Chouteau Jr.'s ornate offices.

"Ah, Straus, my condolences. I hope you got my wreath," said Cadet.

"I did."

Chouteau's gaze settled on Hiliodore after raking Fitzhugh briefly. A question formed on his face.

"You had an engage named Raffin," said Hiliodore.

"Ah, perhaps. I don't know the names of them all. So many, *oui?*"

"You knew him well."

"Shall I order tea, gentlemen?"

"No," said Guy. "We have only a question or two. What are you doing about Julius Hervey?"

"Hervey? Hervey? Oh. At Fort Cass, I believe. Should I be doing something?"

"Yes. You could discharge him. It would

help your company."

Billedeaux said, "We have a murder warrant for him. And another warrant. Will you instruct him to come down the river for trial?"

"Why, of course. Let the man face judge and jury. But I don't think he's guilty of anything. He's a good man, what little I know of him."

"You'll discharge him if he fails to appear?"

"Certainly. We tolerate no lawbreakers in the company."

"See that you don't," said Guy.

"This is an unfriendly visit, *mes amis.* Won't you have tea? How are your returns, Guy? A good season?"

"We had a good season," said Guy. "But it cost me a son, and Mr. Fitzhugh a wife, and the company horses, oxen, wagons, and other items. But a good profit if Dance's operation succeeded."

"It's a hard business, eh?"

"A hard business," said Guy. "And we lost."

Author's Note

In 1834, the aging John Jacob Astor sold his wilderness giant, the American Fur Company, to two buyers. Ramsey Crooks bought the Northern Department, centered on the Upper Great Lakes, as well as the company name. Pratte, Chouteau and Co. bought the Upper Missouri Outfit, but that company continued to be known as American Fur along the Missouri River.

Whatever the name, the company continued its ruthless treatment of all competitors, resorting to whatever method it could get away with. And since its crimes occurred in a vast wilderness, it got away with much. There were, of course, honorable men in that large company, among them three depicted in this story: Alexander Culbertson, James Kipp, and Peter Sarpy. There were others less honorable. My fictional Julius Hervey is based on the real Alexander Harvey, one of the most brutal men in the fur trade. He devoted his malign energies to the American Fur Company but was more a liability than an asset, and eventually wound up in opposition.

While my story is fiction, I have portrayed some historical fur trade people in it, including Captain Joseph Sire, Black Dave Desiree, David Mitchell, Robert Campbell, and Pierre Chouteau Jr. Big Robber was an important Crow chief. The tactics the fur company used in my story to destroy the opposition are fictional, but historically plausible. The usual method was to attempt a buy-out, and if that failed to resort to less savory methods, up to and including murder, usually by Indian proxies to avoid blame. The memoirs of Joseph LaBarge, as recorded by Hiram Martin Chittenden, describe two such attempts.

Alcohol was the central lubricant of the robe trade, and I have accurately depicted its transportation and use by traders. Congressional prohibition had no effect on the traffic, but did induce a certain caution among traders. The American Fur Company nearly lost its license when a rival trader revealed to authorities that it had a whiskey still operating at Fort Union.

The decision of my hero, Brokenleg Fitzhugh, to barter his Cheyenne wife to save the company, offends modern sensibilities about marriage but is historically plau-

511

sible and accurate for the period. The liaisons between Indian women and trappers and traders were usually casual, although some, such as the marriage of Alexander Culbertson and his Blood wife, Natawista, lasted most of a lifetime. But more commonly these "country marriages" as the French called them were brief. Lewis and Clark's translator Toussaint Charbonneau had numerous wives, of whom Sacajawea was only one. The Jesuit missionary Father Pierre-Jean DeSmet tried to regularize these liaisons, and did succeed in many cases. To this day one can find French names among the mixed-bloods enrolled in the reservations of Montana. Plains Indian marriage itself was casual, and it was no great dishonor to an Indian wife to find her possessions outside the lodge door. Usually she found another husband.

While this story is pure fiction, I have stayed close to history and the realities of the robe trade of a century and a half ago.